The Prince Brothers: Satisfaction Guaranteed!

Three red-hot brothers...
Three sizzling Hollywood affairs...

Three glitzy, glamorous romances from
reader-favourite Carole Mortimer!

In October 2009 Mills & Boon bring
you two classic collections, each
featuring three favourite romances
by our bestselling authors

CHOSEN BY THE GREEK TYCOON

The Antonakos Marriage by Kate Walker
At the Greek Tycoon's Bidding
by Cathy Williams
The Greek's Bridal Purchase
by Susan Stephens

THE PRINCE BROTHERS: SATISFACTION GUARANTEED!

by Carole Mortimer
Prince's Passion
Prince's Pleasure
Prince's Love-Child

The Prince Brothers: Satisfaction Guaranteed!

CAROLE MORTIMER

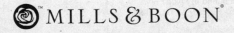
MILLS & BOON

All the characters in this book have no existence outside the imagination of the author, and have no relation whatsoever to anyone bearing the same name or names. They are not even distantly inspired by any individual known or unknown to the author, and all the incidents are pure invention.

First published in Great Britain 2009
Harlequin Mills & Boon Limited,
Eton House, 18-24 Paradise Road, Richmond, Surrey TW9 1SR

THE PRINCE BROTHERS: SATISFACTION GUARANTEED!
© by Harlequin Enterprises II B.V./S.à.r.l 2009

Prince's Passion, Prince's Pleasure and *Prince's Love-Child* were first published in Great Britain by Harlequin Mills & Boon Limited in separate, single volumes.

Prince's Passion © Carole Mortimer 2005
Prince's Pleasure © Carole Mortimer 2005
Prince's Love-Child © Carole Mortimer 2005

ISBN: 978 0 263 -87141 8

05-1009

Printed and bound in Spain
by Litografia Rosés S.A., Barcelona

PRINCE'S PASSION

Carole Mortimer was born in England, the youngest of three children. She began writing in 1978, and has now written over one hundred and forty books for Harlequin Mills & Boon. Carole has six sons, Matthew, Joshua, Timothy, Michael, David and Peter. She says, 'I'm happily married to Peter senior; we're best friends as well as lovers, which is probably the best recipe for a successful relationship. We live in a lovely part of England.'

Don't miss Carole Mortimer's exciting new novel, *The Infamous Italian's Secret Baby,* **available November 2009 from Mills & Boon® Modern™.**

PROLOGUE

'SO WHAT did your elusive author have to say to my offer this time?' Nik prompted the publisher as the two men faced each other across the other man's desk, his American accent muted with deceptive boredom.

Deceptive, because Nik was anything but bored when it came to acquiring the movie rights to J. I. Watson's emotive book...

James Stephens looked uncomfortable. A man in his mid-fifties, head of Stephens Publishing since his father had retired over twenty years ago, James had obviously seen it all when it came to the often unpredictable temperaments of the authors who wrote for him.

But Nik's assessing gaze beneath lowered lids could see that the other man was as baffled by the attitude of the author J. I. Watson as Nik was himself.

What was so difficult about him wanting to acquire the movie rights to the book that had taken the publishing world by storm six months ago? Surely it was every author's dream to have their book turned into a movie? A movie—and even if Nik did say this himself!—to be produced and directed by none other than the Oscar-winning Nikolas Prince?

But no, of the four letters sent to the author in the last two months, the first two had gone unanswered, the third one had resulted in a polite but terse refusal of the proposal, and Nik had yet to hear a response after the fourth. But from the resigned look on James Stephens's face, it was yet another refusal.

To be truthful, Nik had found the last two months of waiting to meet J. I. Watson increasingly frustrating. A month ago he had even wined and dined the female senior editor here who dealt with the author in the hopes that he could bypass James Stephens altogether and get straight to the author himself. After several dinners Jane Morrow had become relaxed enough in his company to confide in him, after making him promise not to reveal his source, that the author's real name was Nixon. But she had gone on to admit that this little nugget of information wouldn't be too much of a help to him, because the publishers always corresponded with the author through a PO box.

'He turned my offer down again,' Nik guessed grimly now.

'Yes,' James confirmed, obviously relieved not to have to say the words himself.

'What's wrong with the man?' Nik stood up forcefully, a big man, well over six feet tall, his dark hair overlong and slightly unkempt, glittering grey eyes dominating his hard-hewn features. 'Does he want more money? Is that it?' he speculated. 'I'll give him whatever he wants. Within reason.'

James sighed, a slightly built man with receding brown hair, only the shrewd light in his blue eyes to belie his otherwise amiable appearance. 'Perhaps if I show you the latest letter we've received...?' He opened a file on his desk, picking up the top sheet of paper to hand it to Nik.

There was only a single line printed on the paper: 'Not even if Nik Prince were to ask me himself!'

Succinct. To the point. An unmistakable refusal.

And yet, irritating as it certainly was, it wasn't that one-line refusal that caught and held Nik's attention as he continued to look at the letter. For printed at the top of the letter was the PO box number Jane had mentioned, and it was right here in London, of all places. A fact that James Stephens had probably forgotten when he'd offered to let Nik look at the letter…

Nik looked up at the publisher, silver gaze narrowed as he handed back the letter without comment; he had no doubts that James Stephens was an honourable man, that if he realized he had breached his author's anonymity by letting Nik see the place of the PO box, he would most likely contact the man immediately and get him to change their point of contact.

'Have you tried talking to the man face to face—no?' He frowned as James shook his head.

James sighed heavily. 'I've never met him—'

'Never?' Nik echoed incredulously; this was turning into something of a farce. James had stonewalled him from the beginning concerning meeting J. I. Watson, but Nik couldn't have guessed that that was because the other man had never met the author, either!

The publisher grimaced. 'Never met him. Never seen him. Never spoken to him,' he rasped. 'No telephone number ever supplied, you see. In fact, our contact has only ever been through the mail.'

'I don't believe this!' Nik dropped back down into the chair facing the desk, totally bemused by what he had just learnt. Thanks to Jane Morrow he knew about the PO box, but he had thought that point of contact had been set up after meetings between the author and publisher. 'All this time I've assumed this reclusive thing was just a publishers' publicity stunt!'

'I wish!' James muttered frustratedly. 'But the truth is we received the unsolicited manuscript almost eighteen months ago. A junior editor eventually read it, quickly passing it on to a more senior colleague once she realized the quality of writing and storyline. The manuscript finally arrived on the senior editor's desk after being in-house for almost three months—that's actually not bad!' he defended as Nik gave him a scathing glance.

'If you say so,' Nik murmured, still stunned by the knowledge that no one at this prestigious publishing house had ever met the author who made millions for them, as well as for himself, over the last six months.

Jane Morrow certainly hadn't chosen to confide *that* important snippet of information to him!

'I do say so.' James sat up straighter in his high-backed leather chair. 'We have, of course, asked to meet Mr Watson on several occasions, but all to no avail,' he continued firmly as Nik would have made another scathing comment. 'Every approach has been met with a firm refusal.'

Nik shook his head. No wonder he was having such difficulty trying to do a deal with the author if the man refused to even meet with his own publishing house!

'It's true,' James Stephens assured him, obviously misunderstanding the reason for the shake of Nik's head. 'The contract, editorial suggestions—although I have to admit there weren't too many of those,' he acknowledged admiringly. 'Everything was done through the post.'

'But what do you do about fan mail, things like that? Do you send all that off through the mail, too?' Nik asked.

James shook his head, pulling another file on his desk towards him, a file filled to overflowing. 'We send him a selection every now and then, just so that he knows how his public feels about the book. But none of the nastier ones, of course; those are all dealt with in-house.'

'Nastier ones?' Nik raised an eyebrow.

'The insulting ones.' James shrugged. 'Death threats,'

he clarified. 'This much overnight success tends to bring out the worst in some people.'

Oh, Nik could believe that; he had received more than his own fair share of nasty letters over the years. 'The contract.' He picked up on the one point in James's earlier statement that might have relevance to his own needs. 'Surely—'

'The clause concerning film and television rights was taken out,' James cut in as he easily guessed Nik's next question. 'At the author's request, of course.' Blue eyes twinkled merrily.

'Of course.' Nik scowled; why shouldn't the other man's eyes glitter with laugher—after all, Stephens Publishing was already laughing all the way to the bank!

James grinned unrepentantly. 'We wanted the book, under any terms we could get it.'

Nik felt sure that a book like *No Ordinary Boy* only came along once in a publishing lifetime, so he couldn't blame the other man for grabbing the manuscript, regardless of any terms the author cared to make. If he hadn't, then another publishing house certainly would have done.

Not that any of that was of help to Nik now; he wanted to make a movie of the book, and without the author's cooperation there was no way he was going to be able to do that.

'You think *you* feel frustrated?' James shook his head. 'Can you imagine the mileage we've lost by not being able to produce the author, to provide personal interviews, book signings, things like that? Watson's reclusive attitude has probably lost us millions in sales.'

'But you've made millions, anyway,' Nik drawled knowingly. 'And I don't suppose my acquiring the movie rights would do you any harm, either.'

'No,' the other man acknowledged with a smile. 'But as you *aren't* going to acquire the movie rights—'

'Who says I'm not?' Nik cut in ruthlessly, his expression once again grim as he stood up.

James looked up at him curiously. 'What makes you think *you'll* be successful in meeting and talking to the man when we've been trying for months to no avail?'

'That's easy.' Nik smiled confidently. 'I don't play by the same rules as you do, James.' And now that he had the PO box number, and its point of origin, he had every intention of pursuing J. I. Watson—or should he say Nixon?—in any way open to him. 'Watson's claim "not even if Nik Prince were to ask me himself" is shortly going to become fact,' he assured James grimly. 'And, I should warn you, I never take no for an answer!' Nik added harshly.

Neither did he intend doing so this time. As J. I. Watson was shortly going to find out!

CHAPTER ONE

'THANKS for inviting me, Susan.' Jinx smiled brightly at the other woman as she opened the door to her, the sound of a party audible in the background.

The two women had been at school together, and Susan was now married to a partner of an accountancy firm, their two small children safely asleep upstairs. Or, if they weren't, the live-in nanny would make sure they didn't interrupt the party being given to celebrate their parents' fifth wedding anniversary.

Susan gave a disbelieving snort. 'Don't give me that, Jinx; you and I both know you would much rather be at home with a good book, that I had to practically twist your arm at lunch earlier this week to get you to agree to come tonight! But thanks, anyway; it simply wouldn't have been the same without the presence of our one and only bridesmaid.' She moved to kiss Jinx warmly on the cheek before standing back and looking at her frowningly. Jinx was small and slender, the black dress she wore perfect with her long, flowing, fiery red hair. 'Tell me, how is it that you seem to get younger every year and I just get more matronly?'

'Flatterer,' Jinx scoffed, handing her friend the peach-coloured roses she had brought with her as a present; the same colour roses that had adorned Susan's bouquet at her wedding five years ago.

'Oh, Jinx, they're beautiful!' Susan beamed. 'But tell me, how's Jack?'

Jinx's smile didn't falter, although her eyes shadowed

11

a little. 'About the same.' She shrugged. 'But where's your handsome husband?' she prompted mischievously, deciding the subject of her father was something better not discussed at her friend's celebration party.

'Here I am,' Leo announced happily, moving past Susan to easily sweep the diminutive Jinx up into his arms and kiss her firmly on her lips. 'It's still not too late for us to run away together, you know,' he told her *sotto voce*, blue eyes twinkling merrily as he received a playful punch on the arm from his grinning wife.

'Sounds like a good party.' Jinx nodded in the direction of Susan and Leo's drawing-room where the sound of chatter and laughter, the chinking of glasses, could easily be heard.

'We have a surprise guest,' her friend told her excitedly as she linked her arm with Jinx's to walk down the plushly carpeted hallway in the direction of the noisy enjoyment. 'You know we had Stazy Hunter design our drawing-room last year?' she prompted as Jinx did her best to look interested; as Susan knew only too well this sort of scene really wasn't her idea of fun.

As the decoration of the now-beautiful gold and terracotta room had been Susan's main topic of conversation six months ago, of course Jinx was aware that the famous Stazy Hunter had been the designer.

Susan nodded, not really requiring an answer. 'Well, we've stayed friends, so of course I invited Stazy, and her husband Jordan, to join us this evening, and then an hour ago Stazy telephoned to ask if she could possibly bring her brother with her as he had arrived unexpectedly, and of course I said yes, and you'll never guess who Stazy's brother turned out to be—'

'She'll pause for breath in a minute,' Leo reassured Jinx dryly as he fell into step beside them, draping his arm affectionately across his wife's shoulders. 'But you know Jinx isn't interested in that sort of thing, Susan. Now if this chap were a university professor or an archaeologist, something like that, then she might be more interested, but as he's only a—'

'Leo is only being so negative because the man's gorgeous,' Susan huffed. 'Absolutely gorgeous,' she repeated enthusiastically. 'Six foot three of pure sexual magnetism—'

'And what am I?' Leo interrupted.

'Oh, you're gorgeous too, darling,' Susan assured him distractedly.

'Just not as gorgeous—or sexually magnetic!—as our esteemed guest,' he acknowledged ruefully.

'Well…I'm married to you.' Susan pouted. 'It isn't the same.'

'No, I can see that it isn't.' Leo grimaced. 'Are you sure you wouldn't like to run away with me, Jinx?'

Jinx gave the expected dismissive laugh. 'You know as well as I do that you love Susan to distraction!'

Leo shook his head. 'That could change if she's going to go around enthusing about famous film directors!'

Jinx's eyes widened in alarm. 'Stazy Hunter's brother is a film director?'

'Yes, he's—sorry.' Susan gave a rueful smile as the doorbell rang again. 'Catch up with you later.' She squeezed Jinx's arms before grabbing her husband's hand and dragging him off to answer the door with her.

Jinx turned to enter the drawing-room—and instantly found herself face to face with what she was pretty sure was Susan's 'six foot three of pure sexual magnetism'!

Well…not exactly face to face—she was only five feet one inch in her stockinged feet, the two-inch heels on her shoes still making her a foot shorter than the man who returned her gaze with compelling silver-grey eyes, his mouth hard and unsmiling.

A man she easily recognized as Nik Prince. One-time actor, now an extremely successful film director, the eldest of the three brothers who owned PrinceMovies, one of America's most prestigious film companies.

A shutter came down over her eyes of violet-blue, that curious shade between blue and purple, her pointed chin rising challengingly as Nik Prince looked down at her with an assessment that was totally male. And for that brief moment, a mere matter of seconds, it was as if the two of them were the only people in the room, the noisy chatter, the laughter, the background music all fading away as steely silver-grey clashed with violet-blue.

Jinx became very conscious of the flowing red hair down her back, the perfect fit of her knee-length black dress above long, silky legs. But most of all the man's size, the sheer animal magnetism emanating from him despite the civilized attire of black evening suit and snowy white shirt, made her aware of each nerve and pulse in her own body, every part of her seeming to tingle with awareness, her breasts rising pert and aroused beneath the silky material of her dress.

As if drawn by a magnet, that intent grey gaze dropped down to the level of her breasts, lingering, as tangible as any caress, as if the man had reached out and physically touched her there.

But it was the amusement that glimmered in those hard grey eyes, the knowing smile that curved the perfect symmetry of that cynical mouth, as if completely aware of the effect he was having on her—and why shouldn't he be? This man was almost forty years old, obviously experienced, his affairs over the years with his leading ladies legendary! That was what enabled Jinx to break the force of his gaze, her own mouth curving derisively now.

'Well?' she challenged him.

Dark brows rose. 'Well, what?' The voice was low and husky, the American drawl giving it a sexy quality that made a nonsense of the actual words he said—his tone said 'let's go to bed', so sensual was its inflexion.

Jinx's direct gaze didn't falter for a second. 'Do you like what you see?'

He smiled fully now, showing even white teeth, lines etched beside his eyes and mouth. 'Wouldn't any man?' he taunted her.

'I wasn't asking "any man",' Jinx snapped. 'I was asking *you*.'

Nik Prince took a step towards her, bringing him dangerously close, so close she could feel the heat from his body, smell the tangy aroma of his aftershave. 'Yes, I like what I see,' he murmured huskily. 'But, then, you already knew that,' he added. 'How would you feel about the two of us making our excuses and getting out of here?'

Jinx blinked, the only sign she gave—she hoped!— that she was stunned by his suggestion. It would be surprising coming from any man on such short acquaintance, but Nik Prince was no ordinary man!

She usually made a point of avoiding parties like this one, had only made the effort to come this evening because she was so fond of Susan and Leo. But if Nik Prince thought she was the sort of party girl who allowed herself to be picked up by men like him, then he was in for a disappointment.

'Wouldn't that be rather rude to Susan and Leo?' she retorted critically.

'Are they our host and hostess?' he asked with an uninterested glance in their direction as they stood further down the hallway greeting yet more guests. 'I don't know them and they don't know me; why should it bother me what they think?'

Why, indeed? In fact, from what she had heard of this man, he tended to be a law unto himself, was reputed to be an uncompromising film director, an inflexible head of his family of two younger brothers and a sister, his relationships with women, be they beautiful actresses or otherwise, always short-lived.

In fact, he wasn't Jinx's type at all. If she had a type. It had been so long since there had been anyone in her life in a romantic way that she had forgotten!

She gave a shrug of slender shoulders. 'Because they were gracious enough to extend their hospitality to you on very short notice might be one way of looking at it, don't you think?' she rebuked.

He gave a mocking inclination of his head. 'I stand corrected,' he drawled, grey eyes warm as he smiled down at her.

That genuine smile, when it came, was well worth waiting for. In fact, Jinx felt slightly breathless and not a little shaky at the knees. Not a very sensible response given the circumstances!

'Good,' she bit out with more force than she had intended, deliberately turning away from him as she took a step back, once again widening the distance between them. 'Now, if you will excuse me, Mr Prince—' She broke off abruptly as he reached out a hand to lightly grasp her arm, his fingers long and strong, their warmth seeming to penetrate her silky skin.

'You obviously know my name, but I don't know yours,' he said huskily as she looked up at him enquiringly.

Jinx felt shaken by the effect of his touch, a surge like electricity having coursed through her. Her breathing suddenly became shallow and uneven, and her eyes widened with surprise at her own response.

Nik Prince tilted his head to one side. 'Let's see... You don't look like a Joan. Or a Cynthia. Or a—'

'Tell me, does this chat-up line usually work?' Jinx cut in, having finally come to her senses enough to know that this man was dangerous—with a capital D!

Nik Prince didn't look too put out by her mockery; in fact, he was standing far too close again, those grey eyes gleaming with laughter. 'Believe it or not, I don't usually need a chat-up line.'

Oh, she believed it, all right. She was sure this man usually had women lining up to be with him rather than his having to pursue them. 'Perhaps that's as well,' she told him dryly.

Grey eyes warmed as he smiled his appreciation of her deliberate put-down. 'You'll have to excuse me; it's been a while,' he conceded wryly.

Jinx wasn't in the least interested in how long it had been. 'If you wouldn't mind releasing my arm...?' she prompted, having made several unsuccessful attempts to do so herself.

'But I do mind,' he murmured throatily, his thumb moving in a rhythmic caress against her inner wrist now.

'But so do I,' she snapped. 'Now, if you'll excuse me...? I must just go over and say hello to Susan's parents.' Thank goodness she had just spotted their familiar faces across the room.

Nik Prince moved his hand, but only to take a proprietorial hold of her elbow instead. 'How about you introduce me? I can say hello to them too, and then I'll finally know your name.'

She met his gaze unblinkingly. 'My name is Juliet.'

His eyes widened momentarily, as if that wasn't quite what he had expected to hear—as, indeed, it probably wasn't!—and then his considerable acting skills took over and he gave an acknowledging inclination of his head. 'Now that's more like it.'

'That hardly makes you my Romeo, Mr Prince.'

'Pity,' he drawled. 'And it's Nik.'

'Nik,' she accepted shortly.

'Okay.' He smiled his satisfaction with her compliance. 'And what do you do, Juliet?'

'Do?' she delayed warily.

'Careerwise. Or have I committed some sort of social gaffe and you don't do anything?'

The amusement in his tone annoyed her intensely. 'What I do, Mr—Nik,' she corrected irritably as he gave her a reproving look, 'is teach. History. At Cambridge University.' She tried to keep that slight tone of pride out of her voice when she said the latter, knowing she had failed miserably as his firmly sculptured mouth twisted mockingly. 'Although I'm in the middle of taking a year's sabbatical at the moment,' she enlarged.

'And does that make you a Dr Something?'

'It does. Now if you will excuse me? I know I may have arrived on my own this evening, but that really doesn't mean that I am on my own,' she pointed out.

'Well, of course you aren't—I'm here now.'

Jinx gave him an exasperated frown. 'That isn't what I meant and you know it!'

'Do I?'

'Yes,' she easily dismissed his too-innocent expression.

'I see.' He glanced around the room. 'And which one

of the twenty or so men here tonight is going to come over and claim you?'

Jinx felt the colour warm her cheeks. No one was going to 'come over and claim her', because at twenty-eight she was single, had never been married, and probably never would be.

She straightened her shoulders, at the same time shrugging off his hand under her elbow. 'I really don't think that is any of your concern, Mr Prince,' she told him quietly, stepping completely away from him now as she turned and walked across the room.

But she was totally aware, with every step that she took, that Nik Prince was watching the sensuous sway of her hips!

Nik stood and watched the redhead's departure with narrowed, enigmatic eyes.

Damn. He hadn't made too good a job of that, now had he? He really must be rusty when it came to the art of seduction. Because Juliet 'Jinx' Nixon certainly hadn't been seduced!

He'd had to wait days for the man he had hired to watch the post office box to confirm that a girl came to collect the mail at twelve-thirty every day. Nik had then taken over himself, only to realize, on closer inspection, when she had arrived, that she wasn't a girl at all, just a very petite woman. The denims, tee shirt and baseball cap she'd worn had served to disguise her age. Deliberately so? He had thought so.

In fact he'd been totally convinced of it when she'd gone outside to the adjacent car park, unlocked a Volkswagen Golf, and thrown her mail in the back of the car before removing the baseball cap and shaking out the long length of her fiery red hair. Then she'd thrown the cap in the back with her letters before taking out a tailored jacket and pulling it on over the tee shirt.

The transformation from a teenager like almost every other teenager Nik had been able to see walking down the street, to a beautifully elegant older woman, had taken only a little adjustment of the clothing and an application of a deep peach lipgloss.

Nik had followed her as she'd taken a shoulder bag from the back of the car and set off down the street, standing well back when she'd gone into a busy Italian bistro and met a beautiful blonde woman for lunch. Susan Fellows, he had learnt afterwards after quizzing one of the busy waitresses. When, incidentally, his seductive tone had been more than successful!

A couple of conversations with his sister Stazy later—a young lady residing in London herself with her husband and baby son, and more intimately acquainted with the London social scene than he was—and he'd known exactly who Susan Fellows was. Even more interesting than that, he had quickly discovered that her luncheon companion was a very good friend of Susan's called Jinx Nixon.

It hadn't taken too many more enquiries to learn that Jinx's father was Jackson Ivor Nixon, also a university professor who taught history, and an authority on the Jacobite uprisings, author of several prestigious books on the subject. Nik had put two and two together and realized that Jackson Ivor Nixon also had to be J. I. Watson, the author of *No Ordinary Boy*…

Nik had also figured out why he preferred to remain anonymous; Jackson I. Nixon was an extremely well-respected author of several historical tomes. *No Ordinary Boy*, while being a runaway success, was actually a book written for children, but which had been taken up and read by adults and children alike, about a young boy of twelve confined to a wheelchair who suddenly became a superhero. Not exactly Jackson I. Nixon material!

And following Jinx, having her checked out, wasn't the most scrupulously honest thing he had ever done, Nik allowed ruefully, but a necessary evil as far as he was concerned. As had been the seduction scene when Jinx had arrived at her friend's party a few minutes ago.

Not that it had been too much of a hardship; Juliet 'Jinx' Nixon was an extremely beautiful woman.

She hadn't seemed too impressed with him, though! Nik winced inwardly. Never mind, it was early days yet. He wasn't known for his patience when it came to directing temperamental actors and actresses, but when it came to something he wanted, then he could be extremely patient, indeed. And he wanted the movie rights to J. I. Watson's book. Jinx Nixon's father's book…

'Exactly what are you up to, big brother of mine?' Stazy linked her arm through his as she looked up at him knowingly. 'And don't say nothing,' she warned mischievously. 'I know you far too well for that. And I saw you make a beeline for that beautiful redhead the moment she came in the door.'

He never had been able to put too much over on Stazy. At twenty-two she was seventeen years his junior, and had been the single constant weakness in his life from the moment she was born. Her marriage to Jordan Hunter just over a year ago, and the birth of her son Sam three months ago, had given her a confidence that brooked no refusal.

'In fact,' Stazy continued thoughtfully, a beautiful redhead herself, although at five feet nine inches tall she would completely dwarf the petite Jinx Nixon, 'now that

I think about it, it was almost as if you were waiting for her to arrive. Nik, what—?'

'Don't worry about it, honey,' he advised with a pat on the hand she rested on his arm.

'But I do worry about it, Nik,' she persisted.

He gave a resigned sigh. When Stazy got her teeth into something, she was apt not to let go. Since her successful marriage to Jordan she had been more than a little obvious in her marriage-making plans for her three older brothers. And as all three of the Prince brothers were in England at the moment in preparation for baby Sam's christening tomorrow, she was taking full advantage of this opportunity to play matchmaker…!

'I shouldn't,' he murmured softly, his gaze warning her off the subject.

'No?' She arched auburn brows.

'No,' he confirmed firmly.

The last thing he wanted was for Stazy to take an interest in Jinx Nixon; he already had his work cut out trying to maneouvre a meeting with the other woman's father, without contending with Stazy's machinations, too!

'Okay,' his sister capitulated. 'In that case, come over and say hello to some of the other guests.'

Nik eyed her warily for several seconds, not in the least fooled by her easy acquiescence. But other than pursuing the subject himself, something he had no intention of doing, there was nothing else he could say or do to put his mind at rest.

However, he did keep a close eye on Jinx Nixon's movements over the next hour or so. He noted with satisfaction, despite what she had said earlier, that she didn't spend more than a few minutes in any other man's company—while at the same time totally avoiding his!

'Can I drive you home?'

Jinx turned and frowned at Nik when he spoke to her. He'd stood and watched her as she'd slowly edged her way over to the door, seeming on the verge of making her excuses to leave. 'I beg your pardon?'

Nik moved to stand in front of her, effectively blocking out the rest of the room, leaving the two of them co-cooned in a bubble of intimacy. 'I asked if I could drive you home,' he repeated mildly—of course, that was on the assumption that Jordan wouldn't mind getting a cab home for himself and Stazy and letting Nik borrow his car for a couple of hours!

Jinx shook her head, her hair gleaming copper-red in the candlelight that illuminated the room. 'I have my own car. Thank you,' she added belatedly.

He nodded. 'Which you aren't going to drive.'

'I'm not?' Her eyes had widened, deep blue eyes that could appear almost purple in some lights.

In this light, Nik noticed appreciatively. Also her skin was that pale peach of most redheads, smooth and clear, a tiny pulse beating at the base of her throat. A throat he ached to kiss, he suddenly realized.

'No,' he confirmed huskily. 'You've drunk two glasses of wine, which means you're already over the limit—'

'You've been counting?' she interrupted incredulously, angry colour heightening in her cheeks.

'Don't worry about it.' He shrugged. 'I have that sort of mind. For instance, the man standing beside the fireplace has so far drunk a whole bottle of champagne to himself and is now about to start on another. The brunette at his side is obviously the driver for the evening, has only had three glasses of orange juice, and is obviously very pi—annoyed about it,' he corrected wryly. 'The man near the window—'

'Okay, I get the picture,' Jinx snapped. 'But even so…'

'Even so…?' Nik prompted softly.

She looked resentful. 'I'm not sure I like the idea of having someone watching me that closely.'

'The only way you can stop that is to not be quite so watchable—which, with your face and body, just isn't going to happen,' Nik teased her.

She gave him a perplexed frown, obviously not quite sure how to take that last remark, whether to be flattered or insulted by it. In the end, it seemed, she decided to ignore it. 'Nevertheless, I won't be requiring your offer of a lift home,' she dismissed with obvious relief.

Not very flattering to his ego, Nik acknowledged. In fact, Jinx Nixon's attitude towards him hadn't exactly been warm all evening. His only consolation was that she hadn't been warm towards any other man, either!

Apart from perhaps Leo Fellows, their host, Nik corrected himself with an inward frown. The two of them had seemed to be enjoying a flirtatious conversation half an hour or so ago. Could it possibly be that the reason Jinx had arrived here alone this evening was because she was involved in an affair with her best friend's husband? It wouldn't be the first time—in fact it was all too common.

Nik found the thought more than slightly unpleasant when made in connection with the beautiful Jinx Nixon—and no matter what she might have told him her name was, he knew that her closest friends called her Jinx.

And that was his plan, wasn't it? To get close to Jinx, wheedle an introduction to her father, and present him with the contract for movie rights to *No Ordinary Boy*.

What could be simpler?

Well, Jinx Nixon being a little less beautiful and a whole lot less sexy would have been a help!

He had expected to engage in a little light seduction— it was a dirty job, but someone had to do it!—but finding Jinx Nixon so attractive, his senses roused just inhaling her perfume, and other parts of him roused every time he so much as looked at her, had definitely not been part of that plan…

CHAPTER TWO

'WHY not?'

Jinx smiled confidently in the face of Nik Prince's obvious displeasure at having her turn down his offer of a lift home. 'Susan's parents live only half a mile away from me and have already offered to drive me home later.' Although, she had to admit, she had been on the point of forgoing that offer and simply leaving!

She found this man altogether too disturbing, which was why she hadn't looked his way at all since they'd parted earlier, even though she had been conscious of his every move.

In fact, she had never been this aware of a man in her life before. Of course that awareness was on more than one level. On the surface she was aware of the letters received from Stephens Publishing, on this man's behalf, requesting a meeting with the author of *No Ordinary Boy*, in order to discuss acquiring the film rights. But underneath all that she was aware of a physical attraction to Nik Prince that she was trying desperately to ignore.

Obviously, his height and sheer size would dominate any company he was in. The forcefulness of his personality likewise. But it wasn't either of those things that made her skin tingle and heightened her senses just being in the same room with him. No, the attraction she felt towards this man was something she simply couldn't explain, something she had never experienced before.

Or ever wanted to experience again!

'And when you aren't teaching at Cambridge University, home is where?'

Jinx's gaze was guarded as she looked up at Nik. 'London.'

He sighed. 'Which part of London?'

'South west,' she offered unhelpfully, glancing away from the shrewdness in those silver-grey eyes.

As far as she was concerned it was too coincidental, after those letters sent from James Stephens on his behalf, that Nik Prince was here at this party at all. Neither Susan nor Leo had met him before this evening, and he certainly didn't look the type to need his sister to elicit a late invitation, as this one appeared to be, to fill his evening.

No, Jinx had stopped believing in coincidences a long time ago. And Nik Prince being here this evening certainly wasn't one, either. She just wasn't sure how much he knew. But he obviously knew enough—from where, or whom, she wasn't sure—to have arranged to meet her in this roundabout fashion.

But had he been any more prepared than her for the physical awareness that practically sizzled between them?

Somehow she doubted it!

He gave a rueful smile now. 'In other words, you have no intention of telling me where you live?'

'None at all,' she confirmed lightly. That was the very last thing she intended doing!

'Then I had better make the most of my time with you this evening, hadn't I,' he accepted dryly.

Jinx eyed him warily. 'Meaning?'

He gave a shrug of those powerfully broad shoulders. 'There's music in the other room. How about you dance with me as a start?'

A start to what? And did she really want to be that close to him, to feel the heat of his body only inches away from her own, to have him touching her, his hands touching hers, the warmth of his breath against her temple…?

'Scared?' he murmured knowingly.

Jinx straightened immediately, knowing he was goading her in order to achieve his goal, but at the same time unwilling to back down from a man so obviously used to having his own way. 'Not in the least, Mr Prince,' she assured him. 'The truth of the matter is, I can't remember when I last danced; I may have forgotten how.'

'Dancing is like lovemaking,' he told her huskily. 'Once you've tried it, you never forget how!'

So, in spite of her efforts, he was obviously determined to keep this conversation on an intimate level. 'Then I shouldn't have any trouble, should I?' she retorted, turning in the direction of the dining-room where a quartet was softly playing music for the guests to dance to, leaving him to come to his own conclusions concerning her last remark.

She had been right to be apprehensive about allowing this man too close, she acknowledged several minutes later. Nik Prince had ignored all the rules of social etiquette when dancing with a relative stranger, instead pulling her right against him, his arms about her waist, hands linked at the base of her spine, their bodies touching from chest to thigh as they moved slowly to the music.

As far as Jinx was concerned, they might have been the only two people dancing. She was totally aware of Nik as her hands rested on his shoulders, her efforts to maintain a distance between them completely thwarted when Nik reached up and gently laid her head against his shoulder before resting his own head against the silky softness of her hair.

'You smell like flowers,' he murmured close to her ear, his breath as warm as she had known it would be.

'Lily of the Valley soap,' she dismissed pragmatically.

He chuckled softly. 'Are you always this romantic?'

'Are you?' she came back.

'I don't believe it's been one of my character traits to date, no,' he allowed ruefully. 'But that could change,' he added throatily.

This really hadn't been a good idea, Jinx acknowledged with an inward groan. Nik's legs felt hard against her softer ones, the stirring of his thighs unmistakable in such close proximity, the uneven rise and fall of his chest against hers more evidence of his increasing arousal, an arousal that caused a pounding in her own chest and a warmth between her thighs.

'I want you,' Nik groaned, his words accompanied by a gentle nibble against her ear lobe.

Jinx quivered with pleasure, shivers of hot and cold tumbling down her spine. But at the same time she wondered how she could put a stop to this. Because she had to stop it. Now. Before it spiralled out of control.

'There's a woman standing across the room who keeps staring at us,' she told him, hoping to distract him. 'Friend of yours?'

'My sister, Stazy,' Nik answered her without even raising his head, his tongue now tasting the sensitive flesh beneath her ear lobe.

'How can you be sure?' Jinx pursued determinedly, her voice slightly higher than usual as she fought the instinct of her body to curve itself against his, that marauding tongue now seeking the delicate curves of her ear.

Nik chuckled softly, the reverberations only increasing the pleasure of his caresses. 'Stazy has become something of a matchmaker since her own happy marriage a year ago; she's obviously assessing you to see if you're suitable wife material for her eldest—and, may I say, favourite?—brother.'

Jinx pulled back abruptly, staring up at him in disbelief. And then wished she hadn't. He really was the most ruggedly attractive man, and those grey eyes were pure silver now, shining with an intensity of emotion that was unmistakable. Desire. Arousal. For her.

Her own pupils had probably dilated until the black practically obliterated the blue. Revealing desire. Arousal. For him.

She drew in a deep breath. 'In that case, I think it's best that we end this now, don't you?' She stepped back, feeling the momentary tightening of his arms about her before he reluctantly released her, the expression in his eyes one of regret now.

'Why don't we just follow my earlier suggestion and leave here to continue this some place more private?' he asked.

'Like my home?' Jinx challenged.

'Sounds good.' He nodded.

'The home I have no intention of taking you to?' she derided. 'You misunderstood me a few moments ago when I said it's time we end this now, Nik—I meant the charade.'

It was as if a shutter had come down, his eyes no longer silver but a narrowed grey, his expression deliberately—or so it seemed to Jinx—unreadable. 'Charade?' he echoed blandly.

Her mouth twisted humourlessly. 'Look, I know who you are, and you know who I am. I'm not sure how you know—' *yet!* '—but I do know it's totally ridiculous for us to continue with this charade.'

Those grey eyes narrowed even more, several emotions

flickering in their depths, but too briefly for her to analyze.

'Besides,' she added coldly, 'I really see no point in your continuing this seduction act any further.'

'*Act?*' He sounded outraged. 'Do you really think I can just manufacture my attraction to you?'

'I think, Mr Prince, that you are capable of manufacturing anything you feel the inclination to,' she told him candidly, at the same time aware that her attraction to him had been anything but manufactured! 'Now, if you will excuse me, I think my lift is preparing to leave.' She had just spotted Dick and Janet saying their goodnights to the other guests. 'But for the record, Mr Prince,' she paused to add huskily, 'as predicted, having now met you "in person", the answer is still an emphatic *no*! There will be no movie.'

His mouth thinned. 'Isn't that for your father to say, and not you?'

Jinx continued to look at him for several long seconds before giving a slow shake of her head. 'In the circumstances, no, I don't think so,' she answered cautiously.

'What do you mean?' he challenged.

She met his gaze steadily. 'My father isn't a well man, Mr Prince.'

'But all I want is his signature on a piece of paper.'

She gave a humourless smile. 'A signature that would no doubt give you exclusive film rights to *No Ordinary Boy*!'

'Yes,' he bit out, at least sensible enough not to try to deny that was his true interest in pursuing her this evening.

'That isn't going to happen, Mr Prince—'

'Will you call me Nik, damn it?' he cut in harshly. 'In the *circumstances* anything else certainly is ridiculous!'

Jinx didn't need to ask what circumstances he was referring to; their physical response to each other during that dance certainly made a nonsense of any future formality between them.

'Mr Prince. Nik. It's all the same to me.' She gave a dismissive shrug. 'In either case, the answer is still no.'

'As I told James Stephens earlier in the week, I never take no for an answer,' he warned her grimly.

She drew in a sharp breath, unable to hide her surprise at the mention of the publisher. But then how else could Nik have discovered that J. I. Watson's real name was J. I. *Nixon*? 'James Stephens was the one who told you J. I. Watson's real name?'

'James is far too much of a professional to ever do a thing like that,' Nik reproved.

That was something, at least. If Nik Prince's answer had been anything but the one he had just given her then she would have made sure that the second J. I. Watson manuscript, which was even now being prepared for editing, never made it onto James Stephens's desk.

But it was still pretty obvious that someone at Stephens Publishing had to have revealed that confidential information to Nik Prince. The question was, who…?

'Tell me, Mr Prince…' she gave him a considering look '…what is it that you find so difficult to understand about the word no?'

'As far as I can recall, it's not a word that's ever been in my big brother's vocabulary,' a female voice chimed in lightly.

Jinx turned to look at Nik Prince's sister, Stazy Hunter, as she moved to stand next to her brother. The younger woman was extremely beautiful, her red hair almost as bright as Jinx's own. In fact, Stazy Hunter looked a far nicer person altogether than her eldest brother!

'Not at all,' Nik came back smoothly. 'I'm just a positive person rather than a negative one.'

Well, he could be as positive as he wanted as far as Jinx was concerned, because the answer to his request was no, and it would remain no.

'If you'll both excuse me...' She gave Stazy Hunter a vague smile, shot Nik Prince a look of warning, before moving determinedly away from them, inwardly shaken by how close he had got to her.

Too close.

In more ways than one!

Nik frowned frustratedly as he watched Jinx join a middle-aged couple across the room, his gaze narrowing as he considered his two choices of action. One, he could let Jinx just walk out of his life, also taking her knowledge of J. I. Watson with her. Or two, he could make sure that he left with her!

'Do me a favour, will you, Staze?' He turned urgently to his sister.

She looked slightly surprised. 'Of course. If I can. What—'

'Persuade your charming husband that it's time for the two of you to leave.'

Stazy looked nonplussed. 'But it's still early, Nik; what on earth will I tell Susan and Leo—?'

'I don't care what you tell them,' he cut in forcefully, starting to panic slightly as he could see Jinx and the older couple were coming to the end of their goodbyes. 'Your house is on fire. You need to take your husband home and seduce him—'

'Jordan doesn't need any seducing,' Stazy assured him happily.

Nik winced. 'I really didn't need to hear that.' He was

still coming to terms with the fact that his little sister was married at all, let alone to a man as powerful and experienced as Jordan Hunter. 'Okay, find your own excuse, but think of something soon, hmm!'

'Fine.' Stazy held up soothing hands. 'I take it you aren't coming back with us, after all?'

'You take it correct,' he confirmed grimly, his gaze still fixed on Jinx. 'But whatever you're going to do, do it quickly, will you?' Jinx was starting to move towards the door now!

'I'm gone,' his sister assured him—before doing exactly that.

And by the speed with which his sister and brother-in-law made their excuses to their host and hostess, before immediately leaving, Nik had a feeling that the suggestion of seduction might have worked on Jordan, after all!

Nik shook his head. Stazy had made her choice, and it was a choice he wholeheartedly approved of; it was his own problem if he was still having trouble coming to terms with another man being more important to Stazy than he was.

At this moment he had a much more serious situation to deal with!

'Sorry I was delayed.' He hurried to Jinx's side just as she reached the front door, taking a firm hold of her arm before turning to smile warmly at the older couple who accompanied her. 'I hope you don't mind including me in that offer of a lift home?' His tone was deliberately charming. 'My sister was going to drop me at my hotel, but she and Jordan had to get straight back to their house—some sort of emergency...'

The couple shot each other a briefly knowing look before assuring him they didn't mind at all, that there was plenty of room for him in their car.

Not that Nik had thought they would be a problem; it was Jinx's response that could turn this situation around.

He raised questioning brows as he looked down at her, his expression deceptively calm, only the tightening of his fingers on her arm showing evidence of his inner uncertainty as to what her next move would be.

Her eyes were purple as she looked right back at him, anger flaring in their depths, even though she too managed to look outwardly calm.

Come on, Jinx, Nik inwardly encouraged; at least give me a chance.

If he lost sight of her now, then he would have to start all over again tomorrow. Not that he minded doing that, but it would save a hell of a lot of time if she would just be a little more cooperative now.

'Actually—' she turned back to the older couple, smiling '—it really isn't that far. Nik and I can easily walk it.'

'Are you sure, Jinx?' The other woman frowned her uncertainty with the suggestion. 'It's at least a couple of miles,' she explained to Nik.

'But it's such a lovely evening.' Jinx released her arm from Nik's grasp to lightly link it with his. 'I think it would be so much more fun to walk. Don't you, Nik?' she asked sweetly.

Beware the smile of an angry female, he acknowledged ruefully, at the same time happy to fall in with whatever Jinx suggested—as long as it included him. 'Much more fun,' he agreed dryly; a two-mile walk through the Saturday-night revelry of London sounded more like hell to him, but if it ultimately ended up at Jinx's home, the home she shared with her father, then he was willing to put himself through it if she was.

If it ultimately ended up at Jinx's home...

Somehow, after what she had said to him earlier, he had a feeling that wasn't her intention.

'Tell me,' he murmured softly once they had been walking together in silence for some minutes through the balmy streets, Jinx's arm still linked with his own, despite her efforts to release it, 'will we be crossing any bridges on this fun walk home?'

'Several,' she snapped back tautly, obviously not happy with his reluctance to release her.

'That's what I thought.' He grimaced—having a distinct feeling she was considering pushing him over the side of one.

'One thing I can assure you of, Nik,' she bit out tautly. 'I'm not violent.'

'Just private, hmm?' he said knowingly.

'Just private.'

'I've heard several people refer to you as Jinx this evening,' he said in an effort to divert her thoughts.

'Close friends, yes,' she confirmed stiffly—obviously not counting him amongst their number.

Nik disregarded that for the moment; she might not think they were going to be close friends, but he knew better! 'How on earth did you come by such an unusual nickname?'

She shot him a mocking glance. 'Changing the subject?'

'Rapidly,' he confirmed, laughter gleaming in his eyes; the chances of this petitely beautiful woman being able to force his six-foot-three, one-hundred-and-eighty-pound frame over the parapet of a bridge were ludicrous to say the least. Which wasn't to say she wouldn't give it a damn good try!

She gave an uninterested shrug. 'When I went to school the other children quickly latched onto the fact that my initial was J. followed by Nixon, and when you say the two of them together…' She trailed off pointedly, giving him a sideways glance. 'You aren't coming home with me, you know.'

Of course he knew. After the last two months of sending letters to her father, just in the hopes of being able to meet him and discuss the movie rights to his book, of the use of a PO box for that correspondence, of the author never agreeing to so much as meeting with his own publisher, it would be expecting too much now for his daughter to just take Nik home with her and introduce the two men.

'You mentioned earlier that your father isn't well…?' he said instead.

She stiffened, all expression suddenly erased from her face. 'I mentioned it, yes,' she acknowledged guardedly.

'Nothing life-threatening, I hope?' Nik persisted.

'It depends on what you call life-threatening,' she returned evasively, a frown now marring her creamy brow.

He shrugged, having an idea that in the case of Jackson I. Nixon the writing and subsequent success of *No Ordinary Boy* didn't fit in too well with his other literary achievements. Nik didn't happen to agree with him, and neither did the millions of other people who had bought and enjoyed the book, but that was just his opinion…

His mouth twisted wryly. 'It usually means resulting in premature death.'

'Mr Prince—okay, Nik,' Jinx conceded impatiently as he scowled his displeasure at the formality. 'Just stay away from my father, okay?' Her expression was fierce with emotion now.

'But I only want—'

'I know what you want, Nik!' Her eyes flashed deeply purple in the illumination of the street lamp, her tiny hands clenched into fists at her sides. 'You want to make a film of *No Ordinary Boy*. In the hopes, no doubt, of adding yet another Oscar to the five you already have in your trophy cabinet!'

God, this woman was beautiful when roused, whether to anger or passion. And at this moment Nik knew exactly which one he wanted it to be!

'Perhaps I should feel flattered that you know I have five Oscars—'

'And perhaps you shouldn't!'

'Another Oscar would be nice,' he conceded huskily. 'But at this moment I'm damned if I wouldn't settle for a night in bed with you!'

Colour flared suddenly in the paleness of her cheeks, her lips full and inviting, her breasts moving with the same rapidity of her breathing.

'I wasn't aware that was an option,' she retorted, the nerve pulsing in her raised jaw giving lie to that challenge.

Because Nik was experienced enough to know that, no matter how she might try to deny it—and she was denying it!—Jinx was as physically aware of him as he was of her.

'Not as an instead of, no,' he admitted gruffly, moving closer to her, not quite touching, but nevertheless feeling the heat given off from her body. He reached up to touch the pouting softness of her mouth, feeling the quiver his caress invoked. 'You want me too, Jinx,' he said with certainty.

Her eyes were so dark now they appeared black, her mouth trembling moistly, a becoming flush to her cheeks, the hardened nubs at the tips of the gentle sweep of her breasts visible beneath the thin material of her dress. And Nik was sure, if he could have touched the very centre of her desire, that she would be moist there too, as ready for him as he was for her.

And they hadn't so much as kissed each other yet!

But that was easily rectified, Nik decided, no longer able to resist the urge to take her into his arms, to mould her body fiercely against his, to let her feel the surge of his desire against her warm thighs, before he bent his head and his mouth took hers—and his previously well-constructed world fell apart!

Drowning.

It was like drowning.

Every other woman he had ever known was instantly consigned to a black void and could never be recalled. Only Jinx existed, only the touch, the warmth, the smell, the taste of her.

This woman, this tiny, stubborn, five-foot delicacy of a woman, was taking possession of him, body and soul…!

CHAPTER THREE

WHAT was she doing?

Whatever it was, Jinx knew she couldn't stop it. Not yet. Oh, please, not yet!

Nik was kissing her as if he wanted to make her a part of him, to devour her, to take her completely inside him. Or for him to be completely inside her. His thighs were moving restlessly against hers, rubbing, tormenting, frustrating, until Jinx wanted nothing more than to throw off all their clothes and be taken by him right now, the two of them lost in the heat of the sexual arousal that drew them nearer and nearer to a climax that was completely beyond their control.

'Let's go to a hotel!' Nik managed to take his lips from hers long enough to groan achingly, long hands framing her face as he looked down at her with glittering silver eyes. 'I don't know what you're doing to me, Jinx Nixon, but if I don't make love to you soon then I'm going to self-combust!'

She knew it, could feel the force of his need. A need she easily matched.

'Feel it, Jinx.' Nik's thighs moved erotically against her, hard, pulsing with desire.

A desire that made her own thighs moist, burning, aching, throbbing with a need that she knew would explode if Nik's flesh should so much as touch hers.

But she couldn't just book into a hotel with a man—*especially* not this man! And while her body might think

40

that it recognized and knew his, she knew she had every reason to distrust him. More reasons than he realized.

'No!' Nik protested as he seemed to feel her moving emotionally away from him, his arms tightening about her as he tried to hold onto the moment. 'Jinx, I know you want me too!' he groaned.

Oh, yes, she wanted him. But she would never give in to that want—she had too much to lose if she ever did.

She straightened determinedly away from him. 'And do you always get what you want, Nik?' She sighed.

'Almost always,' he confirmed, his arms falling back to his sides.

'Then a little self-denial could be good for you.'

'It isn't self-denial, it's Jinx-denial,' he corrected huskily. 'And men have been known to go insane trying to draw back from the brink you just took me to!' His eyes glittered with the intensity of his feelings.

'Women too, or so I'm told,' she came back dryly, some of her own normal reserve returning now that she was no longer held in his arms. Although the desire he had aroused hadn't abated in the slightest...

'Then why—'

'Because it would be a mistake!' she cried frustratedly. 'Can't you understand?' she continued as he looked at her blankly. 'You are positively the last man on earth I ever want to become involved with!'

He became very still, his expression guarded now, a shutter coming down over grey eyes, his mouth a grim line. 'Because I want to make a movie of *No Ordinary Boy*?'

'Because you want to film *No Ordinary Boy*,' she agreed flatly.

'Damn it, woman—'

'Nik, swearing at me isn't going to help this situation one little bit—'

'Maybe not,' he admitted grimly. 'But it makes me feel a hell of a lot better!'

She gave him a bleak smile. 'I'm sure it does,' she conceded. 'But it isn't going to change a thing. Because I'm not stupid enough to go to a hotel or anywhere else with you. Neither do I have any intention of taking you home with me—'

'You really are the most stubborn—'

'And if you attempt to follow me home,' Jinx continued as if he hadn't spoken, 'then I shall contact the police and have you arrested for stalking me.'

'Wouldn't that rather null and void this phobia you have about your father's privacy?' he mocked. 'I'm quite well known, Jinx; there is no way having me arrested wouldn't appear in some tabloid newspaper or other.'

Nik Prince's much-photographed face and highly recognizable profile were aspects of this situation that she was well aware of. They were yet more reasons she intended avoiding him at all costs.

'That's your problem, not mine,' she dismissed with much more confidence than she actually felt. 'My priority is to keep any publicity from even touching my father. It's the reason a pseudonym was used, for heaven's sake!' Her eyes flashed warningly.

Nik's frown deepened. 'What exactly is wrong with your father?'

Jinx turned away. 'Just stay away from us, Nik.'

'And if I can't do that?' he challenged.

She shrugged. 'Watch this space.'

'Damn it, he wrote the book; surely it must have occurred to him, to both of you, that it might be a best-seller—'

'Of course it didn't occur to us!' Jinx protested heatedly, the colour back in her cheeks now. 'Writing a book is a very personal thing.' She shook her head. 'Who could possibly have imagined that *No Ordinary Boy* would be as popular as it was?'

'As it still is.'

'Yes,' she conceded quietly.

'Aren't you being just a little selfish, Jinx?' he pursued relentlessly. 'You've made your own feelings about my filming *No Ordinary Boy* more than clear, but until I've actually spoken to him I have no way of knowing that's your father's opinion too...'

Jinx looked up at him, tears glittering in her deep blue eyes.

'Why don't you just leave us alone?' she choked.

'Because I can't do that.'

One of the tears spilled over onto her cheek and she immediately brushed it away. 'How I wish none of this had ever happened!'

'Oh, come on, Jinx,' he scorned. 'All that money your father is earning has to have its advantages for you too. That dress you're wearing, the diamond earrings—'

'That's enough!' she exclaimed.

'Quite enough,' he agreed.

'I bought these things myself,' she told him angrily. 'With my own money. Earned by my own endeavours.'

'If you say so.'

'I do,' she snapped.

'Fine,' he replied.

Jinx looked up at him searchingly, knowing by the determined glitter in his eyes that he wasn't the sort of man to back off just because she asked him to. Considering the lengths she knew he must have gone to in order to meet her this evening, she shouldn't be surprised by that.

And she wasn't. Surprise certainly wasn't her primary emotion.

'If I so much as *think* you're following me home I *will* contact the police, Nik,' she declared.

He gave an inclination of his head. 'I know that.'

'And?'

'And I'll find some other way,' he answered unhesitantly.

Looking at him, she could see that he would, as he had arranged their meeting this evening, by fair means or foul.

'I have to go,' she told him coldly.

He shrugged. 'Your prerogative.'

She suddenly realized from the harshness of his expression, that whatever had happened between them a few minutes ago was definitely over now as far as he was concerned.

Which was what she had wanted. Wasn't it…?

Of course it was. Any relationship with Nik Prince was dangerous. To her own peace of mind, as well as her father's.

She nodded abruptly before turning and walking away, knowing from the way she felt no tingling of awareness down her spine that Nik wasn't watching her this time. And why should he? He had failed in his objective, which meant she was of no further use to him.

What would Nik say, Jinx wondered, if he were to ever learn the truth?

He was less than proud of himself, Nik acknowledged uncomfortably as he sat across the dinner table from Jane Morrow, the pretty blonde thirtyish-year-old making no effort to hide the attraction she felt towards him, touching him constantly as they talked.

The last six days of searching for Jinx's home address had proved even more frustrating than the previous two months.

There were several J. Nixons listed in the London telephone books, none of them the right ones. Jackson Nixon's previous publishers—of those serious historical tomes—had informed him that Professor Nixon had recently moved and hadn't yet supplied them with his new address. Although, they had also added firmly, they wouldn't have been able to reveal that information even if they did have it!

Nik hadn't been any more successful when he'd decided to turn his attention to investigating Jinx instead of her father.

Cambridge University had been of no use at all in supplying him with an address for Dr Juliet Nixon, claiming they weren't at liberty to give out that information, although they had offered to forward any letter he cared to send to Dr Nixon at the university. Very helpful!

A visit to Jinx's friend Susan Fellows two days after her party, on the pretext that he had lost a cufflink on Saturday evening, had proved totally unfruitful, both with regard to the non-existent cufflink and in garnering any information on Jinx. Apart from confirming that, yes, the Nixons had moved in the last year—with no address forthcoming, naturally!—and that Jinx's father had been ill for some time, the beautiful blonde hadn't wanted to discuss her friend at all.

None of Stazy's friends seemed to know Jinx personally, let alone where she lived. Which had brought Nik full circle and left his only possible source of information to be Jane Morrow at Stephens Publishing...

But, strangely enough, even though he had felt no qualms about calculatingly charming this woman a month ago, he now felt distaste at the possibility of taking it any further. As Jane seemed to want him to do. Oh, Jane was attractive enough, but his reason for asking her out again was certainly less than honourable.

Honourable…

Now there was a word to be reckoned with, Nik acknowledged self-derisively. Was he an honourable man? He had always thought so. But his behaviour these last few weeks concerning meeting Jackson Nixon was certainly questionable. In fact, since meeting Jinx, it seemed to have become something of an obsession with him.

As had Jinx!

In fact, Nik had found himself thinking altogether too much about Jinx Nixon the last six days, about the way she had felt in his arms that night, and not enough about her father, and the movie he wanted to make of the man's book.

'—had some really good news today.' His attention returned to Jane Morrow as she spoke excitedly, her almost boyish slenderness due to the nervous energy that marked all of her quick movements.

'Tell me about it,' he invited.

'J. I. Watson sent in his second manuscript this morning!' Jane told him, her face flushed with the triumph of being able to tell him that. 'James has it, so I haven't had the chance to read all of it yet, but the little I have tells me it's going to be another runaway success. Which doesn't always happen with second books, you know…'

'Is it another *No Ordinary Boy* book?' he asked.

'Oh, yes,' Jane confirmed. 'Of course, it won't have that title, but it has all the same characters, and…'

She continued to talk, but Nik had faded her out after

her initial announcement that they had received the second J. I. Watson 'Boy' manuscript.

Was Jinx aware that her father had written a second book? From her vehemence on Saturday evening concerning the commercial success of the first one, he would have thought she would rather her father never put fictional pen to paper again. Or fingers to keyboard, depending on which method Jackson Nixon preferred to use in order to write his books, Nik allowed ruefully.

But this second manuscript made it even more urgent that he meet the other man; the publication of the second book, coinciding with the possible release of the movie of the first book, would be tremendous publicity for all concerned.

If only he could get past Jinx and talk to her father!

'I suppose he's requested the same conditions as before?' he quizzed Jane lightly, knowing she had been as puzzled by the author's behaviour as James Stephens was.

In fact, Nik having learnt that the J in the author's name stood for Jackson, the I for Ivor meant that he probably now knew more about the author than the publishers did!

Jane made a face. 'No publicity? No interviews? No book signings?' She nodded. 'Pretty much. Except there was rather an interesting footnote this time...' She broke off teasingly as she gave him a pointed look.

Nik moved uncomfortably under that predatory gaze. 'Yes...?'

'Well, it's strange, really,' Jane confided huskily, once again touching his hand. 'You're actually mentioned by name too this time.'

He stiffened warily. 'I am?'

'"Absolutely no further correspondence from Nik

Prince to be forwarded on'' was how I believe it was worded.' She gave him an assessing look. 'I think you must have really upset him with all your approaches regarding making the film.'

No, he hadn't upset Jackson Nixon—how could he have done when it was virtually impossible to meet the man? The person who was so annoyed with him was his daughter, Jinx. And Nik wasn't altogether sure that it was a totally impersonal annoyance, either.

There was no getting away from the fact that the two of them had had an explosive response to each other on Saturday evening. In fact, in any other circumstances, Nik was sure his pursuit of Jinx Nixon would have culminated in the most passionate affair he had ever been involved in. Something he was sure Jinx had been only too aware of, too.

Jackson Nixon's adamant refusal now to have any further contact with Nik, he was sure, had been instigated by his daughter's reluctance to have any further contact with him!

Making Nik all the more determined that he wouldn't back off, either from Jackson Nixon or his beautiful daughter. The sooner he got Jinx into his bed, the easier this might all be resolved! In fact, just the thought of that slenderly curvaceous body curled nakedly in his arms was enough to arouse him.

Which accounted for the reason, he told himself, that he felt so reluctant to accept Jane Morrow's invitation to join her for coffee when he took her back to her apartment later that evening. 'Coffee' in this case, he knew, was really Jane's way of inviting him into her bed— something, for all her touching and innuendos, he had so far managed to avoid. And intended continuing to do so!

Because at the moment all of his desire was centred on a tiny, rebellious redhead with violet-blue eyes...

He gave a regretful shake of his head. 'Perhaps another time; I have a really early appointment in the morning that I need to be fully awake and alert for,' he invented to nullify any insult Jane might feel at his refusal.

Jane moved closer towards him, her hand resting lightly on his chest as she looked up at him, her tongue moving suggestively across her lips. 'I'll make sure to set my alarm,' she persisted.

'I really can't, Jane.' He smiled to take the edge off his rejection.

'Why not?' She frowned her disappointment, her smile fading. 'Or is it that I've served my purpose now that I've told you as much about J. I. Watson as I know?' she guessed astutely, eyes starting to glitter with anger.

She was too close to the truth for Nik's comfort, he acknowledged self-disgustedly. He also didn't like that slightly possessive edge he detected in her tone; a couple of dinners together certainly did not give her that right. 'I truly am sorry—'

'Not as sorry as I am.' Her voice was sharp with fury.

Nik didn't like her tone at all now, finding it slightly threatening. It only confirmed his decision that to have pursued any further sort of relationship with this woman would have been a mistake.

However, he also knew that his own reluctance wasn't entirely due to any noble sentiment on his part—it had more to do with the haunting memory of a pair of violet-blue eyes, poutingly kissable lips, and a slenderly seductive body.

Although Jane Morrow was already angry enough at his reluctance to share her bed, without knowing that he was actually attracted to the daughter of J. I. Watson!

'Hell hath no fury'…and all that, Nik thought with an inner wince.

Jane's pretty face was no longer pretty at all. 'I should have known that Nik Prince wouldn't really be interested in me, but rather in what I might be able to tell him about the elusive J. I. Watson!' She gave a disgusted shake of her head, agitatedly searching through her evening bag for her apartment key now. 'Well, if it's any consolation,' she bit out, having found the key at last and unlocked the door, 'I have a feeling the reason J. I. Watson shuns the limelight may be because he has—slightly feminine tendencies, shall we be kind and say?'

Nik, having been about to apologize yet again, became suddenly still instead, his eyes narrowing. 'What makes you say that?'

She shrugged too-narrow shoulders as she paused in the open doorway. 'Either that or someone else writes his letters for him; the last two we've received definitely had a female perfume about them.'

Jinx's perfume…?

That elusive, but at the same time heady perfume of Lily of the Valley that he had commented on on Saturday and that Jinx had so summarily dismissed?

'Did you recognize—'

'No, I didn't!' Jane turned to glare at him indignantly, her face twisted in anger now. 'You really are all that they accuse you of in the press, aren't you?' she accused scornfully.

Arrogant. Hard. Cold. Calculating. Single-minded. Brilliant. Gifted. He really had lost track of the names the press had bestowed on him over the years, rarely read anything they wrote about him nowadays, although he did know that the latter two comments were usually the exception to the rule. Most reporters preferred to dwell on his cold arrogance or the latest woman in his life rather than the skill that had earned him those five Oscars Jinx had referred to so scathingly on Saturday evening.

Jinx, again…

He really was becoming obsessed, wasn't he? Although, what Jane said about the perfume on those last two letters was interesting. More than interesting, in fact. Perhaps, as he was reported to have been ill for some time now, Jackson Nixon had had more than a little help from his daughter in the writing of *No Ordinary Boy*? Perhaps—

Nik froze as another—totally amazing!—alternative suddenly occurred to him.

No—it couldn't be!

They couldn't all have been so wrong.

Could they…?

CHAPTER FOUR

'Juliet India Nixon.'

The name, softly but firmly spoken by Nik Prince as he sat opposite Jinx in the lounge of this large, impersonal London hotel, hung in the air between them like a dark, threatening cloud.

Or maybe that was only the way it seemed to her, Jinx allowed heavily; after all, Nik had absolutely no reason to feel in the least threatened by this meeting. In fact, the opposite, she would have thought.

As evidenced by his air of satisfaction as he leant further over the coffee-table that divided them, that silver gaze easily holding hers as he murmured, 'That is you, isn't it, Jinx?'

She forced herself to turn calmly away from those all-seeing eyes, not in the least surprised to see the woman sitting alone two tables down in this hotel lounge staring avidly at Nik Prince; he was the sort of man who attracted female attention wherever he went! Not that Nik seemed at all aware of that interested female gaze—no, all of his attention was firmly fixed on her.

Jinx gave the other woman a sympathetic smile before turning away, deliberately adding sugar to one of the two cappuccinos they had ordered, to give herself a little time before answering Nik.

Not that she thought for a moment that time was going to be of any help to her whatsoever; it had already been two days—two excruciatingly tense days!—since the letter had arrived in the post office box from Nik Prince with, 'Juliet India Nixon or just J. I. Watson? I think we need to talk, don't you? Reception, The Waldorf, Wednesday at 10.30 a.m.' written on it. And Jinx was no further now towards knowing how to deal with this forcefully determined man than she had been then!

She could try continuing to bluff her way out of it, of course, although she didn't hold out much hope of this astutely intelligent man putting up with that for too long. She could try telling him the truth and appealing to his better nature—but did he have a 'better nature'? The press seemed to think not—and, judging by his tenacity in tracking her down this last week, Jinx was inclined to agree with them.

Her chin rose slightly. 'What do you want from me?'

Silver eyes gleamed. 'The truth, of course.'

Her mouth twisted contemptuously. 'Would you know that if it were to jump up and bite you on the nose?'

That silver gleam became slightly opaque now as his gaze narrowed. 'Tell me, is this dislike personal, or just a general one towards movie directors?'

A week ago she would have said the latter, but Nik's behaviour over the last week and a half hadn't endeared him to her in the slightest. 'Tell me, Mr Prince, exactly how did you come to the conclusion that I am J. I. Watson, rather than your initial assumption that it was my father?' She made no effort to keep the derision from her voice.

He looked so much in control sitting across from her, so sure of himself, so—so damned arrogant. Because he was arrogant. And ruthless. A man who didn't care about the how or why, as long as he got what he wanted. And this week he wanted to meet J. I. Watson. In fact, he believed that was exactly what he was doing.

She had no intention of telling him how wrong he was...

But even now, disliking him as much as she did, it was impossible to deny that just looking at him, so self-assured in casual trousers and a cream silk shirt, made her pulse race, sent a shiver of awareness down the length of her spine.

It had been this way since she'd first looked at him at Susan and Leo's party. This complete awareness, just his gaze resting on her mouth—as it was now!—making her feel as if he had actually touched her there, caressed her.

'Does it matter how I found out?' He shrugged those powerful shoulders dismissively. 'It is you, isn't it?' It was a statement rather than a question.

How to answer that?

She had never expected to have to answer questions like this. Because she had never thought the book would become such a runaway bestseller, with cries from all directions for the appearance of the author. And an offer to buy the film rights from such a prestigious director as Nik Prince...

He was still and silent as he waited for her to answer him, like a stalking tiger with his prey, that silver gaze almost hypnotic.

Jinx gave a deliberate smile, if only to show him that she wasn't in the least mesmerised. Or in the least daunted by the fact that he believed he had discovered her real identity. 'And what if it is?' she evaded. 'Surely I've made it more than obvious that I'm even less inter-ested in your offer for the film rights than my father would have been?'

He arched one dark brow. 'You haven't heard my offer yet.'

'Because I don't need to.' She gave a shake of her

head, red hair silkily vibrant. 'I've said no. Several times. As James Stephens has obviously informed you.'

Nik Prince once again sat forward in his chair, seeming to fill the whole of Jinx's vision now. 'What are you so afraid of, Jinx? Maybe if you tell me that—'

'You'll give up on the idea for the film and just go away?' she scorned.

'Well, no...I couldn't exactly say that,' he conceded wryly.

'I thought not,' she rasped.

'But I might be able to understand your stubborn refusal a little more,' he continued.

'Really?' Jinx gave a disbelieving snort. 'And why do you imagine that I need your understanding?'

He drew in a harsh breath, his expression grim now, eyes narrowed, lips thinned. 'Right now, taking your paranoia into account, what you need is my silence, young lady,' he rapped. 'Let's go from there, shall we?'

'Are you threatening me, Mr Prince?' she said slowly, replacing her cup and saucer back on the table.

'No, I'm—' He gave an exasperated sigh. 'No, Jinx, I'm not threatening you—'

'It certainly sounded as if you were.' She met his gaze unflinchingly.

Nik gave a sigh of obvious frustration. 'I didn't ask for this meeting with you today in order to argue with you—'

'You didn't ask for this meeting at all, Mr Prince— you demanded it,' she reminded him forcefully. 'And you did it with the belief that you had the leverage to talk me into allowing you to purchase the film rights of *No Ordinary Boy*. So how do you think you're doing so far?'

'Badly,' he conceded heavily.

'Very badly,' she confirmed.

'That's because you—' He broke off, staring at her impatiently. 'Jinx, what do you have against the movie being made?'

'By you?' she delayed.

'By anyone.'

How astute of him to realize that her stubbornness really wasn't personal, that she would have been just as adamant in her refusal concerning the approach of any film company.

Although she had to say, since meeting Nik Prince, her determination had grown where he was concerned.

Because she recognized his powerful force? Because she knew he wasn't a man who took no for an answer? Or was it simply that the fierce attraction she felt towards him, from that first moment of meeting him at Susan and Leo's, made her doubly wary?

She couldn't remember the last time she had felt attracted to any man, let alone one as forcefully compelling as Nik Prince. She had a good idea where such an attraction could lead if she allowed it to. Which was why she was determined to hold this man, in particular, completely at arm's length.

'Jinx?'

She looked across at him, frowning as she tried to remember what his last question had been. 'Have you read *No Ordinary Boy*?'

His expression darkened. 'Well, of course I've read it! The whole damn world has read it—'

'I think that's somewhat of an exaggeration,' she scoffed.

'It's been published in over ninety countries, in twenty-five languages—'

'Having received one set of royalties already, I do have all that information,' she cut in.

'Then you must also realize that the majority of the people who have read the book believe that J. I. Watson is a man—'

'As you did,' she pointed out.

'As I did,' he agreed. 'The book is about a twelve-year-old boy confined to a wheelchair who suddenly discovers he has super mental abilities—'

'I know what the book's about, thank you! But you think me incapable of imagining being a twelve-year-old boy?' she challenged, her unease increasing if that should prove to be the case.

That silver gaze swept over her with slow deliberation, lingering on the curve of her breasts in the cream silk blouse, before moving down the slender length of her legs in fitted black trousers.

Again, it was almost as if he touched her, as if those big, capable hands had actually caressed her, leaving heat wherever they touched.

'I think,' he finally said huskily, 'that you might have trouble imagining being a boy of any age!'

Her heart gave a leap at the warmth she could see in his eyes, the complete awareness of her treacherous body making her answer him sharply. 'How typically sexist of you, Mr Prince!'

He shrugged broad shoulders. 'Not at all, Jinx.' It seemed he deliberately used her nickname, the name only close friends used. 'Merely stating it as I see it.'

'Well, it would appear that you see it wrong, wouldn't it?' she taunted.

He looked at her with narrowed eyes now. 'It would appear so…' he slowly echoed her words.

Too much, Jinx, she reprimanded herself, she had said far too much; she wanted this man completely out of her life and that of *No Ordinary Boy*, not to make him all the more curious about its author!

She shook her head. 'I simply don't believe that the book would transfer to the big screen.'

He looked derisive now. 'You don't?'

Her cheeks flushed angrily at what she sensed was his amusement at her lack of faith in his ability as a film director. Oh, she knew all about this man's successes, the awards, the Oscars—just as she knew that *No Ordinary Boy* was so personal to her that she couldn't allow a third party to rip it apart in order to make a 'marketable' film.

'No, I don't,' she snapped.

'Why don't you let me be the judge of what does and doesn't transfer to the big screen?'

He was laughing at her, damn him. When she found little or nothing about this situation in the least amusing. 'My answer is no, Mr Prince,' she told him with finality, bending to pick up her bag from the carpeted floor. 'It will remain no.'

She was leaving!

This tiny slip of a woman, with ice in her eyes and fire in her hair, was walking out on him!

That definitely had to be a first...

He had thought at the weekend, once he had established that Juliet India Nixon was more probably the author of *No Ordinary Boy* than her father, that he finally had her at a disadvantage, that it would simply be a case of meeting with her today to tie up the loose ends regarding the movie rights. But Jinx Nixon was anything but amenable, was just as determined as she ever had been to thwart him.

'Just what is it with you, Jinx?' he challenged as she stood up. 'Could it be that it's beneath the highbrow Dr

Juliet Nixon to be associated with a work of fiction like *No Ordinary Boy*?'

If he had thought her eyes cold before, they now turned to fire, her beautiful face flushed with the same anger as she flicked that blazing red hair back over one slender shoulder to glare down at him.

Nik had hoped to evoke some sort of response by his challenge—he just hadn't been quite prepared for the one he got.

This woman was so beautiful when roused, so vibrantly alive, that he immediately saw her aroused in a completely different way, the image of her lying naked and wanton in his arms causing him to shift uncomfortably as his body responded to that image.

It was totally amazing; he hadn't physically responded like this just at the thought of a woman in his bed since his college days, but ten minutes in Jinx Nixon's company and he was doing exactly that.

Something, given the circumstances, he stood about as much chance of achieving where Jinx was concerned as flying to the moon!

He grimaced. 'I apologize for that remark.' He sighed, shaking his head. 'I just don't understand you.' Something else that hadn't happened in a long time.

Perhaps he had become jaded over the years, too accustomed to women wanting something from him, from the power he wielded as head of PrinceMovies, but nothing he said or did seemed to make any difference whatsoever to Jinx's resolve not to have anything to do with him or his movie company. By itself that was enough to frustrate the hell out of him, but taking his personal—physical!—response to this woman into account, it only made the situation more explosive.

Jinx seemed to be confused herself now, as if she wasn't quite sure what to do next, either.

Nik knew exactly what she wanted to do—tell him goodbye and walk out of here!—but he could also see by the perplexed frown of indecision on her creamy brow that something was holding her back from doing that.

What could it be?

What was this woman still hiding from him?

God, he was arrogant, wasn't he? Nik recognized with self-disgust. There must be any number of things this woman wasn't telling him. Probably not just him either; Jinx Nixon came over as a very private person, indeed. In fact, he had a feeling Jinx was the sort of woman it could take a lifetime to get to know.

Hell! It was dangerous to even think about the words 'Jinx' and 'lifetime' in the same sentence. It wasn't that he was particularly anti-commitment; after all, his parents had been happily married right up until the day his father had died, and his sister Stazy was certainly happy in her marriage; it just wasn't an option Nik had ever considered for himself.

So why was he considering it now?

He wasn't, came the blunt answer. Not seriously. Damn it, he barely knew Jinx Nixon, and the little he did know, that she was stubborn, sassy and highly intellectual, totally nullified the fact that she was so incredibly beautiful.

Nevertheless, Nik still had a feeling, for his own self-preservation, that the idea of seduction was no longer an option where this woman was concerned.

'Please sit down again, Jinx,' he persuaded, still sensing her indecision.

She sat, looking down at her hands now, the fiery curtain of her hair falling forward to caress the paleness of her cheeks as those hands clenched tightly together.

What was it? What had he missed? Because Nik was more convinced than ever that he was missing something, that he just had to find the right button to press and Jinx Nixon would be like putty in his hands. He just had no idea what that button was!

'Jinx, will you have dinner with me this evening?'

Now where the hell had that come from? Nik wondered dazedly. The idea hadn't even formed in his mind, let alone been processed for viability—if it had he would have told himself what a bad idea it was for him to spend any more time alone with Jinx, that he just wanted her signature on a contract and then he would be on his way.

She was looking at him now, her head tilted thoughtfully to one side, a slight smile curving that deeply kissable mouth. 'You didn't mean to say that…'

'No,' he admitted with a wry smile. 'But having said it…?'

She laughed softly, a huskily evocative sound. 'I don't think that's a good idea, Nik.'

Neither did he—just the sound of his name on her lips was enough to send a sliver of awareness down the length of his spine. 'Perhaps not,' he conceded. 'But I'm asking, anyway.'

How his two brothers would laugh if they could see him now—the arrogantly self-contained Nik willing this tiny woman to have dinner with him tonight. Zak and Rik would find it highly amusing that he had to ask twice at all, let alone exert all of his pressure of will in order to get the positive answer he wanted.

And he did want it. That cautious self-preservation told him to stay as far away from this woman as it was possible for him to be, but all of his natural instincts told him he wanted to be with her again. That he wanted so much more than that.

And he wasn't averse to using every means at his disposal to achieve his objective!

'Surely your father won't mind your going out and leaving him for one evening?' he prompted softly, closely watching her response to this mention of her father, knowing by the way her expression suddenly became blankly unreadable that he had touched a raw nerve. 'Just how ill is your father, Jinx?' he pressed at her continuing silence.

She seemed to flinch at his persistence, her smile having faded long ago, once again withdrawing behind that coolly dismissive mask. 'I have no intention of discussing my father with you, Nik,' she snapped. 'Either now or at any other time,' she added firmly.

In other words, she wasn't going to have dinner with him this evening. Damn. Good move, Nik! He cursed his own stupidity in having moved too far, too fast. So much for his finding the right buttons to press...

'I heard that he had some sort of nervous breakdown a year or so ago?' he murmured, still sure that Jackson Nixon was the key to this woman's acquiescence.

Then why did he feel such a heel as her face paled even more, her eyes huge blue pools of pain and confusion as she looked at him incredulously?

'And where, exactly, did you *hear* that?' she demanded, her whole body defensively taut as she sat up straighter in the chair, those tiny breasts unknowingly thrust provocatively forward.

A fact that Nik tried his best to ignore—and failed miserably, able to see the outline of her nipples against the silky fabric of her blouse; indeed, almost able to discern their rosy hue. 'One of his colleagues at the university mentioned—'

'You had *no* right to go anywhere near my father's colleagues!' She gasped. 'This is *exactly* what I didn't want! *Exactly* what I knew would happen once people started snooping about in an effort to meet the author of *No Ordinary Boy!*' Two bright spots of colour had appeared in the paleness of her cheeks as she breathed deeply in her agitation. 'Stay away from my father, Nik! Stay away from anyone who knows him! Most of all—' she stood up again forcefully '—stay away from me!'

He couldn't do that. Didn't want to do that. More than ever he wanted this woman to have dinner with him this evening. Forget dinner—he just wanted her with him this evening.

'Jinx, please sit down—'

'No way,' she told him angrily, once again flicking back the fiery length of her hair. 'I can't believe you did such a thing! Can't believe anyone could sink so low as to—'

'You weren't exactly cooperating,' Nik pointed out as he stood up to face her.

Jinx looked at him incredulously. 'And that was enough for you to pry into my private life, my father's private life, like some cheap—'

'Excuse me, Mr Prince—it is Nik Prince, isn't it?'

Nik had turned sharply at the first sound of the female voice, his angry gaze narrowing warily as he took in the woman's appearance—short dark hair, deep brown eyes, a pleasantly smiling mouth—as she looked at him enquiringly.

'The film director?' the woman pressed brightly.

Nik felt the faint stirrings of unease; in his experience there was only one profession he knew of who pushed their way into other people's lives in this intrusive way. And as he saw the woman nod to a man who had just entered the lounge, the familiar camera slung about his neck, Nik knew that his guess had been the correct one.

Hell, Jinx was skittish enough already, without finding herself face to face with a reporter and her photographer!

CHAPTER FIVE

'WHAT do you think you're doing?' Jinx squeaked indignantly as she suddenly found her arm grasped in Nik Prince's vice-like fingers as he began marching her across the room. 'Nik—'

'Move!' he instructed harshly as she attempted to push his hand away from her arm.

'But I don't—' Jinx broke off in alarm as a light was suddenly flashed in her face, momentarily blinding her.

Nik just kept on walking, pulling the semi-blinded Jinx along with him.

What on earth was going on? she wondered dazedly. Who was that woman? The same woman who had been staring at Nik so avidly across the lounge earlier...! Why had Nik wanted to get away from her so quickly? Most puzzling of all, what had been the source of that light that had blinded her?

'She was a reporter, Jinx,' Nik told her as he pulled her into the lift and pressed the button to ascend.

But not before another light had flashed brightly, almost in their faces this time, Jinx able to see clearly that the flash had come from a camera being thrust between the rapidly closing lift doors.

'And he—' Nik reached out to grab the camera just as the doors closed, the other man's cry of protest instantly cut off mid-flow '—is her associate!' He released Jinx to open the back of the camera and take out the film and thrust it into his trouser pocket. 'Damn, damn, damn!' he muttered grimly as he closed the camera.

A reporter…

Not just a reporter. Paparazzi!

The scourge of the true reporter, whose aim was to report the real news, these other, less professional members of the press weren't really looking for truth, but went in search of sensationalism.

Jinx felt slightly sick at the realization that she had been in the presence of just such a reporter the last half an hour or so, that she had been completely wrong in her assumption earlier that the other woman had been looking at Nik because she'd recognized him and found him attractive; this woman was out for a story, and didn't particularly care how she got it.

Her teeth began to chatter uncontrollably in reaction to what had just happened.

If Nik hadn't realized— If he hadn't spotted the photographer— If he hadn't grabbed the camera in that way—!

'It's okay, Jinx.' Nik spoke soothingly as he moved to stand in front of her, touching her gently as he moved the fringe of hair back from over her horrified eyes. 'It's okay,' he repeated encouragingly.

Of course it wasn't okay. Nik was a personality, a highly photographic one, and if he hadn't retrieved that film then Jinx knew she would have appeared beside him in a photograph in one of tomorrow's newspapers—probably with a speculative comment about who this latest mystery woman was in his life. After that, it would only be a matter of time…!

'Come on,' he urged as the lift doors opened.

Jinx followed him out of the lift, only to come to an abrupt halt as she saw they were on one of the upper floors. A floor containing bedrooms, she realized as a maid came out from cleaning one of them.

'Could you see that this is taken down to Reception and returned to its owner?' Nik handed the camera over to the rather surprised maid. 'You can't miss him—he's the one who looks as if he just found a cent but lost a dollar,' he added with grim satisfaction before turning back to Jinx.

A Jinx who stared back at him accusingly. This was all his fault—

'This isn't my fault, Jinx.' His words harshly echoed what she was thinking.

Her eyes widened. 'Then whose fault is it? Mine?' she asked scornfully. 'Reporters and their photographers don't usually follow me around, I can assure you—'

'They would if they knew you were J. I. Watson!' he assured her scathingly before turning to open the door across the corridor, standing back to allow her to enter first.

Jinx hung back reluctantly. Did she really want to compound this situation by going into a hotel bedroom with Nik Prince—?

'Jinx, it's my guess it isn't going to be safe for you to leave here for some time yet,' Nik informed her dryly as he saw her obvious reluctance. 'In fact, I may have to have some help in creating a diversion.'

'I beg your pardon?' Jinx queried as she marched past him.

Into what turned out not to be the bedroom she had been expecting, but a sitting-room obviously attached to a bedroom. Of course; she should have known that a man like Nik Prince would have a suite, not just a bedroom!

'Don't worry about it, Jinx,' Nik reassured her as he strode across the room to pick up the telephone receiver. 'I'll sort this out in just—'

'Don't *worry* about it?' she repeated with suppressed

violence as she threw her shoulder bag down onto one of the sofas. '*You'll* sort it out? It's because of you that I'm in this mess in the first place!' She glared across the room at him, eyes gleaming deeply blue, her cheeks flushed. 'Did you organize for that reporter to be there? Is this some trick to force me into giving you the film rights to *No Ordinary Boy*?'

'Of course not,' Nik rasped.

'I don't believe you!' Jinx dissolved into floods of tears, her face buried in her hands.

As if by doing so she could shut out Nik Prince altogether, could fool herself into believing none of this were really happening!

'Jinx, it was me the reporter spoke to, not you,' he reminded her. 'It was me she was after, not you.'

'Are you sure?' She so much needed to believe him!

His expression softened, and he murmured her name as he took her into his arms. Arms that felt strong and protective as they completely enveloped her, and Jinx reacted instinctively as she clung to him like a rock in a storm. A storm that seemed to be gaining momentum and force with each passing second.

'Jinx...!' This time her name was a husky groan, one of Nik's arms tightening about the slenderness of her waist, the other hand moving to cup her chin as he raised her face to his, his eyes looking deeply into hers as he slowly lowered his head.

There was only time for the briefest moment of doubt, before she gave herself up to the seductive claim of his mouth on hers.

Emotions swirled and grew as she kissed him back with all the pent-up feelings inside her, her lips parting beneath the pressure of his, senses leaping as he began a slow exploration with the tip of his tongue, first along the edge of her bottom lip, then the moist softness within.

His arms tightened as Jinx tasted him with her own tongue, his thighs hard against hers now. Her blouse came loose from the waistband of her trousers as her arms moved up to curve about his neck, his hair soft and silky to the touch as her fingers caressed his sensitive nape.

His hands slipped under her blouse and felt warm against her bare skin as they moved to touch the arch of her back, moving featherlight across her ribcage before tenderly cupping both her breasts.

Jinx's back arched when Nik's mouth left hers to travel the length of her neck, lingering in the hollows at its base, nibbling erotically on her ear lobes, before licking the sensitive skin below.

His chest was covered in fine dark hairs, Jinx's fingers making their way beneath Nik's shirt and lacing into their silkiness, easily finding the sensitive nubs nestled there. Nik's sharply indrawn groan of breath was evidence of his own pleasure at her searching touch.

Nik unbuttoned and then pushed aside her silky blouse, his mouth moist against the upper curve of her breasts, his hands still cupping, caressing, unerringly finding the fiery tips as he bent to suckle through the lacy material of her bra that was all that separated him from her nakedness.

Heat. Consuming her. The warmth between her thighs was the hottest moist heat imaginable, dragging at her lower limbs with sweet demand, her hands moving to cling to the broad width of his shoulders as she felt weak with need. A need she knew Nik could satisfy, assuage, as no other man could.

His eyes were smoky grey as he raised his head to

look at her searchingly. 'Is this what you want, Jinx?'
His voice was husky with his own arousal. 'I hope it is—
because I want you very much!' His lips once again
sought hers, his kiss lingering, seeking, persuading.

There was no doubting what Nik was asking. No
doubting that he wanted her. Or that she wanted him.

But…

It would be so easy to dismiss that *but*, to forget it, if
only briefly, and *yet*…

But. And *yet*.

Both expressions of doubt. A doubt that was growing
stronger the longer Nik looked at her so compellingly as
he waited for her answer.

Entering into a relationship, any relationship, with Nik
Prince would be a mistake, Jinx finally accepted painfully, every inch of her protesting as she forced herself
to move out of his arms, to turn away to rebutton her
blouse with shaking hands.

That task finally completed, she was almost afraid to
turn back and look at Nik. She knew that he hadn't
moved, could feel the heat of his gaze on her back.

She deliberately walked away from him to stand in
front of the window looking down into the busy street
below, her back stiffening slightly as she finally heard
him move.

But it was only to once again pick up the telephone
receiver as he punched out the number with suppressed
violence.

Really meant for her? Probably, she accepted huskily.
What must a man like Nik think of her, a twenty-eight-
year-old woman, too afraid of the physical intimacy they
had both craved such a short time ago, because she feared
the emotional intimacy that would follow?

'Zak?' he barked into the receiver as his call was obviously answered.

Zak...? His brother, Zak Prince? The legendary golden film star everyone—but especially women!—raved about?

What on earth was the point of Nik telephoning him now, of all times?

'No, I think you have the wrong number,' a distracted voice sounded down the earpiece of the phone.

'Very funny, Zak,' Nik snapped in answer to his younger brother's witty reply, all the time his gaze fixed on Jinx as she stood so aloofly remote in front of the window, the sunshine giving her hair the appearance of living flame. 'Are you in the hotel?' he demanded impatiently of Zak, knowing he was unfairly taking out his foul temper on his brother, but too angry with himself—and Jinx—at that moment to do anything else.

'Uh-oh,' Zak murmured knowingly, obviously giving Nik all of his attention now. 'What—or should I say who?—has upset you, big brother?'

'I'll tell you later,' Nik dismissed—knowing he wouldn't tell Zak any such thing. The fact that he was frustrated as hell, first by Jinx's accusations, and then by her shying off just now, was not something he intended discussing with his little brother. For one thing, it was simply too personal, and for another—Zak probably wouldn't stop laughing for a week at the idea of his big brother being turned down in that way! 'What I need right now is for you to find a beautiful woman—'

'No problem,' Zak assured him. 'Why do you think I'm still in the hotel?' he added mockingly.

Nik would just bet it wasn't a problem for his brother to find a beautiful woman; at thirty-six Zak went through women like other men went through socks! 'Is she single?' he prompted cautiously.

'Of course,' Zak came back slightly indignantly. 'That only happened the once, Nik—and only then because she forgot to mention she was a married woman.'

'Okay,' Nik conceded. 'In that case, I would like the two of you to go down to Reception, making sure you're seen. There's a reporter and photographer waiting down in Reception. I want you to distract them long enough for me to get the hell out of here!' he explained impatiently as Zak would have interrupted.

'Hmm,' Zak mused. 'And can I ask who's going to be leaving with you?'

'No,' Nik snapped.

'And you asked me if I'm with a married woman—'

'Zak!' he warned.

'Okay, okay, give me ten minutes. I'll call you as I'm about to go down. If it rings three times and then stops, that means it's me—'

'Zak, you aren't supposed to be enjoying this!' Nik growled, knowing his brother was doing exactly that—and that he would want some sort of explanation later on today!

'Just give me ten minutes,' Zak told him good-naturedly.

It was probably going to be the longest ten minutes of his life, Nik realized as he slowly put down his receiver, Jinx still turned away from him. Although she couldn't have helped but overhear his half of the telephone conversation, at least.

Not that it would have been much help, he acknowledged ruefully; he wasn't especially known for explaining himself to people, even less so when all he really wanted to do was pull Jinx back into his arms, take her to his bed, and keep her there for a week!

He tensed as she finally turned around, a shutter coming down over his emotions as he took in the paleness of her face, her eyes seeming like huge blue lakes in that paleness. Damn it, she looked like an injured butterfly, all elusive fragility.

'That was very kind of you.' She spoke huskily, her gaze not quite meeting his.

His mouth twisted. 'I've never thought of myself as particularly unkind.'

'I didn't mean—never mind.' The hand she had raised in protest dropped back down to entwine awkwardly with the other one, her expression guarded beneath dark lashes. 'I'm sorry about just now—'

'About what?' Nik tried to sound unconcerned. Damn it, it was bad enough that just one word of encouragement from her and he would be back in her arms, without having her apologize for turning him down!

'It's a woman's prerogative to change her mind, isn't it?' he drawled.

'I was referring to my accusations concerning the reporter, not—' She broke off, sudden warmth colouring her cheeks. 'Never mind,' she mumbled.

No, never mind. The fact that every time he met this woman he was left a frustrated mess was his problem, not hers. It was just that she seemed to get under his skin...

If it weren't for the fact she was J. I. Watson, then he would get the hell away from her—and stay away.

Which, from how she was looking at him, was obviously exactly what she was thinking too!

'Um.' She swallowed hard, almost squirming with discomfort. 'Do you think your brother will be long?'

Of course, she hadn't heard that part of the conversation. 'Ten minutes should do it. Seven now,' he added after a brief glance at his wrist-watch. 'Can I get you a drink while we're waiting?' he offered almost desperately; this was obviously turning out to be the longest ten minutes of his life!

Her tongue moved to moisten her lips, Nik's pulse leaping along with it, although he was pretty sure that Jinx had no idea how provocative the gesture was. There was no way she would have done it if she had!

'A cola, or some other soft drink?' he elaborated as her frown deepened. 'Don't worry, Jinx,' he added scathingly, moving to show her the mini-bar that stood in the corner of the sitting-room, stocked with drinks, nuts and chocolate. 'I have no intention of trying to get you drunk in the middle of the day in order to have my wicked way with you!'

'No,' she confirmed flatly—giving him no idea what she thought of that particular suggestion! 'Does that happen a lot? The thing with the reporter and photographer,' she explained quickly, once again not meeting his gaze.

Just in case he should misunderstand and assume she meant her having turned him down flat!

He grimaced. 'All the time.' He shrugged. 'We all came over a couple of weeks ago for our nephew's christening,' he explained at her questioning look. 'And we've all been avoiding the media ever since,' he added dryly, 'but my little brother Zak, who's still in town because he's discussing his next film with the director, makes much more interesting reading than I do. Talk of the devil,' he said as the telephone began to ring.

Three times before ringing off. As promised.

He really should have a word with his little brother about his knowledge of such subterfuge...

'Right, let's get out of here!' Nik closed the mini-bar, striding over to open the door. 'Jinx?' he prompted as she didn't move; in fact, she seemed rooted to the spot.

She looked at him guardedly. 'You're sure this is going to work?'

No, he wasn't sure this was going to work! Oh, he had no doubts that Zak and his companion would prove a suitable diversion; that wasn't the problem at all. The problem was that he had really annoyed that photographer earlier by taking his camera, and members of the press, once annoyed, tended to stay that way. He also didn't underestimate the intelligence of the reporter or the photographer; Zak arriving downstairs in this way could seem just a little too convenient to one or both of them...

'I'm sure,' he said with more hope than certainty, although there was no way that the reporter could know that Jinx was J. I. Watson. 'Now, once we get downstairs, walk straight through the reception area, don't look left or right, just keep on walking, and then once we're outside we'll get into a taxi and—what?' he rasped as she slowly shook her head, her expression unmistakably sceptical now, the look in her eyes derisive.

'You've done this before, haven't you?' she said knowingly.

'Avoided reporters?' He frowned. 'All the time—'

'No, not that,' Jinx said slowly, no longer looking either apprehensive or remote; in fact, it was difficult to tell how she looked at this moment! 'The telephone call to your brother. The easy way he agreed to help out. The fact that you have some sort of message to let you know he was on his way downstairs.' She indicated the now-silent telephone. 'Nik, just how often have you had to sneak a woman out of your hotel room?'

Now he could tell exactly how she looked—disgusted best described it.

And he wasn't sure whether that emotion was directed at herself or him!

CHAPTER SIX

WHAT a fool she had been!

It was so easy to forget, when Nik held her in his arms, when he kissed her, when he made love to her, exactly what sort of man he was. But the smoothness with which he had dealt with that reporter and photographer earlier, as well as now—with his brother's help, of course!—had very quickly reminded her. Thank goodness!

'Jinx—'

'You have so many things worked out, don't you, Nik?' she scorned. 'The way that you engineered that meeting at Susan and Leo's last weekend, for example. Just how did you know I was going to be there, Nik?' She could tell by the impatient discomfort in his expression that he would rather she hadn't asked that particular question.

'Jinx, you're wasting valuable time—'

'It's my time to waste.' She shrugged.

'And mine—'

'I don't give a damn about your time, Nik—and I'm not leaving here until you answer my question!' Her eyes flashed deeply blue.

He glared at her frustratedly. 'You have to choose *now* to ask me that particular question?'

'Yes!'

He sighed. 'You're not going to like the answer.'

'I didn't think for a moment that I would,' she assured him scathingly. 'I can reason that you were able to write directly to me to organize this morning's meeting, because you discovered the PO box that was used for corresponding with Stephens Publishing—although I have yet to find out who your source was,' she added coldly, deciding it was past time she had words with the publisher. 'But it doesn't follow that that would tell you I would be at Susan and Leo's the weekend before last— Wait a minute! You had me followed from the post office earlier that week when I had lunch with Susan, didn't you?' she realized slowly as Nik looked decidedly uncomfortable now. 'Which means, to know about her anniversary party on Saturday, you must also have had Susan checked out...'

There was no other way he could possibly have found out what her own plans were for that weekend. She had realized his being there at all was too much of a coincidence, but she certainly hadn't realized the lengths to which he had gone—!

'Didn't you?' she breathed incredulously.

'Jinx—'

'You did.' She nodded furiously. 'And my name is Juliet. Or Dr Nixon, if you prefer. Never Jinx as far as you are concerned,' she bit out, grabbing her bag from where she had placed it earlier and walking determinedly to the door. She paused there, turning to glare at him. 'If you—or anyone employed by you,' she added scornfully, 'attempt to come near me again, then that harassment charge I threatened you with last week will become a reality!'

She was so angry that at that moment she could cheerfully have hit him—and felt all the better for it. She simply couldn't believe that anyone could behave in such an underhand way. Or that she could have allowed herself to kiss, and be kissed, by such a man.

He shook his head. 'You're being totally unreasonable—'

'*I'm* being unreasonable?' she hissed. 'Your own behaviour borders on obsessional. Hit a raw nerve, did I?' she spat out as he seemed to pale slightly.

Good, came her inner—childish?—response. But it was about time he knew what it felt like to be on the receiving end for a change. She felt as if she had only just been managing to keep half a step in front of him for the last week and a half—it seemed only fair that she had now decided to turn and challenge him!

What was the old saying—'attack is the best form of defence'…?

Well, where Nik Prince was concerned, attack was the only defence left to her.

'Not at all,' he dismissed stiffly. 'As I pointed out to you last week, such a course of action would only bring about exactly what you're hoping to avoid. Publicity,' he reminded at her questioning look.

Her eyes widened. 'Are you threatening me?'

'Believe it or not, no. No,' he repeated firmly as she continued to look at him sceptically. 'But even if that reporter earlier had no idea who you are, I've made no secret of the fact that I'm looking for J. I. Watson. And if I could find you, then so can someone else.'

Oh, he was unquestionably right about that. Except they weren't talking about 'someone else' at the moment, they were talking about him!

'Let's concentrate on you for the moment, shall we?' Her voice was saccharine-sweet. 'Because if you force me into making this into a legal matter, then I can assure you I will never give you the film rights to *No Ordinary Boy*. In fact,' she added as he would have spoken, 'I'll find out who your biggest rival is and give them to him!'

Nik's gaze narrowed as he looked at her for several long minutes. 'You really would do that, wouldn't you?' he finally said.

At this moment? Angry with herself. Angry with him. Oh, yes, right now she was more than capable of doing something like that.

Tomorrow might be something else entirely...

Although she had no intention of letting the arrogant Nik Prince see that. 'If I'm forced to.' She nodded abruptly.

He drew in a harsh breath. 'Fine. Let's get you out of here, then, shall we? And then—'

'I'm more than capable of getting myself out of here,' she assured him. 'After all, as you've already pointed out, it's you the press are after, not me!'

Although just how long that would last was anybody's guess. Which meant she had some very serious decisions to make during the next couple of days. Decisions she was no nearer making now than she had been a year ago...

'It's only a matter of time, Ji—Juliet,' Nik corrected pointedly as his words echoed her thoughts. 'It was bad enough the first time around, but the mad clamour to find J. I. Watson will start all over again, more intensely, once the second ''Ordinary Boy'' book is published...'

'What do you know about the second ''Boy'' book?' she cut in sharply, every inch of her tensing warily as that icy grey gaze suddenly eluded hers.

Nik made an impatient movement. 'Well, of course there will be a second book—'

'There's no ''of course'' about it,' she said slowly, becoming more sure by the minute that he knew she had already submitted the second manuscript. Just as she was sure that only someone at Stephens Publishing could have told him that...

'Oh, for—' Nik broke off his angry exclamation as the telephone began to ring.

Three times. Just as before. And then ringing off. Just as before.

'Your brother seems to be becoming a little—anxious, at the delay,' Jinx said derisively. 'I suggest you go down and alleviate that anxiety for him.'

'And you?' Nik frowned. 'Where are you going?'

'I don't believe that is any of your business! But I actually intend going out exactly the way I came in—straight out the front door! You're the one they want a story on, Nik—not me. And as far as I'm concerned, they can have you!' she declared before letting herself out of the suite and heading for the lift.

She certainly wasn't going to be part of Nik's story. Either now or in the future. Although she had come very close to becoming exactly that, Jinx realized heavily as the lift descended. She had been so close—too close!—to giving in to the desire he had aroused in her, to just forgetting everything else.

How he would have liked that! Not only would he have managed to find J. I. Watson where everyone else had failed, but he would also believe he had managed to get her into his bed!

Jinx closed her eyes, swaying slightly as she thought of her arousal earlier, her need for the feel of Nik's body against hers, inside hers, loving her, possessing her, until she could think of nothing else.

Had it been only the loneliness of the last eighteen

months, that necessary feeling of distance between herself and other people, that had caused her intense reaction to Nik? Or had it been something else?

Please let it not be anything else!

Falling in love with a man like Nik Prince, besides being a totally insane thing for her to do, would also be complete anathema to the anonymity of J. I. Watson.

If she needed further proof, the crowd of people gathered around Zak Prince and the stunning blonde at his side as Jinx stepped from the lift into the reception area, the reporter of earlier included, was more than enough to convince her of that!

Jinx strode straight through the reception area, outside to where a row of taxis stood waiting, nodding her thanks to the doorman as he opened the back door of the first one for her to get inside. Only starting to breathe easily again once that door had been closed behind her.

'Where to, love?' the driver prompted cheerfully.

'Fold Street, please,' Jinx told him. 'Stephens Publishing on Fold Street,' she repeated firmly before sitting back to stare sightlessly out of the window.

Well, that went well, Nik told himself disgustedly as the door closed decisively behind Jinx, having had no choice but to stand impotently by and watch as she walked out of his life.

Or thought she did.

There was no way, absolutely no way he was letting Jinx just walk away from him like that. Because she was J. I. Watson. Because he still wanted the movie rights to *No Ordinary Boy*.

At least, that was what he told himself. But another

part of him knew that it was because he wanted Jinx Nixon, wanted her in his bed, with no interruptions, for as long as it took to sate both himself and her. Maybe then he would be able to get her out of his head, out of the dreams he had been having about her this last week, naked and willing as he made love to her in every imaginative way he could think of.

He had never allowed a woman to get between him and his work. And Jinx Nixon was going to be no exception.

'What the hell happened to you?' Zak demanded a few minutes later as Nik opened the door to let him into his suite. 'I kept the press busy for as long as I possibly could—much to Damson Grey's delight. Yes, that is who spent the night with me.' Zak grinned at Nik's disgusted snort. 'And, believe me, her body more than lives up to her name!' His grin widened as he threw himself down into one of the armchairs to look up at Nik.

He was one of the scruffiest men Nik had ever seen, both on and off the screen. It never ceased to amaze Nik how his brother drew women to him like a magnet. Of course, it could have something to do with Zak's golden good looks: overlong blond hair, laughing blue eyes set in a face so handsome he was almost beautiful, his body long and loose-limbed in the faded denims and baggy black tee shirt.

'So where is she?' Zak prompted as he looked conspiratorially around the suite. 'Still hiding in the bedroom?'

To Nik's self-disgust, he found himself tensing resentfully at this offhand remark directed at Jinx. 'She was never in the bedroom,' he bit out reprovingly.

'She wasn't?' Zak's eyes widened speculatively. 'So where is she now?' he asked before Nik could give him another cutting reply.

'I have no idea,' Nik answered him honestly. 'She walked out of here about five minutes ago. In fact, you may have seen her on her way out.' He frowned as the thought occurred to him.

Zak gave the idea some thought, his brow clearing suddenly. 'Tiny little thing? Long red hair, very deep blue eyes? A very kissable—'

'That's enough!' Nik growled.

Zak's eyes widened. 'Yep, I guess that was the one,' he teased. 'And you never made it as far as the bedroom? Maybe that's why you're in such a foul mood, big brother. Self-denial isn't good for a man of your advanced years!'

Zak could say that again! Not the part about his advanced years, of course, but this constant frustration certainly wasn't doing anything for his mood.

Although Nik's discomfort was nothing compared to his concern now for Jinx and what she would do next. Because he didn't doubt that she intended doing something.

'Will you excuse me, Zak?' he murmured distractedly. 'I have to go out for a while.' He picked up his brown leather jacket and pulled it on over his shirt, checking in his trouser pockets for his wallet.

'Going after the beautiful—what is her name?' Zak queried.

'Her name is Juliet. And stay away from her, little brother. Well away.' He scowled darkly.

Zak's grin was wider than ever. 'Wow, this is a first!

Can I use your phone? I have to ring Rik at Stazy's and tell him—'

'Use your own phone,' Nik snapped. 'And tell Rik what, exactly?'

'That our BB has been bowled over by a five-foot nothing of a woman with the body of Venus, of course.' Zak stood up, heading for the bar, taking out a cola and drinking it straight from the bottle.

'Help yourself!' Nik drawled, giving an impatient shake of his head. 'And I would hold off telling Rik anything, if I were you,' he added as he headed for the door. 'Things aren't always what they seem, Zak.'

His brother frowned meditatively. 'Now you've really got me curious…!'

That wasn't quite the idea; the last thing Nik needed right now was Zak and Rik on his case. He was confused enough about Jinx as it was!

'Feel like telling me where you're going?' Zak quirked mocking brows.

'Nope.'

Zak shrugged. 'Maybe I'll catch up with you later.'

'Maybe,' he echoed, frowning heavily as he left the hotel suite.

Where would Jinx have gone after she left him? Home? Or somewhere else? Bearing in mind how angry she had been when she'd left, he had a feeling it wasn't the former. If he were in Jinx's shoes, he'd go—

'Fold Street,' he told the taxi driver as he got in the back of the black vehicle. 'Stephens Publishing,' he added tersely.

The journey seemed interminable, the taxi meeting every conceivable hold-up possible, from someone falling off their bicycle to a set of failed traffic lights. All of which only served to increase Nik's impatience to boiling point.

Jinx had been in a furious mood when she'd left— because of him, admittedly, but he had a definite feeling that anger might spill over onto whomever she spoke to next. If his guess was correct, and Jinx had gone to Stephens Publishing, then, after months of never even meeting his author, James wasn't going to know what hit him!

Maybe they would be lucky and James would be out of the office!

No such luck, Nik groaned inwardly after the receptionist had called James Stephens's secretary and okayed him to go up.

Maybe he was wrong, after all, Nik reasoned on the way up in the lift; the secretary would hardly have allowed him up if there were a full-scale battle going on in James's office.

In which case, he had better do some quick thinking as to what he was doing here!

'You can go right in,' James's secretary looked up to tell him smilingly as he strode into the office.

Great; besides feeling rather foolish for having rushed over here in order to save Jinx from herself by telling James Stephens exactly what she thought of him and his publishing company, Nik was also no nearer to knowing what to tell the other man about his own reason for being here!

'Come in, Nik,' James welcomed him brightly, having stood up to come round his desk and shake Nik by the hand, effectively blocking Nik's view of the rest of the office so he couldn't see whether or not Jinx was actually here.

James smiled at him warmly. 'How fortunate that you should arrive just now.' He beamed. 'You're not going to believe this, but I can actually introduce you to our author J. I. Watson at last!' He finally stepped to one side, leaving Nik with a clear view of Jinx as she sat in the chair facing the other man's desk.

She was sitting sideways in the chair at the moment, that clear violet-blue gaze coldly mocking as she looked up at him challengingly.

Affording Nik little pleasure in knowing he had been right in his surmise as to where she had gone after leaving him…!

CHAPTER SEVEN

'MR PRINCE.' Jinx nodded to him coolly, exerting every ounce of will-power she possessed to remain calmly seated, when every instinct she had screamed for her to stand up defensively as Nik looked down at her with narrowed grey eyes.

The fact that he was here at all was enough to set her nerve endings jangling—even though she'd had prior warning of his imminent arrival when James Stephens's secretary had called through a couple of minutes ago.

But the question was, why was Nik here?

Had he followed her here? Or had he come for reasons of his own?

More to the point, was he going to acknowledge that the two of them already knew each other?

She had arrived here earlier with the sole purpose of telling James Stephens exactly what she thought of his publishing company before demanding her second manuscript back, but the publisher had been so pleased and excited to meet her at last, so obviously genuine in his pleasure, like a little boy who had been given an early Christmas present, that she simply hadn't had the heart to say all those unpleasant things to this genially friendly man.

'Miss Nixon,' Nik greeted her abruptly.

'Can you believe that J. I. Watson has been a woman all this time?' James murmured incredulously as he moved to sit back behind his desk.

'Miss Nixon and I have already met, actually,' Nik admitted.

'You have?' James Stephens looked disappointed as he glanced first at Nik and then back to Jinx.

'Only briefly.' Jinx was the one to expand on that statement. 'But long enough for me to inform Mr Prince that I have no intention of giving him the film rights to *No Ordinary Boy*,' she added tightly.

'Ah,' James breathed softly, grimacing his disappointment.

Jinx's eyes widened. 'I take it that you are in favour of Mr Prince making the film?'

The publisher looked uncomfortable now, obviously debating which of them he should offend—because he had to be aware that whichever way he answered he was going to offend one of them!

He seemed to choose his words carefully. 'If the film were to be made, then I have to say I couldn't think of a finer director than Nik here!'

Jinx had to smile inwardly at the man's tact. 'But the film isn't going to be made,' she said firmly, 'so whether or not Mr Prince is a fine director or not is totally irrelevant.' She raised mocking brows as Nik's mouth tightened grimly at the ambiguity of her remark.

Deliberately so. She knew he was a brilliant director; the whole world knew he was a brilliant director; she just had no intention of adding to his fan club by admitting as much!

'Yes,' James Stephens accepted slowly. 'I—' He broke off as the internal telephone rang on his desk. 'Excuse me.' He smiled apologetically before taking the call.

Probably relieved to get a few moments' respite from the building tension he could sense around him, Jinx guessed ruefully. She—

'What are you doing here?' Nik murmured in a forceful undertone.

Her eyes widened. 'I have a perfect right to visit my publisher if I so wish,' she told him coldly.

'But you never have before.'

'And I probably never will again!' Jinx stood up restlessly, moving across the room to stare out of the window, sensing Nik's presence inches behind her as he followed her. 'What are *you* doing here?' she demanded insultingly.

'Believe it or not, saving you from yourself,' he came back dryly.

She turned to look at him with wide eyes. 'I beg your pardon?'

Nik grimaced. 'You were in a reckless mood when you left the hotel earlier—'

'I wonder why that was!' she snapped.

'Jinx—' He had reached out to touch her, but held his hand up defensively as she flinched away from him. 'Juliet,' he bit out tautly. 'I didn't want you to do something…impulsive, where James was concerned, when it's me you're really mad at!'

He was right, of course, she had come here intending to tell James Stephens that one of his many employees couldn't be trusted, before demanding the second manuscript back.

Because she was mad at Nik.

And herself…

But she would think about that later, when she was alone, not here and now, when Nik was much too close for comfort.

'I'm not mad at you, Nik. I don't know you well enough to be mad at you,' she said insultingly.

His face darkened. 'That isn't true, and you know it—'

'Sorry about that,' James Stephens apologized as he concluded his call. 'Coincidentally, that was your editor, Miss Nixon. I've told her that you and Mr Prince are here, and asked her to join us.'

Jinx hadn't come here with the idea of her visit turning into a social event! In fact, she regretted coming here at all now...

But once again James Stephens looked so pleased with himself and the way things were turning out that Jinx didn't have the heart to disappoint him.

'I'm afraid I can only stay a few more minutes; I have a previous engagement for lunch.' She smiled to take the sting out of her words.

'I was hoping you might let me take you out to lunch.' James frowned. 'Having met you at last, I really don't want to lose you again so quickly,' he added charmingly.

Jinx avoided looking at Nik as he gave a sceptical snort. 'Another time, perhaps.' She was deliberately vague, having no intention of there ever being 'another time'.

She should never have come here, never have blown her anonymity in this way. It was Nik Prince's fault that she had done so. He—

'Ah, Jane.' James Stephens stood up as a tall blonde woman entered his office after the briefest of knocks. 'I want you to meet our author, J. I. Watson,' he announced triumphantly as he moved forward to lightly grasp Jinx's arm.

As if afraid she might try to escape, or at the very least evaporate in front of his eyes, if he didn't hold onto her!

The beautiful blonde Jinx could now identify as her editor, Jane Morrow, moved forward to shake Jinx by the hand, although her smile was bland as she turned to look at Nik.

But it was Nik's response to the other woman's presence in the room that caught and held Jinx's attention; she was able to feel his tension as he looked at the other woman guardedly. A tension he did his best to hide as he seemed to sense Jinx's interest, giving her a tight smile before turning to gaze out of the window at the London skyline.

A view Jinx was almost certain he didn't even see!

She gave her editor a closer look, noting the smooth beauty of the other woman's face, her slender curves in the black business suit she wore, her fingers bare of rings, her legs long and shapely. Attractive enough for Nik Prince to have used his practised charm upon?

The other woman's smile warmed as she turned back to Jinx, blue eyes glowing with enthusiasm. 'It's such a pleasure to meet you at last!' she gushed.

No, Jinx decided, the arrogant Nik Prince wouldn't find this gushing, clinging woman in the least attractive. So what had been the reason for his tension when the other woman had come into the room? Surely Jane Morrow, her own editor, couldn't be the one to have leaked information concerning her identity? That just didn't make sense. But, then, what did make sense about any of this situation she now found herself in?

'Thank you,' she accepted lightly. 'I was actually just telling James that I have to go now.' That she should never have come here in the first place!

'Surely not?' Jane Morrow frowned her disappointment. 'We have so much to talk about, so many questions I would like to ask you. The second manuscript is wonderful, by the way,' she added delightedly. 'So many second books aren't, you know, that...'

Jinx tuned out the other woman's praise, instead turning to look curiously at Nik as she once again sensed the tension in his rigidly straight back.

'It's so kind of you to say so—' Jinx nodded to Jane Morrow as the other woman paused to draw breath '—but I really do have to get going.'

'But you will come back?' Jane Morrow asked.

She swallowed hard as both Jane Morrow and James Stephens looked at her expectantly. They were both nice people, Jinx accepted that, not at all the hard-bitten monsters of the publishing world that she had imagined, and certainly neither of them could be the 'mole' she had told James about before Nik's untimely arrival. But, nice as they were, Jinx knew she had no intention of repeating today's visit…

She moistened dry lips as she formed a polite refusal in her mind. 'I don't really think—'

'I think Miss Nixon is slightly overwhelmed,' Nik was the one to cut in firmly as he turned away from that sightless contemplation out the window. 'Maybe it might be better to let her contact you, James, when she feels up to another visit?'

If it weren't for the fact that he made her sound like a simple-minded idiot scared of her own shadow, Jinx might have felt grateful for Nik's intervention. As it was, he made her feel like a nervous spinster thrown into total confusion by having so much attention paid to her!

'I think, Mr Prince,' she bit out tartly, 'that I am more than capable of deciding that for myself, thank you very much!'

He raised dark brows impatiently before giving a dismissive shrug. 'Fine,' he grated, once again turning away.

She turned back to James Stephens. 'I—I'll call you, shall I?'

The publisher didn't look at all happy with this idea, but one look at the determination on her face seemed to tell him that it was the best he was going to get.

'Fine,' he said regretfully. 'And I will look into that other matter we discussed,' he added.

'Good,' Jinx replied.

'What other matter?' Nik queried.

Jinx shot him a resentful glare. 'Nothing that concerns you, I can assure you, Mr Prince.'

James Stephens once again took her hand in his. 'In the meantime, please feel free to drop in again any time,' he encouraged warmly. 'Let me take you out to lunch next time. Jane, too, of course.'

'Lovely,' Jinx answered noncommittally. 'It was nice to meet you, Miss Morrow,' she added in parting to the other woman, deliberately not so much as glancing in Nik's direction as she hurried out of the office.

As if the hounds of hell were at her heels!

And she didn't relax again until she was seated in the back of yet another taxi taking her home, resting her head back against the seat, her eyes closed, almost able to hear the rapid pounding of her heart.

Never again!

Never again would she allow her emotions to rule her head in that way. She knew what she had to do, knew the dangers attached to revealing the identity of J. I. Watson. And today she had almost blown that.

Because of Nik Prince.

Because he had made her angry.

Because, against all the odds, she knew she was falling in love with him…!

'Well, well, well,' Jane Morrow drawled as she and Nik left James Stephens's office together. 'Who would have thought that J. I. Watson would turn out to be a woman?'

'Yes,' he returned neutrally, anxious to be gone. If he hurried he might still be able to catch up with Jinx before she left. He knew without a doubt that it would be his only chance of finding her again! Whatever had driven her to come here at all—and he had a distinct feeling it was anger towards him!—he knew, even if James Stephens didn't, that she would never come here again.

Jane quirked teasing brows at him. 'Makes your life a lot easier, though, doesn't it?'

'Sorry?' Nik deliberately kept his expression bland, having no idea yet where this conversation was going. Having little interest, either, if he was honest.

'Oh, come on, Nik.' Jane laughed huskily as she touched him lightly on the chest. 'You know how good you are at charming women.'

His mouth tightened, even while he inwardly acknowledged that he probably deserved that remark from this woman. He had set out to charm her, although, to be fair, Jane had given every indication that she wanted to be charmed!

'Possibly. If you'll excuse me, Jane? I'm afraid I have to meet someone.' He knew he probably sounded rude, but he was very conscious of the precious seconds ticking away on the clock.

'Of course.' She slowly removed her hand from his chest, blue eyes hard now. 'You know where I am if you feel like company.'

She knew where he was too, but the likelihood of either of them actually contacting the other was extremely remote.

Although that wasn't to say Nik wasn't completely conscious of her glacial gaze on him all the time he walked down the carpeted corridor to the lift, that feeling confirmed as he turned once inside the lift and saw her still standing exactly where he had left her. She raised a mocking hand in parting, and Nik was relieved when the lift doors closed and shut out her image. After the way they had parted last time, he had been a little surprised by her initial friendliness, although it hadn't taken too long for her to revert back to derisive anger at his obvious lack of interest.

Not very gallant of him, he accepted, but, for some reason he couldn't completely explain, Jane Morrow's hand on his chest just now had given him a distinct feeling of distaste.

It couldn't be because he was falling for Jinx, could it? a little voice mocked inside his head. A little voice that sounded decidedly like Zak's voice teasing him!

And the answer was...no, he wasn't falling for Jinx. She seemed extremely vulnerable to him, very much alone, which probably brought out the same protective instinct in him that he felt towards his sister Stazy, but he certainly *wasn't* falling for her.

Protesting too much, BB?

Zak's voice again, damn it. And he had told both Zak and Rik repeatedly not to call him Big Brother.

But then, if he wasn't falling for Jinx, exactly what was he doing chasing all over London after her in cabs?

Securing the movie rights to a book, that was what!

Lame, Nik, extremely lame. He might as well admit it, to himself if to no one else: the movie had become secondary in his pursuit of Jinx. She was what he wanted right now, every satiny inch of her naked beneath him, her legs wrapped about his hips as they took each other to the heights and back.

He was so lost in thoughts of that image as he came

out of the building onto the pavement that he almost missed Jinx's cab pulling away from the kerb. Mentally cursing himself for his daydreaming, he rushed forward to hail another cab, climbing inside to tell the driver to follow the cab ahead.

The sideways glance he received from the cabbie in the overhead driving mirror, even as he turned the vehicle out into the flow of traffic, was enough to make Nik feel like a character in a second-rate movie. And he had never made a second-rate movie in his life, let alone starred in one.

'The lady left her purse behind,' he leant forward to mutter.

He received another sideways glance for his trouble. 'Course she did, mate!' the cabbie said skeptically.

Nik decided to ignore the driver and instead concentrate on the cab ahead. He could just see Jinx's head above the back seat, that fiery red hair unmistakable. She wasn't going to like the fact that he was following her, so he would have to make sure—

'I 'ate to say this, guv'ner,' the cabbie cut in on his thoughts a few minutes later, 'but I 'ave a feeling that someone's following you too. The taxi be'ind is sticking pretty close, if ya know what I mean?'

Nik did know what he meant, having glanced back to see another black cab almost driving on the bumper of this one, two passengers visible in the back of the vehicle, even if their features were indistinguishable. But every turn that this cab took as it followed behind Jinx, the one behind followed.

Reporters again? Nik couldn't think of anyone else it could be. And if it was the same two from earlier this morning, they were obviously ticked off with him enough to be dogged in their pursuit.

'Can you lose them?' he asked his driver.

'I can try,' the man came back with a cheeky grin, obviously relishing the thought. 'But I might lose sight of the cab in front if I do that.'

Continue to follow Jinx? Or lose the cab behind?

After this morning's fiasco, Jinx certainly wasn't going to thank him if he should lead a reporter directly to her door. But if he had the driver divert from following her, in an effort to divert the cab following his, Nik had a feeling he might never find Jinx again.

Something that didn't please him at all.

Neither choice was a good one as far as he was concerned.

'Okay,' he sighed heavily. 'Turn off at the end of the next block and let's lose these guys.' And he would lose Jinx…

He gazed regretfully after her cab as his driver took the next left turn, her own cab continuing straight on.

'Uh oh,' his driver murmured a few seconds later.

'What is it?' Nik demanded sharply.

The man shrugged. 'Guess they weren't following you, after all.'

'What do you mean?'

'Take a look.' The man grimaced.

Nik turned to look out the back window, the other cab no longer in sight. 'Where did they go?'

Surely they couldn't both have been wrong, after all? If they had, and the cab just happened to have been going the same way that they were, that meant he had lost Jinx for absolutely no reason.

'They continued to follow the other cab, I'm afraid, guv,' the man told him apologetically.

Nik frowned at the empty road behind them. 'Are you sure?'

'Positive.'

Nik didn't hesitate. 'Turn back onto the other road, will you, and see if you can catch them up again?'

While he tried to work out exactly what was going on!

He had assumed, both he and Jinx—after a little persuasion on his part—that the reporter from this morning was following him in the hopes of getting a story, that Jinx's presence there just happened to be coincidental. But what if they had both been wrong...?

Now that he thought about it, he remembered that the woman who had turned out to be a reporter had already been in the hotel when he'd met Jinx in Reception this morning, sitting in one of the chairs there apparently reading a newspaper.

She had then followed them through to the lounge, again seemingly reading a newspaper as she drank a cup of coffee.

But what if following Nik was only a means to an end, in the hopes that he'd lead the reporter and her photographer to the mysterious author J. I. Watson...?

Something he had undoubtedly done!

CHAPTER EIGHT

JINX heaved a sigh of relief as the taxi pulled in next to the kerb beside her home, so weary now that she didn't even want to think about—

'Get out of the cab and go into the house, Jinx! Quickly!' Nik Prince instructed grimly as he wrenched open the door beside her.

She stared up at him dazedly. Where on earth had he come from? More to the point, how had he got here? If he had been following her again—

'I don't have time to explain now, Jinx,' he muttered impatiently, starting to pull her out of the taxi. 'Just go inside and lock the door!'

She blinked up at him incredulously as she suddenly found herself out on the pavement beside him. 'Now just listen here, Nik—'

'Now, Jinx!' he rasped, taking her firmly by the shoulders and turning her in the direction of the house.

One glance at the reporter from this morning, the photographer at her side—obviously with a replacement film if the fact that he was focusing the machine on her was any indication—as the two of them hurried across the pavement towards her was enough to send Jinx hurtling in the direction of the house as if the devil were at her heels.

She almost dropped her door key in her hurry to unlock the door, shooting one last frantic glance in Nik's direction as he stood arguing with the reporter and photographer, before she escaped into the house and closed the door firmly behind her.

Only to lean weakly back against it, breathing heavily, the pounding of her heart sounding loudly in the hallway.

She had thought—hoped!—that things couldn't get any worse after this morning, but this was worse, so much worse, than anything she could have imagined!

Her home, the privacy she so valued, was now completely violated.

They would have to move again, she realized, get completely away from here. There was no way—

A loud pounding sounded on the door behind her. 'Open the damned door, Jinx! Now!' Nik ordered.

As if he had any right to tell her to do anything! As if—

'For God's sake, Jinx!' He rapped loudly on the door again.

She didn't want to let him in. Didn't want his presence in her home. Didn't want to remember his ever having been here. Didn't—

'I know you're there, Jinx—' his voice was menacingly soft now '—so just let me in and we can talk about this.'

Talk? What was there to talk about? Not only had he followed her here, but he had brought a reporter with him.

'Unless you would rather just leave me alone out here with this reporter?'

Her fingers fumbled with the lock as she turned the knob, suddenly finding herself pushed to one side as the door immediately sprang open and Nik forced his way inside, slamming the door behind him.

Jinx just stared at him, her eyes accusing, her face pale.

'Don't look at me like that!' he growled, closing his

eyes briefly before raising his lids to look at her with glittering grey eyes. 'No matter what you may think, I am not responsible for—for that!' he told her grimly, moving restlessly away from the door.

Jinx took a step backwards, effectively blocking the hallway, as if to stop him going any further inside. She couldn't help herself, the move purely instinctive.

'Jinx…!' Nik groaned almost pleadingly.

'You—' She broke off as a knock sounded on the door behind him, her expression scathing now. 'Shouldn't you answer that?'

His eyes glittered angrily. 'Don't make this any worse than it already is, Jinx—'

'Is that possible?' she snapped, wondering how this nightmare was going to end.

Not only did Nik Prince know where she lived, but a reporter did too!

'Probably not,' he conceded. 'But, I repeat, I am not responsible for bringing that reporter here.'

Of course he was responsible; she certainly hadn't invited a reporter to her home. If Nik hadn't followed her—

'Why did you follow me?' she accused.

He looked uncomfortable now. 'You know why,' he muttered.

Oh, yes, she knew why; Nik had been all too aware that once she left James Stephens's office none of them— but Nik especially!—would ever see her again.

She shook her head. 'You've only made this so much worse, Nik. Are they ever going to go away?' She groaned as the knock sounded on the door once again.

'Not for a while, at least.' He grimaced, taking a firm hold of her arm. 'Let's go somewhere where we can't hear them—'

'Let's not,' Jinx contradicted, pointedly removing her arm from the hold he had of her. 'Do you think they managed to get a photograph?' She frowned at the thought.

He winced. 'Maybe not...'

'In other words—yes,' Jinx sighed. 'This is such a mess. I don't know what to do next. I—' She broke off as the door opened at the end of the hallway.

'Juliet, is that you, dear?'

She pushed past Nik, smiling brightly as she walked down the hallway to meet her father. He was a tall, spare man, iron-grey hair brushed neatly back, dressed in his familiar tweed suit and checked shirt, but the whole effect was slightly marred by the carpet slippers he was wearing with them. 'Yes, it's me, Daddy,' she confirmed gently. 'Where is Mrs Holt?'

Her father looked slightly vague. 'In the kitchen preparing lunch, I think. I—there appears to be someone at the door.' A frown furrowed his brow as another knock sounded on the door. 'I—that was quick.' He smiled enquiringly as he spotted Nik standing just in front of the closed door. 'How do you do, young man?' He moved forward to hold out his hand to Nik. 'I'm Jack Nixon.'

Jinx was dismayed. Nik was an intelligent as well as astute man, and it wouldn't take him too long to realize in exactly what way her father 'wasn't well'...

'Nik Prince, sir,' Nik returned respectfully as he shook the other man's hand, a good thirty years younger than Jinx's father. 'I hope we're not disturbing you?'

'Not at all,' the older man assured him. 'We get so few visitors nowadays,' he added wistfully. 'Perhaps you would like to stay to lunch? I believe Mrs Holt said it's chicken salad. I like chicken salad. Do you like chicken salad, young man?'

Jinx felt her heart contract at her father's childish pleasure in such a small thing as having chicken salad for lunch, her gaze instantly becoming guarded as Nik turned to her with a frown.

'Mr Prince isn't staying to lunch, Daddy,' she was the one to answer quickly. 'In fact, I believe he was just on his way...?' She gave him a pointed glare.

Nik's expression was deliberately bland. 'I'm not in any particular hurry,' he said slowly.

'Good. Good.' Jinx's father beamed, his blue eyes pale and watery now, lacking the sharp intelligence they had once had. 'I'll just go and tell Mrs Holt that there's one extra for lunch.' He shuffled off in the slightly overlarge carpet slippers.

Silence followed his departure. Jinx was loath to look up at Nik and see the questioning look she was sure would be on his face, and Nik remained quietly patient as he waited for her to say something.

But what could she say? Excuse my father, but he isn't quite himself nowadays?

Not quite himself! Her father had once been one of the foremost experts on Jacobite history in this country, had taught the subject for over forty years, was consulted by other learned minds as to his opinion on certain events.

But that had been once...

Nowadays her father seemed to have trouble remembering what day it was, let alone what year, and if he still had his knowledge of history then it was buried somewhere behind the vagueness of his expression.

But how could she say any of that without having Nik feel sorry for her father?

Because she didn't want Nik to pity her father. Didn't want anyone to pity him, when he had once been a man so respected and revered by his peers.

'Jinx…?'

Her head rose defensively as she finally looked up at Nik, her gaze challenging him to say anything that could be interpreted as pitying or—worse!—condescending.

Whatever he said next had to be the right thing, Nik knew, or Jinx would cast him from her life and never see him again. And that, he realized, was totally unacceptable to him.

Because of the movie he wanted to make of *No Ordinary Boy*?

The movie didn't even come into it! In fact, if he was honest, it hadn't been a factor for some time now. Jinx was what mattered. And at this moment, the reporter outside apart, he was walking on very shaky ground where she was concerned…

'What happened?' he asked gently.

'What makes you think something happened?' If anything her chin rose even higher.

But unless Nik was mistaken, the new brightness to her eyes was due to unshed tears and not the anger of a few minutes ago. 'I—your father—' He drew in a deep breath, very aware of that knife edge he was balanced upon. 'Did he have a breakdown of some kind?' He decided briskness was probably the way to go; pity he knew Jinx would totally reject, gentleness probably the same.

'Of some kind,' she admitted, every inch of her seeming to be covered in defensive prickles. 'What are we going to do about the reporter and photographer outside?' she abruptly changed the subject.

Nik shrugged. 'Have lunch with your father, and then see if they're still there?' He was pushing it, he knew, but he really did want to find out more about this situation than he knew now.

Although just seeing Jinx's father answered a lot of questions for him. There was no way that Jack Nixon could withstand the sort of publicity that would prevail if it were known that his daughter was the author of *No Ordinary Boy*. The press could be dogged, intrusive, stripping one's life down to the bare bones, and still carry on looking for more. Nik had no doubts that Jack Nixon's delicate mental health wouldn't be able to cope with something like that.

Something he was sure Jinx was all too aware of, too...

'I have a better suggestion,' she came back tartly now. 'You leave, taking the reporter and photographer with you, and I'll go and have lunch with my father!'

Nik grimaced, having expected her to say something like that. And on the face of it, it must seem like the practical thing to do. Except that it had been Jinx the reporter and photographer had been following.

Which meant they must have some idea that she was the author J. I. Watson.

As far as he was aware only three people, possibly four, knew that Jinx was the author J. I. Watson: himself, Jane Morrow, James Stephens, and possibly James Stephens's secretary, none of whom benefited in any way by revealing that information to the press.

But, nevertheless, Nik was sure that the information had leaked out somehow.

He just wasn't sure it was a good idea to tell Jinx that just yet. She was already as jumpy as a cat, and furiously angry with him. If she thought that he was somehow responsible—!

He smiled. 'I think I like my plan better.'

Her cheeks flushed angrily. 'Well, that's too bad, because—'

'Lunch is ready!' Jinx's father came back into the hallway to announce brightly.

Nik's gaze narrowed thoughtfully as it rested on the other man. Jinx hadn't answered his question earlier concerning what had happened to make her father like this. Because he was pretty sure that something had. Something of a highly emotional nature.

Something that had affected Jinx, too...?

He wasn't sure yet. But he definitely wanted to find out.

Which was extraordinary in itself, he admitted wryly. Most people would call his single-mindedness where his work was concerned arrogant, but he preferred to think of it as being focused. Maybe that was an arrogance in itself? Probably, but it was the way he worked. One thing at a time, everything compartmentalized.

But Jinx, with her fiery hair, violet-blue eyes, and a body that answered his, made a nonsense of that compartmentalization, causing everything that was important to him at this moment to overlap itself; the movie of *No Ordinary Boy*, the puzzle of Jackson Nixon, but, most of all, Jinx herself.

She interested him more than any of those other things!

'Lunch is ready,' he told her.

She shot him an impatient glance, but was obviously very aware of her father waiting for them at the end of the hallway.

'Jinx...?' Nik prompted.

'Fine,' she snapped. 'But you and I will definitely talk later,' she muttered so that only he could hear.

There were much pleasanter things he could think of to do with Jinx than talking, but if that was all that was on offer at the moment—and he was pretty sure that it was!—then he would take what he could get.

'I'll look forward to it,' he assured her huskily, raising innocent brows as she looked up at him with brief suspicion before following her father through to the back of the house.

The three of them had lunch outside sitting at a table under a sun umbrella in the well-maintained back garden—a garden that was, thankfully, completely closed in by a six-foot-high fence. Nik knew better than most exactly how tenacious reporters could be once on the scent of a story—they were quite capable of looking through windows and over fences in order to get what they wanted. And they obviously hadn't given up on Jinx yet…

Despite the fact that Jinx obviously wished him well away from here, that her father's conversation lacked the intelligence he was so well known for, Nik enjoyed the next hour spent in their company.

He saw a gentler side of Jinx as she conversed with her father, that gentleness obviously a calming influence on the older man as he took childish pleasure in her company. Not that Nik had ever found Jinx to be an aggressive person; it was just that she was usually so on the defensive when he was around that this softer side was a revelation to him.

Everything about Juliet India Nixon was a revelation to him, the attraction he felt towards her like nothing he had ever felt before. And it seemed to be getting more intense the longer he was around her, rather than diminishing as it usually did when he spent too much time in one woman's company.

He loved to watch the elegance of her slender hands as she ate, or pushed the coppery swathe of her hair back from her cheeks. The gentle curves of her body, curves he longed to touch. The way a little dimple appeared in one cheek when she smiled at her father—not at Nik, because she hadn't smiled at him once all the way through the meal!

Not that her father seemed to have noticed any strain between Jinx and Nik, just enjoying their company completely oblivious of the tension between them.

'Time for your nap, Daddy,' Jinx told her father as Mrs Holt came to clear away the remains of the meal.

Jack Nixon rose slowly to his feet. 'Never get old, Nik,' he warned ruefully even as he followed the housekeeper back into the house. 'The man becomes the child again!'

Nik's gaze was speculative as he watched the other man enter the house. That last comment had been quite an intelligent observation for a man who seemed totally unaware of his surroundings most of the time, let alone anything else.

'There are the occasional flashes of—of his old self, shall we say?' Jinx said, obviously having watched Nik watching her father. 'But unfortunately they don't usually last for long,' she added sadly.

Nik frowned; Jinx was too beautiful, too lovely a person, to be sad. Surely something could be done...? 'Has he seen anyone? A specialist, something like that?' he asked—and as quickly wished that he hadn't as Jinx stiffened resentfully.

'He had several months in a nursing home, after the initial shock,' she finally answered distantly. 'But, quite honestly, it did no good. He's better off at home, anyway.'

Nik nodded. 'Mrs Holt watches out for him when you have to go out?'

'Yes. Nik, I really think that you should go now. The

reporter and her friend have probably given up by now
and gone home—'

'Doubtful,' he dismissed from experience. 'What was
the "initial shock", Jinx?' he queried astutely, knowing
by the way she became even more coldly aloof that he
had touched on a subject she would rather not talk about.

But if he were to help either of these people—and he
really thought that he must—he had to know what trauma
Jackson Nixon had suffered.

The same trauma that had also helped to create the
fiercely private woman Jinx was now…?

CHAPTER NINE

JINX stared at him, unsure of what to say in answer to that particular question. On the one hand, the less Nik Prince knew about her or her family, the better she was sure it would be. But if she stood any chance of making him go away—and staying away!—then she knew she had to at least tell him some of what had happened eighteen months ago.

She drew in a ragged breath. 'Come through to my father's study with me—oh, yes, he has a study,' she confirmed heavily as Nik raised surprised brows. 'Not that he's ever used this one.' She sighed. 'But I still brought everything with me when we moved six months ago.'

Just in case, she had been telling herself this last eighteen months. Just in case her father made some sort of miraculous recovery and decided to finish the book on the Jacobite uprising that he had been working on when— When—

'This way.' She led the way further down the hallway, opening the door at the end and ushering Nik inside.

'Study' was probably rather a complimentary way of describing the room that they entered. The shelved walls, and most of the floor space, were covered in books, both for reading and reference, and the desk was awash with papers and framed photographs.

It was one of the latter that Jinx picked up and handed to Nik, at the same time keeping her gaze deliberately averted from his.

She knew exactly what he would see in the photograph: a family sitting on a blanket eating a picnic beside a river, all of them smiling happily into the camera.

Her mother. Her father. Her brother. Herself.

Just a normal family snapshot.

Except that it wasn't the whole picture...

'Where are your mother and brother now?' Nik asked with that astuteness Jinx had come to expect of him.

'They died eighteen months ago,' she answered flatly. 'In case you're interested, my mother's maiden name was Watson,' she added dryly.

Nik continued to look at her, his stillness letting her know he expected her to add something to that remark. But what could she say? Her mother and Jamie were both dead. There was nothing else to say.

'The shock was too much for my father,' she added abruptly when she couldn't stand that expectant silence a moment longer. 'I—he's been like this—' she raised her hands helplessly '—ever since.'

Nik gave the photograph another long look before replacing it back on the desktop. 'Wasn't that just a little selfish of him? After all, it wasn't just his wife and son who died, but your mother and brother too.'

'You don't understand!' Jinx snapped, deeply resentful of this criticism of her father. 'You know nothing about the situation at all, Nik, so how dare you come here and presume to sit in judgement—?'

'Calm down, Jinx,' Nik soothed. 'I was only—'

'I know what you *were only*,' she accused. 'I think it's time you left now.' She turned away. 'Past time!'

She had been stupid to have ever hoped for Nik's understanding; after all, his only interest in her was the film rights to *No Ordinary Boy*. Something she kept forgetting!

Because every time she was around him all she could think about was how attracted she was to him. It was there all the time, a thrum of awareness beneath her skin. As for what had happened between them at his hotel earlier…!

'I want you to leave, Nik,' she repeated.

'Do you?'

When had he got so close? At what point in their conversation had he moved so that he was now standing only inches away from her? Causing that thrumming sensation beneath her skin to increase so that every inch of her was tinglingly alive!

She moistened dry lips. 'Yes. I—'

'I don't think so, Jinx,' he murmured throatily, standing so close now he was actually touching her.

Causing fire to leap and flame through her veins like molten lava, her breathing ragged as she looked up at him.

Grey eyes shimmered like mercury, his gaze intense as it rested on her lips, his own breathing rapid and uneven.

'No, Nik—' Jinx only had time to protest achingly as his head lowered and his mouth took possession of hers.

Oh, yes, Nik, her body disagreed as it instinctively curved against the hardness of his. Jinx was the one to initiate the deepening of the kiss as she forgot everything else but the pleasure of being in this man's arms.

It had only been a few hours since they were last together like this, but even so they were hungry for each other, Nik's arms like steel bands about her waist, Jinx's hands moving restlessly up and down the long length of his spine as their lips and tongues explored and possessed, Jinx easily matching the desire that Nik made no effort to hide from her.

Nik was finally the one to pull back, his expression

regretful as he looked down at her, his hands still lightly
linked at the base of her spine. 'Much as I'm enjoying
this—and, believe me, I am enjoying it,' he drawled, 'at
this particular moment I believe there may be several
other things that need our immediate attention more.'

Jinx looked up at him with passion-drowsy eyes. 'Such
as?'

He grimaced. 'The fact that there is a reporter and
photographer outside—who, no matter what you might
hope, aren't likely to be going anywhere soon. Which
means—'

'Yes?' She had stiffened warily now, stepping back as
she moved out of his arms to self-consciously straighten
her hair, embarrassed at the way she kept falling into his
arms.

Yes, she was attracted to him. Yes, she wanted him.
But he was the last man she should keep responding to
in this way.

Nik's look of regret deepened at her obvious withdrawal. 'Which means that you and your father will have
to be the ones to leave. If only temporarily.'

Her eyes widened. 'That's ridiculous. It's you they're
after, so when you leave, they will leave with you.'

She had moved house six months ago because continuing to stay at the family home had seemed to be badly
affecting her father, his lapses more extreme as he shut
himself off even from his surroundings; to move him
again now—even temporarily!—was out of the question.

Nik raised dark brows. 'And if they don't?'

'They will,' she said flatly.

He shook his head. 'I wish I could be as sure of that
as you appear to be...'

Jinx looked at him sharply. 'What do you mean?'

He shrugged. 'Just a hunch I have. Jinx, does it really

matter why they're hanging around out there?' he continued impatiently as she made to protest once again. 'The fact remains that they are there, and they have a lot more patience than you do. And your father isn't going to remain asleep upstairs for ever,' he added softly.

No, he would be down within the hour, and when he did come down he was unlikely to understand why it was she didn't answer the knocking on the front door. But where on earth was she supposed to go in order to avoid those people outside? Nik just didn't understand. There was no way she could take her father to the impersonality of a hotel, and it wasn't fair to just invite themselves to stay with friends, either.

She drew in a ragged breath. 'I still think that they will leave when you do,' she told him stubbornly.

He raised an eyebrow, signaling his disagreement with that statement. 'Shall we give it a try?'

Jinx looked at him with narrowed eyes, suspicious of his confident tone, as if he knew the reporter and photographer were waiting for her and not him.

But that couldn't be so. The only interest a reporter could possibly have in her was if they were to know of the J. I. Watson connection, and there was no way—

What about her meeting with Nik Prince this morning in the very public lounge of a large London hotel—a man already reported to be on the trail of the author J. I. Watson so that he could acquire the movie rights? What about her visit to James Stephens's office this morning?

She felt her heart sink as she faced the possibility that she could have been the one to lead the press to her home. It would be just too ironic if that were the case.

It was, also, primarily Nik Prince's fault, she decided angrily. If he hadn't been so persistent in the first place—

If he hadn't discovered the connection— If he hadn't followed her here—

'Don't bother,' she snapped, glaring her displeasure at him. 'Where do you suggest we go, then?' she demanded pointedly.

'Well, I've already given that some thought—'

'Why am I not surprised?' Jinx huffed.

Grey eyes gleamed warningly. 'There's no need to get angry with me—'

'Who else can I get angry with?'

Dark brows rose mockingly. 'And that's reason enough, is it—because I happen to be here?'

'For the moment—yes!' Her eyes flashed deeply violet. 'I'm still not convinced this wasn't all your fault. Everything was just fine before you came into my life—'

'Everything was *not* just fine!' he rapped out, eyes now a shimmering silver. 'Your father is very ill, and likely to remain so if he doesn't get professional help. Your own life is a mess—'

'I beg your pardon?' She stiffened resentfully.

'Look at you, Jinx. You have a job as a university tutor, but you can't do that at the moment because of taking care of your father. You're a famous author, but for the same reason you can't lay claim to that either.' He gave an impatient shake of his head. 'As for your personal life—'

'Stay out of my personal life, Nik!' she cut in coldly.

'I'm already in it—'

'Then I suggest you get *out* of it again!' she practically shouted. 'I don't need you, Nik, or your amateur psychiatry concerning my father; I believe I am the best judge of what is and isn't good for him! I just don't need you in my life…full stop!' She glared at him.

He drew in an angry breath. 'That wasn't the impression I got a few minutes ago—'

'Oh, let's bring that into it, shall we?' she scoffed. 'So I'm attracted to you; so what? Why is it that men feel they can differentiate between love and lust, but we women can't? Because I assure you that we can, Nik.' She gave a humourless laugh, angry with herself as much as him for the way she had once again given in to the desire she felt for him. '*I* can,' she claimed, her gaze challenging now as she met his.

Nik wanted to shake her. Wanted to grasp her shoulders and shake her until her teeth rattled.

Lust. She lusted after him?

No woman had ever said anything like that to him ever before—even if it had happened to be the truth! And, coming from Jinx, he found that he didn't like having it said to him now, either!

'What's the matter, Nik?' she taunted his silence. 'Don't you like having the tables turned on you?'

No, he damn well didn't! It was an unpleasant experience to be told that someone—Jinx!—lusted after him.

At the same time he could accept the irony of it. Wasn't it how he had always conducted his own personal relationships, feeling desire without the love?

Maybe it was, but that was still no explanation for the resentment he felt at having this five-foot-one-inch of a woman say the same thing to him...

He drew in a controlling breath. 'Not particularly,' he acknowledged. 'I'm also not sure it's the way for a nicely brought up young lady to be talking,' he mocked, knowing by the way the colour suddenly blazed in her cheeks that he had scored a direct hit with his barb.

But did he really want to score direct hits where Jinx

was concerned? Wasn't that just guaranteed to alienate her even more?

It was too late to realize that, Nik admitted ruefully as her expression became haughtily remote, violet eyes turning to icy blue. 'Probably not,' she accepted tersely. 'Now I really think it's time for you to leave, Nik.'

After which she would be at great pains to make sure the two of them *never* met again.

It was there in the resolve of her expression, in the coldness of her eyes, the defensive stance of her body.

But he knew where she lived now; he could always—

No, he couldn't, he accepted heavily. That would make him as bad as the reporter and photographer lying in wait for her outside.

Which brought him back to his initial point…

'Jinx, you really can't stay here—'

'I really can, Nik,' she insisted. 'In any case,' she continued firmly as he would have spoken, 'whether I decide to go or stay is really none of your business.'

He wanted to make it his business, wanted to pick Jinx up, throw her over his shoulder and carry her away from here. Be a regular caveman, in fact—which would go down with Jinx about as well as a lead balloon!

But the alternative was leaving her and her father here at the mercy of the press…

He drew in a deep breath. 'I have a friend—well, he's more like family, I suppose—it's a bit complicated,' he tried to explain, sure that now wasn't the right time to be discussing his sometimes complicated family tree. 'Have you ever heard of Ben Travis?' he asked instead.

'Should I have done?' Jinx returned cautiously.

'Probably not—although he is married to Marilyn Palmer.'

Jinx's eyes widened. 'The famous Hollywood actress?'

'The one and only.' Nik nodded. 'And Marilyn's daughter, Gaye, is married to the brother of Stazy's husband, Jordan Hunter.'

'The acting world is almost incestuous, isn't it?' Jinx scorned.

Nik felt the anger flare in his gaze, his mouth tightening to a thin line. 'Ben is a psychiatrist—'

'I've already told you, my father doesn't need a psychiatrist,' Jinx interrupted. 'Time and love are all he needs. And a little peace and quiet to go with it,' she added pointedly.

Meaning she really wanted him to leave now. Not that he hadn't thought she'd meant it in the first place, but now she absolutely wanted him out of her home. And her life…? Unfortunately, yes.

Nik sighed. 'Can I call you later?'

Jinx's gaze narrowed suspiciously. 'Why?'

He made an impatient movement. 'So that I can check that everything is okay!'

'And why shouldn't it be?'

'Jinx, will you just try being a little less defensive for a few minutes and actually think?' Nik exploded in frustration. 'If I leave—when I leave,' he amended as Jinx raised mocking brows, 'if, as I suspect, the reporter and her buddy continue to hang around outside, then I'm going to need to know about it—'

'Why?'

He really would strangle her in a minute! Which would achieve precisely nothing. But it might make him feel a lot better. If only fleetingly.

'Okay, let me put this another way,' he bit out, inwardly wondering how he could have been so aroused by her a few short minutes ago and now felt like throttling her! 'I am going to call you later to see how everything is.'

'You are?'

'Yes, I ar—am,' he corrected himself irritably.

She arched dark brows. 'And exactly how do you intend doing that when you don't have my telephone number?'

Go, Nik, he told himself. Now. Before you actually do reach out and do something you're going to regret!

'But I do have your telephone number, Jinx,' he couldn't resist assuring her triumphantly, at the same time congratulating himself on his perspicacity.

'I don't see how—'

'It's right there on your telephone,' he pointed out, at the same time giving a rueful wince as he waited for the explosion that was sure to come.

'You—you—' Jinx stared at him in disbelief. 'You really are one devious bast—'

'When are you going to realize I'm trying to *help* you?'

'When are you going to realize I don't *want* your help?' she returned furiously.

Nik stared down at her frustratedly, his hands clenched at his sides. 'Fine,' he bit out tersely, turning away abruptly, breathing deeply in an effort to calm down. Almost an impossibility when around this woman. 'I *will* call you later, though,' he added determinedly even as he left the study and strode forcefully down the hallway to the front door.

'Don't hold your breath on getting a reply,' Jinx called after him.

Nik came to a halt as he reached the door, forcing

himself not to retaliate, to just open the door and leave.
But it wasn't easy.

In fact, as he was quickly learning, nothing was easy
when it came to Jinx Nixon…

CHAPTER TEN

'HELLO…?' Jinx at once berated herself for sounding so hesitant as she answered the telephone call later that evening. After what he had said earlier, Nik Prince was sure to be the caller, and being hesitant around that man could only lead to him attempting to walk all over her—only attempting, of course, because he wouldn't succeed!

But he had been right about the reporter and photographer; the two of them were still waiting outside. In fact, the photographer had left for a brief time and returned with a car, in which the two of them now sat. It looked as if they were even eating hamburgers and drinking cola now, too. And waiting. And they appeared to be able to carry on doing just that for as long as it took for Jinx to have to finally leave the house, if only in order to buy food.

'Juliet?' a female voice answered. 'Juliet Nixon?'

Jinx's wariness increased at hearing this unfamiliar voice. 'Yes…'

'This is Stazy Hunter,' the woman responded. 'We met briefly at Susan and Leo's the other weekend.'

As if Jinx needed any reminding of who the other woman was! And where they had met wasn't the relevant point at the moment—the fact that this woman was Nik Prince's sister was!

She straightened defensively, unsure yet as to whether the other woman had got her telephone number from her brother or from Susan. 'What can I do for you, Mrs Hunter?'

'Please call me Stazy,' the other woman invited, her American accent softer and less pronounced than her brother's. 'And I believe your friends call you Jinx…?'

Yes, they did—but she very much doubted this woman was ever going to become her friend. 'I don't wish to sound rude, but exactly why have you telephoned me, Mrs—Stazy?' she corrected awkwardly; she would so much rather have kept things formal between the two of them, but at the same time Stazy Hunter sounded a genuinely warm and friendly person. So unlike her eldest brother!

The other woman gave a husky laugh. 'Don't worry, I don't have Nik breathing down my neck listening in on the conversation!'

That was something, at least! 'But he did ask you to telephone me?' Jinx said sharply.

'Yes, he—he's concerned about you…' Stazy Hunter told her ruefully.

'Then he has no right to be,' Jinx snapped. 'Something I have already told him once today!'

'So I believe,' Stazy chuckled appreciatively.

How much had Nik told his sister about the two of them? Not that there was a 'two of them', but she didn't particularly enjoy the thought of Nik discussing her with his sister at all.

'Is the reporter still there?' Stazy asked.

Jinx thought briefly of lying to the other woman, but what would be the point of doing that? Nik, when told of the conversation by his sister—as Jinx was sure he would be, even if he wasn't breathing down Stazy's neck right now!—would be sure to know that she was lying.

'Before you answer that,' Stazy Hunter continued warmly, 'may I just say how much I enjoyed your book. It made me cry as well as laugh,' she added sincerely.

Nik really had been confiding in his sister, hadn't he? Although it would probably have been a little difficult explaining his 'concern' for Jinx without telling the other woman of her connection to J. I. Watson.

Nevertheless, Jinx felt a warm glow at the other woman's praise for *No Ordinary Boy*. The books, five of them in all, had been written from the heart, and had made Jinx 'cry as well as laugh' too.

'Thank you,' she accepted huskily. 'And, yes, the reporter is still here, but it really isn't a problem.' At the moment...!

If the pair outside were set in for the duration, then it could definitely become a problem. And Jinx had a feeling that was exactly what they were going to do.

'Are you sure?' The frown could be heard in Stazy's voice. 'I know how intrusive the press can be.'

Well, she would, wouldn't she? Jinx acknowledged; Damien Prince, the legendary Hollywood actor, although dead for some time now, had been Stazy's father as well as Nik's, which meant the other woman had probably grown up surrounded by that intrusive press.

'They really aren't a problem,' Jinx repeated. 'It's very kind of you to have called in this way, Stazy,' she added briskly, 'but—'

'Kindness has little to do with it,' the other woman assured her. 'But I didn't just telephone to check up on the reporter. Nik thinks, and I have to agree with him, that it would be a good idea if you came here and stayed with me for a few days. You and your father, of course.'

Jinx frowned, totally speechless just at the idea of Nik putting forward the idea of inviting her to stay at the home of his sister.

'Then he has no right to think any such thing!' she finally answered incredulously. 'For one thing, I wouldn't dream of intruding on you and your family in that way—'

'Oh, you wouldn't be intruding,' Stazy Hunter assured her. 'In fact, Jordan is away on business for a few days, so I would quite enjoy having some female company.'

'For another, it's totally unnecessary,' Jinx added firmly. 'I don't mean to sound ungrateful, Stazy, it's just that—I'm well aware of whose idea this actually was! But please assure Nik that I don't need his help, that I'm perfectly capable of taking care of myself.' She hoped she didn't sound too rude to the other woman; she just wanted to make sure that Nik got the message she wanted him to receive—which was, 'Leave me alone!'

'Okay,' Stazy accepted, obviously not in the least offended. 'But I'll leave you my telephone number, anyway, shall I? Just in case.'

In case of what, Jinx had no idea, but she wrote the other woman's telephone number down anyway before saying goodbye.

She continued to sit by the telephone for several minutes after ending the call, a frown marring her creamy brow. Nik just couldn't stop interfering in her life, could he? Well, hopefully, that last message, relayed to him via his sister, might make him falter a little in his tracks. Although, knowing Nik, Jinx wouldn't count on it.

And did she really want him to just disappear completely from her life? She could be honest with herself, at least!

The answer was no, that even the last few hours of thinking about never seeing Nik again had left her with a heavy, oppressive feeling.

Could she really be falling in love with him?

Or was she already in love with him?

She heaved a big sigh, unable to deceive herself any

longer. She loved Nik, but the problem of *No Ordinary Boy* apart, there could never be a future for them together. Nik wasn't a man interested in for ever, and she was a woman who wouldn't settle for anything less.

Impasse.

Better to just leave things as they were. She would get over this in time. Wouldn't she…?

Not that there seemed much chance of her having that time when she looked out the window the next morning and found, not just the one reporter and photographer outside, but a dozen or more, cameras at the ready, at the moment all focused on the tall man getting out from behind the wheel of a dark green Jaguar.

Nik!

His expression was grim as he strode through the reporters and photographers, looking to neither left nor right, totally ignoring the barrage of questions being thrown at him, although it was impossible to stop the cameras flashing away.

In the circumstances, Jinx felt she had no option but to at least open the door to him, stepping out of the way as Nik turned to shut the door in the face of the more determined reporters who had followed him down the pathway. He looked cool and assured in a black shirt and faded denims, dark hair still looking wet from where he had taken a shower.

Which was more than could be said for Jinx. Having only just got out of bed, she was wearing a silky peach-coloured robe over a matching nightgown, her hair still tousled from sleep, her face completely make-upless.

'What on earth is going on?' she gasped. 'Where did they all come from?' She gave an airy wave in the direction of the front of the house.

Nik's expression remained grim. 'Have you seen the newspapers this morning?'

'Not yet. Mrs Holt usually brings it with her when she comes in the mornings, and it isn't time for her to arrive yet.' Which wasn't surprising, considering it was only eight o'clock in the morning!

He gave a shake of his head. 'If she has any sense, she won't bother!' he rasped. 'How long will it take you to collect up the things you and your father might need for at least a couple of days away?'

'Five minutes,' she answered dazedly. 'What was in the newspapers, Nik?' she asked as some of her normal composure started to come back to her.

'Actually, so far it's just the one—the one the initial reporter works for, presumably. But that won't remain the case after today. And you can definitely say goodbye to any idea of anonymity; there's a photograph to accompany the article speculating whether or not you're J. I. Watson!' He looked pointedly out of the window at the people milling around outside the house, obviously just waiting for a glimpse of the famous but elusive author.

Jinx put her hands up to her face as the enormity of what was happening washed over her. 'This is awful,' she groaned. 'Just awful!'

'Yes.' Nik didn't even attempt to soften the blow. 'You do realize you should have got out of here last night when Stazy asked you to?'

Her hands dropped back to her sides, her face pale now as she looked up at him. 'Don't you mean, when *you* asked me to?' she challenged.

'Me. Stazy. What the hell difference does it make who suggested it?' he growled. 'You should have damn well taken the opportunity to get out of here! As it is, the house is now surrounded like a three-ring circus!'

She could see that—she also had no idea how her father was going to react to all this when he came down in half an hour or so.

Her father.

No matter what she might personally want, she knew it was her father she had to think of now. And getting him away from here, from reporters and photographers, had to be her first priority.

'What do you want me to do?' she said briskly.

Nik raised surprised brows at her sudden acquiescence. 'Now you start being cooperative!'

Jinx felt the colour warm her cheeks. 'I had no idea it was going to—to escalate like this!' she defended impatiently.

'No, in your naivety, you probably didn't.'

Her eyes flashed deeply violet. 'We aren't all as world-weary and cynical as you, you know!'

Nik became suddenly still, looking down at her with hooded eyes. 'Is that how you see me?' he asked slowly. 'As world-weary and cynical?'

'Well, aren't you?' Jinx flushed uncomfortably, knowing she was behaving ungratefully after the way Nik had taken the trouble to come here—in spite of her clearly telling him to go away and stay away!—and try to help her out of this mess.

Despite what she was saying to Nik, she was grateful for his help. She knew that she would never have known how to handle this situation on her own.

She just couldn't tell Nik how grateful she was—not when she was also in love with him!

Nik, giving her accusation some thought, totally missed that briefly bewildered expression on Jinx's face.

World-weary?

And cynical?

Yes, he was both those things. But when he looked at Jinx, so incredibly young-looking without make-up and her hair all tousled from sleep, none of that seemed to matter any more.

'Jinx…!'

She gave a startled look at the groan of longing that escaped him, the colour slowly draining from her face as she continued to stare at him.

This wasn't the time for this, Nik knew. He should be concentrating on getting Jinx and her father away from here. But at the moment, having spent a totally sleepless night because of the way the two of them had parted yesterday and the fact that Jinx had refused Stazy's offer of help, Nik felt that if he didn't take Jinx in his arms, feel the softness of her lips against his, the warmth of her body curved against him, he might go quietly insane!

She felt as good against him as he remembered—better! Her lips were soft and delicious beneath his. The fluttering caress of her hands against his nape before she clung to him spread a sensual warmth through the whole of his body. As for how Jinx felt beneath the silky material of her robe…!

God, he wanted this woman!

He might try to deny it, keep telling himself that his interest in her was purely business, but his body knew better. As for his heart—

Nik pulled back sharply, total denial in his face as he stared down into her drowsily aroused face. He didn't have a heart—goodness knew enough women had told him that in the past! What he felt for Jinx was desire, pure and simple. It didn't need to be complicated by things like love!

'I think you had better go and get dressed,' he said

gruffly, moving away and thrusting his hands into his denims pockets so that he shouldn't be tempted to reach for her again.

His own feelings apart, hadn't Jinx made it perfectly obvious how she felt about him? Of course she had. She only 'lusted' after him. God, how he still wanted to shake her for saying that!

Jinx flinched as if he had physically struck her, her face paler than ever as she hastily tightened the belt on her robe. 'Yes,' she acknowledged woodenly. 'I— How am I supposed to get out of here, without running into— into those people outside?' She gave a hunted look in the direction of the front of the house.

'Leave it to me,' he assured her. 'While you're upstairs dressing,' he added impatiently as Jinx stared at him levelly, obviously having no intention of going up the stairs until he had explained exactly what he intended doing, 'I intend going outside and telling them that a statement will be forthcoming in the next fifteen minutes or so—'

'No way!' She shuddered with feeling, at the same time seeming to sink back into her robe. 'I have no intention of going out there and—'

'Of course you don't,' Nik grated. 'If you listened to what I said, you will realize I didn't actually say *who* would be making that statement.'

She blinked, staring up at him uncertainly now.

'Right.' He nodded. 'Hopefully all the reporters will then gather at the front of the house in anticipation of the statement. And while I'm outside making that statement, you and your father will be leaving by the back door.'

Jinx still looked bewildered. 'Leaving how?'

He wanted to take her in his arms again, wanted to smooth away that worried frown, to reassure her that everything was going to be all right. But his own confused emotions kept him from doing that. And the fact that those violet-blue eyes, as if she were aware of exactly what he wanted to do, were now glittering warningly!

'My brother will have arrived out the back in a second car by then—'

'Zak?' She looked and sounded horrified.

'Not this time,' Nik drawled, scowling slightly as he wondered if Jinx's horror was because of who Zak was or because she was yet another woman besotted with his glamorous younger brother.

He was being paranoid, he told himself pityingly. That, and jealous at the thought of Jinx finding any other man attractive.

'This will be my youngest brother, Rik,' Nik told her.

'The screenwriter?'

'The one and only.'

'My, my,' Jinx taunted. 'And to what do we owe the honour of all these Princes?'

Nik's mouth tightened. 'I already told you that we all came over initially for our nephew's christening. But Zak stayed on to discuss his next movie. Rik is visiting with Stazy for a few weeks. And I—'

'I think we all know why *you're* still here!' she snapped.

He gave a dismissive shrug; having an argument with Jinx now wasn't going to help anyone. 'Rik has never been as keen as Zak to have his photograph splashed all over the newspapers.'

Her mouth twisted ruefully. 'Then that makes two of us!'

'Yes,' he confirmed tersely.

'Doesn't Rik mind? After all, he doesn't know me from Adam.'

'I know you,' Nik stated without apology for his arrogance. They were a close family, always had been, and what affected one affected all of them. So when he had asked Rik for his help today his brother hadn't questioned the 'whys', had just got in the second car and followed him here. 'Time is ticking on, Jinx,' he reminded her.

'Yes.' She nodded, once again looking up at him uncertainly. 'This really is very kind of you, Nik.' Her voice was husky.

Sensually so, Nik realized with that now-familiar ache. Damn it, did everything about this woman have to arouse him?

'Not really,' he dismissed curtly. 'The photograph in the newspaper is of you leaving the publishing house yesterday, so I guess I owe you one.'

'Oh. Right.' She smiled shakily. 'Fine. I—I'll go and get dressed, then.'

'I should,' he mocked. 'Unless you want to cause even more of a sensation!'

Nik watched her as she hurried up the stairs, admiring the brief glimpse of a shapely leg as she reached the top before disappearing into a bedroom.

He turned away, his hands tightly clenched at his sides as he drew in a controlling breath, knowing he couldn't go with his instinct to follow Jinx upstairs to her bedroom, take her into his arms and make love to her until they were either sated with each other or simply died from lack of food.

In any case, he had a feeling Jinx Nixon was going to be the death of him—one way or another!

CHAPTER ELEVEN

JINX gave the man seated beside her a sideways glance as he drove behind the wheel of the silver Mercedes that had been waiting for them at the back of the house. Just as Nik had promised it would be.

But, then, she wouldn't have expected anything else, would she?

This man, the youngest of the Prince brothers, was much more like Nik to look at than Zak, being dark-haired, too, although his eyes were blue. But other than getting out of the car to put the single bag that Jinx had brought with her into the boot, and to see her father safely seated in the back of the car—her father actually seemed to be enjoying this change in his routine, quite happy as he sat back looking out of the car window!—Rik Prince hadn't said a word.

Jinx cleared her throat before speaking lightly. 'You must wonder what on earth is going on!'

He shrugged broad shoulders, his attention remaining on the road ahead. 'I'm sure if Nik wants me to know then he'll tell me in his own good time.'

She raised auburn brows. 'Is that the way it usually works?'

Rik gave her a sideways look. 'The way what usually works, Miss Nixon?'

Jinx gave him an uneasy glance, realizing that there was a lot more to Rik Prince than initially met the eye. He was more like Nik than she had realized, and not just in looks. He had managed to convey quite a lot in that

133

question than had actually been said. He didn't smile as easily as Nik, either—and Nik wasn't exactly known for his jollity!

'This.' She gave a pointed shrug, that one word encompassing the press gathered outside her home, her escape out of the back door while Nik kept the press otherwise occupied at the front of the house, this drive through London to goodness knew where—she had completely forgotten to ask Nik where his brother was taking her!

'This is a first for me, Miss Nixon,' Rik Prince told her evenly. 'For Nik too, I suspect,' he added with a touch of wry humour in his voice.

Jinx's eyes widened. 'But you're all so famous; you must have problems like this with the press all the time.'

His mouth relaxed into a rueful smile. 'I wasn't referring to the need to avoid the press.'

'Then what—? Never mind,' she dismissed quickly, having decided she probably didn't want to hear the answer to that particular question; it was bound to involve Nik in some way, and she was desperately trying to keep things in perspective as far as he was concerned.

For one thing, she had to try and remember that Nik had an ulterior motive for helping her in this way, and that that motive wasn't exactly unselfish. For another, she had to keep remembering that, although she had realized she was in love with him, Nik certainly wasn't in love with her.

Which wasn't all that easy to do when he kept coming to her rescue in this way!

'Can I ask where you're taking us?' Jinx opted for a neutral question rather than pursuing the previous subject.

'Initially to my sister Stazy's. But after that I'm sure

Nik will take you wherever you want to go,' he said before Jinx could protest this plan.

Which she had been about to do! At the moment she felt as if she had slightly lost control of what was happening in her life, as if she and her father were being drawn in by the Prince family, to be cocooned in their protective circle.

The only problem with that was they were just as likely to be spat out again afterwards, when they were of no more use.

'Fine,' Jinx accepted tautly, turning to look out of the car window herself now.

She could always go to a hotel with her father, she supposed, although, as she had already told Nik the previous day, it was far from an ideal solution with her father the way that he was. Maybe Susan and Leo would—

'I really wouldn't worry about it, Miss Nixon,' Rik assured her softly. 'At least talk to Nik first before making any immediate decisions.'

She turned back to him, her smile derisive. 'We both know that if Nik has already decided I will stay at your sister Stazy's house, then that is precisely where I will be expected to stay!'

He raised dark brows. 'Is that really such a problem?'

'When it comes to conceding to Nik's arrogance—yes!' she said with feeling.

Rik gave a humourless smile. 'Aren't you being a little ungrateful, in the circumstances?'

Jinx felt the warm colour in her cheeks at this man's gentle rebuke. Yes, she knew she must sound ungrateful, it was just that— Just that nothing, she acknowledged heavily. Nik hadn't had to come and help her out this morning; he could just as easily have left her to her own devices. In which case she would still be a prisoner in her own home!

'I'm sorry,' she sighed. 'It's just—Nik can be a little overbearing at times.'

'Tell me about it!' Rik's smile warmed. 'But, in his defence, I would like to add that he usually means well. He just doesn't always ask before following a particular course of action.'

Jinx returned his smile, starting to like this youngest of the three Prince brothers. Quieter, more serious, he had a reserved sense of humour, a quiet reassurance, that appealed to her.

'I'm the screenwriter of the family, by the way,' he told her gently, one dark brow raised questioningly.

Jinx sobered, her expression noncommittal. 'I know.'

'I would love to work on *No Ordinary Boy*,' Rik murmured.

She stiffened, well aware of her father seated in the back of the car, even if he did still give every appearance of sitting back and enjoying the drive. 'Look, Rik, I—'

'You don't want to talk about it.' He nodded understandingly. 'No, I can see how that might be a problem for you.'

Jinx blinked at his easy calm. 'You can…?'

'Oh, yes.' He gave her a sympathetic smile. 'My big brother still has it wrong, doesn't he?'

Jinx felt herself go cold as the colour drained from her face. 'What do you mean?' Although she was very much afraid she knew exactly what he meant!

'Nik explained before we left this morning about your family—tragedy.' He glanced pointedly in the driving-mirror at her father seated in the back seat.

Jinx was so tense she ached. 'And?'

'I'm a writer too, Jinx,' he told her softly.

'And?' she prompted again.

'We can talk later,' Rik murmured huskily. 'This obviously isn't the time to talk about this.'

No, of course it wasn't, not with her father within earshot. But the two of them did need to talk. Rik Prince was implying that he had guessed the real truth behind the writing of *No Ordinary Boy*—something that no other person had.

She swallowed hard. 'Rik—'

'It can wait, Jinx.' He reached out and briefly covered her hand with his. 'We're at Stazy's now,' he added briskly as he waited for the electronic gates to open before driving up the long gravel driveway to the imposing Victorian house owned by the Hunters. 'Stazy needs the room for the half a dozen kids she plans on having,' he explained affectionately as the three of them got out of the car.

'I hope her husband feels the same way!' Jinx joined in the easy conversation, while all the time she was deeply aware of Rik's earlier comments.

She didn't know how, or why, but it was pretty obvious that Rik Prince had guessed the truth about *No Ordinary Boy*, that he somehow knew she was no more the author J. I. Watson than her father had been!

Not that Jinx had too much time to think about that as Stazy Hunter came out of the house and down the steps to greet them, almost immediately followed by the crunch of gravel on the driveway as the green Jaguar, with a grim-faced Nik behind the wheel, arrived only seconds behind them.

'I went a circuitous route, just in case,' Rik explained as Jinx looked surprised to see Nik there so soon. 'And stop looking so worried,' he whispered so that the others didn't overhear. 'For the moment it's just our secret, okay?'

No, it wasn't okay! How long was that 'moment' going to last? Did Rik intend speaking to her again first before confiding in his older brother?

'All right, Jinx?'

She blinked up at Nik as he stood beside her, a concerned frown between enigmatic grey eyes. 'Fine. I— Was everything okay? At the house, I mean?' she said awkwardly, aware of his watching—and listening— brother and sister.

Nik gave a humourless smile. 'Well, I've probably totally annoyed the majority of the tabloid press by helping you to escape out the back door—but other than that...? Yes, everything's fine.'

Jinx hadn't really given any thought to the fact that by helping her in this way Nik was leaving himself open to a deluge of publicity...

But she thought of it now. 'I don't believe I've thanked you properly yet for coming to my aid this morning,' she said huskily.

He raised a mocking eyebrow. 'I believe you did mention "how kind it was of me"!'

Jinx looked up at him blankly for several seconds, and then she began to smile as she realized he was teasing her for how pompous she must have sounded earlier. Considering the man had just thoroughly kissed her seconds earlier, doubly pompous!

'Er—if I could just interrupt for a few seconds...?' Stazy inserted. 'I believe your father might like to go inside and have a cup of tea and possibly some breakfast?'

Jinx dragged her gaze away from Nik's with effort, turning to look at her father as he stood beside Rik admiring the fish in the pond in the front garden. Colour warmed her cheeks as she acknowledged what Stazy had obviously realized; for the duration of those few minutes' conversation with Nik, she had completely forgotten everyone else but him! Including her father...

'Of course. Sorry.' She grimaced. 'You must think me very rude.' She smiled hesitantly at Stazy.

'Not at all,' the other woman dismissed. 'Nik has this effect on people, I believe.'

'Ha ha, very funny,' he drawled, at the same time taking a light hold of Jinx's arm. 'As it happens, Stazy, I don't think any of us have had time for breakfast this morning.'

She really had inconvenienced everyone, hadn't she? Jinx realized with a frown. The least she could do now was be a little more gracious considering the help Nik and his family had given her this morning.

Although that wouldn't change the fact that she had to talk to Rik Prince, in private, at the earliest opportunity!

Nik could see the different emotions flittering across Jinx's beautiful expressive face; knew, despite her thank-you of a few minutes ago, that she was still having difficulty coming to terms with the fact that it had been him who had come to her rescue this morning.

His mouth tightened ominously as he remembered almost choking over his morning coffee as he'd seen the photograph and headlines on the first of the pile of newspapers he had delivered to him in his hotel room every morning.

COULD THIS BE J. I. WATSON? the headline had shouted, and beneath had been a photograph of Jinx as she'd left Stephens Publishing yesterday.

And it was unmistakably Jinx, her red hair gleaming

like copper, her expression intense as she hurried to get
in the waiting taxi. Hurried to get away from him…

Not that the last part had seemed in the least important
earlier this morning; Jinx needed his help, and, whether
she wanted it or not, she was going to get it!

Although now that she was away from the chaos that
existed at her home she definitely looked less than
pleased at finding herself here.

'Breakfast,' Nik told her decisively, maintaining his
hold on her arm as he urged her to follow the others into
the house. 'Nothing ever looks as bad on a full stomach,
my mother used to say,' he added teasingly as Jinx
looked up at him.

'Mine too,' she acknowledged heavily. 'But mothers
can't always be right, can they?'

'Mine usually was,' Nik insisted, seeing Jinx seated at
the breakfast table before reaching over to pour her a cup
of coffee. 'Maybe coffee will do the trick,' he said, receiving a sceptical grimace for his trouble. 'What would
your father like?' he asked, the older man still looking
completely unruffled by his new surroundings as he
smiled benignly.

'I'll see to him,' Jinx answered abruptly, getting up to
move to her father's side.

Nik's gaze narrowed on the older man as he turned to
respond to Jinx's gentle enquiry. Jackson Nixon had been
an intelligent man and Nik simply couldn't accept that
there wasn't a way to help him get back to that.

'Perhaps you shouldn't interfere, Nik.' Rik spoke
softly at his side.

Nik turned and scowled at his brother. 'Don't you
think that someone has to?' he grated.

Rik seemed to give the idea some thought. 'Not necessarily, no,' he finally answered slowly.

'Not necessarily!'

'Calm down, Nik,' Rik soothed. 'I merely meant that it isn't really any of your business. Or is it...?' he queried softly.

Nik's mouth tightened, his gaze impaling his youngest brother. Rik had always tended to keep things to himself, didn't talk too often, but when he did people took notice of him. As Nik was doing now.

Perhaps Rik was right, and Jackson Nixon's mental health wasn't any of his business, but—

But what?

With her father like this, and Jinx being the only close family that he had left, there was no way that she would ever allow herself to have a life of her own. And that included becoming involved with anyone. With him...

Nik suddenly decided that he didn't like the too-innocent expression he could see on Rik's face. 'Have you talked to Zak recently?'

His brother raised dark brows. 'Should I have done?'

Nik gave a humourless smile. 'When are you two going to grow up?'

Rik gave an unconcerned shrug. 'When we finally see our big brother topple as he falls in love?'

Nik gave a derisive snort. 'You'll have a long wait!'

'Do you think so?' Rik mused before turning to give Jinx a smile as she sat back down at the table, not next to Nik this time, but on Rik's other side.

Nik stiffened. Now why had she done that? It was further away from her father—but further away from him too, Nik acknowledged frustratedly. Damn it, he had never met a woman who was so stubborn.

Never met a woman like Jinx ever before...

And that was his problem, he decided as he watched Jinx through narrowed eyes. She was unique. Totally unlike anyone else he had ever met. Forced a response from him that he had never known before, either!

Even now, just sitting in the same room as her, he was totally aware of her, of the slender elegance of her hands as she buttered a croissant, of the soft pout of her lips as she put the croissant down untouched to sip from her coffee-cup—damn it, was it normal to feel jealous of a knife and a piece of china?

Because Nik did. He wanted the gentle caress of her hands on him, wanted the feel of her lips crushed beneath his, the slenderness of her body curved perfectly into his.

No, this wasn't normal, Nik decided as Jinx turned to give Rik a look beneath long lashes and a wave of black rage instantly washed over him. It wasn't normal to be jealous of Jinx just looking at another man. Not just any man, but his own brother, for goodness' sake!

'You aren't eating, Nik,' Stazy prompted from his other side.

He drew in a deeply controlling breath before turning to face his sister. 'Sorry, no appetite,' he apologized.

Stazy glanced past him. 'Is Jinx going to stay here, do you think?'

He shrugged. 'You would have to ask her that,' he rasped. 'I'm the last person Jinx would confide her plans to!' He knew that he sounded bad-tempered and impatient—and not a little petulant? he questioned ruefully—but that seemed to be becoming the norm where Jinx was concerned.

Stazy shot him an amused glance. 'Finally met your match when it comes to stubbornness, have you?'

'I don't even come close to Jinx's bloody-mindedness!' He scowled darkly.

If anything, Stazy looked even more amused. 'Oh, I wouldn't be too sure about that,' she said.

'Thanks!'

'You're welcome,' Stazy returned cheerily.

Nik turned to give Jinx another glance, only to find her once again looking at Rik. A Rik who turned at that moment and gave her a gently reassuring smile as he softly encouraged her to eat her croissant, Jinx responding to that encouragement.

Hell, what had happened between these two during that half-an-hour car journey?

Because something certainly had; he had never seen Rik this tenderly solicitous, or Jinx this compliant!

He was completely jealous of his own brother, Nik realized disgustedly.

Now that really was a first. And to be jealous of Rik, too. As a family, they had come to expect Zak to flit from one woman to another, but, as far as any of them were aware, Rik hadn't been seriously interested—and that was the only sort of interest Rik ever showed!—in a woman for years.

Although, if the admiration in his gaze as he looked at Jinx, and the warmth of his manner as he poured her another cup of coffee, were anything to go by, Rik was certainly interested now!

No!

Every particle of Nik rose up in protest at the thought of Rik ever being involved with Jinx. She was *his*, damn it—

Exactly what did that mean?

His? In what way was she his? In no way, came the unequivocal answer!

And yet the thought of Jinx with any other man, his brother Rik included, was enough to fill him with murderous rage. Well…maybe not murderous—but he would certainly want to do someone physical damage if he ever saw Jinx with another man!

'Are you sure it isn't going to inconvenience you?' Jinx was obviously answering something Stazy had said to her now.

'Not in the least,' Stazy replied. 'As I told you on the telephone last night, Jordan is away for a few days, and I would appreciate the company.'

'What does that make me?' Rik put in mockingly.

'I meant female company, silly,' Stazy chided, the two of them grinning at each other affectionately.

Meaning that both of them missed Jinx's reaction to the fact that Rik was staying here at Stazy's too.

But Nik was all too aware of the look of relief that flitted across Jinx's expressive face.

Filling him with a depth of anger he had never known before.

CHAPTER TWELVE

JINX could feel the relief wash over her as Stazy finally left her to the privacy of the bedroom she was to occupy for the duration of her stay here. A short duration, if she had anything to say about it.

The last half an hour, as Stazy had lingered over her cup of coffee before baby Sam woke up and demanded her attention, had seemed like pure purgatory as far as Jinx was concerned, all too aware of Nik's brooding silence as he sat further down the table.

What on earth was wrong with him?

It had been his idea to bring her here, but his silence seemed to imply that he now regretted that impulse.

Because it brought her closer into his family? Because he had realized it might somehow give her the idea that the attraction he felt towards her was more than that?

He need have no worries on that score! She knew exactly what his interest in her was—she wasn't so simple-minded as to imagine that the attraction between them would ever lead to a wedding dress and orange blossom!

But he had been singularly uncommunicative—even for Nik!—since their arrival here. Didn't—?

Jinx turned sharply as the bedroom door suddenly opened, every inch of her tensing as Nik stood silhouetted in the doorway. 'I always thought it was polite to knock...' She frowned across at him.

'Sorry,' he bit out unrepentantly, at the same time stepping further into the room and closing the door softly behind him.

A deceptive softness, as the grim expression on his face was anything but calm. Or reassuring.

Jinx straightened, eyeing him warily. 'What do you want, Nik?'

'What do I want?' he repeated mockingly. 'What I really want is never to have met you! What I really want is to forget that I ever did meet you! What I really want—'

'I think I get the picture, Nik,' she cut in sharply, inwardly flinching with every word he uttered.

She was in love with this man—and he wished that he had never met her!

'I doubt it,' he growled, thrusting his hands into his trouser pockets. 'Jinx, exactly what is going on between you and my little brother?'

She frowned. 'Zak?'

'You know exactly which brother I'm referring to, Jinx, so stop playing games!' Nik scowled. 'You and Rik exchanged coy looks all through breakfast—'

'Now you're being ridiculous!' Jinx interrupted. Coy looks? She hadn't been aware of Nik's gaze on the two of them, but she did know that on her part they were more likely to be wary looks than coy ones; Rik Prince had implied he knew altogether too much!

'Am I?' Nik challenged, his face all hard angles. 'Hell, the two of you were only alone together for half an hour or so in the car, and yet my little brother can't seem to take his eyes off you!'

'That's rubbish, and you know it—' She broke off as Nik moved to stand far too close to her than was comfortable, her breath catching in her throat as she looked up at him. 'I barely know Rik,' she protested.

Nik's mouth twisted derisively. 'You barely know me either—but I have trouble keeping my hands off you!'

As if to prove his point he reached out to put his arms around her and pull her into the hardness of his body. 'Don't mess with my younger brother, Jinx,' he warned her, grey eyes glittering silver.

She couldn't breathe at all now, totally aware of the hard length of Nik's body as she curved softly against him.

His gaze narrowed. 'Did you hear me?'

'I heard you!' she assured him, her voice rising slightly in her confusion at being held so close to this man. She shook her head. 'Rik isn't interested in me, Nik. And I'm not interested in him, either,' she added quickly as she saw the way his eyes darkened dangerously. 'If you must know, I— He reminds me a little of you!'

Nik became suddenly still, his eyes like silver shards of glass as he seemed to look into her soul. 'What's that supposed to mean?'

Jinx shrugged. 'You're the one with all the answers— you work it out!'

Although a part of her hoped that he never would. It was one thing to know that she was in love with him, quite another for Nik to realize it too!

Nik continued to look at her searchingly for several long seconds. 'You have a very kissable mouth, do you know that?' he finally murmured huskily.

She swallowed hard. 'So do you,' she answered softly, her gaze transfixed on the sensuality of his full lower lip.

His eyes widened. 'I do?'

She fought the impulse to reach up on tiptoe and explore that sensuality with her lips and tongue. 'You do.'

He drew in a sharp breath. 'Jinx, when all this is over—'

'Will it ever be?' she dismissed heavily, looking away,

the moment of intimacy passing as quickly as it had arrived.

'I hope so.' He nodded grimly before giving an impatient sigh. 'I have to go out and see to a couple of things,' he rasped, releasing her to move abruptly away. 'Will you be okay here while I'm gone?'

Jinx gave a scornful laugh, towards herself as much as him as she felt the loss of his warmth. 'Well, I'm not going to wither and fade away because you aren't here, if that's what you mean?'

He snorted. 'No, that's not what I meant! What I'm really asking is if you can delay making any other plans until I come back later?'

He was asking? Not telling, but asking? That had to be a first!

She gave an inclination of her head. 'I'm sure I can do that,' she answered slowly.

'Good.' He nodded his satisfaction before striding over to the bedroom door. He paused after opening it. 'Try to stay out of trouble for a couple of hours, hmm?'

'Try to—!' Jinx spluttered indignantly. The most 'trouble' she intended getting into was asking Rik for an explanation of his earlier remarks.

'It does seem to follow you around,' Nik drawled.

She glared at him. 'Only since I met you!'

'Well, it's nice to know I've had some sort of impact on your life!' He chuckled throatily, closing the door carefully behind him as he left.

Well, really! First he accused her of flirting with his younger brother, and then he had the cheek to tell her to stay out of trouble!

Until she'd met Nik Prince she had never been in trouble, her life quietly uneventful.

Boringly so?

She had never thought so. Although it was certainly going to become so once Nik had gone from her life.

She sat down heavily on the bed just at the thought of it. He was just so overpoweringly there, larger than life, that it was impossible to be anything other than completely aware of him.

Much as she fought against his arrogance and his domineering attitude, she had no idea how was she going to feel when he was no longer around.

Although she could take a guess...

Arriving back at Stazy's three hours later, and finding Jinx and Rik ensconced in the kitchen preparing lunch together, was not conducive to calming Nik's already volatile mood!

'Well, isn't this cosy?' he rapped out with barely suppressed fury.

'Oh, hi, Nik.' Rik turned to greet him, smiling blandly. 'Stazy's upstairs bathing Sam.'

He didn't give a damn where Stazy was—the fact that Rik and Jinx were here together, after he had warned Jinx earlier this morning to stay away from his brother, was enough to make his blood boil.

Especially as he had just spent a frustrating morning trying to get to the bottom of this latest development in Jinx's already complicated life!

'Hello, Nik,' she said huskily, at the same time eyeing him warily.

As well she might! He had been chasing all over London on her behalf for the last three hours, trying to track down the original reporter, and her source. The fact that Jinx didn't know that was what he had been doing was totally irrelevant!

'Hello,' he grated, his gaze meeting hers challengingly.

She blinked. 'I— We're having chicken curry for lunch.' She made an ineffectual gesture towards the apple she was dicing to add to the mixture frying on the hob.

His mouth twisted. 'I can smell that.'

'Had a good morning, Nik?' Rik broke into the tension that was thickening by the second.

Nik turned glacial eyes on his brother, wondering if Rik could possibly have guessed what he had been doing this morning. 'As it happens—no,' he rasped. 'I need to talk to you later, Jinx,' he added firmly.

'I—er—fine.' She nodded, frowning her puzzlement.

'Where is your father?' Nik looked around pointedly at the otherwise empty kitchen.

'In the garden.' Jinx's frown deepened at his obvious hostility. 'He likes watching the fish in the pond—didn't you see him when you came in?' she realized sharply, her body tensing in alarm.

The garden and driveway had been completely empty when he'd come in seconds ago; he would certainly have seen Jackson Nixon if he had been there.

'Oh, no!' Jinx cried as she easily read the denial in his face, dropping the knife she was holding to run out into the hallway.

Nik put his hand on Rik's arm as he would have hurried after her. 'I want to talk to you later, too,' he told his brother grimly.

Rik looked completely unperturbed. 'That sounds like fun! Now shouldn't we help Jinx look for her father?' he suggested as Nik opened his mouth to assure him of just how little fun it was going to be.

His jaw clamped together in annoyance. 'Yes,' he grated, the two of them following Jinx out the front door.

Jinx was obviously frantic, her face pale, unshed tears almost blinding her as she looked up at Nik. 'He isn't here!' she choked. 'I've looked everywhere, and—' She broke off as two men came round the side of the house, one her father, the other man known to Nik but not to Jinx. 'Oh, thank God,' she breathed her relief as she turned into Nik's arms, her face resting against the hardness of his chest as she held onto him. 'Thank God!'

Well, at least it was him she had turned to in her distress. Although the look of mocking derision on Rik's face as he glanced at his brother over the top of Jinx's fiery head seemed to taunt Nik for thinking she would have done anything else.

But what was he to think? Rik was the most reserved of the three brothers, preferring to keep himself and his life totally private. He didn't make friends easily, and yet he and Jinx were comfortable enough in each other's company for it to seem as if they had known each other for years.

Exactly, the deepening mockery on Rik's face seemed to say.

Because the last thing Nik felt was comfortable in Jinx's company; often angry, always frustrated, his senses heightened and attuned to her every movement, but never, ever comfortable!

'There you are!' Jinx released herself to hurry over to her father, smiling brightly in an effort to try to hide her anxiety of a few seconds ago.

'Jackson and I were just taking a stroll round the garden,' the other man told her soothingly.

'That's nice,' she returned absently, her whole attention centred on her father at the moment.

Although Nik had a feeling that wasn't going to last for too long, and once she learned the other man's identity…!

Nik winced as he imagined the fireworks that were

going to follow once she did know. He also knew it would be no good claiming his innocence; Jinx seemed to take delight in thinking the worst of him, and his motives.

'Are you here for lunch, Ben?' Rik asked.

'Not today, no,' the older man answered smilingly. 'I just thought I would look in on Stazy and Sam on my way to meet Marilyn for lunch.'

Rik nodded. 'Stazy was upstairs bathing Sam, but I expect she's finished by now.' He fell into step beside the older man as they began to walk towards the house, shooting Nik a knowing look before nodding pointedly towards Jinx and her father, obviously intending for Nik to accompany the pair into the house.

In truth, Nik was reluctant to look at Jinx, could feel her accusing glare from ten feet away, knew from that glare that she had already added two and two together where Ben was concerned and come up with the correct answer of four. Except it wasn't quite correct. Yes, Ben was the Ben Travis he had already mentioned to Jinx as a possibility for trying to help her father. But no, the older man certainly wasn't here at Nik's invitation; he knew Jinx well enough to know she wouldn't thank him for his interference. Not in that situation, anyway...

Although the furious expression on her face when he finally did chance a glance in her direction assured him that she wasn't going to give him the opportunity to even try to explain...

CHAPTER THIRTEEN

'How dare you? How dare you?' Jinx was so angry, she was shaking with the emotion.

It didn't matter that Ben Travis had spent the whole of his half an hour visit playing with baby Sam and talking mainly to members of the Prince family; Jinx was still very aware of who he was, what he was, and the fact that the man studied her father whenever he thought no one else was watching him.

Jinx had picked at her lunch, eating little, talking even less, just waiting for the opportunity when she could speak to Nik alone. Like now!

'I told you I didn't want any help for my father,' she continued forcefully, the two of them alone in the sitting-room, her father taking his afternoon nap, Rik having opted to accompany Stazy while she went shopping. 'I told you that quite categorically,' she snapped. 'And yet you still went against my decision and invited a psychiatrist here—'

'I didn't invite him, Jinx,' Nik denied, completely relaxed as he sat in one of the comfortable armchairs watching Jinx as she impatiently paced the room.

'I don't believe you!' She glared. 'It's too much of a coincidence that we should have to come here this morning, and that a couple of hours later Ben Travis just *happened* to call round—'

'For reasons I'm not about to go into, Ben calls around all the time,' Nik cut in, grey eyes starting to glitter silver. 'And I don't appreciate being called a liar, Jinx,' he

153

added coolly. 'If I had invited Ben here to take a look at your father to see if there's anything he can do, then I would tell you so. But as I didn't…' He gave a dismissive shrug.

Jinx's resolve wavered slightly at his complete implacability, but then she remembered the way he had disappeared this morning, on the pretext of 'having things to do', and the fact that Ben Travis had arrived here so conveniently, and she knew, no matter what Nik might claim to the contrary, that it couldn't just be a coincidence, not when Nik had already mentioned the possibility of consulting the other man concerning her father's condition.

'He spoke to me before he left, you know,' Jinx bit out. 'Took me quietly to one side and told me that if I would like him to try talking with my father at any time, Stazy has his telephone number.' An offer that she had politely, but firmly, refused!

Nik gave an impatient sigh. 'I can guess what your answer was to that suggestion. But whether or not I'm responsible for Ben's visit here today—which, incidentally, I'm not,' he insisted, 'what is so wrong with the idea of Ben talking with your father?'

'I— It— You—'

What *was* so wrong with it? Just the fact that it was Nik who had suggested it? Or did she genuinely believe that it would be a waste of Ben Travis's time as well as her father's?

'As it happens, Ben spoke to me before he left too.' Nik spoke quietly as she desperately sought the answers to her own questions.

'What a surprise!' Jinx taunted.

Nik drew in a sharply angry breath, his mouth thinning with the same emotion. 'Believe what you like, Jinx, but

I would have thought that you would want to do something about your father's mental health—'

'Of course I want to do something about it!' she cut in furiously.

'Just not at what you believe is my instigation?' Nik guessed scornfully.

Machination more aptly described this man's behaviour when it came to getting something that he wanted. As she already knew only too well!

'You're irrelevant,' she dismissed with deliberate rudeness, knowing she had scored a direct hit as a nerve began to pulse in Nik's rigidly clenched jaw. 'The fact of the matter is that I don't want to make my father's condition any worse than it already is—'

'And his talking to Ben is going to do that?'

'I don't know, do I?' she wailed.

These last eighteen months of being completely responsible for her father's health and well-being had taken their toll on her own nerves, but the last thing she wanted was to make her father's life any more difficult than it already was.

Nik sat forward in his chair, his gaze compelling. 'Then shouldn't you at least give it a try? Jinx, you can't believe he can actually stay the way that he is?' He gave a disbelieving shake of his head. 'In fact, Ben has already warned me that he probably won't,' he continued determinedly. 'It was the trauma of your mother's and brother's deaths that put him in this state. Another shock could just as easily bring him out of it—or put him further into a state of denial.'

She already knew that, had heard as much from the doctor who had initially dealt with her father. It was for that very reason that she had taken such extreme measures, such as moving house, and her dealings with

Stephens Publishing all made through a PO box, to keep all of the publicity concerning the author J. I. Watson away from him.

'He doesn't need to see a psychiatrist,' she insisted stubbornly. 'And you had *no* right to interfere after I had expressly told you not to do so.'

'Jinx, I told you, I *didn't*— Damn it!' He finally stood up, his height and sheer physical presence immediately dominating the room. 'Do you like being mad at me? Is that it? Is that what this is really all about?' he queried shrewdly. 'Get mad at me, stay mad at me, and the attraction between us can be kept at a distance, too?'

Her eyes had widened at the accusation, the colour receding from her cheeks now as she realized the truth behind his words. It was easier to be angry with him, and to stay angry with him, than it was to fight the attraction she felt towards him. Than to accept the love she felt for him...

'Do you really believe that, Jinx?' Once again Nik was standing far too close, his warmth reaching out and touching her, his breath gently stirring the tendrils of hair at her temples.

She swallowed hard, her expression defiant as she looked up at him. 'You're changing the subject, Nik—'

'No, I don't believe I am,' he returned slowly, his eyes probing the steadiness of her gaze. 'Why do you need so desperately to push me away, Jinx?'

'There's nothing desperate about it!' she denied resentfully.

'Oh, I think that there is,' he murmured consideringly. 'Why, Jinx?'

'Why do you think?'

He shook his head. 'You tell me.'

She didn't want to tell him, didn't want to acknowledge this complete weakness she had where he was concerned. Nik Prince was a man who indulged in brief, meaningless relationships; what she wanted was a lifetime, an eternity, of a passionate, loving marriage. But that was unobtainable. Laughable when put together with Nik. She would have laughed at herself if loving him didn't hurt so much!

'We're completely different, Nik—'

'I'm a man, you're a woman; I believe it's a combination that usually works,' he taunted.

Her eyes flashed deeply blue at his levity. 'Laugh if you want to, Nik, but I—'

'I find very little to laugh at about this situation,' he assured her grimly. 'In the past I've met a woman, we've been attracted to each other, we've satisfied that attraction, and moved on. With you everything is so complicated—'

'I'm sorry,' she choked, biting hard on her bottom lip as the tears that suddenly burnt her eyes threatened to fall hotly down her cheeks. 'We could always be attracted to each other, miss out the middle bit, and just move on.'

He reached out to grasp her arms, not hurting her, but not about to release her, either. 'Can we?'

She felt like a moth mesmerized by the flame, held fascinated in the sheer intensity of that silver gaze, at the same time knowing she wanted nothing more than to lose herself in the burning pleasure of Nik's kisses, to know the hard desire of his body against hers, a desire she more than matched.

'Jinx…!' Nik groaned throatily before his head bent and his lips claimed hers, at the same time enfolding her softness against the contours of his body.

Fighting this man was impossible when she wanted him as much as he obviously wanted her. Jinx gave up any idea of even trying to do so as her lips parted beneath his to allow his marauding tongue access to the moist warmth beneath.

His hair felt like silk beneath her fingertips as they curled into his nape. She slid her body up his as she moved to return the intimacy of his kiss, gasping slightly as the sensitive tips of her breasts brushed against the hardness of his chest, feeling heavy and full in their arousal.

Staying 'mad' at him wasn't even an option at this moment!

Every inch of her felt as if it were on fire, totally alive and attuned to Nik's caresses, his hands cupping her breasts now, thumbs moving rhythmically across the hardened nipples.

Jinx gasped her pleasure, Nik at once taking advantage of her open mouth as his tongue probed even deeper, searching out every tingling nerve ending, filling her, claiming her.

She couldn't breathe—forgot to breathe!—the warmth between her thighs building to a raging fire, a fire that only grew more intense as she moved restlessly against his hardness.

Her neck arched as Nik's lips trailed across her cheek to the exposed column of her throat, sending a shiver of longing down her spine as he nibbled the lobe of her ear before continuing his exploration of the creamy hollows at the base of her throat, licking, tasting her there, before moving lower.

She had no idea who had unbuttoned her blouse, Nik or herself. She only knew that her bra was no barrier to Nik's questing lips and tongue as they moved from the swell of her breasts to capture first one roused nipple and then the other, Jinx at once feeling a rush of warm moisture between her thighs that sent her completely over the edge.

She began to unbutton his shirt, and then lost patience, simply pulling the garment apart, hearing the tearing of the silky material as a couple of the buttons actually popped off, but unheeding of it as she bared his chest to her own searching hands and lips. She reveled in the feel of the silky hair covering his tanned skin, hearing his own gasp of pleasure as her tongue teased the hardened nubs she found nestled there, at the same time as she felt the leap of his hardened shaft move suggestively against her.

One of her hands moved down the length of his chest, down over the flatness of his stomach, desperately needing to touch him, to know the joy of that pulsing flame as he—

Nik's hands moved suddenly as he cradled each of her cheeks so that he could raise her face to look intensely into her eyes. 'Be absolutely sure this is what you want, Jinx,' he groaned. 'Because I'm rapidly reaching the point of no return!'

She had passed it long ago, long before today, before yesterday, probably the first time she'd looked at him. This was the man she was destined to love, the only man she was destined to love, and she wanted him with a fierceness she hadn't known she was capable of.

She steadily held his gaze as her hand continued its downward path, touching him, caressing him, letting him know with every caress how much she wanted him.

Nik closed his eyes briefly, breathing deeply, his eyes almost black as he looked down at her once again. 'Let's go upstairs, hmm?' he prompted huskily, reaching down to take one of her hands in his as he walked towards the door. 'I very much want privacy when we make love for the first time.'

The first time...

That seemed to imply there would be other times, too. Not that it mattered; at this moment Jinx just knew she had to be with the man she loved, had to know him completely, had to give herself to him completely. Nothing less would do.

'—must be starting a cold,' Stazy murmured worriedly as she came in through the front doorway carrying baby Sam in her arms, Rik following closely behind.

Nik hastily stepped back into the sitting-room, closing the door softly behind him, silver gaze full of regret as he looked down at Jinx. 'I don't suppose it will do any good for me to ask if we can continue this at my hotel later?'

Jinx looked up at him with darkened eyes, pausing in the act of refastening her blouse to reach up and gently touch the hardness of his cheek. 'It's probably not a good idea, is it?' she murmured just as regretfully.

'I still need to talk to you,' he reminded her gruffly.

Jinx gave a rueful laugh. 'And is that what we would do if I came to your hotel later this evening—talk?' she teased. 'Somehow I don't think so.' She shook her head, finishing buttoning up her blouse. 'Some things just aren't meant to be, Nik.'

His face darkened. 'That's rubbish, and you know it!'

Did she? Seconds ago she had been prepared to take whatever Nik had to give to a relationship, no matter how little, but for some reason the fates had decided otherwise.

Nik reached out and grasped her arms. 'We make our own luck in this world, Jinx,' he rasped, as if able to read her thoughts. 'Meet me at the hotel later!' he urged forcefully.

She looked up at him, at the fierce determination in

his face, tempted, so tempted… 'I can't, Nik,' she refused breathlessly. 'My father is here. My responsibility is here,' she added more firmly.

He slowly released her, although his expression had darkened even more.

'This isn't over, Jinx,' he warned her as the murmur of voices outside could be heard approaching the sitting-room. 'Not by a long way!'

She wished that it weren't, wished that they could just go back to the way it had been a few minutes ago, aware only of each other, of pleasuring each other. But it wasn't to be. They weren't to be!

She stepped away from him, her chin raised as she bravely met his gaze. 'It's over when I say it's over, Nik,' she said, knowing by the way his mouth tightened that his desire was rapidly changing to anger.

Sometimes the only way for her to survive with this man was to make him 'mad' at her!

Nik continued to look at her for several tense seconds, once again wanting to shake her and kiss her all at the same time.

In the end he did neither, the door opening behind them to admit Stazy and Rik, his sister fussing over the baby as he grizzled in her arms. 'What is it?' Nik demanded as he took the baby from her and he instantly stopped crying.

'Just a cold, I think.' Stazy grimaced as her young son lay quietly in Nik's arms. 'But my shopping wasn't really that important.' She gave him a pointed look, the two of them knowing that she had actually 'gone shopping', and taken Rik with her, at Nik's instigation; he had said he needed to talk to Jinx on her own.

He still needed to talk to her!

Although he had definitely enjoyed what had happened between them more than he would just talking to Jinx. It was when they talked that things seemed to go wrong between them.

Which didn't for a moment change the fact that his real reason for being alone with Jinx, the conversation he needed to have with her, still remained unspoken.

'I was just trying to persuade Jinx into having dinner with me this evening,' he told Stazy, his gaze speaking volumes.

'What a lovely idea!' Stazy smiled brightly at the other woman. 'I'm sure your father will be absolutely fine with Rik and myself,' she added before Jinx could comment.

He never had underestimated his sister's intelligence, but at this moment Nik could have kissed Stazy for the way she had dismissed Jinx's reason for refusing before it even materialized.

'Absolutely fine,' Rik echoed softly, blue eyes brimming with amusement as he looked at Nik. 'What happened to your shirt?' he teased. 'You look as if you've been in a fight. Or something,' he added speculatively.

Or something…

Nik didn't so much as look at Jinx, but nevertheless he knew that her face had flushed fiery red as Rik drew attention to the fact that Nik's shirt was completely unbuttoned, that several of those buttons were actually lying on the carpet. Having fallen there when Jinx had wrenched them off earlier…

'I caught it on the door handle.' He easily held his younger brother's gaze, challenging him to take the subject any further.

'Really?' Rik smiled mockingly.

'Yes—really,' Nik insisted, silver eyes like shards of glass as he gave his brother a warning look. 'Sam seems to be okay now, Stazy.' He handed her back her sleeping son. 'It was probably having Rik along that upset him,' he taunted.

'I wondered how long that would be in coming,' his brother murmured, obviously having been well aware that he wouldn't escape retribution for the shirt remark.

'Then you weren't disappointed, were you?' Nik drawled.

Rik grinned. 'I rarely am where you're concerned.'

The two men shared a smile of mutual affection before Nik decided that Jinx had had long enough to get over her feelings of embarrassment in front of his brother and sister. 'I'll call for you at about seven-thirty, shall I?'

She gave him a frowning look. 'I don't think, after that reporter yesterday morning, that going to your hotel is a good idea.'

Nik's mouth tightened at her reference to the reporter; that was what he needed to talk to her about. And preferably before anyone else had a chance to do so. 'We won't be eating at my hotel. Besides,' he added firmly as she would have spoken, 'I've changed hotels.'

Jinx blinked. 'That was rather sudden, wasn't it?'

'But necessary,' he bit out grimly, knowing that once the press realized they were wasting their time by staking out Jinx's home they would turn their attention to his hotel. He could see by the suddenly dismayed expression on Jinx's face that she realized it too.

'I can never understand why he doesn't stay here like Rik does,' Stazy said.

'Can't you?' Rik teased.

'You could always move in here now.' Stazy ignored Rik's remark and turned to Nik. 'After all, Jinx is here, and—'

'I think we'll leave things as they are for the time

being, Stazy,' Nik interrupted before taking a light hold of Jinx's arm. 'Walk me to the door, hmm?' he prompted huskily.

She nodded, needing to escape from Stazy's and Rik's knowing gazes, if only for a few minutes.

'They know, don't they?' Jinx sighed once they were alone in the hallway.

'That you were about to rip my clothes off when they arrived back so unexpectedly? Oh, yes, I think—'

'I wasn't!' she instantly protested, her look of apprehension turning to a rueful smile as she looked up and found Nik smiling down at her. 'Well…okay, I was,' she conceded awkwardly, at the same time trying to pull the ragged edges of his shirt back together. 'I'll have to buy you another shirt.' She winced. 'This one is beyond repair.' She seemed slightly dazed that she could have been the one responsible for that.

Nik reached up and put his hand beneath her chin, looking down into the fragile beauty of her face. 'You can rip as many shirts off my back as you please, Jinx,' he assured her huskily.

'Don't!' She groaned her renewed embarrassment.

He bent his head and gently brushed his lips against hers. 'Do,' he encouraged softly.

Her gaze suddenly avoided his. 'I—I'm afraid I'm not as—as experienced, as the other women in your life have probably been—' She broke off as Nik put silencing fingers against her lips.

He looked at her consideringly, that blush in her cheeks, the slight look of bewilderment in her eyes. 'You aren't experienced at all, are you?' he realized slightly breathlessly, more pleased than he could ever have guessed if that was the case.

In the past he had always been involved with women

who were experienced, deliberately so, wanting no unwanted complications in his life, and yet the possibility of being Jinx's first lover—her only lover...?—somehow exhilarated him.

Jinx's gaze didn't quite meet his. 'There never seemed to be the time. First school. Then university. Teaching.' She shrugged awkwardly. 'I didn't—'

'Don't apologize, Jinx,' he cut in decisively.

'I'm not apologizing,' she snapped indignantly. 'And I'm not completely inexperienced, either. Just because I said I wasn't as experienced as your other women doesn't mean—'

'Don't tell me any more, Jinx.' He winced, really not wanting to hear any of the details.

What was this woman doing to him? What had she already done to him that he could feel such burning jealousy for faceless men who might so much as even have kissed her?

Maybe he needed to at least have figured that out before they had dinner together this evening!

'No, you're right,' she conceded. 'We really don't need to exchange stories about our individual sexual experiences. It could take several hours to list all yours— and if we're going to have dinner this evening, I would like to find some time for eating!'

Nik's gaze narrowed ominously at what he guessed was a deliberate attempt on Jinx's part to put distance between them.

Not that he could exactly blame her; his own response to her surprised the life out of him, so how much more disturbing must she find her attraction towards a man like him?

But at least she had agreed to have dinner with him this evening; it was definitely a step in the right direction.

Of what he still wasn't absolutely sure. But he did know he had no intention of letting Jinx slip out of his life…

CHAPTER FOURTEEN

JINX had no idea how she had come to be having dinner with Nik this evening. One minute she had been refusing the invitation, and the next the Prince family had seemed to have the entire thing worked out—including Stazy loaning her a dress to wear for the evening.

This dress, Jinx frowned as she looked at her reflection in the full-length mirror that adorned one wall of the bedroom she occupied in the Hunters' home. It was a simply designed dress, a black silk sheath that reached down to just above her knees—it must have been microscopically short on the much taller Stazy!—and yet Jinx knew that it carried a designer label, that its demure styling was deceptive, that the silk material clung to breasts and thighs as she moved.

But when they had hurriedly left the house earlier this morning there hadn't been time to pack more than the minimum of essentials—and a dress she could wear for a dinner date had not been included in that description.

A dinner date...

Was this really a dinner date with Nik? Of course it was. But it was because he needed to talk to her, and he couldn't do it here in front of his brother and sister.

Just keep remembering that, Jinx, she warned herself as she went downstairs to meet Nik and found him standing in the hallway looking up at her with admiring grey eyes.

Amazing. Incredible. She had fallen in love with this

man, was in love with him, and yet the two of them had never even gone out on a date together.

'You look lovely,' Nik complimented her huskily as she joined him at the bottom of the wide staircase.

'It's Stazy's dress,' Jinx instantly blurted out—and then wondered why she had done such a thing; it was certainly a good way to put an end to that particular conversation.

Although some of her flustered response, she knew, was due to her complete awareness of Nik in the black evening suit and snowy white shirt; he looked gorgeous! Lethally so…

Nik gave a rueful smile, as if he was well aware of what she was trying to do. 'Setting the tone for the evening, Jinx?' he drawled, taking a light hold of her elbow as they walked to the door.

'Sorry?'

He shrugged broad shoulders before opening the car door for her to get inside. 'If I say, "It never looked as good on Stazy", then I'm insulting my sister, and if I say nothing, then I'm insulting you.' He walked around the car and got in beside her. 'I can't win either way.'

Was that really what she had been doing? If so, she didn't think she had meant to. Her defensive instincts seemed to have kicked in automatically this time!

'Sorry.' She grimaced.

Nik chuckled. 'It's not a problem,' he assured her, putting the car in gear and driving away from the house.

She frowned. 'It isn't?'

'No.' He still smiled. 'It's a lovely evening, Jinx. I have you at my side, a table booked for the two of us at a romantic Italian restaurant I know; I have no intention of allowing you to annoy me into losing sight of that!'

When he put it like that…!

Although that wasn't the reason they were here, was it? 'I thought you said we had something we needed to talk about this evening,' she reminded him.

His mouth tightened slightly before he forced himself to relax again. 'You're dogged, Jinx, I'll give you that,' he conceded with a slight edge to his voice. 'Yes, we do have something we need to talk about, but I believe that can wait until after our meal.'

By that time she might be so under his spell that it wouldn't matter whether he talked or not—she would just want him to kiss her!

But maybe that was the plan...?

'Nik—'

'Let's just call a truce until after we've eaten, hmm?' he cut in deliberately. 'Indigestion is something to be avoided, not a prerequisite to the evening!'

He was right, Jinx knew he was right, and yet she was too aware of Nik as he sat beside her, in every way. He looked so tall and handsome, a fact borne out by the way the other women turned to look at him as they entered the restaurant together a short time later. And it was all too easy when she looked at the elegant strength of his hands to remember the way he had touched her earlier today, the caress of those hands against her bare skin. The fact that knowledge was reflected back at her in the warmth of his eyes every time he looked at her certainly wasn't helping, either!

'Let's order, shall we?' he encouraged as she would have spoken.

This was unreal. He was unreal. She would wake up tomorrow morning and realize that all of this had been a dream. A warm, wonderful dream.

Except she didn't want to wake up. Not unless it was

in this man's arms, the two of them intimately entwined in the comfort of a huge double bed, both of them naked.

'You've gone very quiet,' Nik murmured once they had given the waiter their order.

Her brows rose over steady blue eyes. 'I thought that was what you wanted.'

'Jinx, you aren't ready yet to hear what I want!' he grated frustratedly.

He might be surprised about that—because it was probably what she wanted too! Damn tomorrow. It could take care of itself. For once in her life she just wanted to forget caution, forget everything but Nik and the touch of his skin against hers.

It had been like this from that first evening, she realized slightly dazedly, a complete awareness of Nik as the man she wanted to be with, the man she wanted to make love with, the man she was in love with.

She drew in a deep breath. 'Nik, perhaps we shouldn't bother with dinner—'

'Jinx, I'm not about to let you run out on me again now!' he rasped, his hand reaching across the table to tightly clasp hers. 'Just give me a chance, hmm? You might find that you like me after all!'

Like him? She loved everything about this man, from the way he looked, the way he had come to her rescue, not once, but twice, his gentleness with her father, to the obvious close relationship he had with his sister and two brothers.

She smiled. 'Nik, you misunderstood what I was going to say. I—the thing is—' God, there had to be a better way than this, a more sophisticated way, to tell a man you wanted to go somewhere private with him and make love! Except sophistication had never been something she was good at…

'I—oh, damn!' he muttered grimly as the mobile phone in his jacket pocket began to ring. 'You aren't going anywhere,' he told Jinx before answering the call.

Jinx was very pleased not to be the person on the other end as Nik scowled into the telephone receiver. To say he was terse as he took the call would be a definite understatement, although his initial aggression calmed down as he made just yes or no answers.

Jinx was left with the dilemma of whether or not she resumed her conversation once his call was over, or simply steered it onto a safer subject.

Coward, she instantly rebuked herself.

Maybe, but wasn't she just going to be more hurt when the relationship was over if the two of them had made love? Maybe she should have thought of that earlier! Because if she knew anything at all about Nik, then he wouldn't let the subject go until he had got the truth out of her...

And the truth was that she was in love with him.

Why it had to be this man, she had no—

'Jinx.'

She looked up at the sound of her name, having been so lost in thought that she hadn't realized his telephone conversation had come to an end. But the expression on his face, compassion mixed with concern, was enough to jolt her out of that pleasant dreamworld where she had been imagining that Nik returned the love she felt for him.

'What is it?' she demanded.

'Your father,' he said economically, turning to signal to the waiter that the two of them were leaving. 'It's nothing for you to panic about,' he added hastily as she began to do exactly that, dropping her bag in her rush to leave. 'Stazy just thinks it might be a good idea for us to return home now.'

Jinx was no longer really listening, haphazardly pushing the things back into her bag that had fallen onto the floor, before standing up to walk dazedly towards the door.

Her father. What could possibly have happened? And why did Stazy think it might be 'a good idea' for them to forgo dinner and return immediately?

'Did Stazy say what's happened?' she demanded of Nik as soon as he joined her beside the car.

'Something about Sam. And your father. And—'

'Sam?' Jinx echoed. 'What on earth does Stazy's baby have to do with anything?'

'I don't know,' Nik answered, having already manoeuvred the car out into the London evening traffic. 'She was babbling, okay?' he explained as Jinx frowned at him. 'She said your father was crying—'

'*Crying?*' Jinx gasped. Her father hadn't shown any emotion other than smiling benevolence for eighteen months!

He nodded. 'Something to do with someone called Jamie. But as I don't know anyone called Jamie—Jinx?' He turned briefly and saw the way her face had paled to a ghastly grey colour. 'Jinx, do you know who this Jamie is?' he queried.

Oh, yes, she knew exactly who, and what, Jamie was. Or had been.

She just hadn't thought that her father would ever remember him again...

By the time he turned the car into the driveway to Stazy's home Nik was so tense at Jinx's stubborn refusal to talk about Jamie that he could barely contain his emotions.

The fact that Jinx barely waited for him to park the car before getting out and running into the house didn't help his mood, but he made sure that he was only a couple of strides behind her, determined to get to the bottom of this situation.

Rik came out of the sitting-room as they hurried down the hallway. 'They're upstairs in the nursery,' he said before falling into step beside Jinx on the wide staircase. 'Sam woke up crying.' He spoke softly to Jinx. 'Your father heard him, went to investigate, and—he's okay, Jinx.' Rik put a reassuring hand on her arm.

Nik's tense frustration turned to burning anger as he saw his brother's hand on Jinx's arm, a red-hot wave of fury washing over him, almost making it impossible for him to think logically. He—

Rik glanced back at him. 'Cool it, Nik,' he said reprovingly. 'This isn't the time or the place.'

No, of course it wasn't. Jinx was the one they had to think of now. But that still didn't change the fact that Nik was filled with burning rage because it was his brother who seemed to be able to offer Jinx comfort, or that Rik seemed to know the reason why she needed that comfort.

What had he missed?

Because he had certainly missed something—he had a feeling that this man Jamie was the key to a lot more things than Jackson Nixon's returning emotions!

Nik stood in the doorway of the nursery as Jinx hurried across the room to where her father sat in the rocking-chair cradling a now-sleeping Sam, Stazy sitting on the carpeted floor at his feet.

Jackson Nixon looked up, his gaze no longer vague but filled with a pain that looked bottomless. 'He's very like Jamie was at this age, isn't he, Juliet?' He spoke gruffly before looking back down at the baby. 'So tiny. So defenceless.' He shook his head, that pain increasing in his eyes, his face lined with strain.

'Just listen, okay,' Rik said quietly at Nik's side as he made a move to go towards the ashen-faced Jinx. 'You're going to learn something,' he insisted at Nik's warning scowl.

'I hadn't noticed—but, yes, he's very like Jamie,' Jinx agreed huskily, reaching out to touch the baby's creamy cheek as she sat down on the carpet in front of the rocking-chair.

Her father closed his eyes briefly, seeming to be fighting back the tears. 'We loved you both so much, Juliet, your mother and I.'

'We both knew that, Daddy,' Jinx assured him emotionally.

'We married late, you see, and never thought that we would have a family.' Jackson continued to talk as if he hadn't heard Jinx's response. 'But first there was you. And then there was Jamie. Our two darling children.' He smiled at the memory. 'We wanted to wrap you both up in cotton wool and keep you safe for ever.' He shook his head, seeming unaware of the tears now falling hotly down his cheeks.

'We always knew how loved we were.' Jinx's hand tightened on his.

Jackson drew in a deep breath before continuing. 'It was so awful when Jamie was twelve and had his accident, when he could no longer walk, but had to sit in that wheelchair all day long; we felt as if we had somehow let him down. But when he died all those years later of pneumonia it was even worse, as if part of us had died too. Three days later your mother did die,' he choked out. 'They said she had a heart attack, but I know better.

She had spent so many years caring for Jamie, making his life as normal as possible, that when he died her heart was broken.' He shook his head, swallowing hard.

'Are you learning?' Rik murmured beside Nik.

Oh, yes, he was learning, learning what Rik had somehow already guessed. Jamie had been Jinx's brother. Jackson's son. And he had been confined to a wheelchair for years before he'd died. Like the twelve-year-old hero of *No Ordinary Boy*...

Was that where Jinx had got her idea for the book from? Was it because of her brother, a sort of memorial to him and the courage he had shown—?

'In this case two and two do make five,' Rik gently interrupted his churning thoughts.

Two and two made—?

And suddenly he knew what Rik had somehow guessed: Jamie Nixon wasn't just the hero of *No Ordinary Boy*—he had written it! Jinx's brother Jamie was the author J. I. Watson!

CHAPTER FIFTEEN

JINX sat in an armchair eyeing Nik warily as he stood in front of the unlit fireplace in the Hunters' elegant sitting-room, the two of them alone.

For eighteen months Jinx had prayed for this day, had willed her father to get better, knowing that it was the shock of, first Jamie's unexpected death, quickly followed by her mother's, that had put him into the cocoon-like state where nothing and no one could harm him.

Denial, the initial doctor had called it, a diagnosis backed up by Ben Travis a short time ago after he had spent an hour or so talking with her father, Jinx having finally agreed to having the other man called in.

Her father was asleep now, aided by medication from Ben Travis, the other man promising to return first thing in the morning. Although he had assured Jinx that he believed they were through the worst of it now, that her father was well on the way to a complete mental recovery.

Stazy and Rik had drifted off to their respective bedrooms once Ben Travis had left, which just left herself and the now-pacing Nik...

Only!

She had been too busy with her father for the last couple of hours to pay much attention to his reaction to what was going on, but she had known that couldn't last, that she owed him some sort of explanation. Where to start—that was the problem!

'Did Jamie write more than two books?' Nik spoke before she had the chance.

Her eyes opened in alarm as she stared up at him. 'You know…?' she gasped softly. 'Did Rik—?'

'No, my little brother kept your secret,' Nik assured her grimly, obviously far from pleased.

'He guessed.' Jinx shrugged. 'While you were out this morning the two of us talked. He's a writer too. He told me that he knew those books hadn't been written by a woman. You had told him about my family, about my mother and Jamie. He guessed the truth,' she recited flatly.

In fact, once she'd got over her initial dismay when she'd spoken to Rik earlier today, when he'd told her how he knew the truth, she had felt relieved that at last someone other than herself did.

She stood up restlessly. 'There are five books in all,' she revealed. 'I had no idea Jamie had written them until after— He left them for me in his will,' she hurried on, not wanting to dwell on the death of her beloved younger brother. 'With a request for me to send them to a publisher. He wanted to try and reach out to other people in his position, to help them, and able-bodied people, to realize that the wheelchair wasn't everything, that there were still people inside the wheelchair. The stories are a sort of legacy, I think, something he could leave behind him.'

The dilemma of her brother's request, when taken into account with their father's fragile mental health following Jamie's death quickly followed by that of her mother, had consumed her for days, weeks, before she had finally typed the first story up and sent it to James Stephens. She had simply had no idea that the book was going to be so popular, that the whole situation was going to explode in her face.

'All of the royalties from the books are to go to charities that help people like Jamie,' she added.

Nik's face softened slightly. 'Why didn't you tell me the truth?'

Jinx looked at him beneath lowered lashes. 'That I'm not the author J. I. Watson any more than my father is? That it was my dead brother who wrote them?' She shook her head. 'That wouldn't have helped me to keep the circus of the publicity away from my father.'

'But I could have helped,' he insisted. 'Damn it, Jinx!' He sighed frustratedly. 'You should have told me,' he repeated heavily.

She looked at him searchingly. 'But you were only interested in the movie rights—'

'Have I so much as mentioned them the last few days? Have I?' he demanded, grey gaze easily holding hers.

'No...' she finally conceded. 'But that doesn't mean you aren't still interested—'

'Jinx.' He reached out and grasped her arms, his fingers gentle but still immovable. 'The only thing I'm interested in is you,' he admitted. 'Just you. Forget the book. Forget the movie. Forget everything else.' His voice lowered huskily. 'Just you,' he repeated gruffly.

Jinx gazed up at him wonderingly, her gaze searching now, finding only gentleness and understanding in his expression. And something else. Something she was almost afraid to put a name to...

'I love you, Jinx.' Nik obviously felt no such fear. 'I love you, and I want to marry you. And if you think I've been determined where the movie rights to *No Ordinary Boy* are concerned, you're going to find that's been quite mild to the campaign I'm going to make on your heart!' He gave a self-derisive smile. 'I'm just going to hang around and make a nuisance of myself until you can't do anything else but fall in love with me!'

Jinx felt as if she had been in shock since the moment Nik had first said he loved her, but at this last statement she couldn't help but smile, albeit a tearfully happy smile. 'More of a nuisance than you've already been?' she asked shakily.

'Oh, much more,' he assured her.

She smiled through her tears. 'Then it's just as well I'm already in love with you, isn't it?' she teased.

'You're already—!' For once in their acquaintance Nik looked stunned. Although that didn't last long as he began to smile, love lighting up his eyes now as he took in the full import of what she was saying.

Jinx nodded shyly. 'Why do you think, in the restaurant earlier, I was about to suggest that I would like to leave so that we could go somewhere private and make love?'

His eyes widened. 'That's what you were about to say?'

'Oh, yes,' she breathed softly, moving into the warmth of his arms, her face raised invitingly to his. 'I love you very much, Nikolas Prince. And I would love nothing more than to be your wife,' she told him seconds before his head lowered and his mouth claimed hers in a kiss so filled with love it made her heart ache with happiness.

Heaven. Nik was her own piece of heaven. The man she had been searching for all her life. Her Prince.

* * *

How he loved this woman! She was the other half of him. The 'something' that had been missing all of his adult life. She was the love of his life!

All of which he had realized earlier today when he'd sat down to analyze what it was he felt towards her. Analyze! Love wasn't something that could be analyzed. It just was. And he loved Jinx more than life itself, knew that he could only be complete with her at his side, as his beloved wife.

'Mmm,' she murmured happily some time later as he reluctantly released her lips, smiling up at him with such love he felt as if he were going to burst with the emotion. 'Do you think Stazy and Rik would notice if you were to stay the night in my bedroom?'

'They might not, but I would—and I have no intention of us sharing a bedroom until you are officially my wife,' Nik told her firmly, at the same time wondering at himself for these newly realized protective feelings.

He wanted everything to be right for Jinx, everything done exactly as it should be, wanted her to wear a white gown as she came down the aisle to him, wanted their wedding night to be the first they shared together.

Damn it, against all the odds, since meeting Jinx he had discovered he was just an old-fashioned romantic, after all!

Jinx chuckled softly as she correctly read the slightly dazed expression on his face. 'Bet you can't believe you said that, can you?' she teased lovingly.

'No,' he admitted wryly. 'But I do mean it, Jinx. It will just have to be the most rapidly arranged wedding in history!' He groaned as her soft curves nestled lovingly against his.

'It will be.'

Nik put Jinx determinedly away from him as he could feel his emotions—and his body!—rapidly spiralling out of control. Although he couldn't release her completely, needing to touch her, to know that she was there, that she was his. He twined his fingers with hers as the two of them sat down on the sofa, Jinx's head resting against his shoulder, his lips against the silky softness of her hair.

He still couldn't believe this was happening, had felt sure that Jinx must hate him after the way he had hounded her over the movie rights of *No Ordinary Boy*, had resigned himself earlier to winning her love, to showing her that he wasn't the man the press said he was, deciding that he would have to embark on an old-fashioned courtship. Not that he was completely aware of exactly what that was, he just knew that Jinx deserved to be wooed, that he would win her love, no matter how long it took.

He still found the fact that she was already in love with him completely overwhelming.

But he would be grateful that she did until the day he died…

'You were going to tell me something at the restaurant earlier,' she reminded him drowsily.

He had forgotten all about that the last half an hour or so! Not surprising really, with Jinx lying so warm, soft, and loving in his arms. But it was one last explanation that she probably deserved.

Even if he did come out of it in a less than positive light, he allowed with an inward grimace of apprehension.

'Nik?' Jinx sat up to prompt concernedly.

He reached up to cradle each side of her face with his hands as he looked at her. 'Jinx, I haven't always been— fair, shall we say, in my dealings with women—'

'I thought we had agreed on not having those sort of confessions,' she teased.

'We have.' He nodded. 'Except that one of the women I was briefly—involved with, was Jane Morrow.' He looked at her anxiously, half fearing Jinx's reaction to his confession, and yet knowing he had to make it.

'My editor? *That* Jane Morrow…?' Jinx said slowly, a frown now appearing between her glorious violet-blue eyes.

'Yes.' Nik swallowed hard. 'It wasn't anything serious, a couple of dinners, a few kisses.' He grimaced in self-disgust. 'But my motives weren't exactly honourable.' Anything but, he could now acknowledge with distaste, knowing that loving Jinx had changed him in ways he could never have imagined, that he never wanted to do anything that would hurt, upset, or disappoint her. And his brief relationship with Jane Morrow, the reasons behind it, were guaranteed to do all three of those things.

He watched Jinx anxiously, her eyes narrowed, her thoughts all inwards. If he should lose her now—!

Finally she nodded. 'Jane Morrow was the one who told the press about me, wasn't she?' she realized astutely. 'That's why that reporter was at the hotel following you, hoping you would lead them to me. Why they were able to follow me from the publishing house yesterday. She telephoned them before coming to James Stephens's office and told them the author J. I. Watson was there, didn't she?'

'She did,' he confirmed heavily; as long as the two of

them continued talking, perhaps it would all come out right after all.

'But why?' Jinx frowned. 'I'd never done anything to her—'

'No, but I had,' Nik put in flatly. 'I used my friendship with her to find you. And once I had, I—well, let's say that Jane had good reason not to feel particularly friendly towards me.'

'She wanted to get back at you,' Jinx realized. 'She was trying to hurt you, wasn't she?' She shook her head. 'Jane Morrow believed that if she made it look like you were responsible for bringing publicity to J. I. Watson, someone who had made it perfectly plain he didn't want any, then he would categorically refuse to let you have the film rights to *No Ordinary Boy*. That's it, isn't it, Nik?'

He nodded. 'Earlier this morning I managed to locate the reporter from the hotel. She didn't want to talk to me at first, but while discussing the large sum of money that had been paid to her source for supplying information on J. I. Watson she inadvertently revealed who that source was.'

'But I thought reporters didn't reveal their sources?' Jinx frowned.

'They don't usually. This one wouldn't have done, either, but once she mentioned that her source was a senior member of Stephens Publishing staff, and as such entirely reliable, it didn't take too much intelligence to guess that it was Jane Morrow. Besides, the reporter didn't exactly luck out; she wasn't averse to extracting a price herself for having given me the information.'

'What sort of price?' Jinx's eyes were wide.

'An in-depth interview with Zak,' he revealed with satisfaction. 'Not that he knows about it yet…!' And his little brother was going to be far from pleased when he did know, but at the time of asking Nik hadn't hesitated in giving the reporter exactly what she wanted. Besides, the reporter was quite attractive; Zak might just enjoy the experience. Although Nik wouldn't count on it! 'But that isn't important at the moment.' He dismissed the argument he knew he was going to have with Zak, sitting up to look anxiously at Jinx. 'The thing is that, although Jane Morrow may have made those telephone calls, and accepted that money for doing so, I'm really the one responsible for bringing the press down on you. If I hadn't—' He broke off, Jinx's fingers pressing lightly against his lips.

Jinx shook her head. 'We hadn't even met when you were involved with Jane Morrow.'

'But I was only involved with her as a way of getting to you—'

'Nik, she's a grown woman in her thirties, hardly a child that you seduced and then abandoned!' Jinx reasoned. 'Okay, so your behaviour was—less than honourable, and I'm sorry that it happened, but your behaviour is no excuse for hers. What she did was totally vindictive. She's my editor, for goodness' sake—'

'Was,' Nik put in softly. 'Once James Stephens became aware of what had happened, he dismissed her.'

Jinx shrugged. 'I could never have worked with her again anyway after she had betrayed my trust in that way.'

Nik swallowed hard. 'You aren't going to change your mind about marrying me?' He felt as if he had the sword of Damocles hanging over his head as he waited for her answer.

'Oh, no,' she reassured him without hesitation, moving to kiss him lingeringly on the lips. 'Although I am going to make sure that nothing like Jane Morrow ever happens again,' she added warningly.

Nik's arms tightened around her possessively as he began to breathe again. 'You won't need to,' he assured her with certainty. 'I love you, Jinx Nixon. Only you. For always.'

'Mmm, I like the sound of that,' she murmured, her lips only centimetres away from his.

So did he, he decided as his lips claimed hers in a kiss that left neither of them in any doubt that what they had between them was for ever.

EPILOGUE

'DO YOU think the two of us can leave any time soon?'

Jinx turned to smile warmly at her husband. Her husband of only six hours. Her husband Nik. Her husband Nik Prince.

She had sat in the hairdressers' this morning as her hair had been styled and curled, tiny white rosebuds amongst the curls in place of a veil, and practised saying that phrase, 'My husband, Nik'. Daydreaming, really, and yet the whole of the last three weeks had passed as if a wonderful dream.

First had come telling their families of their intention to marry. Then had come the arrangements for the wedding, something Nik had managed to sort out with ease. Then had come the family statement to the press concerning the real identity of the author J. I. Watson, a statement that had been met with only warmth and understanding. In fact, if anything it had renewed the sales of *No Ordinary Boy*, while at the same time creating a clamouring for the second book to be published.

Her father still found the attention afforded to his dead son a little overwhelming on occasions, but as each day passed, with gentle guidance from Ben Travis, he was getting stronger, his pride in his son helping with that recovery.

If Jinx could have known this would be the result of explaining exactly who the author J. I. Watson really was, then she would have done it much sooner!

'Very soon,' she answered Nik, leaning into his body,

the warmth of her gaze telling him exactly how much she longed for them to be alone, too. 'Hasn't it been a beautiful day?' she murmured dreamily as she glanced around at all the happily smiling wedding guests.

In fact, the wedding list that Nik had drawn up for his side of the family read like a 'who's who' in the world of celebrities, a fact that held her more staid family and friends in thrall.

'Why is Zak scowling like that?' Jinx frowned as she noticed her new brother-in-law's less-than-happy demeanour.

Nik was grinning with satisfaction as she turned to look up at him enquiringly.

Her eyes widened. 'You didn't choose today of all days to tell him about that in-depth interview you promised on his behalf?' she guessed, knowing he had been putting off the dreaded moment.

Nik's grin widened as he nodded. 'I didn't think even he would hit me on my wedding day! Besides, he won't stay too mad at me once he knows you've requested that he take the part of the father when we make the movie of *No Ordinary Boy*.'

Jinx began to smile herself, that smile turning to a chuckle as her arms slid up her husband's chest to link her hands at his nape. 'I'm ready to leave if you are,' she told him throatily.

'More than ready,' he murmured with promise. 'In fact, if I don't make love to you soon, Mrs Prince, I may just go quietly insane!'

One of her hands moved to caress the hardness of his cheek. 'And we can't have that, can we?'

'Not for another forty or fifty years at least!' he agreed huskily.

Forty or fifty years. A lifetime. For ever.

With Nik.

PRINCE'S PLEASURE

CHAPTER ONE

'WHY was I under the impression you were a man?' Zak's mouth tightened as he stared at the woman standing outside his hotel suite.

Her brows rose over eyes so deep a brown they were like smooth melted chocolate. 'I have no idea, why were you?' she retorted.

He scowled, knowing exactly who was responsible for his erroneous impression. 'My brother Nik had something to do with it, I suspect!'

'Do I *look* like a man?' the woman teased.

In a word—no!

But, then, Zak hadn't known what she was going to look like, had he? He had simply been informed by Nik that he had agreed, on Zak's behalf, for a reporter named Tyler Wood to spend a week with him doing an exclusive interview. Nik, with his usual arrogance, had forgotten to mention that the reporter was young, beautiful, and female!

'Not in the least,' Zak allowed dryly, not knowing who he was angrier with, his brother, or this beautiful woman. 'Nik also forgot to mention that you're American.' He frowned, knowing he was going to find it much harder to keep a fellow countrywoman at a distance than he would have the typical English male hack he had been expecting.

Tyler Wood shrugged. 'Obviously your brother is a man of few words.'

Obviously.

And Zak hated being wrong-footed, damn it!

Despite the fact that Tyler Wood was dressed in green combat trousers, and a fitted black tee shirt, her short dark hair moussed into the spiky asexual style that was the fashion at the moment, there was no way she could be mistaken for anything other than female. Those mesmerizing long-lashed dark eyes apart, she had beautiful gamine features, with a small, snub nose and full, pouting lips, and her petite five foot two frame was definitely that of a woman, the trousers resting low on curvaceous hips, her breasts full—and obviously braless!—beneath the clinging material of her tee shirt.

'What's an American doing working for an English newspaper?' Zak was curious, knowing there were more than enough newspapers and journals in America to keep a reporter busy, without going to the trouble of crossing the Atlantic.

Tyler Wood stared at him for several minutes before answering rather casually, 'The same as an American actor in England, I suspect—working. Do you think I might come in?' she added pointedly.

Zak was aware that he couldn't keep her standing outside in the hotel corridor all morning, but he was still acclimatizing himself to the fact that the reporter who was to follow him around for a week was a gorgeous American woman.

He hadn't exactly been overjoyed when Nik had told him of the agreed interview, although he had accepted the reasons for it when his brother had explained to him that it had been done to protect Nik's new wife Jinx from the barrage of publicity that had been about to break over her unsuspecting head.

Tyler Wood had been the initial reporter to leak the

story, but after several conversations with Nik she had agreed to back off for a while in exchange for a week of interviewing Zak, an actor rarely out of the headlines, anyway.

But Zak had been expecting a man, and had thought the two of them could just spend a week together on the town. The reporter could then write up his interview, and everyone would go away happy. Discovering that Tyler Wood was a woman certainly put an end to that idea.

He drew in an impatient breath. 'I suppose you had better come in,' he allowed ungraciously as he opened the door wider for her to enter.

She reached to just under his chin, he discovered as she moved past him into the hotel suite, her almost elusive perfume that of some fresh-smelling flower.

She turned to smile bewitchingly at him, looking at him from under those ridiculously long, dark lashes.

Zak realized he was annoyed—annoyed because although he had always had a healthy relationship with the media, it had always been a relationship he had kept based on his own terms, and he had certainly never found one of their number attractive before. How the hell was he supposed to spend a week in this woman's company and keep her at arm's length at the same time?

She tilted her head to one side, looking at him speculatively now. 'I have to say, I always got the impression you were more—laid-back and charming than this…'

Zak was fully aware that that was the side of him he chose to present to the media. A side he was going to find increasingly difficult to present to Tyler Wood if he had to spend too much time in her company. Which, it appeared, he did…

He attempted to heal the slight breach he'd created. 'It's nine o'clock in the morning, I didn't get to bed until four o'clock; exactly how laid-back and charming do you want me to be?'

She gave a husky laugh. 'I'm sorry, Mr Prince. I didn't mean to imply that you were being less than gracious.'

Zak eyed her with suspicious blue eyes, knowing that, besides being less than charming, he looked less than his best, too. The party last night had been pretty wild, and he had probably drunk a little too much champagne too. He had literally only crawled out of bed five minutes before she had knocked on the door of his hotel suite.

Consequently he had quickly pulled on the black trousers and white silk shirt he had worn to go out the night before, running a hand briefly through the tousled blondness of his overlong hair, having no time at all to shave. Never one for exactly looking well dressed at the best of time, Zak still knew there was studied casualness and just plain scruffy—and he knew exactly which category he fitted into this morning!

'I am being less than gracious,' he apologized. 'Perhaps it's age? I used to be able to party all night and still be fresh and ready to work on the set by six o'clock the next morning. None of this is for the record,' he added quickly as she reached into one of the cavernous pockets in her trouser legs and brought out a notebook and pencil.

'Oh.' Those brown eyes darkened with disappointment before she placed the notebook back in the pocket to give him a considering look. 'Exactly how old are you?'

'Thirty-six. How old are you?' he came back.

'Twenty-six,' she answered without hesitation.

He nodded, having already guessed she was aged in her mid-twenties. 'And can you still party all night and then go to work in the morning?'

Once again she gave that husky laugh. 'I never could!'

Zak shrugged. 'Then perhaps there's hope for me yet.'

'Perhaps there is,' she agreed. 'Mr Prince—'

'Zak,' he corrected tersely. 'Mr Prince sounds like my brother Nik,' he explained.

And there could only ever be one Nik: arrogant, determined, forceful, a man totally confident of his own worth. Also now a happily married man, Zak acknowledged affectionately.

'I was just wondering, Mr—Zak,' she corrected huskily at his pointed look, 'if perhaps you feel you have been pressured into this interview by your brother and myself?'

'*Feel* as if I have?' he echoed incredulously. 'There's no *feel* about it, Miss—'

'Tyler,' she suggested with gentle mockery.

'Tyler.' He nodded impatiently. 'I was *pressured* into this interview by you and Nik. What's the interview for, anyway? Which publication?' he enlarged as she looked at him blankly. 'I'm pretty sure that the newspaper which carried your last article about Nik and Jinx isn't interested in this sort of exclusive interview.'

Was it his imagination, or did those huge brown eyes suddenly no longer quite meet his? Although he wouldn't be in the least surprised if she felt embarrassed about working for the newspaper that had plastered that story of Nik and Jinx all over its front page; a scandal-mongering tabloid was probably too kind a description of that particular rag!

Tyler gave him another one of those blindingly bright smiles. 'You're right, Mr Pr—Zak,' she corrected herself. 'But *The Daily Informer* does have a Sunday newspaper, with a glossy magazine supplement.'

'And you intend this interview to be published in that supplement?'

She turned to look out of the window at the London skyline. 'This is rather a magnificent view, isn't it?'

'Magnificent,' Zak agreed dryly. 'Tyler, I have the distinct feeling that you—' He broke off as the second knock of the morning sounded on his suite door.

'That will be my photographer,' Tyler Wood turned to reassure him as he scowled in the direction of the door.

'No,' Zak said firmly.

'Oh, but I think it might be,' she said, after glancing at the heavy watch that adorned the slenderness of her left wrist. 'I asked Perry to meet me here at nine-fifteen—'

'I wasn't disagreeing with your guess as to who might be on the other side of that door,' Zak elaborated. 'Merely stating that your agreement with my brother didn't include having a photographer trailing around with me for a week and shoving a camera into my face every minute of the day.' At least, it had damn well better not have included one!

Those deep brown eyes widened protestingly. 'But I'll need photographs to go with the article—'

'And you can have them,' he said. 'At the end of the week. At my convenience.'

Tyler looked as if she would like to argue that particular condition, but one look at his face must have convinced her she would be wasting her time. 'Okay,' she agreed. 'I'll just go and tell Perry, and then we can continue—'

'I'm actually going back to bed, Tyler,' Zak cut in, 'but if you would like to, I have no objection to you joining me there so that we can "continue"…?' He eyed her challengingly, still far from happy at having been pressured into this situation in the first place, and even less happy about it now that he had met the woman who was to be his shadow for a week.

If it weren't for the fact that he loved and respected his older brother, and if he didn't think so highly of Nik's wife, then Zak would have quite simply told Tyler what she could do with this 'exclusive interview'!

In fact, it might still come to that!

Tyler looked at him narrowly. 'I have a feeling you're enjoying playing with me, Zak,' she said finally.

'Under other circumstances, I'm sure that I would,' he taunted, rewarded by the sudden flush to her cheeks. 'But today? Right now? With a photographer standing on the other side of the door?' He shook his head. 'All I want at this moment is to go back to bed. Alone,' he added with finality.

'Of course,' she agreed lightly, walking over to the door with long, determined strides. 'Perhaps we can meet up again later this afternoon? Without the photographer.'

'Perhaps we can,' Zak conceded. 'Be sure to telephone first, though, hmm?' he added mockingly. 'I would hate to shock your delicate sensibilities by having you find me here with someone.' He raised dark blond brows.

Tyler Wood paused with her hand on the door handle. 'My sensibilities really aren't all that delicate, Zak. In fact, it was a pleasant surprise to find you here alone this morning.'

'Touché.' Zak nodded an appreciative acknowledgement of her sharp comeback.

She paused before opening the door. 'Tell me, when you worked with John Devaro last year—'

'Not another John Devaro fan!' he groaned before answering her. 'Yes, he really is as good-looking as he appears on screen. Yes, he really is a very funny guy. Yes—'

'I was actually only going to ask you if you felt in the least threatened by the fact that his name appeared above yours on the credits,' Tyler interrupted dryly.

Zak was taken aback at the unexpectedness of the attack—for attack it certainly was. 'The two of us talked it over and decided we would go alphabetically.'

'Oh.' She nodded. 'See you later, then!' A slight smile curved her lips as she let herself out of the hotel suite.

Perhaps there was more to Tyler Wood, after all, than a pair of melting chocolate-brown eyes and a stunning smile? Maybe he had underestimated the fact that she was a woman, an American one at that, trying to make it in a country that wasn't her own, in a profession that was often dominated by men.

And what if he had underestimated her? As he saw it, he had two choices where she was concerned.

Considering the way she seemed to get his hackles up without even trying, he could carry on being this obnoxious and uncooperative, or he could give in to the attraction he felt towards her and try charming her into his bed. He was damned if he didn't, and damned if he did!

Not much of a choice, really.

CHAPTER TWO

'ARROGANT bastard!' Perry scowled as the two of them made their way across the large hotel reception area to the huge revolving door that led out onto the street.

Tyler couldn't exactly blame him for being disgruntled at Zak's decision not to have a photographer following him around all week; the two of them had worked together on and off for six months now, and nothing like this had ever happened to them before.

Posing the question, had Zak realized there was more to this interview than at first appeared?

'Don't worry about it,' she assured Perry as they stepped out into the warming sunshine. 'I'm sure you'll be able to manage without his cooperation; you always have in the past.'

'And I'm sure I will this time,' Perry acknowledged with satisfaction. 'Although I would much rather have spent the time openly with the two of you rather than creeping around in the background.'

Tyler was well aware that for most of the last six months Perry had wanted to make their relationship into something more intimate, which she had so far resisted.

It wasn't that she didn't like Perry, and he was certainly a good-looking guy with his overlong dark hair and warm blue eyes, she just didn't feel that way about him and considered him more like a brother than anything else. Much to his chagrin.

But she couldn't in all honesty become involved with someone, especially a friend like Perry, without telling him everything about herself—and that she had no intention of doing. No one was to know who or what she was; as far as anyone in England was concerned she was just Tyler Wood, rookie reporter, and that was the way she wanted it to stay.

'Although I should watch yourself with Zak Prince this week, if I were you,' Perry added teasingly. 'From what I've heard the man can't be alone with a woman for five minutes without trying to seduce her into his bed!'

Tyler grimaced. 'Going on his mood this morning, I don't think he can succeed too often!'

She knew that wasn't true, though... Of the three Prince brothers Zak was the good-natured charmer. The oldest, Nik, had remained arrogantly aloof from involvement until his recent marriage. The younger brother, Rik, was the more reserved of the three, keeping himself to himself most of the time.

But obviously nine o'clock on a Monday morning, after what had obviously been a full weekend, was a time when Zak was all out of charm!

It had been Nik Prince, before disappearing on his honeymoon yesterday, who had been the one to set up this morning's meeting for nine o'clock...

Had it been deliberate? That would have been a little unkind on Nik's part—to both Tyler and Zak. But, then, kindness wasn't an emotion very often attributed to the legendary Nik Prince!

He *had* done it on purpose, Tyler realized with dismay. It wasn't an auspicious beginning to a week spent in Zak Prince's company.

*   *   *

'Tell me,' she asked later that evening once she had finally managed to meet up with Zak Prince again in the hotel lounge; he had still been sleeping when she had rung him at four o'clock. 'I know what I'd done to anger your brother enough to arrange such an early meeting that it was guaranteed to annoy you, but what did you do?' She quirked dark brows over mischievous brown eyes.

'Very astute of you, Tyler.' Zak Prince smiled, much more relaxed this evening as he lounged back in one of the capacious armchairs, wearing ragged denims and a loose black tee shirt. 'With Nik—' he shrugged '—who knows? Although I actually think it was his idea of a joke.'

'Ha ha.' Tyler grimaced.

'Yeah.' Zak grinned.

Tyler could see exactly why this man had won three Oscars. His smile was charismatic, almost mesmerizing when taken into account with the rest of his looks: overlong hair the colour of ripe corn, eyes the blue of a perfect summer sky, his features rugged, as if hewn from stone.

Whoa! Tyler brought herself up short. She was here to find a new angle on Zak Prince for her story, not fall under his spell herself.

Because she was sure there was more to this man than the charismatic charmer he was usually portrayed as. There had been rumours, of course, of involvements with married women, and even the possibility that the success of the Prince brothers' movie company owed much to connections with the shady underworld—which was patently absurd! But there were always rumours about anyone successful; Tyler wanted to get to the truth.

'Anyway—' she straightened briskly '—I apologize for any misunderstanding this morning and I suggest we move on.'

'Move on to where exactly?' he teased.

Tyler frowned, knowing she hadn't quite phrased that correctly somehow. 'Background stuff this evening, I thought,' she ploughed on. 'Where you were born, family, what you're working on at the moment, things like that.'

'Look, Tyler, I don't want to tell you how to do your job—'

'But you're going to anyway?' she guessed.

He shrugged broad shoulders, seeming completely impervious to the female attention his presence was engendering. Most of the other women in the lounge were unable to take their eyes off him, not quite with their tongues hanging out, but pretty close, Tyler noted disparagingly.

'Most people already know the background stuff,' he dismissed, pausing to smile up at the waitress as she brought over the two mineral waters they had ordered.

He was right, of course; the three Prince brothers and their younger sister were the children of the legendary Damien Prince, an actor who had held the public in thrall for over thirty years, before his premature death over twenty years ago.

During the brothers' youth, Zak had always been the bad boy of the family, in and out of trouble during most of his teens, dropping out of school to take up acting like his father, and then finally finding his niche and settling down to being the charming rogue that he was now known for worldwide.

But all three Prince brothers, the principals in the

movie company PrinceMovies, were as successful in
their own individual fields, Nik as movie director, Rik
as screenwriter.

'You're right.' Tyler nodded, accepting that he was
just stating a fact rather than being arrogant. 'I can
probably look all that up.' She settled back in her armchair. 'So what do you have planned for this week?'

'Planned?' He took a sip of his mineral water.

She had seen Zak being interviewed, had watched
several recordings of him on one of the leading chat
shows. She knew that he wasn't usually this much
hard work, that he normally responded easily and
smoothly to questions put to him, his charm always in
evidence.

But it wasn't this evening—again.

Did he know something? Did he suspect that this
interview wasn't quite as straightforward as she
wanted it to appear?

'The reason why you're here in England.' She
smiled, determined not to let him know she was bothered by his lack of cooperation. 'After all, you're usually based in the States, so—'

'My older brother was married at the weekend,
Tyler; isn't that reason enough for me to be here?'

She felt embarrassed colour warm her cheeks. 'Of
course,' she acknowledged evenly. 'I just wondered at
the reason for your *still* being here.'

'You did?' he murmured incredulously.

She shrugged. 'I doubt anticipation of this interview
was enough to keep you here!'

'You doubt correctly,' he said. 'The première of
Gunslinger is showing on Saturday; I think I'm expected to be there!'

She had done it again, Tyler recognized with an

inner groan. Of course the English première of Zak's most recent movie was taking place this coming Saturday. She had known that. She had just forgotten it.

Because she was too anxious to get to the real story? Probably. Well, she wouldn't make that mistake again. She needed an exclusive—something new to the market, a different angle, a story no one had written before. And she was convinced that this interview with Zak could give her the exclusive she was after.

'I'm sorry, Zak,' she apologized. 'I—'

'Tyler—' he sat forward in his chair, his expression almost pitying '—might I suggest, in an effort not to waste any more of my time, that you go away and do a little more research before we continue with this?'

She deserved the rebuke, she knew she did, but that didn't alter the fact that he didn't need to have made it. The legendary Prince charm! Huh, so far she had seen little evidence of it!

Which only convinced her all the more that this man was hiding something, that there was more of a story behind Zak Prince than anyone had ever discovered. But she *would* discover it!

She straightened. 'That won't be necessary, Mr Prince,' she told him tartly. 'I'm aware of the première at the weekend, I was simply enquiring as to whether or not you are working on something else in England at the moment?' She met his mocking gaze unblinkingly.

She had guts, he would give her that. Guts, and a little anger too at the moment, if that glint in those chocolate-brown eyes was anything to go by.

Not surprising, really. He wasn't exactly giving her

an easy time of it this evening. But then it wasn't in his job description to make life easy for reporters. The fact that he normally did didn't mean that he had to do so in the case of Tyler Wood.

He had no idea why she should be so different, and yet something about her made his hackles rise, his normally relaxed approach to the media deteriorating to this barbed exchange of barely concealed animosity.

He shrugged. 'I'm meeting with a director for lunch tomorrow to discuss the start of filming next week— no, you cannot be present at the meeting,' he added as he saw her eyes light up in anticipation.

A light that instantly went out as her gaze narrowed angrily. 'My agreement with your brother was that I would be allowed complete access to you for a week—' She broke off as he raised a sardonic eyebrow. 'Not *that* sort of access, Mr Prince,' she snapped.

'I usually make my own choices when it comes to *that* sort of access,' he gibed. 'And your agreement was with my brother, not me.' His voice had hardened. 'So there will be no inclusion in my meeting tomorrow.'

She opened her mouth as if to argue the point, and then closed it again to stare across at him in total frustration.

Zak gave her a considering look. 'Tell me again what sort of magazine this interview is for, Miss Wood?'

'The usual sort of Sunday supplement,' she answered abruptly.

Was it his imagination, or had those brown eyes become slightly guarded again? 'The "usual" sort,' he repeated softly, once again having the feeling that

Tyler Wood was acting evasively. And she wasn't very good at it.

Her chin rose challengingly. 'I thought *I* was the one conducting the interview, Zak, not the other way round!'

'I'm just curious to know a little more about the woman I'm expected to take around with me all week. After all,' he added as she would have spoken, 'most people are going to assume that you're the latest woman in my life.'

'The latest in a *very* long—' She grimaced her dismay as she realized what she had just said. 'I shouldn't have said that. It's just that—'

'It's the truth...?' he jeered.

'No! I mean—well, yes, it is the truth. But I still shouldn't have said it.'

'No, you shouldn't,' Zak acknowledged dryly. 'But it's probably the most honest thing you've said all evening!'

Her eyes widened. 'I beg your pardon?'

'Granted.'

Her mouth firmed. 'I have no idea what you're talking about, Mr Prince. Are you implying I've been dishonest with you?'

Were her hands trembling slightly? He couldn't be sure as she hastily clasped those hands together. 'You aren't the only one with connections, Tyler,' he added, sure now that she had definitely gone paler. 'And this afternoon I made a few phone calls in order to check up on you.'

The colour did drain completely from her cheeks now. 'Oh, yes?' she said airily. 'And what did you learn?'

Zak looked at her with narrowed eyes, more convinced than ever that she was hiding something. 'Not a lot, as it happens. The press, it seems, can be pretty close-mouthed when it comes to one of their own. However, I did learn that you're considered a good reporter, if a little inclined to get too emotionally involved.' He paused before making his next statement. 'Also, that you had a blazing row with your editor a couple of weeks ago, which apparently culminated with him threatening to fire you...'

Her eyes were huge brown pools of melted chocolate as she met his gaze unflinchingly. 'Well, he doesn't seem to have carried out that threat, does he? Because I'm still employed,' she retorted.

'Apparently not,' he conceded, his mouth tightening. 'Out of interest, what did the two of you argue about?'

Tyler shook her head. 'I really don't think that is any of your business.'

He shrugged. 'I just wondered if it might have had anything to do with the little agreement you came to with my brother?'

'Of course not,' she snapped. 'Now if we could stop talking about me and concentrate on you...?' she said pointedly.

He sat forward. 'I'll keep asking until I find out the truth about you, Tyler,' he warned.

Tyler closed her notebook with a decisive snap before secreting it away in one of those many pockets on her combat trousers. 'Until today, I really believed all the things written and said about you in the media: that you're charming, not in the least difficult to work with, affable even!' She gave a disbelieving snort of derision. 'When in fact you're really exceptionally rude, extremely difficult to work with, and not even the tiniest bit affable!'

Zak reached across the tabletop and easily clasped her arm as she would have stood up, his fingers like steel bands. 'Is that what you intend writing in your article?' Despite the fact that he had set out to be as unpleasant as possible, he wasn't used to people disliking him, and found that he didn't particularly like the experience.

He also discovered that he liked the feel of Tyler's skin against his fingers. It was soft and silky to the touch, making him wonder if the rest of her body felt as sensuous and warm.

'Relax, Tyler,' he told her gently. 'We haven't finished talking yet.'

She looked across at him coolly. 'Do you want me to hang around just so that you can insult me some more?'

His mouth twisted into a smile. 'I'm all out of insults at the moment—but if you give me a few minutes...! Besides, we're drawing attention to ourselves.' He looked pointedly around the lounge to where quite a lot of people, several men included now, were openly staring at them.

'You're the one drawing attention to us,' she corrected him tautly, at the same time sitting back abruptly, releasing her arm from his grasp as she did so.

Zak watched as she ran the fingers of her other hand over the spot where he had held her. Both of her hands were completely bare of rings, and were long and slender, with delicately tapered fingers. He found himself wondering what it would feel like to have those fingers moving caressingly over his bare chest and back. And other parts of his body...

'We were discussing the argument you had with your editor,' he reminded her, angry with himself for having those thoughts about Tyler; she was a reporter, for goodness' sake!

She shook her head, her spiky hair gleaming almost auburn in the overhead lighting. '*You* may have been, I don't believe *I* was.' She met his gaze boldly over the rim of her glass as she took a sip of the mineral water.

Zak suppressed his feelings of irritation with difficulty, finding that this woman pressed buttons in him that he normally kept well away from the public eye—and he didn't mean physical ones! Although God knew she was attractive enough...

'What shall we talk about, then?' he mocked. 'The fact that you and the handsome photographer Perry Morgan are apparently inseparable? Or shall we—? Going somewhere, Tyler?' he asked as she put her glass down on the table with obvious force before moving to stand up.

Except she didn't quite make it, all the colour draining from her face before she collapsed back into the chair, her eyes closed, her breathing shallow.

'What the hell?' Zak had been propelled forward as she fell, moving down on his haunches beside her chair now. 'Tyler!' He shook her shoulder slightly. 'Tyler, speak to me, damn it!' he ground out forcefully.

She seemed to find the strength to open one eye and glare at him. 'Go away,' she muttered weakly.

He ignored that, and straightened before bending down and easily sweeping her up into his arms.

She weighed next to nothing, he discovered as he began to stride purposefully across the lounge with her still in his arms, totally immune to the avid stares the two of them were receiving, his expression one of grim determination.

'What do you think you're doing?' Tyler gasped, both eyes open now as she began to struggle in his arms.

'I would have thought that was obvious!' Zak didn't even glance down at her as he stepped into the waiting lift.

'It is, but—where are you taking me?' She was struggling even harder to sit up in his arms.

'My hotel suite,' he informed her. 'And stop struggling like that; you'll only end up hurting yourself,' he said as his arms tightened about her. He had no idea what was wrong with her yet, and until he did she wasn't going anywhere!

'You're definitely making an exhibition of us now,' Tyler protested as the two people waiting to get into the lift stared at them in shocked surprise as Zak stepped out with her still cradled in his arms.

'Do I look as if I care?' he dismissed impatiently as he used the key-card to get into his hotel suite, kicking the door shut behind him to stride over to the sofa and lay her down on it. 'Don't move,' he instructed her before moving over to the mini-bar, all the time keeping one eye on her as he searched through the array of alcoholic drinks there.

Although she didn't seem to be making too much of an effort to get up now, once again lying back with her eyes closed, her cheeks still deathly pale.

Either she really was ill, or this was some sort of elaborate ploy on her part to keep this interview alive.

It certainly wouldn't be the first time a woman had tried something like this on him in order to get into his hotel room, although, he had to admit, it wasn't usually with an interview in mind!

But if it should turn out that was what Tyler Wood was doing, then she was going to find out exactly how 'exceptionally rude' he could be!

CHAPTER THREE

'WHAT are you doing!' Tyler gasped, eyes wide as Zak raised her head and tipped some liquid into her mouth. Fiery liquid that burned as it went down her throat. 'No!' she protested, desperately trying to push his hand away, and not succeeding as he forced another mouthful of the foul-tasting liquid down her throat. 'What was that?' she groaned as he placed her head back on the sofa.

'Brandy,' he told her with satisfaction. 'Guaranteed to—'

'Make me ill,' she finished heavily. 'Even more so on an empty stomach.' A very empty stomach. In fact, it was because she hadn't eaten anything, since a hurried slice of toast for breakfast this morning, that she had collapsed in the first place.

She had been dismayed when she had first moved to London at how high the cost of living was here, her reporting job not exactly earning her big bucks. So, in order to survive on those wages, as she had sworn she would when she'd walked out of her sumptuous home in New York with claims to her family that she could make it on her own, she had had to economize on things. Like eating.

Bread, milk and cereals were cheap, as well as being quite nourishing, which was just as well, because it was what Tyler had mainly been living on for the last six months, with the odd hamburger thrown in here and there as a treat.

'Why do you have an empty stomach?' Zak probed, shrewdly attacking the relevant part of her statement. 'It's nine o'clock at night, so why haven't you eaten dinner yet?'

Because dinner was a luxury she could rarely afford. Lunch, either, for that matter. Although having eaten either wouldn't have lessened the effect the brandy was going to have on her any second now.

'I have an allergy.' She ignored his questions, trying to sit up. 'And if you don't get me to the bathroom in the next ten seconds I'm going to be ill all over this expensive carpet!'

'An allergy?' Zak Prince repeated with a dark scowl, making no effort to step forward and help her. 'What sort of allergy—damn it, Tyler…!' he rasped in disbelief as she put her head over the side of the sofa and was indeed ill all over the carpet.

As predicted.

It had been the surprise of her life to discover, on entering college, and the round of parties that had followed, that alcohol of any kind caused this reaction in her.

'What—how—what sort of allergy?' Zak Prince queried as he came back from the bathroom with a couple of towels, handing one to Tyler and throwing the other one over the mess on the carpet.

'To alcohol,' she had time to answer him before she was ill once again.

Not that this could last for too long; there was really nothing in her stomach for her to be ill with except that slice of toast and liquid!

Although it was unpleasant enough while it lasted, Tyler acknowledged half an hour later, equally exhausted and devastated that she had been sick in front

of Zak Prince of all people. The fact that he was the
one responsible for giving her the alcohol in the first
place didn't lessen that feeling in the slightest!

'Damn it, you only had a couple of sips of the
stuff!' he protested as he helped her to the bathroom
to wash her face and clean her teeth, before easing her
back onto the sofa.

'The amount doesn't seem to matter,' she explained.
She was already feeling the start of the headache that
usually followed one of these bouts. Not that there
were any now that she simply avoided drinking alcohol.

Unless it was literally forced down her throat!

Sleep was the best thing for her now, although there
wasn't too much chance of that until she had got herself back to her apartment...

It was dark when she woke up. Very dark. And very
silent. Apart from the sound of steady breathing.

Tyler held her breath.

The sound of breathing continued.

Where was she?

More to the point, who was that breathing beside
her?

She sat up with a start, groaning as she felt the
pounding pain in her head.

'Are you okay?'

There was a movement beside her, and Tyler
quickly closed her eyes as a light was switched on, its
brightness only increasing the pounding in her head.
As did the easy recognition of that voice!

'Tyler?' Zak repeated with concern.

What was she doing lying in bed beside Zak Prince?

How had she got here? More to the point, what was she still doing here?

The last thing she remembered was being violently ill, knowing she had to sleep, and then—nothing.

'Tyler, open your eyes and talk to me,' Zak Prince instructed forcefully, at the same time grasping her arms and shaking her slightly.

'If you don't stop doing that my head is going to fall off!' She gently lowered herself back onto the pillow.

Zak instantly stopped shaking her. 'Sounds like you have a hangover to me.' He sounded amused. 'Are you sure you hadn't been drinking before you met me last night?'

Her eyes shot open as she ignored the pain in her head to glare at him indignantly. 'I told you, I'm allergic to alcohol! One mouthful and I'm violently ill.'

'You sure are!' He grinned, leaning on his elbow to look down at her. 'In fact, I've never seen anyone as ill as you were last night. Before you blacked out, of course,' he added.

'I fell asleep,' she defended, and then winced at the loudness of her own voice. 'I fell asleep,' she repeated huskily, suddenly very aware of where they were, and of how close Zak Prince actually was. 'What time is it?' She turned her head slightly, having trouble trying to focus on the luminous clock on the bedside table.

The bedside table! She really was lying in bed with Zak. Both of them were fully dressed, she was relieved to see, but it was still a huge double bed the two of them lay in.

Zak peered past her at the clock. 'A few minutes after eleven o'clock,' he supplied.

'Oh, that's not so bad!' She sighed her relief. 'I've only been asleep for an hour or so—'

'A few minutes after eleven o'clock in the *morning*,' Zak enlightened her with a teasing smile.

'It can't be!' she protested, half struggling to sit up, and then falling back down again as she realized how close she was to Zak. 'If it's morning, then why is it still so dark?'

He shrugged broad shoulders. 'I always stay in this particular suite when I'm in London. If I'm working I never know when I'm going to get to bed and the curtains in here are so thick they cut out all the daylight.'

Tyler stared up at him now, her mouth open, her eyes wide with shock. Eleven o'clock in the morning! Did that mean she had been here all night?

Zak chuckled softly. 'Well, this isn't the usual reaction I get from a woman after we've spent a night in bed together!'

Tyler felt her face pale even more, her lips feeling slightly numb too. 'We—we haven't spent a night in bed together,' she finally managed to stutter.

'No?' He looked pointedly at their surroundings.

There was no denying that they were in a bedroom, nor that the two of them shared the same bed, but they certainly hadn't—they hadn't—had they…?

Her eyes were wide with anxiety as she looked up into Zak's face for some sign of exactly what had happened here last night, but his expression was unreadable as he looked at her beneath mockingly raised brows.

'You know, Tyler—' Zak reached up and pushed the short hair back from her brow, his fingers leaving a trail of fire where they touched '—I actually consider it extremely insulting that you could imagine I might take advantage of a woman who had just been violently ill all over my hotel suite!' His blue eyes looked as hard and gleaming as sapphires.

It did sound a little insulting, Tyler realized. In fact, a lot insulting. Although, considering his much-publicized reputation with women— No, she had better not even go there. Not if the now-dangerous glint in his eyes was anything to go by!

'Although the same certainly can't be said about twelve hours later!' he rasped just before his head swooped down and his lips claimed hers.

Tyler melted. Just melted. Her lips softened and clung to his, and her body responded avidly as he half lay across her, her hands moving up to thread her fingers in the silky softness of his corn-coloured hair.

Zak's mouth gentled, sipping, tasting, tenderly biting, causing first her lips to tingle, before the sensation spread to the rest of her body.

Then she felt as if she had been engulfed in flames as he suddenly deepened the kiss, her mouth opening wider to allow the hot, passionate intrusion of his tongue.

Her breasts, the nipples firm and inviting, pressed against the muscled hardness of his chest, a chest she longed to touch. Her hands thrust eagerly under his tee shirt, first stroking then lightly dragging her nails down—

'Housekeeping!' A sharp rap on the door accompanied the bright announcement.

Zak, whose fingers had just started to caress Tyler's generous, unfettered breasts beneath her top, shot away from her as if he had been stung. 'Damn, damn, damn!' he muttered. 'I forgot to put the ''Do Not

Disturb'' notice on the door last night before we went to bed!' He was scowling darkly as he swung his long legs off the bed and got up to walk over to the door.

Tyler lay back on the bed in total shock. Zak Prince, the golden boy of the big screen, had just very thoroughly kissed her. She had always wondered what was meant by that phrase, and now she knew. She had just been so 'thoroughly' kissed she still tingled all over and her legs felt shaky!

Not the best move he had ever made in his life, Zak rebuked himself even as he dealt with the cleaning lady standing out in the hallway. First and foremost, Tyler was a reporter, and reporters, in his experience, were after only one thing: a story.

Something he had just given her in spades!

Somehow, and he wasn't quite sure how, he was going to have to take a step backwards—no, several steps backwards. He groaned inwardly as he remembered the softness of Tyler's breasts beneath that little tee shirt. She had felt so good, her skin like velvet to the touch, her lips soft and responsive beneath his.

But of course she had been responsive, he acknowledged with self-disgust. Claiming that he had seduced her during this week's interview would be the icing on the cake as far as any female reporter was concerned!

'If you're hoping for a repeat performance I'm afraid you're going to be disappointed!' he gritted out as he turned from closing the door and found Tyler still luxuriating in the bed. 'I have that lunch appointment I told you about in—just over an hour,' he announced after glancing at his watch. 'But maybe we can pick this up again later?' he added with a deliberately insulting raise of an eyebrow.

The colour flooded Tyler's cheeks as she scrambled to sit up, turning away from him as she did so. 'Where are my shoes?' she asked as she looked around dazedly.

'Your *boots* are in the other room,' Zak said. He still remembered his amazement the night before, when he had gone to remove her footwear before putting her into bed and found she'd been wearing a pair of yellow desert boots. 'Tell me, Tyler, do you wear military clothes to make up for your lack of height and stature?'

She stood up abruptly and frowned. 'And do you take lessons in rudeness along with acting, or does it just come naturally?'

'I've never really thought about it.' Rudeness wasn't usually a part of his character; only Tyler Wood, it seemed, brought out that side of his nature. 'Er—I think maybe you should take a shower or something before you leave,' he advised as she turned to march determinedly through to the adjoining sitting-room.

'No, thank you,' she answered tightly, sitting down to pull on one of her boots, wrinkling her nose delicately because he hadn't quite managed to erase the smell from the carpet the night before.

'Don't worry about it,' Zak dismissed. 'I'll call Housekeeping back and get them to shampoo the carpet while I'm out.'

'You know...' she paused to glare up at him, obviously not happy at being reminded of her illness the evening before '...if you had anything of the gentleman about you then you wouldn't have slept in the same bed as me last night!'

'There's only the one bed,' Zak protested, leaning against the doorjamb between the two rooms as he watched her, his arms folded across his chest.

'Then you should have slept on the sofa in here!' she snapped, pulling her second boot on and tying it so tightly Zak was sure it must be cutting off the blood circulating to her foot.

'It happens to be *my* bed,' he reminded her.

'Yes, but—I would have been happier if you had left me on the sofa,' she insisted, standing up.

'Oh, I couldn't have done that,' he assured her mockingly. 'What if you had been sick again? You might have choked on your own—'

'Please don't talk about that any more!' Tyler practically shrieked, picking up from the table all the articles Zak had emptied from her pockets the night before.

'I really think you should take advantage of the bathroom facilities before you leave, Tyler,' Zak reiterated as he once again took in her appearance.

Her eyes flashed as she looked up. 'I don't—oh, no!' she groaned as she caught sight of herself in a mirror, reaching up a hand to her hair as it stood up in the best likeness to an annoyed porcupine Zak had ever seen. 'You could have told me!' she growled as she marched past him into the adjoining bathroom.

'I thought I just did,' he called out over the sound of water running, grinning unabashedly as she came back from the bathroom, her hair now wet and spiky. 'Not much of an improvement, really,' he teased.

'You—' Tyler broke off, drawing in a controlling

breath before speaking again. 'I didn't notice my appearance putting you off a few minutes ago!'

'No. Well, a woman in your bed is worth two that aren't,' he deliberately misquoted.

Her eyes flashed deeply brown. 'I wouldn't have thought you were that desperate!'

Zak's smile widened at her attempts to insult him, easily guessing the reasons behind it—embarrassment, mainly—but having no intention of helping her out. The fact that she didn't appear in a very good light either should be enough to discourage her from writing about it. *Should* be...

His mouth firmed as he straightened away from the doorframe. 'I'm sure you'll be relieved to know I'm not even the slightest bit desperate,' he assured her. 'Now, if you will excuse me, I have to shower and change before my luncheon appointment.'

'I—of course.' Tyler looked flustered now. 'Can we meet up again later today?'

'Okay,' he said, wondering now about her personal life. Did she have parents still alive? Did she have siblings? Where had she gone to school? Was there a current man in her life? Those thoughts were immediately followed by the question, why did he want to know?

He had been forced into agreeing to have Tyler Wood in his life for a week, and when that week was over he had no intention of ever setting eyes on her again. So why should he care about the answer to any of those questions?

He sighed. 'I've been invited to a party later this evening, so you may as well come with me.'

'If you're sure I wouldn't be intruding—'

'I thought you were already doing that,' Zak responded with brutal honesty.

Tyler winced. 'I'm sure there must be someone in your life at the moment—'

'If there is I can assure you that you aren't ever going to meet her!' Zak cut in harshly.

'If you resent my being here so much, why did you agree—?' She broke off as he steadily returned her gaze, blond brows raised. 'You didn't agree, did you?' she acknowledged with another wince.

He gave a derisive smile. 'You already know that I didn't.'

Tyler grimaced. 'I thought your initial—lack of co-operation was because I wasn't the man you thought you had agreed to be interviewed by. But now I realize it's much more deep-rooted than that.'

'Much more,' he confirmed grimly. 'Although that doesn't change the fact that the agreement was made, with or without my consent,' he continued as she frowned. 'Now, I suggest you come back to the hotel about eight o'clock this evening. That way I can be sure that you have dinner before we go on to the party. God knows what the speculation would be like if you were to faint halfway through the evening!'

Her cheeks coloured furiously. 'I'm perfectly capable of feeding myself, thank you—'

'Really?' Zak was deeply sceptical. 'I haven't seen much evidence of that so far!'

Her eyes flashed. 'I told you, it was the brandy that made me ill; the fact that I hadn't had dinner yesterday evening had nothing to do with it!' She glared across at him.

His gaze narrowed on her speculatively, taking in the hollows of her cheeks, the slenderness of her body, her wrists so delicately thin they looked as if they might break if any pressure was exerted on them. In fact, Tyler Wood was altogether too slim.

'Tyler, I gave you the brandy because you almost fainted, presumably from lack of food. Which brings us back to the fact that you still haven't told me why you didn't eat dinner yesterday,' he probed.

'There wasn't time.' Once again her gaze seemed to be avoiding meeting his.

Zak didn't buy that explanation; there had been plenty of time for her to eat in between their parting yesterday morning and meeting up again in the evening. Unless she had been expecting him to give her dinner yesterday evening? That would certainly explain why she looked so uncomfortable about the subject...

'Just be back here, and dressed for an evening out, by eight o'clock this evening, Tyler,' he ordered. 'If you're not, then I will have already left without you,' he warned as she would have protested.

She bit down on her bottom lip, looking as if she would like to tell him exactly what he could do with both his dinner and his evening out, but at the same time that impulse obviously warring with the consequences of doing so, namely losing the interview.

Maybe it was a little unfair of him to take advantage of her obvious wish to do the interview, but at the moment, impatient with the situation, puzzled by some of her behaviour, and—yes—frustrated as hell from their passionate kiss earlier on, he wasn't in a mood to be fair!

Worse, he had a distinct feeling this was only the beginning of his feelings of frustration where Tyler Wood was concerned...

CHAPTER FOUR

'WHERE have you been all night? Or need I ask?' Perry scowled at Tyler darkly as he got up from where he had been sitting on the staircase to the next floor of her apartment building.

Tyler frowned, slightly out of breath herself after having just staggered up the two flights of stairs to her apartment. She had been ill last night, didn't feel a hundred per cent now, a fact not enhanced by a journey on the hot and claustrophobic London tube; the last thing she needed at the moment was to be asked about last night. Anything about last night!

'Perry,' she greeted lightly, putting the key in the lock to her apartment and opening the door, at once feeling soothed by the untidy comfort of her sitting-room, the furniture old, the sofa sagging slightly, books taking up every conceivable piece of space. But it was her own little world, nonetheless.

A world she would have preferred to retire to alone, after that second run-in with Zak this morning, in order to lick her wounds in private, if for no other reason. Something she knew wouldn't be possible as, without being invited to do so, Perry followed her inside.

'Tyler, I asked you a quest—'

'Perry,' she cut him off, her look of quiet intensity enough to silence him, for the moment. 'As you can see, I have just got home,' she continued softly, 'so do you think we could possibly delay this conversation

39

until after I've at least showered and changed into some clean clothes?'

Not that she really owed Perry an explanation; no matter what he might wish to the contrary, their relationship had only ever been a working one. But it was that working relationship, and the fact that he had also been hauled over the coals a couple of weeks ago, with the threat of dismissal if they didn't come up with something sensational, pictures included, where Zak Prince was concerned, that made her feel an obligation to him.

'Fine,' he accepted tersely. 'I'll just sit here and wait for you.' He dropped down onto the sagging sofa. 'Tyler, you do know that Zak Prince is—'

'Not now, Perry,' she warned—very much at the end of her tether when it came to the subject of Zak Prince. 'Help yourself to coffee,' she invited before turning in the direction of her bedroom. 'I'll try not to be too long.'

'I'm not going anywhere,' he assured her.

Tyler breathed a sigh of relief once she reached the relative sanctuary of her bedroom, the first time she had really been able to relax since waking up this morning and finding herself in bed with Zak.

In bed with Zak!

Just the memory of that was enough to make her drop down weakly onto her bed.

It was bad enough that she had woken and found herself in bed with him, but it was what had followed that disturbed her the most: Zak Prince very thoroughly kissing her.

And her kissing him right back...

If the woman from Housekeeping hadn't interrupted them when she did...!

Then what?

What did she think would have happened? That the two of them would have carried on making love?

Tyler gave a groan of self-loathing. What a stupid, stupid thing for her to have allowed to happen. Zak had made it more than obvious that he had very little respect for her as a reporter as it was. After she'd fallen into his arms like that, he probably had none at all for her as a woman now, either.

'Tyler?' A knock on the bedroom door accompanied Perry's query. 'Are you all right in there? Only I can't hear the shower running.'

'I'm fine,' she answered sharply, glaring at the closed door. 'But I could be a while, so why don't you—?'

'I'm staying right here, Tyler,' Perry informed her doggedly.

She got wearily to her feet, still frowning her irritation with Perry's badgering as she grabbed some fresh clothes and went through to the adjoining shower-room.

Not that she felt too much better half an hour later, freshly showered and dressed in a clean white tee shirt and faded denims, her hair washed and moussed. All surface dressing in an effort to boost her bruised morale, knowing that, after what had happened between them this morning, Zak was going to be more obnoxious that ever when she met up with him this evening.

And she still had a disgruntled Perry sitting in her lounge!

'Coffee?' she offered as she came through from the bedroom and saw that he hadn't made himself a cup after all.

'No, thanks,' he refused tersely, standing up. 'I re-

ally wasn't exaggerating, was I, when I said Zak
Prince can't be alone with a woman for five minutes
without trying to seduce her into his bed? Only in your
case it doesn't seem to have taken even five minutes!'
He looked at her scornfully.

Tyler felt the colour drain from her cheeks. 'Perry,
you have absolutely no right—'

'No right!' he exclaimed, shaking his head in disgust. 'Tyler, I stood outside the hotel last night for
over five hours waiting for one or both of you to come
out. Then I tried calling you when I got home. Then
again at two o'clock. Then again at six o'clock this
morning.' His mouth twisted derisively. 'The fact that
you were still wearing your clothes from yesterday
when you arrived home, and looked as if you had just
fallen out of bed—literally!—is more than enough reason for me to have added two and two together and
come up with the appropriate answer of four!
Wouldn't you say?' His eyes glittered with accusation.

Tyler drew in a sharp breath. It was probably as
well Perry hadn't been inside the hotel when Zak had
swept her up in his arms and carried her away to his
hotel suite! 'Perry, I think you had better leave before
you say anything else you're going to regret,' she
warned.

He dismissed the warning with a wave of his hand.
'Is that all you have to say to me? Tyler, I thought the
two of us meant something to each other. As friends,
if nothing else,' he added as she would have argued
that point.

'Oh, Perry, of course we're friends.' She groaned.
'But nothing happened between Zak Prince and me
last night,' she told him heavily, knowing that wasn't
quite true of this morning, but having no intention of

sharing that humiliation with anyone—including Perry.

'I hope for your sake that it didn't,' he snapped. 'We're supposed to be digging up the dirt on Zak Prince—I would hate for you to be part of it!'

That was the choice her editor had given her after Tyler had effectively blown the story on Jinx Nixon; deliver as much scandal on Zak Prince as she could, or else she could look for another job. Having walked out on her home and family six months ago with the brave declaration she was perfectly capable of making it on her own, she had no intention of getting fired from her very first job as a reporter.

Although that didn't stop her inwardly cringing at the knowledge that this interview with Zak was intended as lurid fodder for the tabloids, rather than the restrained Sunday magazine supplement article that she had told Zak it would be. This type of journalism was not exactly what she had had in mind when she'd made those grand announcements to her family!

'I was ill last night, and Zak Prince was kind enough—'

'You were ill?' Perry moved to her side to look down at her with concern. 'What happened? Why were you ill? Do you need to see a doctor?'

A head doctor, maybe—for being stupid enough not to have rebuffed Zak this morning when he'd kissed her!

'No.' She gave a humourless laugh. 'I don't need to see a doctor. I—inadvertently drank some brandy—'

'Oh, no,' Perry groaned in sympathy, well aware of her allergy to alcohol. 'But how on earth—?'

'It was an accident, okay?' she told him sharply. 'I

drank it. I was ill. And Zak Prince took care of me. End of story.' As far as explaining herself to Perry it was, but she had a definite feeling that Zak would have other ideas on the subject!

'You poor love,' Perry sympathized. 'And all I did when you finally managed to stagger home was hurl accusations at you. Will you let me make you some coffee to make up for my boorish behaviour?'

'Fine,' she accepted as she dropped down into an armchair, just wanting to forget this awkwardness between them; goodness knew she had made few enough friends since moving to London without alienating Perry too. And she really didn't need any more confrontation—she was only just starting to feel a little better.

Although, she had to admit, the thought of meeting Zak Prince again at eight o'clock this evening was enough to make her feel ill all over again!

'You're looking good,' Zak complimented her as he opened the door to his hotel suite at exactly eight o'clock that evening and saw a transformed Tyler standing outside.

She did look good. Very good, in fact. The red dress she wore clung in all the right places as it emphasized pert breasts and the curve of her hips—she was obviously wearing very little clothing underneath the figure-hugging dress. Its above-knee length showed off a long expanse of shapely tanned legs, and the high heels on the matching red shoes she wore added a good three inches to her diminutive height.

His practised eye told him she was wearing more make-up than usual too—those dark lashes surrounding her huge brown eyes looking longer and silkier than ever, a delicate blush emphasizing her cheek-bones, and a red gloss on her lips adding to their full-ness.

'Dressed for battle, hmm?' he guessed.

'A party, I thought,' she came back lightly as she walked past him into the suite.

Zak grinned appreciatively as he turned to watch the sway of her hips. He hadn't been quite sure what to expect when Tyler arrived this evening—the spitfire of their first and second meeting, or the young woman this morning who had seemed confused and not a little upset at their response to each other in bed; he certainly hadn't been expecting this beautiful siren. She had obviously sat back when she'd got home earlier, regrouped, and this dynamically beautiful woman was the result.

'You're looking pretty good yourself,' she returned the compliment as her gaze travelled slowly up the length of his body.

Zak frowned, finding he was uncomfortable with the way Tyler had looked at him with such feminine as-sessment as she took in his appearance in the cream silk shirt and brown trousers he wore this evening. As he had looked at her own changed appearance seconds ago in the red dress with complete male assess-ment…? Hell, yes, but— But nothing. What was good enough for him, her challenging gaze now said, was good enough for her, too.

There was more, much more, it seemed, to Tyler Wood than he had at first given her credit for…

'Thanks,' he accepted as casually as he could. 'I won't bother to offer you a drink before we leave—we both know where *that* could lead!' he taunted, blue eyes challenging *her* now.

Tyler didn't even blink at his deliberate reminder of last night and this morning. 'You mentioned that we would be having dinner before the party...?'

'O'Malley's.' He nodded. 'If that's okay with you?'

'Oh, I think I'll be able to cope,' she said dryly.

The restaurant he had chosen was the in-place at the moment, a cross between an Irish pub and a superb English-cuisine restaurant. But, despite what Tyler might think to the contrary, that wasn't the reason Zak had chosen it. O'Malley's was more relaxed than the other fashionable London eateries, and Zak didn't particularly enjoy dining in formal restaurants. From the brief time he had spent in Tyler's company, he hadn't thought she would either, but her appearance this evening told him very firmly that she would be comfortable no matter what her surroundings.

'Good,' he said as he opened the door for her to leave, still feeling strangely wrong-footed by this stunning woman—something that didn't happen to him too often, he had to admit.

He caught a faint whiff of her perfume as she moved smoothly past him out into the corridor, a heady mixture of clean flesh and that elusively floral concoction.

Tyler was most definitely not his type, he told himself firmly as he accompanied her to the lift. For one thing he abhorred short hair on a woman—he couldn't stand that almost as much as the unfeminine combat trousers Tyler had worn yesterday. Worst of all, she was that loathed of all things, a reporter!

Then why, if he disliked all those things about her, had the memory of her this morning, soft and pliant in his arms, her body warm and inviting, been intruding into his thoughts all day?

'Are you okay?'

He turned sharply at her huskily spoken query. 'Why shouldn't I be?'

'No reason.' Tyler shrugged. 'It's just that the elevator has stopped at the ground floor and you don't seem to want to get out…?'

The lift had indeed stopped at the ground floor. Several people were standing outside waiting to get in, although the recognition in their eyes as they looked at him seemed to say they were in no particular hurry for him to leave.

'Sorry.' His smile of apology encompassed them all as he took a firm hold of Tyler's elbow to step out into the reception area, keeping a hold of her arm as they walked over to the doors at the front of this sumptuously elegant building.

'Are you sure you're okay?' Tyler repeated once they were seated in the cab on the way to the restaurant.

No, he wasn't sure he was okay! Women came and went in his life, with rapidity, if the recent comments of his two brothers were anything to go by, and while he enjoyed their company—and other things!—for the duration of the relationship, he never gave any of those women a second thought once the relationship came to an end. In fact, he had found himself thinking more about Tyler in the last twenty-four hours than he had about any of those women. He could still feel the softness of her skin beneath his hands, the inviting warmth of her lips beneath his.

It was because they weren't in a relationship, he told himself firmly. It was just frustrated lust, that was all. And it was because he had to be careful what he said and did around Tyler—otherwise he might just find that the result of being incautious was being plastered across the front page of a tabloid newspaper.

'I really am fine,' he assured her confidently, glad he had sorted that particular problem out in his mind. 'What have you done with your day?' he changed the subject promptly.

'Done with my day?' she echoed sharply. 'What on earth should I have done with it?'

Zak gave her a quizzical smile. 'I'm just making conversation, Tyler.'

'Oh.' She looked uncomfortable now, her gaze not quite meeting his, her previous air of confidence starting to look a little shaky. 'Well, I—I tidied my apartment, if you really want to know.'

His mouth quirked upwards a little. 'Very domesticated,' he teased, thinking of the complete disarray they had just left behind in his hotel suite. 'Do you live alone?'

'Yes—I live alone!' she snapped. 'Although I can't imagine what business that is of yours.'

Neither could he, if the truth were known, but for some reason he had been curious to know whether she lived with her boyfriend, Perry Morgan. The latter could have proved a little embarrassing considering her non-appearance at home last night!

'Besides,' she continued firmly, 'I'm the one who's supposed to ask *you* the questions.'

'I was just showing an interest, Tyler, attempting to get to know you a little better.'

'Well, I would prefer it if you didn't,' she told him tartly.

Obviously, Zak noted. 'That hardly seems fair when you already know so much about me.'

'Mr Prince—Zak,' she corrected as he raised mocking brows, 'your life is an open book—anyone and everyone can read about it!—and that's the life you chose. Whereas I chose—'

'To be one of those who exposes other people's lives,' he gibed. 'While keeping your own life completely private.'

She shrugged. 'That's my prerogative.'

He turned on the bench seat to look at her, his arm resting along the back behind her. 'And if *I* want to know more about *you*?' His hand moved to rest on her shoulder now, his fingers gently caressing behind the lobe of her ear.

The air in the back of the taxi was so tense between them that it seemed to literally hang there, so thick it felt as if it held them within a cocoon of—of what? Zak wasn't sure. And for the moment he didn't particularly care, either, all of his attention focused on Tyler. On how addictive her kisses were. On how he wanted to caress her breasts again so badly that—

'Zak, are you playing some sort of game with me?' She interrupted his unwittingly lustful imaginings with her question. 'Look, I know I made a bit of an idiot of myself last night—okay, a big idiot of myself last night—being so ill,' she corrected herself. 'But that doesn't give you the right to—to—?'

'Yes?' he prompted huskily, barely able to repress his smile at her obvious feelings of awkwardness over last night. Even if his own thoughts did run more to what had happened this morning rather than last night!

She spotted his smile. '*You* gave me the brandy!' she reminded him indignantly.

Yes, he had, and he really hadn't enjoyed seeing the way it had made her so ill. He just couldn't find it in himself to really regret holding her in his arms this morning...

'How was I to know the effect it would have on you?' he reasoned.

'You weren't,' she acknowledged with a sigh. 'But that's still no reason for you to assume that we—'

'Yes?' he asked, utterly fascinated by the way she always hesitated when it came to mentioning anything about sex—and especially the sexual attraction that existed between the two of them.

Why was that? he wondered. Most of the time Tyler was the confident, accomplished woman that she obviously was, but at the mere mention of anything sexual she seemed to shy away, as if she were embarrassed by the subject. Almost as if—

'You aren't gay, are you?' he wanted to know. Now that would bring a smile to his brothers' faces: Zak having been to bed with a woman who wasn't even interested in men!

'Did it seem that way this morning?' Tyler asked, outraged. 'But even if I were, I don't see why it should be any of your business,' she added hurriedly, instantly regretting mentioning what had happened that morning.

He didn't think it was any of his business either. Not really. Because, no matter how tempted he was, and no matter how much time he had to spend with her over the next week, he had firmly decided that he had no intention of taking the sexual attraction he felt towards her any further than he already had. If he wasn't careful, that would become the story!

'Good point,' he accepted, moving back to his own side of the bench seat. 'Although it could have given you an interesting slant on what you choose to write about me.'

Tyler gave a dismissive snort. 'So far I haven't found anything to write about you that hasn't already been said!'

'Good,' he said with satisfaction, his gaze narrowing slightly as he sensed a certain disappointment in her tone. 'You know, Tyler, maybe you chose the wrong brother to write about. Nik isn't of much interest now that he's married and settled down, but I have a feeling that you would find Rik's reserve hides something much more interesting than anything you will learn about me!'

'At this particular moment I would find Donald Duck more interesting than you,' she jeered.

'Then I suggest you consider writing something about him—because I guarantee you are going to learn absolutely nothing new about me to interest your readership!'

Zak hadn't realized how angry he was about being pressured into this until he started talking about it.

Or had this depth of anger only arisen since he had actually met Tyler and realized how attractive she was?

Oh, he had been angry with the press before, but his anger was usually directed towards the media in general, at the way it seemed any of them would do anything, use any method, to obtain a story. But since Zak had met Tyler, that anger had become much more personal.

In fact, he realized, he found the idea of her, in particular, using such methods to obtain a story more than a little distasteful and incredibly disappointing.

Although he had no idea what that meant!

CHAPTER FIVE

'TYLER…? My God, Tyler, is that really you?'

Having only arrived at O'Malley's a few minutes previously, Tyler was in the process of sitting down at their table when she immediately stood up again and froze, almost afraid to turn around and look at the person who had just spoken to her.

Because she had instantly recognized that precise English voice. And it belonged to someone who knew more about her than she wanted Zak to know!

'It *is* you!' Gerald Knight suddenly popped up in front of her. 'Darling!' He grabbed hold of her and held her at arm's length. 'You've lost so much weight I hardly recognized you! And the short hair is gorgeous!' He beamed at her before kissing her on both cheeks. 'How long have you been in England, you naughty girl?'

'Several months,' she answered.

'And you haven't called me?' He gave her a look of affectionate reproval. 'Shame on you!'

He released Tyler just in time for her to turn and see the expression on Zak's face as he looked at the other man.

Her hackles instantly rose in Gerald's defence, knowing that his rather effeminate manner was just something he had developed over years of working exclusively with women.

Despite this, she still wished she hadn't bumped into Gerald this evening, swiftly realizing she had no

52

choice but to introduce the two men. 'Gerald Knight, this is—'

'The actor, Zak Prince,' Gerald finished, at the same time shaking the other man's hand enthusiastically.

'Gerald Knight, the fashion designer?' Zak said slowly as he released Gerald's hand.

'You've heard of me!' Gerald beamed with delight even as his professionally critical gaze took in Zak's clothing. Short and slim himself, Gerald always designed and wore his own suits and shirts, and was dressed in a brown suit this evening, matched with the palest of pink shirts.

Tyler had no doubts that Zak's clothes boasted a label of similar pedigree, but he somehow still managed to look casually untidy against Gerald's dapperness.

'But of course,' Zak answered the other man. 'Your New York shows are always worth going to.'

Gerald threw back his head and gave one of his hearty chuckles, prompting several other diners to turn and look curiously at the standing trio. 'Naughty, naughty,' he reproved Zak teasingly. 'Those clothes aren't designed for men to ogle.'

'No?' Zak raised a mocking eyebrow. 'Does that mean I've been wrong all these years in assuming a woman dressed with the intention of looking good for men?'

'Totally wrong. Women dress to impress other women. And may I say, darling Tyler, that I'm very disappointed in you for wearing a Vera Wang. What's wrong with a Gerald Knight? Especially now that you've lost all that baby fat,' Gerald continued admiringly. 'You're looking absolutely marvellous. I had no idea there was this fantastic figure underneath all that—'

It was round about here that Tyler stopped listening and concentrated on what Zak must be thinking instead. She was dreading the questions that must surely follow Gerald's rather tactless remarks!

'Earth to Tyler.' Gerald's face suddenly appeared in her vision as he bent down to waggle his eyebrows at her. 'Hello—anyone home?'

'Sorry, Gerald.' She dragged her attention back from a slightly dazed-looking Zak. 'What were you saying?' She forced a bright smile of interest.

'I said how does Rufus feel about the new you? And the new boyfriend, of course,' he asked suggestively.

Tyler's eyes widened, not just at the mention of Rufus, but at Gerald's assumption that Zak was her boyfriend! She might even have laughed at the idea— if she hadn't thought it would turn into a hysterical cackle!

'Oops, got to go,' Gerald announced suddenly after a quick glance at the gold Rolex on his wrist. 'I should have been at the theatre fifteen minutes ago. Oh, well, never mind; I'm sure they've started without me! Now, Tyler, how much longer are you in London? Do call me, darling. We must meet up for lunch and have a really good natter. Must dash! Bye, Zak.' And with a brief wave of one slightly limp hand he disappeared out of the restaurant.

Leaving absolute chaos in his charming wake as far as Tyler was concerned! She sank down weakly into her seat, feeling a little as if she had just been run over by an express train. She didn't dare so much as glance at Zak to see how *he* was feeling!

What had Gerald said exactly? Tyler fretted.

Well, he had easily recognized her dress as a Vera Wang, for one thing. How many rookie reporters could afford to buy a Vera Wang?

Gerald had also made the erroneous assumption concerning her relationship with Zak.

And, worst of all, he had mentioned Rufus...

In fact, none of it had been good!

'Whew,' Zak breathed heavily as he sat down opposite her. 'Is he always like that?'

'Always,' she said ruefully. 'A little of Gerald tends to go a long way, if you know what I mean?'

'Oh, I know exactly what you mean! So how come you and Gerald Knight are such old friends?'

'Oh, I wouldn't go that far,' she dismissed airily, looking up to smile her thanks at the waiter as he handed her a menu.

'No, thanks,' Zak refused his menu. 'I'll have the garlic king prawns to start, followed by the duck—'

'I'm afraid the menu was changed last week, sir, and the duck is no longer on it,' the waiter said apologetically. 'But I can recommend the pheasant—'

'I don't like pheasant,' Zak cut in sharply.

'Then perhaps the—'

'I'll have a steak, medium to rare, with a green salad, and a side order of fries,' Zak almost barked the order out.

Tyler listened to the exchange with interest; admittedly Zak had been rude to her from the beginning, but she hadn't seen or heard him be anything but charming with everyone else. Including the doorman at the hotel, the cab driver on the way over here, and the man who had shown them to their table. He had even been pleasant to the often overwhelming Gerald.

So why was he being such a pain in the butt to this

waiter, especially when the problem wasn't even the guy's fault? She gave her order—the garlic prawns like Zak, but followed by the baked sea bass—in a carefully polite voice and accompanied by a smile, to make up for Zak's curtness.

Zak turned back as the waiter disappeared with their order. 'I had my heart set on the duck, okay?' he muttered as he saw Tyler's questioning look.

'Yeah. Right.' Tyler turned away, looking around at the other diners, most of them easily recognizable, either from the big or small screen.

'Tyler?'

She took her time responding, trying to get her disappointment under control. Because she was deeply disappointed with Zak. Okay, she was supposed to write as scandalous an article on this man as she could, but a part of her was secretly hoping there wouldn't be any scandal to write about.

Even if she then lost her job?

Even then, she acknowledged heavily. Because, despite the way he behaved towards her, she actually liked Zak Prince.

His resentment towards her and the methods she had used to obtain this week-long interview with him were understandable, she had decided earlier as she'd got ready for their evening out. But his behaviour just now, to a man who was only doing his job—and was probably only getting paid peanuts to do it, too!—she hadn't liked at all.

'I really wanted the duck, okay,' he repeated at her continued silence.

'I already said it was okay,' she dismissed.

'No, what you actually said—'

'Zak,' she interrupted quietly, 'why should it matter

what I did or didn't say? We're a reporter—an un-wanted one, at that!—and an actor, out to dinner, not some long-married couple who are answerable to each other for their actions!' She didn't really want to go any further with this subject—although there was def-initely a bonus to it; while they were talking about Zak, it kept the conversation away from their encoun-ter with Gerald Knight!

Zak drew in a sharp breath, his expression remote. 'You're right, it doesn't matter.'

But it obviously did. To him. He seemed incredibly uncomfortable with her—or anyone else?—thinking badly of him. Interesting...

'I should go easy on the red meat, though, if I were you.' She eyed him mockingly over the rim of her glass as she sipped from the glass of sparkling water she had ordered to accompany her meal. 'It may make you even more aggressive.'

'I am *not*—' He broke off, his gaze narrowing on her speculatively. 'You're deliberately trying to irritate me now, aren't you?'

Tyler opened wide innocent eyes. 'Would I?'

'Oh, yes.' Zak began to smile. 'I keep underesti-mating you, don't I?'

'Do you?' She maintained her innocent expression.

'Yeah.' Zak was openly grinning now. 'But luckily I've just realized why.'

'You have?'

He gave a rueful shake of his head. 'I'll grant that you did succeed in diverting my attention for a while there, but not indefinitely, unfortunately for you.'

Damn!

Tyler kept her own smile on her lips. 'No?' she retorted mildly.

'No,' he confirmed. 'You were hoping that I would be diverted enough to forget all about asking for an explanation as to how you know a fashion designer of Gerald Knight's acclaim. Or exactly who Rufus is. And just how—large you were the last time Gerald saw you. Let me also assure you, there is no way you wouldn't be noticed in that spectacular dress—Vera Wang, or otherwise!'

There was also the fact, Tyler thought semi-hysterically, that he hadn't noticed Perry getting out of a cab just behind theirs when they'd arrived at the restaurant a short time ago, and that the other man was still lurking about outside somewhere, hoping he might get a photograph or two when they left!

'Well?' Zak prompted expectantly as no answer was forthcoming on any of the three statements he had just made.

Tyler was certainly turning out to be more of a surprise than he could possibly have realized before actually meeting her—and he was no longer just referring to the fact that she had turned out to be female!

He had known that she looked good when she'd arrived at the hotel earlier, couldn't help but notice how the red dress clung in all the right places. Though, not being interested in clothes himself, he couldn't tell a designer dress from one bought in a high-street store!

But it had been totally obvious that Tyler and Gerald Knight were old friends from way back, that the man knew her well.

And just who the hell was Rufus? An old boyfriend? A current boyfriend, even! Her brother? Just another friend? Although Gerald's remarks certainly hadn't seemed to imply the relationship was anything that casual.

Although why should he care one way or the other when Tyler was nothing but a nuisance of a reporter who had bargained her way into his life?

Because, Zak realized unwillingly, she had stopped being just a nuisance reporter this morning, when he'd taken her in his arms and kissed her...

'Well what?' Tyler finally replied, not even looking up at him, her attention on the pattern she was tracing on the frosted outside of her glass of mineral water. She only glanced up when Zak didn't respond and simply continued to watch her.

Tyler seemed to think quickly and finally offered an explanation. 'Gerald and I met some time ago in New York when I did a feature on one of his fashion shows. For some reason he took a liking to me and we've been friends ever since.'

Zak could quite easily see how that had happened—he was starting to like her himself. Which was the worst thing he could do, considering who and what she was.

Maybe if he tried to picture a much larger Tyler...? No, that wasn't going to work; he thought Tyler was far too thin now and could do with putting on ten pounds or so. The fact that Gerald Knight, a man who surrounded himself with wafer-thin models, had found Tyler's new slenderness attractive was enough to confirm that opinion.

Besides, thin or slightly fuller in the figure, she would still have those melting chocolate-brown eyes, and the more time Zak spent in her company, the more he liked her mischievous sense of humour.

But there was still the question of Rufus...

'And what about Rufus?' Zak raised blond brows. 'Did he take a liking to you too?'

Those chocolate-brown eyes suddenly filled with tears, only to be rapidly blinked away as Tyler's expression changed to one of anger. 'I wouldn't know— the two of us haven't spoken for six months!' she snapped.

Quite what Zak would have said next, he had no idea, but their first course had arrived to be placed on the table in front of them. 'Thanks.' He gave the waiter a warm smile, not at all happy with himself at having snapped at the man earlier. As Tyler clearly hadn't been either.

Zak had his reasons for reacting to the menu change in the way that he had. But he had no intention of explaining those reasons to Tyler. They were private and not to be splashed over the tabloid papers!

The waiter's obviously relieved, 'You're welcome,' didn't make Zak feel any less uncomfortable with his earlier behaviour.

Neither did glancing across the table and seeing the derisive expression on Tyler's face.

'Does that smile usually work?' she asked.

Zak instantly lost his appetite for the king prawns they were both eating. Yes, that smile usually succeeded in making up for any slight he might have given when under stress. As he had been earlier...

'I made a mistake,' he admitted. 'I'm sure even you must make them on occasion?'

'Frequently,' she replied. 'But I hope I'm usually big enough to apologize for them.'

Damn it, she knew nothing about him, had no idea what might have been the reason for his earlier bad humour. And considering the way she had pushed herself into his life, she certainly had no right to lecture him on his behaviour. She—

'I hope you're enjoying your meal, sir, madam.' The waiter had returned to place two bowls of warm lemon water and two napkins on the table for them to use to clean their hands after eating their prawns.

Zak shot Tyler a narrow-eyed glare before turning back to the waiter. 'I'm sorry if I seemed—abrupt, concerning the duck earlier. I shouldn't have taken my disappointment out on you.'

'Please think nothing of it, Mr Prince,' the middle-aged man assured him. 'Your reaction to the change of menu was mild in comparison to the lady last week who threw her glass of wine over me when I broke the news to her! I've mentioned the two incidents to the chef, and I believe he is even now considering putting the duck back on the menu.' There was a definite twinkle in his eyes as he departed to let them finish their starters.

Zak glanced triumphantly across at Tyler, his eyes widening with suspicion as he saw she was desperately biting her bottom lip in an effort not to laugh. But those mischievous brown eyes gave her away. 'Are you laughing at me?' he exclaimed.

'No—but I'm going to!' She burst out laughing, not the soft, affected laughter he heard so often from other famous people, but a deep-throated chuckle that owed nothing to soft and everything to earthy.

Her eyes sparkled, her creamy cheeks glowed, her smile was radiant; in fact, she looked beautiful.

And Zak wasn't the only man in the restaurant to think so, either.

Several male heads turned in their direction, most of them known to Zak, some of them friends of his. Although not such good friends he would welcome them coming over to say hello, his warning expression clearly told them.

Tyler finally stopped laughing to give a rueful shake of her head. 'I have no doubts that the menu will quickly be adjusted to include the duck! You really can be incredibly charming when you want to be, can't you?' she said with unhidden admiration.

He grimaced. 'Meaning I haven't succeeded in being so too often around you!'

She shrugged, still smiling. 'I did say when you *wanted* to be…'

And he hadn't wanted to be around Tyler. He still didn't. She was just too dangerous, too much in his face. It was better if she wrote that he wasn't always as charmingly relaxed as previously reported than she root out the makings of a real story on him.

Not that it was anything he was ashamed of; it just wasn't something he had ever talked about in public. He'd had problems as a child, and had rebelled as a teenager because of those childhood difficulties. He had managed to put things behind him after he'd attained success as an actor, and it was only sometimes, like this evening, that the difficulties once again raised their head.

Nik had told him he should have come clean years ago, but the longer Zak left it, the harder it became to talk about something so personal to him. And he certainly didn't want it splashed all over the tabloid rag Tyler worked for!

'As my mother used to say—eat your prawns,' he muttered gruffly as he picked up one of the prawns on his own plate and began to take the shell off.

Tyler's brows rose incredulously. 'Your mother used to say that a lot, did she?'

'I think it was usually in reference to vegetables or salad.' Zak shrugged. 'But the principle is the same.'

'Shut up and eat?'

'You got it,' he drawled.

CHAPTER SIX

As THEY continued with the rest of their meal Tyler
was relieved to have succeeded in diverting Zak's attention away from the subject of Rufus, and what he
meant to her.

Momentarily, that was.

Because she had no doubts that Zak would return
to the subject when he felt so inclined. She would just
have to make sure she had a suitable answer ready for
him when he did.

Quite what, she had no idea yet—the truth simply
wouldn't do on this occasion.

This was all getting so complicated!

It had all seemed so simple when she had initially
made her decision to come to England and make a
success of herself as a reporter. All she'd had to do
was find somewhere to live, get a job with a newspaper, and then write a sensational story that would
make her name known on both sides of the Atlantic.
Then she could go home in triumph.

Well, she had come over here, found herself an
apartment and a job—but when the 'sensational' story
had presented itself to her in the form of revealing Jinx
Nixon's connection to the famous writer J. I. Watson,
she had made a complete hash of it!

It had been mainly due, she knew, to that tendency
to become emotionally involved that Zak had mentioned earlier today. Nik Prince had appealed to her
finer instincts and asked her not to write the story on

Jinx, and like an idiot she had given up her first chance at success.

Something she simply couldn't do a second time where Zak Prince was concerned!

She had wanted to be a reporter ever since she could remember—except in her family you didn't work for a newspaper or a television station. You might own them, and pay other people to work in them, but you certainly didn't work there yourself.

As an only child of extremely wealthy parents, she had pretty well had her life mapped out for her before she could even talk—the right school, the right college, the right friends—and then some time helping her mother to run their numerous homes and the many charities she was involved in, before meeting the right man, marrying him, and starting the process all over again with her own children.

In a word, her life had been massively constricted.

But it had been her parents' choice of husband for her six months ago that had made Tyler finally decide that enough was enough—and she had just packed her bags and walked out, her flight to England booked that same day.

And everything had been on schedule for her to succeed in her plans until she'd met the Prince family!

'Did you know you get tiny lines between your eyes when you frown like that?' Zak murmured, obviously having been watching her for some time if his relaxed pose was anything to go by.

Tyler shot him a fiery glance. 'Everyone gets lines between their eyes when they frown!'

'True. I was actually wondering what had caused you to frown...'

'Nothing that need concern you.'

'Fair enough.' He shrugged. 'If you've finished your main course, I suggest we leave.'

'Don't you want dessert?' She held out the menu that the waiter had given her a few minutes ago, for him to look at.

Zak didn't even glance at it. 'I never eat dessert. But you go ahead,' he invited at her look of disappointment.

'No.' She put the menu reluctantly to one side; she loved dessert. 'I wouldn't want to regain all that *baby fat* of mine!'

Zak grinned across the table at her. 'You never did tell me how much larger you once were...'

No—and she hadn't meant to remind him of Gerald's conversation, either. 'A dress size or so— okay, two dress sizes,' she admitted as Zak raised sceptical blond brows. 'But I never had any complaints.' She looked at him challengingly.

He held up placating hands. 'You aren't getting any now, either.'

Tyler gave him a confused look, unsure whether he was flirting with her or not.

'Exactly whose party is it we're going to?' Tyler voiced her curiosity a few minutes later as they made their way out of the restaurant.

'Calum McQuire's.'

'*Calum McQuire's!*' Tyler practically squealed, grabbing his arm in sheer excitement. 'I've always wanted—' She broke off as she saw the pitying look on Zak's face. 'I sound like a kid still in high school, don't I?'

'You do,' Zak confirmed with a grin. 'Although it's good to know you aren't so used to your sophisticated friends that you wouldn't be impressed at the thought of meeting Calum.'

Her eyes widened. 'No one could *not* be impressed at meeting him! Calum McQuire has defined the meaning of the word "private". No one, and I really mean no one, gets to meet him, or his family, if he doesn't want them to.'

In fact, the Scottish actor guarded his privacy so well that he hadn't given an interview, or so much as spoken to a member of the media, in the five years since his son had been born. And Zak was taking her to meet him! Maybe this would turn out to be the exclusive she needed…

'Don't even *think* about it, Tyler,' Zak growled, coming to a halt outside on the pavement as he accurately read her thoughts. 'You will be there as my guest, and I advise you not to abuse the privilege.'

He might not have actually voiced the words, but the threat was there in his voice, anyway: take advantage of the meeting this evening with Calum McQuire, and Zak would make sure every other door was closed to her—indefinitely.

Damn it, she was getting a little tired of people threatening her. First her editor on *The Daily Informer*, Bill Graham, and now Zak was getting in on the act.

Pretty soon she was going to lose her cool at being told what to do all the time, and then they had all better stand well back!

But not tonight, she realized, holding her disappointment in check. Calum McQuire, although media-shy, was supposed to be a nice guy who just wanted his wife and son left out of the limelight that followed him around, to allow his son to have as normal a childhood as possible.

Tyler could relate to that!

She gave Zak a bright smile. 'You can count on my discretion,' she assured him as she turned to go.

His hand on her arm held her beside him. 'Look on this as a test of faith.'

'The man is a movie icon, Zak.' Tyler glared up at him indignantly. 'Everyone loves him. God, when I was a teenager, even I used to fantasize—' She broke off awkwardly. She was doing it again: giving him too much information!

'You ''used to fantasize''…?' he prompted with interest.

Tyler felt the colour warm her cheeks. Not because she had admitted to fantasizing about someone that all the girls of her school had had a thing about, but because the comment had reminded her all too forcibly that she had used to fantasize about Zak too…

'I was fifteen, okay!' she protested, turning away, glancing around surreptitiously for Perry now; while she had been inside enjoying the best meal she had eaten in six months, he had been standing outside here probably having had nothing to eat at all.

But she knew from Zak's comments that there was no way Perry was going to get into Calum McQuire's, so maybe she should try and signal to him in some way to let him know he would be wasting his time following them any further, that he might as well go and get something to eat himself.

But even though she sensed that Perry was outside somewhere, she couldn't actually see him. That was the whole point, of course, but even so—

'Have you lost something?'

Tyler turned guiltily at Zak's softly spoken query, her eyes widening as she found herself almost nose to nose with him as he bent his head towards her. It wasn't easy to be so close to him when seconds ago she had been remembering those girlhood fantasies about him.

But she had been a child then. She was a woman of twenty-six now. Except she still wanted him to kiss her…!

She had been fighting this ever since she'd first gone to Zak's hotel suite yesterday morning. No—even before that. Ever since the moment Nik Prince had offered her the deal that entailed her backing off Jinx's story and accepting an exclusive with his brother instead.

She had known at the time that she shouldn't do it, that she was probably committing professional suicide, but the temptation to not only meet Zak Prince, but to spend a whole week in his company, had just been too much for her to resist.

Because there was something she had been keeping from Nik Prince, Bill Graham, Perry, even Zak himself—especially Zak! Her girlhood dreams about this man had never really left her…

When she had been ill in front of Zak last night she had just wanted to die. When he had kissed her this morning she had thought she had died—and gone to heaven!

She had tried so hard to be professional with this man. Had tried to leave her attraction towards him in the past where it belonged—and, to be completely honest, Zak had been so rude and mocking most of the time that she hadn't had too much trouble resisting him. But tonight he seemed less the movie star and more the man behind the image, and, as such, much more approachable.

Considering the major crush she had had on him in her teens, that probably wasn't a good idea. Despite how it might have appeared to Zak at the hotel yesterday morning, she probably knew almost as much about him as his brothers did. Because, as well as covering her bedroom walls with pictures of him, she had collected articles on every interview he had ever given, and had virtually been a walking encyclopaedia on him. Depressingly, she probably still was…

So it totally wasn't a good idea to find herself standing only centimetres away from him, their gazes locked, their breaths shallow and intermingled.

Every inch of her body felt alive, and all her senses were acutely aware of Zak—of the silky softness of that overlong blond hair, the deep, deep blue of his eyes, and his beautifully sculptured mouth, with its sensuous lower lip.

How she longed to kiss that mouth, to run her tongue over his sensuous lips, to taste him, and to feel the strength of his shoulders beneath her hands as she strained against him, to know the—

Tyler blinked dazedly as a bright light suddenly split the darkness, momentarily blinding her.

'What the *hell* was that?' Zak's voice was grim as he turned in the direction the light had come from. But now there was just darkness, only the sound of a car door slamming, quickly followed by the starting of an engine, to show that the incident had happened at all.

It must have been Perry making a hasty getaway after taking their photograph, Tyler realized with dismay as Zak turned back to her, his expression fiercely angry. She took a hasty step back as she saw the murderous glitter of his eyes.

Zak was so furious at what had just happened, and

felt so utterly betrayed after the lively dinner he had just shared with Tyler, that he was almost prepared to strangle her!

'You set that up!' he accused her. 'You deliberately, *calculatingly*, arranged for that photographer—probably your boyfriend Perry—'

'He *isn't* my boyfriend,' she denied. 'And don't be ridiculous. How could I possibly have—?'

'You set *me* up!' At that moment Zak was too angry to listen to anything she might have to say. 'No doubt a photograph of you looking up at me all dewy-eyed and dreamy will appear in tomorrow's newspaper—'

'I was *not* looking at you all dewy-eyed!' Tyler gasped, her face pale in the moonlight.

'Your eyes were begging for me to kiss you,' he jeered.

'They most certainly were not!' she insisted indignantly. '*You* were the one about to kiss *me*—'

'In your dreams!' Zak scorned—knowing even as he said it that he was lying, to himself as well as Tyler.

He *had* been about to kiss her. Had been longing to kiss her all evening. Even when he'd been verbally holding her at arm's length. Even when he'd been angry with her.

She looked absolutely wonderful in that red dress, even her cropped spiky hair no longer the turn off it had been. And as for those melting brown eyes…!

But she had flinched back at his last comment, those dark eyes huge in the otherwise paleness of her face. 'I'm sorry to disappoint you, Zak,' she snapped. 'But no way have you ever featured in any of my dreams!'

He hadn't meant it literally, damn it. He was just so livid with her, and that photographer, that—

'Tyler Wood?'

Zak turned irritably to glare at the woman who had just got out of the cab that had pulled up outside the restaurant. A woman who looked vaguely familiar to him, although for the moment he couldn't place where he had seen the tall, very slender blonde before. He did know he wasn't at all pleased by her interruption.

Tyler didn't look too thrilled at seeing the other woman either, her expression becoming positively guarded even as she took a step backwards.

Zak's gaze narrowed as Tyler gave him a quick glance, before licking her lips and hastily turning away again.

He looked at the blonde once more, eyeing her suspiciously now, knowing by Tyler's behaviour that she wished herself far away from here. And from the sudden widening of the other woman's eyes as she obviously recognized Zak, she was surprised to see whom Tyler was with too.

Who the hell was she? he wondered. Another reporter? That would certainly explain his own feeling of having seen the other woman before. And yet he couldn't think, if that were the case, why Tyler should look almost as green as she had last night—just before she'd been ill.

Unless she was afraid the other woman might try to muscle in on her exclusive with him? Although even as that idea occurred to him he realized it didn't make much sense. Over the last seventeen years or so he had given hundreds of interviews; Tyler's interview, he had already determined, was going to provide nothing new.

'Yes, I'm Tyler Wood,' she finally answered the other woman. 'But I'm afraid we're in rather a hurry, so if you'll excuse us…?'

'But I just wanted to say—'

'I'm sorry, but we really do have to go now.' Tyler linked her arm with Zak's before turning them both determinedly in the other direction. Which was no easy thing, Zak acknowledged wryly, when he probably weighed almost a hundred pounds more than she did, and was also over a foot taller! A determined Tyler was obviously a force to be reckoned with!

Well, not this time. He was still angry with her over the photographer lurking outside the restaurant, and had no intention of going anywhere else with her this evening. Besides, there was still the puzzle of where he had seen the tall blonde before. Because, wherever it was, he had a feeling he didn't particularly like her.

And from the slight trembling he could detect in Tyler as she linked her arm with his, he didn't think she liked the other woman, either. Curiouser and curiouser.

'Aren't you being just a little rude, Tyler?' he murmured as she marched the two of them away from the restaurant—and the unidentified blonde.

Tyler shot him a warning glance, even as she kept on walking. 'I happen to think she was the one who was being rude,' she snapped. 'We were obviously in the middle of a conversation when she interrupted.' She suddenly looked as if she would have liked to bite off her own tongue for reminding him of that conversation.

As if he needed any reminding!

It wasn't as if he really cared who the other woman was—his only interest was in Tyler's reaction to her. And that was of no real importance when compared to the incident with the photographer.

He came to an abrupt halt. 'Forget it, Tyler. We aren't going anywhere.'

She blinked up at him in the illumination of the overhead street lamp. 'But you said—Calum McQuire—'

'I know what I said. But that was before.'

'Before what?' She glanced in the direction of the blonde, the other woman giving a rueful shrug before entering the restaurant.

'Before the photographer,' Zak reminded her grimly.

Tyler swallowed hard as she looked up at him. 'I told you I had nothing at all to do with that—'

'No?' he mocked. Who the hell else could have set that tender little scene up? 'Well, I guess we'll find out the truth of that tomorrow morning, won't we?'

He couldn't remember the last time he'd been so angry. Quite a lot of it was directed towards himself, Zak had to admit. He had been thrown slightly off balance by Tyler from the moment he'd met her.

She moistened gloss-covered lips. 'Tomorrow morning?' she repeated warily.

'Yes—if a photograph of the two of us appears in your scurrilous rag tomorrow morning, you can consider our deal null and void!'

It was what he wanted, anyway, to have this woman completely out of his hair, to call his life his own again, not to have to guard everything he did and every word he said, to wake up tomorrow morning and know that he never had to see Tyler Wood ever again.

Wasn't it?

CHAPTER SEVEN

TYLER blinked up at Zak, horrified at the thought of him terminating their interview.

She had to find Perry!

Now. If not sooner. Before he got anywhere near Bill Graham with the photograph of her and Zak, and the whole thing was taken out of her hands.

Not that it would stop her from personally throttling Perry when she caught up with him!

What did he think he was doing, taking photographs of her and Zak together? *They* weren't the story, and, from Zak's reaction to the photograph, he obviously didn't think they were, either. Much as a part of Tyler might wish it were otherwise...

She couldn't help but feel slightly relieved that something had diverted Zak's attention from the woman who had just approached her outside the restaurant; if Zak had realized who she was then he wouldn't wait for tomorrow morning, he would terminate their interview right now!

'I'm certain the photo won't be in *The Daily Informer* tomorrow,' Tyler assured him firmly.

He shrugged those broad shoulders. 'Let's wait and see, shall we?'

'And you really don't intend taking me to the party with you?' She frowned her disappointment; not because she wouldn't get to meet Calum McQuire after all, but because, despite the interruptions, she had actually been enjoying her evening out with Zak.

'I really don't,' he confirmed with a shake of his head. 'In fact, I suggest you take advantage of that cab—' he pointed back to the vehicle the blonde had just got out of '—and take yourself home.'

Tyler looked at him searchingly, realizing from his expression that he was completely serious. But as for his suggestion about her taking the cab—forget it! She had a few pounds with her, no mobile, unfortunately— it wouldn't fit into her small evening bag—and she wasn't about to use what little money she did have on a cab.

Even if she was wearing a Vera Wang dress!

Besides, she couldn't go straight home…

She drew in a deep breath. 'I think I'll walk, thanks. Where, and at what time, shall we meet up tomorrow?'

Zak's mouth twisted humourlessly. 'Pretty confident, aren't you?'

In a word—no! But she wasn't about to let Zak see that. 'I told you,' she reiterated. 'I had nothing to do with the taking of that photograph.' Even if she had a pretty good idea who did!

'And as I said, we'll see. If you don't intend taking the cab, then I will.' And without another word he got inside the idling cab, leaning forward to give the driver the address, before sitting back in the seat, not sparing Tyler so much as another glance as the cab moved out into the busy flow of evening traffic.

Tyler exhaled deeply, her shoulders slumping dejectedly now that she was alone. She was going to kill Perry when she caught up with him! After she had told him exactly what she thought of him, of course!

Her mood certainly hadn't improved an hour later when she finally limped into the newspaper office. The tube had been crowded, her red evening dress and high-heeled shoes earning her more than a little attention, mainly from leering males. Other women had given her pitying glances at being forced to travel on the tube in such a beautiful outfit.

But the walk from the tube station had to have been the worst of all, the high-heeled red shoes not meant for long walks on hard pavements, blisters forming on her heels, and her ankles aching.

'What the hell happened to you?' Bill Graham frowned as he looked up from his computer screen.

Tyler gave him a scowl for his trouble. 'Have you seen Perry?'

'This evening?' Bill shook his head. 'I thought he was supposed to be with you.'

'So did I,' she muttered, wondering where Perry could have gone after leaving the restaurant so hurriedly if he hadn't come here, after all. Home? Her apartment to wait for her? It looked as if she would have to try both places.

At least he didn't seem to have rushed straight over here with his photograph. That was something, but it in no way lessened Tyler's anger towards him. He had totally blown her evening out with Zak, and ruined her chances of a meeting with Calum McQuire. Although she had to admit it was the former that really bothered her…

'Where are you going now?' Bill could have added, Dressed like that? but didn't after a brief glance at her face dared him to do so.

Tyler grimaced. 'Home, I guess.' If only to change out of these clothes before continuing her search for Perry.

'Here, get yourself a taxi.' Bill reached into his

pocket and took a twenty-pound note from his pocket, throwing it across the desk towards her. 'It wouldn't look too good if one of our reporters got picked up by the police on suspicion of prostitution!' he explained at Tyler's obvious surprise at this kind gesture. 'Don't worry, I'll simply claim the twenty on expenses,' he dismissed before going back to his computer screen.

Tyler glowered across the desk at him. She should have known he wasn't just being nice—Bill Graham was never nice!

But to imply she looked like a prostitute!

Did she really look like a hooker in this dress? She looked down at herself in concern. It *was* quite a revealing dress, with its low neckline and ribbon shoulder straps, the style definitely figure-hugging. Even so, she hadn't thought she—

'You look great, Tyler,' Bill growled exasperatedly as he glanced up and saw her still standing there. 'Just get out of here, okay; some of us have work to do.' He pushed the twenty-pound note further across the desk before once again becoming engrossed in his computer screen.

Tyler picked up the money and left—before he changed his mind and decided to take the twenty pounds back!

But she didn't go straight home, instead directing the cab to take her to Perry's apartment. First she would deal with Perry, now that she knew he hadn't gone running straight to the paper with his photograph, and then she might be able to give some time to thinking about that chance encounter earlier with the woman outside the restaurant.

She had recognized the other woman, of course she had. The two of them might only have met the once, and then only briefly, but Tyler wasn't likely to forget Jane Morrow—the woman who had first given her the lead on the Jinx Nixon story.

Obviously Jinx's ex-editor hadn't forgotten Tyler, either. Not surprising really, in view of the fact that the other woman had lost her job through talking to Tyler!

But Tyler hadn't seen the other woman from that day to this. She hadn't particularly wanted to, either. She had little or no respect for Jane Morrow's work ethic once she had betrayed Jinx Nixon's confidence, and for no other reason, it appeared, than because she had had a huge unrequited crush on Nik Prince and was furiously jealous that Nik had only been interested in Jinx.

Luckily Zak hadn't been able to immediately place Jane Morrow, although Tyler wouldn't count on it remaining that way. He'd remember where he'd seen her sooner or later, and no doubt he would have plenty to say on the subject if he should ever recall who the other woman was!

He'd probably immediately jump to the conclusion that the two women were collaborating again on a story about Jinx Prince—or even, heaven forbid, Nik Prince. Tyler shuddered—it was well known that the Prince family were close. Zak would certainly go off the deep end if he thought that was the reason for Jane Morrow's appearance tonight. When the truth was, Tyler didn't have a clue what the other woman wanted!

Being around Zak, Tyler decided, was like balancing on a tightrope—one false move and she was likely to fall off!

It didn't help at all that suspicions were starting to

creep in that her high-school crush on Zak, far from fading away, was threatening to turn into an emotion more real and lasting now that Tyler had met the man himself. She didn't dare name that emotion. Even to herself. Privately. It was *far* too dangerous...

'What are you smiling about so happily?' Zak snapped after opening his suite door to Tyler's knock the next morning. He immediately wished he hadn't snapped at all as her smile faded to be replaced with a look of uncertainty.

But he was in a foul mood. Annoyed by what had happened the night before—especially after such a pleasant dinner together. Irritated at having to go to Calum's party alone, leaving him a target for all the unattached females there. And there had been plenty of them—all stunningly beautiful, all ready for a little fun. None of them making any secret of the fact that it was him they would like to have that fun with.

Unfortunately, without exception, each one of them, however witty or pretty, had left him cold.

Because all he'd been able to think about all night was Tyler. Of how she had teased and charmed him as they'd eaten dinner together. Of how absolutely stunning she had looked in that red dress. Of how he had been anticipating arriving at Calum's with Tyler on his arm. Of how she had set him up outside the restaurant...

But even that wasn't the worst of it—he'd been looking forward to the time after the party when he took her home, when he had intended kissing her senseless. Yes, much as he hated to admit it, it appeared he had committed that sin of all sins for an actor, and allowed himself to become attracted to a reporter!

He came back to an awareness that Tyler was still eyeing him in utter, adorable confusion.

'Is there some reason why I shouldn't be smiling?' she asked warily, dressed in black combats today, with a white figure-hugging tee shirt.

A tee shirt that outlined the perfection of her pert breasts—and which also showed Zak that again she wasn't wearing a bra beneath it!

Great, Zak moaned inwardly—now he was *lusting* after a reporter, too!

Those dark brown eyes looked troubled by his continued silence. 'But there was no photograph in *The Daily Informer*...'

'No, it would appear that you got to your boyfriend in time to stop that.' Zak's scorn was biting.

The colour in her cheeks deepened at his continued reference to Perry as her boyfriend, whether with embarrassment or anger, Zak couldn't be sure.

Tyler drew in a deep breath. 'I can assure you that Perry had no intention of publishing any photographs of you without first obtaining your permission. Admittedly, he was—a little overenthusiastic, last night, but—'

'Is that what you choose to call it?'

'Yes,' she maintained stubbornly. 'But when I saw him last night he assured me—'

'What? What did he *assure you*, Tyler?' Zak taunted. 'That he never intended taking that photograph to your editor? That he was just collecting material for this *exclusive* you keep talking about?' He could feel the anger building inside him, knew that his eyes were now as hard as sapphires, his expression grim. He couldn't have stopped the words that tumbled out of his mouth next if he had tried.

'And did he assure you of this before or after he took you to bed?' Zak ground out furiously.

Tyler blanched—in pain? 'I—he—you have no right to say such things to me!' she finally managed to gasp, those unfettered breasts quickly rising and falling beneath her tee shirt in her agitation.

Zak remained hardened to the appeal in those deep, deep brown eyes. 'No?' he challenged. *'No?'* he repeated, almost shouting now, reaching out to grasp her arm and pull her inside his hotel suite before shutting the door to give them some privacy. 'I think that this...' he picked up a newspaper and thrust it in front of her nose '...gives me the right to say to you exactly what I damn well please!'

Tyler blinked up at him dazedly for several seconds before reaching out with shaking hands to take the newspaper from him, turning away as she scanned the page in front of her.

Zak thrust his hands into his denims pockets in an effort to stop himself from reaching out and shaking her.

Oh, not because of what she was reading, although he had memorized every word.

And speaking of love, it would appear that Zak Prince, that prince of Princes, has a new mystery lady in his life. The two, seen together at the fashionable O'Malley's last night, couldn't seem to take their eyes off each other, and are said to be very close indeed. Could The Prince be thinking of matrimony this time...?

The article in the gossip column was garbage. Utter and complete garbage, even down to that stupid nickname the press had labelled him with a couple of years ago. But it wasn't what was written there that made him so angry. No, that was entirely due to Tyler. He had realized last night that he liked her, really liked her. The way she looked. Her quirky sense of humour. Her openness. Her *openness*! Hah, that was a joke!

Her face was still very pale when she turned back to him. 'But I— This isn't the paper I write for.'

'No, it isn't, is it? Which means that you kept to your promise that our photograph wouldn't appear in *The Daily Informer* this morning. You kept to the *spirit* of that promise,' he amended grimly, 'but that didn't mean that you couldn't chat to a rival gossip columnist, did it?'

Her eyes widened incredulously. 'You can't seriously think that I had anything to do with this article!'

'I'm trying not to think at all, Tyler,' he rasped harshly. 'In fact, I've been trying not to think since the daily newspapers were delivered outside my door at seven-thirty this morning!' The volume of his voice rose again, proof—if he needed it!—of just how furious he was.

But he didn't need proof. Just as he hadn't needed his brother Rik telephoning him from France at nine o'clock this morning, curious to know who the 'mystery lady' was! Apparently, the information that the story had appeared in the papers had hit the internet, which was where Rik had found it.

Not that he had given his younger brother the satisfaction of telling him anything about Tyler—least of all that she was a reporter. But having laboured through Tyler's paper from cover to cover, only to discover that there was no damning photograph, he hadn't exactly been thrilled when Rik had drawn his attention to the gossip in a rival newspaper!

'You were up at seven-thirty this morning?' was all Tyler seemed able to come back with.

He had been up at seven-thirty this morning for the simple reason he hadn't yet been to bed!

Calum's parties, although very infrequent, were always entertaining. Calum was that rare thing in the acting profession: completely his own man. This exclusive with Tyler, forced on Zak against his will, was enough to show him he wasn't that fortunate! But Calum was a man who did his own thing, having as many friends out of the acting profession as he had in it, and the mix of the two groups was always enjoyable.

Except Zak had been in a bad mood when he'd got there, completely unsociable for the first hour or so as he'd consumed several glasses of champagne. But eventually the friendly atmosphere had got to him, and he had relaxed enough to enjoy a lengthy conversation with one of the teachers from Calum's old school. Much to the chagrin of the beautiful women who had fluttered on the edge of his awareness!

It had been late—or early!—when he'd got back to the hotel at three-thirty, but he hadn't been able to sleep, had listened to music instead while he'd drunk all of the pot of coffee brought up to him by Room Service.

He had been waiting for the delivery of the daily newspapers, he had realized as he'd jumped up as soon as he'd heard them land on the carpet outside his suite. When the photo hadn't appeared in them, he had finally begun to relax, dozing off to sleep on the sofa

when he'd found he couldn't even be bothered to un-
dress and get into bed.

Only to be woken by the ringing of the telephone
and a curious Rik's voice in his ear...

Zak knew Tyler had tricked him. He had only said
their deal would become null and void if their photograph should appear in *The Daily Informer*. And it
hadn't, had it? In fact, the photograph hadn't appeared
anywhere. But the gossip about the two of them being
seen out together was just as damning as far as he was
concerned!

'Yes, I was up at seven-thirty this morning, Tyler,'
he ground out between clenched teeth before finally
taking his hands out of his pockets.

Not because he intended strangling her.

Oh, no, he had decided some time ago that that
would be letting her off the hook far too easily.

No, he determined as he reached out to grasp
Tyler's shoulders, if the gossip columnist had been
informed—and it didn't take two guesses to know who
by!—that he and Tyler were an *item*, then that was
exactly what they would be. Why should he be subject
to gossip based on absolutely no foundation?

'Zak...?' Tyler sounded innocently bewildered.

Deceptively innocent—as Tyler herself was!

And he had fallen for it. He had believed himself
to be a man of the world, that he had seen it all, that
he had become cynical even—because he knew every
trick and ploy a woman cared to make to attract his
attention. But Tyler had slipped under his guard, had
fooled him into thinking she was exactly what she
claimed to be—a reporter who just wanted to do an
exclusive on him, one of those 'nice' articles that were
so popular in expensively glossy magazines.

That might still be her intention. He didn't know—and, quite frankly, he didn't care, either. But what he did know was that Tyler wasn't above promoting herself by publicly linking herself with him. No matter how she had to accomplish it.

Some time early this morning, as he had sat fuming over the gossip column, wondering what to do next, he had decided that if that was what Tyler wanted then she could have it.

For a price!

CHAPTER EIGHT

ZAK was going to kiss her!

Tyler realized that only seconds before his head lowered and his mouth claimed hers.

She had dreamt of this—she had lied last night when she had claimed Zak had never featured in her dreams!—since she was fifteen years old. But in those fantasies it had never been like this. No, never like this!

Zak was angry, furiously so if their brief conversation was anything to go by. And that anger was his prime emotion as his mouth literally ravaged hers, the steely strength of his arms moulding her soft curves firmly against his much harder ones.

His fury and contempt for her was palpable, dictating his actions as his mouth demanded a response from hers, demanded and received it, despite the fact that Tyler was mentally screaming a silent 'no'!

This was just too much on top of what had already happened to her the last twenty-four hours: first that awkward meeting with Gerald in the restaurant, then Perry's stupidity in taking that unsolicited photograph, followed by Zak's response to it, and then meeting Jane Morrow. All of which had been followed by the most tremendous row with Perry when she finally had tracked him down at his apartment.

Oh, he had been all apologies, claiming that he hadn't meant to press the button on his camera at all, that the photograph had happened as a result of his shocked realization that she and Zak were about to kiss each other.

An excuse Tyler had listened to with scepticism. Only to have that emotion turn to guilt when Perry had then claimed he loved her, that he had been in love with her from the moment they had first met!

She had thought *that* was the final straw, until the gossip column this morning had quickly taken over that role—but this punishing kiss, here and now, was so much worse than anything that had happened before it.

Tears began to fall hotly down her cheeks.

Zak seemed to become instantly aware of this and raised his head sharply to look down at her with narrowed blue eyes. He held her out at arm's length as soon as he realized exactly how distressed she was.

'I thought this was what you wanted,' he growled. 'An affair with Zak Prince that you could write about in that rag you work for!'

To her mortification, Tyler was crying in earnest now, deep sobs that racked the slenderness of her body, no matter how hard she tried to control them.

No, this most certainly wasn't what she wanted! A return of the attraction she felt towards him would have been nice, a flirtation, possibly even something deeper if she were very lucky, but not—not this!

She drew in a deep breath. 'I had nothing to do with what's written in that gossip column.' She gave the discarded newspaper a disgusted glance. 'I don't know the person who wrote it. I don't want to know the person who wrote it.' Although a part of her was starting to wonder if she didn't know who was responsible for giving the information to the gossip columnist.

There was really only one person it could be—Jane

Morrow. And she had every reason to feel resentful towards Tyler, as well as wishing for vengeance on any member of the Prince family. Including Zak Prince.

But Tyler knew she couldn't tell Zak of her suspicions without bringing the other woman's name into the conversation, something she really didn't want to do if Zak hadn't realized himself yet who the woman outside the restaurant last night had been. And he obviously hadn't, otherwise that would have been something else he could challenge her with this morning.

'That's it, Zak,' she told him steadily. 'That's all I have to say on that subject.' She raised her chin, deep brown eyes clashing with accusing blue ones.

Only he looked perplexed now, frowning down at her for several long minutes, until a reluctant smile began to curve his lips. '"That's all?"' he teased.

Her brows rose in mute challenge. 'That's all,' she confirmed firmly. 'Believe me, or don't believe me, I've really got to the stage where I don't particularly give a—'

'No, don't spoil it, Tyler,' he protested. 'Do you want me to apologize?' He quirked one of his own dark blond eyebrows.

She blinked, then eyed him suspiciously, not sure what he would be apologizing for: kissing her so uncaringly, or for his accusations about her in the first place.

'That's really up to you, isn't it?' she said guardedly, her lips actually feeling a little swollen from the force of his kiss.

'Okay.' He nodded. 'I apologize. Unreservedly.'

That was a great help—she still had no idea what he was apologizing for! Why couldn't he just—?

She flinched back as Zak raised his hand towards her, that hand coming to an abrupt halt as he saw her involuntary movement. He scowled in sudden realization.

But what did he expect? He had just physically overpowered her. In fact, if she had any sense at all she would have walked out of here after proclaiming her innocence!

Zak moved his hand again, slowly this time, cradling her cheek, his thumb moving to gently touch the swell of her lips. 'I hurt you,' he said huskily.

Her tender lips were nothing compared to the hurt she felt inside at his complete lack of faith in her, professionally as well as personally. She tried to brush aside the fact that she was after as sensational an exposé on him as possible—*he* didn't know that! Just as he didn't know that she wouldn't jeopardize her chances of getting that story for a minor bit of tittle-tattle about the two of them that basically amounted to nothing more than embarrassment. For them both.

So he had been seen out with a 'mystery lady' who just happened to be her—so what? It was still no more than idle gossip. Irritating idle gossip, admittedly, but without the name of that mystery lady it was really pretty useless.

Although she, for one, was very relieved that there was no name—if anyone back home had read it and made the connection between the name Tyler Wood and her *real* name of Tyler Harwood, which she'd changed on arrival in England because of her well-known family, then she would really have been in trouble!

Zak looked pained, his thumb still moving soothingly across her lips. 'I really do apologize, Tyler. No matter what the provocation was, that's no excuse for my behaviour just now.'

'No matter what the provocation was?' she echoed. Did he still not believe her claim of innocence?

His mouth twisted wryly. 'No matter what I may have *thought* the provocation was,' he corrected ruefully.

'Better.' She nodded, much preferring him in this repentant mood to the formidable stranger who had met her at the door such a short time ago.

She had actually considered telephoning before coming over here, but had finally decided if she did that then she would just be giving him the opportunity to deny seeing her. She wished now that she had called first; at least that way she would have been forewarned about the gossip column—and Zak's feelings about it!

Although she didn't have any complaints about his behaviour at the moment...

The caress of his thumb against her lips was extremely sensual, so much so that her knees were starting to feel weak, heat building inside her. She was completely aware of how close he was standing to her, of the tangy elusiveness of his aftershave.

Tyler swallowed hard, her gaze locked with Zak's. 'Perhaps...' she stopped to clear her throat as her voice sounded huskily soft '...perhaps you could kiss it better?'

Zak's eyes widened slightly. 'Kiss it better?'

'Hmm.' She nodded, not a hundred per cent sure she knew what she was doing—but doing it anyway!

Minutes ago this man had been a cold, punishing stranger, but even then Tyler had known that wasn't the real Zak Prince. He had been angry, probably justifiably so after what had happened the previous evening and this morning, but once she had made a stand he seemed to have accepted her word that she was in no way to blame for that photograph or the gossip column.

She knew she was playing with fire, but as she had already burnt so many boats by coming to England in the first place, what was one more…?

He arched blond brows. 'You're sure about this, Tyler? I was angry before, now I'm just incredibly aroused,' he admitted gruffly.

She was well aware of that, had noted the way his eyes had darkened from sky- to cobalt-blue as his gaze rested on her mouth, the slight flush against his cheekbones. Besides, he was standing so close to her now it would have been impossible for her not to feel the way his thighs had hardened against hers. With desire. A desire she echoed.

She moistened dry lips, her tongue accidentally stroking the sensitive swell at the base of his thumb, fire leaping in his gaze as he felt that hot, wet caress against his skin.

Tyler raised expectant eyes, still not sure if she quite knew what she was doing, or quite where it might end, but longing to feel Zak's lips against hers again, this time without anger.

One thing she did know seconds later—she was lost the moment Zak's mouth touched hers!

Her arms reached up over the broad width of his shoulders to wind themselves around his neck. She moved involuntarily against him, wanting to be closer still as his mouth worked passionate magic on her lips.

His hands felt hot on her back, as though they could burn through the material of her tee shirt. Then they slipped underneath her top, and she could feel them firm and caressing against the skin of her back, totally aware of wherever he touched her. Tyler gasped breathlessly as one of those hands moved around the front to cup her bared breast. The thumb that seconds ago had stroked her spine now moved skilfully, erotically over her hardened nipple, sending wave after wave of fiery warmth coursing through to deep down inside her.

It felt so good to have Zak touch her in this way, she thought, almost mindless with desire as she pressed herself deeper into his arms. She was on fire, trembling, shaking, the throbbing ache between her thighs becoming almost unbearable. Almost…!

It felt too good for her to ever want Zak to stop. She had never experienced anything like this before, so overwhelmingly aroused she could feel and see nothing else but Zak.

Oh, God!

As the pleasure continued to wash through her with every beat of her pulse nothing else existed. Nothing else mattered except Zak and the incredible passion that only he could make her feel. Her entire body felt as if it were melting, the force of their combined desire taking her to heights she had never known before.

She wanted this never to stop, wanted nothing else, needed nothing else as Zak's lips and tongue now moved moistly over her bared breasts, capturing first one pouting nipple and then the other, drawing it deeply into the heat of his mouth—

'What the hell…?' Zak responded dazedly to the sharp rap he had heard on the suite door. He was completely aroused from the feel of Tyler's caressing hands on his chest and back beneath his unbuttoned shirt. And he was totally absorbed in the perfection of her swollen, creamy breasts with their gorgeous crushed-raspberry nipples.

'There's someone at the door.' He groaned as he reluctantly released her and pulled down her top to avoid the temptation to just carry on where they'd left off—despite the person now standing outside the door! 'I'd ignore it, but if it's Housekeeping again come to clean my room then they'll just let themselves in,' he explained at the look of confusion on Tyler's face.

It had always been convenient for him to live in a hotel whenever he visited England, but just recently he had begun to realize that it also had its draw-backs—lack of privacy being the main one!

He strode over to the door and opened it impa-tiently. 'Yes?' he barked irritably at the man standing outside in the corridor—obviously not Housekeeping!

'David Miller, Mr Prince,' the other man introduced himself briskly at the same time as he thrust out his hand in greeting.

Having absolutely no idea who the younger man was, Zak shook that hand warily.

David Miller smiled brightly. 'I'm following up on the column in the— Mr Prince!' he protested as Zak moved to close the door on him. 'Is that the "mystery lady"?' The man—another reporter!—glanced quickly past Zak into the suite and saw Tyler. 'Hey, don't I know you—?'

The slamming of the door cut off the rest of what the reporter had been about to say, and Zak scowled darkly as he turned to look at a red-faced Tyler.

This was getting ridiculous, Zak decided. He was used to the media being overly interested in his private life, but over the years he had managed to reach an unspoken agreement with most of them: they would basically leave him alone and then when there was something for them to report he would let them know about it. All that mutual goodwill seemed to have evaporated since Tyler Wood had exploded into his life!

God, Tyler! She had felt fantastic in his arms just now, her skin as soft as velvet to the touch, every inch of her body completely responsive to his. As his was to hers...

He had never felt such overwhelming desire for a woman before. Oh, there had been plenty of women in his life, probably too many, he admitted honestly to himself. But never anyone quite like Tyler before.

He wanted her. Desired her. Needed her. But at the same time he had sensed an inexperience about her, as if she were surprised by her own response to him, surprised, but at the same time eager for the feelings to continue. And that, in turn, made Zak feel protective towards her.

Which was probably the most ridiculous thing about this whole situation. Tyler was twenty-six years old, beautiful, feisty, and fighting for her place in a male-dominated career; it was highly unlikely that she was sexually inexperienced!

Or maybe it was just that she had the ability to make a man feel that she was...?

Zak thrust his hands into his denims pockets as he frowned across at her. 'Miller seemed to think that he knew you; does he?' he asked, still not completely sure he bought her claim of innocence concerning that gossip column.

Could this second reporter turning up at his hotel suite out of the blue, conveniently while Tyler was here too, be perhaps too much of a coincidence?

The same thought seemed to have occurred to Tyler as she suddenly looked worried. 'Not personally, no,' she answered slowly. 'But we were briefly introduced at a press conference a few months ago.'

Zak arched blond brows sceptically. 'By whom?'

She shook her head, her gaze no longer quite meeting his as she replied, 'I don't remember.'

Was it just that she didn't remember, or could it be that she actually knew David Miller rather better than she was willing to admit to Zak, of all people?

Whatever, the other man's timely interruption had certainly put a dampener on the passionate interlude in each other's arms—and wherever that had been about to lead!

That could have been the whole intention, of course, Zak allowed wryly. But no—how could they have arranged that when even Zak hadn't known it would happen? It looked as if he was becoming completely paranoid where Tyler was concerned, although, after the last few days of such 'coincidences', he couldn't exactly be blamed for that!

'Whatever,' he dismissed. 'Do you think it likely that Miller will remember where he knows you from?' In his opinion—and at the moment that could be slightly biased, he allowed—no man was ever likely to forget having met Tyler.

'I don't know that, either—I'm not a mind-reader, Zak!' she objected as he gave a derisive snort.

At the moment, that was probably just as well, he conceded ruefully. A few minutes ago he had been thinking quite seriously about taking her to bed for several hours—days!—and just forgetting who and what she was, of forgetting that the rest of the world existed, in fact.

Way to go, Zak, he mentally mocked himself. Very mature and responsible.

Except that mature and responsible were the last two things he felt around Tyler. Slightly wrong-footed and dazed by lust probably best described how he felt whenever he was with her. Which wasn't a good thing to be around any sort of reporter!

The main problem was, he still wasn't sure what sort of reporter Tyler was...

'How do you intend going about finding out where he knows you from?' he prompted curiously.

Her eyes widened. 'Me?'

'Yes, you. You appear to know who he is, so you probably know which newspaper he works for too.'

'Well...yes,' she admitted irritably. 'But if I start asking questions it's only going to add to his specu- lation—'

'Not my problem.' Zak shrugged.

'Well, it certainly isn't mine!' she protested.

'No?' he mused. 'Then you aren't at all bothered at the thought of having your name and face plastered all over some newspaper in connection with mine— you are bothered?' he jeered as her face distinctly paled, her expression panicked before she managed to replace it with one of uninterest.

That same panic he had seen in her earlier when he had first shown her the gossip column...

Tyler Wood was hiding something, he realized shrewdly. Although quite what that could be, he had no idea... Yet.

'My presence in your hotel suite is easily explained as business,' she protested. 'I'll simply give David a call and explain the real situation to him.'

Zak gave a humourless grin. Humourless because,

although she might see her presence here as just 'business', he had ceased to think of her in that way long ago. Probably from the moment he'd first looked into her chocolate-brown eyes.

'That's certainly one way of dealing with it,' he allowed. 'And the sooner the better, don't you think…?' he added pointedly.

Tyler blinked, and then frowned as his meaning became clear. 'You want me to go *now*?'

'Yes, I want you to go now.'

Because if she didn't go soon he was going to forget everything else and start kissing her again—and this time he'd remember to put the 'Do Not Disturb' sign on the door first! And that was a very bad idea. No, he badly needed Tyler to leave. Right now. If not sooner!

Then, hopefully, by the time he saw Tyler again, he would have this desire to kiss her and never stop back under control again. Hopefully!

No woman had ever had this effect on him before, where he felt a need to kiss and shake her at one and the same time. And until he knew more about Tyler— something he intended rectifying the moment she had gone!—it would probably be better for everyone concerned if he did neither of those things.

Tyler, it seemed, was something of a 'mystery lady' after all, if not quite in the way that the gossip columnist had implied. She knew someone of Gerald Knight's fashion-designer status, quite well if their friendly greeting the previous evening was anything to go by. Which seemed to imply there was more to it than her having just written an article on the man.

Also, her relationship with her photographer, Perry Morgan, was rumoured to be a lot more than platonic.

And yet no one he had so far spoken to seemed to know anything about Tyler before she had arrived in England six months ago, intent on making a name for herself as a reporter.

Which posed the questions: where had Tyler been for the first twenty-five and a half years of her life? Where did she come from? Who were her friends? Her family? The main question Zak wanted an answer to—and he already knew he wouldn't get that from Tyler herself—was why none of the people she had met and befriended in England knew anything about her other than the little she had told them.

What was Tyler hiding?

Because she was definitely hiding something…

CHAPTER NINE

'AND so I just wanted to ask you, if by some remote chance Zak Prince should contact you, not to tell him anything you know about my private life.' Tyler looked pleadingly across the table at Gerald Knight as the two of them had lunch together.

At her request. Because there had been something in Zak's manner when they had parted this morning, a spark of suspicion, that made Tyler want to close all the doors behind her before he had a chance to go through them and start asking questions about her.

Somewhere, somehow, during the last twenty-four hours, Zak had neatly turned the tables on her, so that *she* was now the one evading answering questions about herself!

Gerald arched mischievous dark brows. 'By "private life" I'm presuming you mean I'm not to discuss Rufus or the fact that you're calling yourself Tyler Wood now and not Tyler Harwood?'

'Yes, that's exactly what I mean,' she said, at the same time only just resisting the urge to look around them to see if anyone might be listening to their conversation. Was she being paranoid, or what? 'It's bad enough that Zak thinks I'm some flaky female rookie—if he finds out who I really am then he'll never take me seriously as a reporter!'

He laughed softly. 'I would love to be a fly on the wall if Rufus and Zak were ever to meet!'

'They never will,' Tyler vowed, shuddering just at the thought.

'Oh, I wouldn't be too sure about that, Tyler darling,' Gerald mused, wearing a cream suit today, with a yellow shirt and cream tie. 'From where I was sitting last night, and that column in the newspaper this morning, Zak Prince seems to be pretty interested in you.'

She felt the warmth colour her cheeks. 'You're wrong,' she insisted flatly. 'I'm interviewing him, and that's all. Now promise me, Gerald. Please!'

He gave in gracefully, saying, 'You know I never could resist your gorgeous brown eyes.'

One down, Tyler accepted gratefully, only David Miller to go—although she knew it would be a lot more difficult to get any information out of him—such as who had set him onto her and Zak. Tyler hadn't exactly been truthful this morning when she had told Zak she didn't remember who had introduced her to David Miller, but she was sure the person who had introduced them didn't have anything to do with all this. Could Jane Morrow have gone to David Miller then, in an attempt to cause yet more trouble for the Prince family? Tyler hoped finding Miller would answer these questions.

However, in the meantime, dealing with these problems certainly gave her something else to think about other than Zak's lovemaking. She really, really didn't want to go there. At the moment, she couldn't handle where those thoughts might take her...

And she didn't think about it. Not once all afternoon. Until she returned to her desk at the newspaper and glanced across the busy room to see Zak comfortably ensconced in Bill Graham's private office!

Her eyes went wide and her legs trembled. She

reached out to grab the edge of her desk, her face paling, as through the window of the office she actually saw Bill laugh—Bill never laughed!—at something Zak had just said to him.

But that wasn't the only unusual thing about Zak being in Bill's office; the door was firmly closed, and Bill's office door was never closed. He liked to keep his ears as well as his eyes open when it came to his staff.

A staff that might as well not have been there as far as Tyler was concerned, her whole attention focused on Bill's office and what might be happening in there right now.

What on earth was Zak doing here? Men of his calibre and fame never usually stepped into any newspaper office willingly. The media followed him, not the other way round!

'He's even better looking in the flesh, isn't he?' Callie Rhodes, part of the fashion team, winked at Tyler suggestively as she walked past her desk.

The colour flooded back into Tyler's cheeks as she remembered exactly how much of that flesh she had seen on Tuesday morning as well as today. How much of that flesh she had actually touched!

'Lucky old you,' Kelly Adams, a fellow reporter, sighed longingly as she also strolled past, her gaze fixed on Zak.

Oh, yes, lucky old her!

Had Zak come to complain to Bill about her method of reporting?

She hadn't exactly been too successful in interviewing him—her complete awareness of Zak, her response to him, seemed to render her completely incompetent as a journalist every time she was anywhere near him!

Zak was standing up now. The two men were smiling at each other as they shook hands, before Bill moved to open the office door and escorted Zak out into the main office.

Zak walked straight towards her, that smile still curving those beautifully sculptured lips.

Tyler stood rooted to the spot, a look of absolute horror on her face, her eyes still wide with the shock that Zak was here in the first place.

'Hi, Tyler,' he greeted lightly as he neared her desk, his expression totally unreadable.

'Hi, Zak,' she managed to return through barely moving lips.

'Bye, Tyler.' He raised a hand in parting as he continued to walk straight past her desk towards the door.

'Bye, Za— Hey, just a minute!' she burst out of her stupor to protest, moving to hurry after him as he headed towards the lifts. But not before she had noticed Callie, Kelly, and every other female in the vicinity gazing at him with sickening doe eyes.

But then, if Zak had bestowed that smile of warm, lazy charm on her, as he just had on them, she might have joined them!

'Zak!' she called out to stop him from actually getting into the lift, lengthening her stride as she joined him in the corridor. 'What are you doing here?' she demanded to know as he looked down at her.

He shrugged broad shoulders beneath the black tee shirt he wore, fitted denims resting low on his hips. 'I don't mean to sound rude, Tyler,' he drawled, 'but do you really think that is any of your business?'

Angry colour burned her cheeks at this put-down. 'Bill Graham is *my* boss,' she objected.

'And is there some law that says I can't come in and talk to him?'

Her hands clenched into fists as she glared up at him. 'No law, it's just—Bill is my boss,' she repeated ineffectually. But if Zak had some sort of complaint to make about her—and he probably had lots!—she would much rather he had discussed them with her rather than with Bill Graham. 'Does this mean my exclusive with you is at an end?' If she was off the story, then she was out of a job, too... 'Did you ask Bill to take me off the story?' she enlarged with impatience as Zak continued to look puzzled.

'Why would you think that?' he asked.

Any number of reasons! She had a snap-happy photographer following her around. It was because Zak had been seen out to dinner with her the previous evening that his name had appeared in a gossip column this morning. And probably worst of all—and neither of them had referred to it for some time—she had been sick all over the carpet in his hotel room before spending the night recovering in his bed!

She shrugged. 'Things haven't exactly been running smoothly the last couple of days—'

'*Running smoothly?*' Zak exclaimed incredulously. 'Tyler, it's been nothing but one disaster after another since the moment we met!'

Tyler blanched at this blunt statement, but she couldn't leave it there. She barely glanced at the lift as it arrived at their floor, the doors opening automatically. 'That hasn't all been my fault,' she defended herself weakly—knowing that most of the disasters he was referring to had indeed been her fault. Even if she had done nothing personally to cause them!

'Well, it certainly hasn't been mine,' Zak argued as

he stepped into the waiting lift. 'Are you free for dinner tonight, Tyler?' he added unexpectedly.

'Oh! I—er—yes,' she accepted finally, totally taken aback by the invitation; their conversation so far certainly hadn't indicated that he wanted to spend another minute in her company, let alone an entire evening!

'Fine.' He turned and pressed the button for the ground floor. 'And if you happen to have another Vera Wang in your wardrobe, I should save it to wear on Saturday evening,' he advised her enigmatically.

Tyler gave him a startled look. Saturday night? What was happening on Saturday night?

'I'll see you at my hotel at around eight this evening, okay?' he added as the lift doors closed—with him inside, and Tyler still standing in the corridor wondering at exactly what point she had completely lost control of the conversation.

No, that was wrong, she instantly chided herself— she had never *had* control of the conversation in the first place! In fact, she had no idea what Zak had been talking about half the time.

Saturday night was just one more indication of that. What was happening on Saturday night that Zak wanted her to wear something as exclusive as a Vera Wang dress to? she wondered as she wandered back to her desk. She did have another one, as it happened, in fact she had—

'He is one gorgeous man, Tyler,' Kelly gushed effusively as she paused on her way out of the office.

'Yes,' Tyler acknowledged vaguely, although an inner part of her—an unreasonable, jealous part!—resented Kelly's obvious attraction to Zak. He certainly was gorgeous, and there was no doubting that his kisses melted her all the way down to her toes, but she didn't like hearing another woman commenting on his good looks. Which was pretty ridiculous if she thought about it.

For one thing, the way Zak looked was part of his acting success; she very much doubted he would be quite as successful if he looked like Godzilla's uncle! And for another thing, she simply had no right to resent anything where Zak was concerned. No matter how much she might wish it were otherwise.

'Do you know who this mystery lady is in his life?' Kelly probed.

Tyler had always liked the other woman, both personally and as part of the reporting team, but at that moment she dearly wanted to tell Kelly to mind her own darned business!

'I don't think there is one.' She managed a small rueful smile at the other woman. 'Our competitor must have just been short of gossip this morning.' She gave a dismissive shrug, hoping the other woman wouldn't continue the subject.

'Oh.' Kelly looked disappointed. And then she brightened. 'Oh, well, perhaps there's still hope for the rest of us, after all. See you later, Tyler,' she added brightly before hurrying back to her own office on the next floor.

Leaving Tyler feeling decidedly disgruntled. With three people.

With Kelly for her obvious drooling over the man Tyler was more and more convinced she was falling genuinely in love with; it was positively the last thing she wanted, but she was very afraid it was already a fact.

With Zak himself for the totally bewildering conversation they'd just had.

And, finally, with Bill Graham, because he had been chatting away with the younger man, even laughing with him at one stage, and she still had no idea what they could possibly have been talking about! Knowing Bill as she did, he probably wouldn't tell her either, if she were to ask. Which was—

Saturday night!

Tyler dropped weakly onto her chair behind her desk as the full significance of that day finally hit her with the force of a sledgehammer.

It was the reason Zak was still in England after attending his brother's wedding last weekend. The reason he had been able to give her the time this week to do the interview with him at all.

Saturday night was the English première of Zak's latest film *Gunslinger*!

And from the little he had just said to her, he was expecting her to accompany him to it...

There was absolutely *no way* she was going to appear in such a public way with him, to the interest of reporters and photographers alike—*worldwide* reporters and photographers...!

'So although it's a very—gracious thought on your part, I'm afraid that I have other plans for Saturday night, which means I will have to decline your invitation,' Tyler concluded breathlessly as she sat next to Zak in the cab they'd hailed after leaving his hotel shortly after eight o'clock that evening.

Zak listened, with complete indifference, to her refusal to attend the première with him on Saturday evening. Because, no matter what she might think to the contrary, she would be going with him. Either that, or she would have to tell him the real reason she didn't want her own name or photograph appearing in the newspapers on Sunday morning.

Zak was more convinced than ever that this was the real motive behind her refusal. He had been trying all day to find out more about his so-called 'mystery lady', but it was as he had thought; either people—like David Miller—didn't know anything about Tyler before she'd come to England, or others that did—like Bill Graham and Gerald Knight—simply weren't talking. In fact, Gerald Knight hadn't spoken to him at all, because he had been 'unavailable' all day.

So he had come up with a plan that was sure to elicit some sort of response from Tyler, and in so doing perhaps give him an insight as to what—or whom—she was running away from in the States.

Her halting claim to having other plans for Saturday night was certainly a start!

He gave a falsely rueful shrug. 'Then I guess you'll have to change or postpone those plans.'

'I'm afraid I can't do that,' she protested stiffly.

'That's a pity,' Zak said unsympathetically. 'Bill Graham seemed to like the idea when I discussed it with him earlier today.'

Tyler stared at him incredulously. '*That's* what you were discussing with him earlier?'

He arched mocking brows. 'He didn't tell you?' Although he wasn't surprised the other man had left it up to him to discuss this with Tyler; he had the distinct feeling that Bill Graham was one of those people, although he liked to pretend otherwise, who knew a lot more about Tyler Wood than he was willing to divulge, to Zak or anyone else. Possibly even to Tyler herself...

'No, he didn't tell me,' she snapped angrily. 'Unless

it escaped your notice, Bill Graham isn't a man who likes to make life easy for the people who work for him!'

'I did notice, actually,' Zak drawled. 'Nevertheless, he totally approves of your attending the première with me. In fact, I think he likes the kudos of having one of his reporters in the limelight,' he added provocatively.

Because Bill Graham probably guessed—knew…?— that Tyler felt totally the opposite!

Tyler drew in a deep breath, obviously about to launch into yet another refusal to attend the première, when her attention was caught and held by the fact that the cab had turned into a private driveway. Zak gave her a brief smile before getting out of the cab and punching the code into the security device that automatically opened the huge iron gates.

She looked slightly confused as Zak got back in beside her, the cab now driving up to the front of a tall, imposing Victorian house. 'Where are we?' she finally asked as Zak came round to open the door for her to get out of the cab.

Zak answered as he turned back from paying the driver, 'My sister Stazy also saw that gossipy piece about the two of us in the newspaper this morning.' Probably aided and abetted by Rik, he inwardly acknowledged grimly. 'She's invited the two of us for dinner this evening,' he added, at the same time taking a light hold of Tyler's arm.

A move she totally resisted, pulling her arm out of his grasp to step back. 'You have *got* to be kidding!' she cried incredulously, looking absolutely horrified at the thought of meeting yet another member of the Prince family.

But it was a statement that Zak wholeheartedly sympathized with where his sister was concerned; Stazy might be the youngest in their family of four siblings, but as the only female, and happily married herself, she had since become quite formidable in her matchmaking efforts for her three older brothers.

From their brief telephone conversation this morning, Zak had the distinct impression Stazy wanted to know more about this 'mystery lady' in his life, hence the invitation to dinner this evening. But it wasn't an experience Zak intended going through alone!

'Believe me, you don't kid around with someone like Stazy,' he informed Tyler as he rang the doorbell. 'She may not be very old, but she's become decidedly bossy since she married a year ago.' And he had to admit to feeling a certain curiosity about what his sister would make of Tyler.

A Tyler who still looked absolutely horrified at the prospect of having dinner with a member of his family!

'If it makes you feel any better, her husband Jordan will be there too. Jordan Hunter, of the Hunter Brothers hotel chain,' he added, attempting to be reassuring, but only increasing Tyler's trepidation if her now-apprehensive expression was anything to go by.

What she actually looked was incredibly beautiful, the black fitted, knee-length dress suiting her slenderness, her make-up light, and for once her hair not in that spiky style that reminded him of an angry porcupine, but falling softly onto her forehead and curling back behind delicate ears.

He received a glare for his effort at trying to help her feel more relaxed, Tyler giving a disgusted snort before turning as the front door was opened by his sister; Stazy, as a hugely successful interior designer, was wealthy in her own right, and Jordan was a millionaire several times over, but Stazy resisted having any live-in staff in the house, preferring to make a home for her family herself.

Zak stood slightly back as the two women looked at each other, knowing by the way Stazy's eyes widened that she, at least, was pleasantly surprised by Tyler. He wondered briefly what the women he was usually involved with were like, because Stazy had never approved of any of them!

Not that he was altogether sure she approved of Tyler either as Stazy's smile faded to be replaced by a perplexed frown as she continued to look at Zak's companion. Zak could sympathize with the emotion— it was how Tyler made him feel most of the time, too!

Tyler was the one to break the silence that was beginning to stretch out so long it was seriously in danger of becoming awkward. 'Hi, I'm Tyler Wood,' she greeted brightly. 'I believe there's been some sort of misunderstanding concerning my being seen with Zak a couple of times.' She gave a—forced?—laugh. 'The ''mystery lady'' in Zak's life is actually just a reporter doing an exclusive interview with him. Your brother Nik actually arranged it,' she added pointedly.

So much had happened this week since he had first met Tyler that Zak had to admit that he had almost forgotten that little fact!

But obviously Stazy hadn't, her frown fading slightly. 'Of course,' she replied. 'Why didn't you just explain to me earlier, Zak? I'm sure Tyler can't really want to have dinner with your family,' she chided as the three of them went inside the house.

And miss out on all the fun of spending another

evening in Tyler's company? Besides, when Stazy had invited them for dinner, he really had forgotten the real reason Tyler had come into his life when he'd accepted for the two of them! It just showed how complicated his life had become the last few days. Probably because his two prime emotions during that time had been anger and desire—both of them directed at the tiny, beautiful woman at his side.

'We were meeting up this evening anyway. Besides, I didn't want to miss out on a free dinner!' he teased, to direct the attention away from his error.

Stazy laughed. 'Go through and join Jordan, you clown. I'll just take Tyler upstairs so that she can freshen up before we eat.'

Tyler already looked fresh enough to him. In fact, he was finding it hard to keep his eyes—and everything else!—off her. But who was he, a mere man, to question the need to reapply lipstick or whatever?

'Fine.' He nodded, turning off into the sitting-room, where he intended asking his brother-in-law for a whisky and soda. A large one!

CHAPTER TEN

'OKAY, Miss Harwood,' Stazy Hunter said abruptly as soon as she had closed the bathroom door on the two women. 'I believe you have about five minutes to tell me exactly why you're masquerading as a reporter named Tyler Wood!'

Tyler stared in horror at her hostess. Stazy stared right back at her, that implacable Prince will Tyler had already run up against several times with both Nik and Zak clearly in evidence, her grey eyes hard and unblinking, the previously smiling mouth set in a determined line.

Tyler had thought things were going so well—she had got this far in England without anybody discovering her real identity. Maybe she could still save the situation...

'And it had better be good,' Stazy Hunter continued harshly. 'Good enough to convince me not to march straight down those stairs and tell my brother exactly who you really are!'

Tyler swallowed hard, a little shaken by the other woman's challenge. 'So you know who I am?'

'Well, of course I know who you are,' the younger woman snapped. 'And so would Zak if he had ever read any of the society magazines over in America! You're that New York socialite who's practically the arbiter of fashion, make-up and hair-dos over there.'

Tyler gave a rueful smile. 'Hardly Zak's scene, is it?'

'No,' his sister conceded dryly. 'But it's certainly *yours*,' she accused. 'I'm still waiting, Tyler, and the minutes are ticking away.'

She raised an auburn eyebrow in pointed enquiry.

Tyler's thoughts were racing madly. What could she tell her? What could she possibly say, when Stazy obviously knew exactly who she was, that would convince this woman that her own intentions were completely honest where Zak was concerned?

Especially as they *weren't* completely honest, a little voice in her head reminded her reprovingly.

Okay, so maybe they weren't, but her interview with Zak had nothing to do with the reason she was over here working as a reporter under an assumed name, did it?

Of course it didn't. She hadn't even known she would so much as meet Zak Prince when she had made that initial decision six months ago.

So maybe if she just told Stazy the truth about why she had come here six months ago and her reasons for keeping it private—especially from Zak—it would be enough to avert disaster.

Maybe it was the relief of finally being able to talk freely about herself, or perhaps it was just that Stazy looked so set on not moving until she knew what was going on, but once Tyler started explaining, the whole story just came tumbling out.

Stazy didn't show any reaction as Tyler began talking. She just listened, giving Tyler no indication as to whether or not the other woman believed a word she was saying.

'After the most awful row with my parents, in particular my father because I'd rejected his choice of husband for me, I just packed a bag, booked myself a ticket for London, Heathrow, and here I am,' Tyler explained. 'I changed my name because it's so well known both here and in the States, and I didn't want to get a job on the back of that or, even more likely, have job applications refused because I was perceived as an empty-headed bimbo who was only worried about her hair and nails! As for not telling Zak who I am, I figured that if he knew he'd just stop taking me seriously as a reporter—not that he takes me that seriously professionally, anyway,' she finished up ruefully.

Stazy finally moved, shaking her head. 'I wonder why it is,' she mused, 'that dominating men just don't see themselves as being that way.'

Tyler made no reply, the statement not really requiring one; those men just didn't see themselves that way.

But did that comment mean that Stazy believed her?

Stazy sighed. 'Believe it or not, I did something very similar myself eighteen months ago, including changing my name.' She grimaced. 'Three older brothers, who always think they know what's best for their little sister, is just three too many, let me tell you!' She chuckled softly. 'And Zak really has no idea who you are?'

'None,' Tyler confirmed—although she was sure Zak had some suspicions that she wasn't quite what she appeared to be!

'Hmm.' The younger woman considered. 'Well, at this point in time, I'm not sure that he needs to know, either.'

'Do you mean it?' Tyler pounced hopefully. 'Are you really not going to tell him?' It seemed a little too good to be true!

'At this point in time,' Stazy reiterated. 'But if that situation changes, if I think for one moment that Zak is going to be hurt by not knowing—I'll tell him.'

'He won't be hurt,' Tyler hastened to assure the other woman, able to think of no circumstances where her real identity might affect Zak. And she wasn't being dishonest in her claim; the exposé she was supposed to write on Zak might not go down too well, but her real name shouldn't make any difference to that.

'Are you sure about that?' Stazy gave her a searching look. 'This is the first time Zak has ever brought anyone to dinner here.'

'But only because you made a point of inviting me,' Tyler protested.

'And you think this is the first time I've ever issued such an invitation to any of the women Zak has been involved with?' Stazy asked with a smile.

Tyler didn't want to hear about any other woman Zak had been involved with! 'He isn't involved with me,' she assured the other woman, even as she could feel herself blushing once again. Those twin flags of colour, for one reason or another—usually to do with Zak!—seemed to be becoming practically permanent fixtures in her normally pale cheeks. 'I told you, I'm just spending a week interviewing him.'

Stazy still looked far from convinced. 'You have to know that, as far as I'm concerned, Zak always comes first.'

'I wouldn't expect anything else,' Tyler acknowledged, seeing this as further evidence of how close the Prince family really were. 'But by not telling him who I am, I'm not hurting Zak, I assure you.' At this moment she was willing to promise the other woman anything if it prevented Stazy from telling Zak who she was!

Stazy gave a glance at the slender gold watch on her wrist. 'We've been far longer than five minutes,' she announced. 'The men are going to wonder where we've got to.'

Not noticeably so, Tyler thought wryly as the two handsome men, one tall and dark, the other tall and honey-blond, broke off their laughing conversation to introduce Tyler and Jordan to each other.

To her surprise, after that rather shaky start, Tyler found herself enjoying the evening, the conversation flowing easily. The Hunters were obviously a very happily married couple, and Zak's relationship with both of them was pleasantly easygoing too. In fact, despite her earlier apprehension, it turned out to be the most relaxed and enjoyable evening Tyler had spent since coming to England.

'Thank you for including me this evening,' she told Zak huskily on the drive back. 'Stazy and Jordan are nice.'

Zak eyed her teasingly. 'And being my sister, you didn't think Stazy was going to be?'

'No, of course I didn't think that,' Tyler fired up immediately. 'I just—you're winding me up again, aren't you?'

'Only a little,' he assured her softly. 'What were you two women talking about upstairs for so long when we arrived?' he asked innocently.

Too innocently? It certainly seemed so to Tyler. But Stazy had appeared genuine in her promise not to tell Zak about who she was unless absolutely necessary. And certainly nothing had happened yet this evening for that situation to have changed.

'Just fashion and things,' she said evasively. 'Totally boring as far as you men are concerned.'

'Aren't you being a little sexist there?' Zak taunted. 'I'm sure Gerald Knight, for instance, would be very interested.'

'Gerald?' she echoed a little too sharply; after her worries earlier in the day, it seemed a little coincidental that Gerald should be introduced into their conversation.

Zak nodded. 'Ladies' fashions would obviously be of interest to him.'

'Only because it's what he does,' she retorted. 'I meant that, as a general rule, ladies' fashions—'

'—and things,' Zak put in dryly.

'—are of little interest to most men.'

'You're right.' He nodded. 'No interest whatsoever.'

Then what had the last few minutes' conversation been about? He was probably still trying to wind her up. He really was—

'Perhaps you would like to tell the driver your address,' Zak prompted.

Tyler gave him a startled look in the dimly lit interior of the cab. 'My address?'

'Mmm. It occurs to me that, although we've had dinner together twice now, I've never actually collected or taken you back home at the end of the evening. It's time I rectified that.'

She didn't want Zak to take her home! She didn't want Zak to know where she lived. In fact—

'Just what exactly are you hiding, Tyler?' He seemed to guess some of her thoughts, his gaze narrowed now. 'A husband and six kids? Or could it be—' his voice had hardened slightly '—that you share your apartment with someone, after all?'

'Of course I don't—'

'Perry Morgan, for example,' Zak added as if she hadn't spoken, a scowl darkening his eyes now.

'I've already told you I don't share my apartment with Perry,' she reminded him indignantly. 'I don't share my apartment with anyone!'

Zak was quick to take advantage. 'Then there's no problem with my taking you home, is there?'

Of course there was a problem. A big problem. Her apartment was her own space, her very own space, the first she had ever had; if Zak ever went there she would never be able to go home again without remembering him there. And feeling about him as she did, that would be unbearable.

Besides, there was also another factor involved here; earlier this evening Zak had completely overridden her objections to going to his film première with him on Saturday. No matter what he thought to the contrary, she still had no intention of going with him—despite what Bill Graham might or might not have to say about that!—but if Zak actually knew where she lived, he might prove harder to evade than she wished. In fact, hiding out in her apartment seemed to be the only answer to that particular problem!

She was going to fob him off with yet another excuse; Zak knew it before she even spoke.

He had been pleasantly surprised this evening by the easy way Tyler got on with Stazy and Jordan; his sister wasn't known for giving the current woman in any of her brothers' lives an easy time of it!

But maybe the difference here had been the fact that

Tyler had gone to great lengths to let Stazy know she wasn't, in fact, the current woman in his life!

It had deeply irritated him at the time. What exactly constituted being 'in someone's life'? Spending time together? He and Tyler seemed to have done a lot of that the last few days. Kissing each other? Well, he and Tyler seemed to have done that several times too.

In fact, to all intents and purposes, whether Tyler wanted it or not, she was very much in his life!

But she so obviously didn't want to be his current woman. Which was why he knew she was going to make some feeble excuse about not taking her home, let alone actually inviting him up to her apartment!

'The thing is, Zak—' she spoke quietly '—I just don't want to take you there.'

Not feeble at all! Just the straight, unvarnished truth. He had come to admire that about her, in spite of himself.

He gave a rueful laugh. 'Try to spare my feelings, why don't you?'

'I just think it's time we put things back on a busi-nesslike footing,' she explained.

He was very much past businesslike where this woman was concerned. Hell, he had passed that point the moment he had laid Tyler in his bed three nights ago.

She had been ill, and had looked it, but, at the same time, while she'd been asleep that slightly aggressive expression she habitually wore hadn't been in evidence, giving her a delicately appealing look. And he was as vulnerable to that as any other man would be.

Not that he had seen her defences down again in quite that way since; in fact she was usually prickly enough to frighten off most men's interest in her.

Maybe it was arrogance on his part, but he had just never thought of himself as 'most men'…

Admit it, Zak, he inwardly chided himself, you're far too interested in a woman who's running in the opposite direction so fast you have difficulty keeping up with her, let alone getting one step ahead of her! Maybe that was half the novelty to him; he was usually the one doing the running! Whatever the reason, he was so interested in Tyler he could almost believe he was falling in love with her, if that idea weren't so ludicrous. A famous actor, in love with a tabloid reporter…he could see the headlines now!

'Put things back on a businesslike footing?' He repeated her words now. 'Exactly how have we got along with that so far? What do you actually have to write for your article at the moment?' he enlarged as she looked puzzled.

Was it his imagination, or did her cheeks become slightly flushed at his reminder that they'd done more kissing than interviewing to date? Bill Graham had been quite convincing earlier today that there really was an article. In fact he had confirmed to Zak that he had it in mind for the Sunday supplement magazine.

And yet Zak was sure he detected a slight embarrassment in Tyler every time he mentioned the article. Which meant that Bill Graham was either a better actor than he would have given the other man credit for, or Tyler was just embarrassed at her lack of interviewing skills so far.

No doubt it was a little difficult to ask questions when the subject of the interview was kissing you! As he wanted to kiss her again right now…

Once again Tyler looked beautiful this evening, the

plain black dress deepening the brown of her eyes and giving a peachy glow to her bare neck and face. She had also proved to be a very funny dining companion as she'd regaled them with stories earlier about some of the vocabulary mistakes she had made when she had first come to England.

Stazy, he could tell, had liked the other woman very much, and Jordan had been enchanted by her. In fact, if it weren't for the fact that Zak knew Jordan was totally and utterly in love with Stazy, he would have found his brother-in-law's teasingly indulgent manner towards Tyler meritous of a punch on the nose!

He had been jealous.

Even though he had never experienced the emotion before, Zak knew and recognized the feeling for what it was. That destructive, character-changing green-eyed monster he had heard so much about but had never experienced until now.

It was one of the reasons he so badly needed to kiss Tyler again. Away from curious eyes and interruptions, so that the two of them might explore their emotions— Who was he kidding? He wanted to be alone with Tyler so that he could make love to her until she was senseless. Until they were both senseless!

'In retrospect, we haven't been businesslike at all,' she answered his question huskily. 'Which is why I suggest that tomorrow we spend the day together so that you can read through a list of questions I've compiled.'

Spending the day together sounded okay to him; him having to read through a list of questions less so. 'Isn't my just giving answers to a load of pre-written questions going to come across as just a little stilted in your article?' As well as being excruciatingly laborious on his part.

The truth was, he just didn't want Tyler to see him struggling to read the damned questions!

This was his real—his only—secret from the public. He had been labelled a troublemaking rebel during his high-school days, the wild one of the Prince brothers. But what no one had realized for quite some considerable time was that the reason he was always bored and getting into trouble was because most of the classes just went completely over his head, and that textbooks were just a bewildering jumble of letters to him.

Dyslexia. He was an adult before it had actually been diagnosed—along with his IQ of one hundred and sixty!—but once it had been, his reading difficulty had ceased to be much of a problem. With two older brothers, and a very young sister, all of them eager to read things to him and help him memorize his scripts, the issues that had dogged his school life had just faded into the background. In fact, he rarely gave them a thought nowadays.

Dyslexic. What a name to give to someone with reading difficulties—he could barely say it, let alone read it, and it was a sure fact that he couldn't spell it! He was pretty sure that most dyslexics felt the same way. They were people challenged by the formation of a sequence of letters into a readable word, and putting a label like dyslexia on it only served to confuse the people afflicted with it.

And it was something Zak didn't want Tyler, or indeed any other reporter, writing about!

Other successful actors who had been open about their dyslexia had already proved that dyslexics weren't idiots—far from it, they were just letter challenged. But Zak had decided long ago that he didn't need, or want, anything written about him to begin with 'dyslexic this' or 'dyslexic that'; it was a learning disability, and he wanted to just leave it at that.

Tyler's face was still flushed at his previous comment about her article possibly sounding stilted. 'I like to think I have the ability as a reporter to write the article in such a way that it doesn't just appear like a question-and-answer thing.'

'Let's hope so,' he said. 'Coming in for a nightcap?' he invited as the cab came to a halt outside his hotel.

'I won't, if you don't mind,' she refused abruptly, obviously still smarting from what she saw as his implied criticism of her reporting skills.

Zak sat back from paying the driver. 'And if I do mind?' he asked huskily.

She met his gaze unblinkingly. 'I'm still not coming in.'

He couldn't help it, he laughed, once again wanting to kiss her as well as shake her. He could never remember feeling that way about any woman before. 'You're one stubborn woman, Tyler Wood.'

Because of the unhelpfulness of those people who knew her, whether deliberate or otherwise, he still knew little more about her this evening than he had this morning. But that didn't mean he wasn't still determined to find out more. By fair means or foul.

Knowing Tyler as he did, he had a feeling it was going to have to be foul!

She gave a rueful smile. 'It takes one to know one!'

He raised surprised brows. 'You think *I'm* stubborn?'

She gave a derisive smile. 'I think you are many things—and stubborn is just one of them.'

Zak laughed again. 'Maybe you should come inside and tell me some of the other things I am?'

'That *I* think you are,' Tyler corrected dryly. 'And the answer is still no.'

He shrugged. 'You can't blame a guy for trying!'

In fact, he wanted to do more than try with Tyler. Much more. That was the problem. And until he knew more about her, where she came from, who, if anyone, was waiting for her back in the States, he was wary of even attempting to try and take their relationship further.

That was what the rational side of his brain told him, anyway.

The other part, the part that wanted to pick her up in his arms and carry her upstairs to his suite—pretty much as he had on their first evening together, except this time he wouldn't give Tyler any brandy!—said to hell with caution and just go for it!

'I don't blame you for anything, Zak.' She sighed wearily. 'I've just had enough for one night, okay?'

No, it wasn't okay, not really, but from her tone of voice, that slightly defensive air, he knew he didn't have any other choice.

'Okay,' he accepted before leaning forward and kissing her lightly on the lips. 'Thank you for a lovely evening, Tyler; I enjoyed it.' It was the truth, after all; he had enjoyed the evening. He had just hoped to be able to kiss her—no, more than just kiss her—at the end of it.

She had looked slightly disconcerted after he'd kissed her, but now she laughed. 'Goodnight, Zak.'

''Night, Tyler. Same time tomorrow morning?' he added as he got out of the cab.

'Same time tomorrow,' she echoed huskily.

By fair means or foul, he reiterated as he stood on the pavement and watched the cab drive away...

CHAPTER ELEVEN

'OH, NO, not again!' Tyler groaned as she looked down at the newspaper Bill Graham had just slapped down on the desktop in front of her, his expression grim.

She had come into the office early this morning— did Bill never go home?—intending to check on her e-mails and other messages, deal with any other paperwork, before taking the tube over to Zak's hotel.

This photograph, on the front page, no less, in yet another rival newspaper, of her and Zak getting into a cab, Stazy and Jordan Hunter standing in the doorway of their home as they waved goodbye at the end of the previous evening, told her that wasn't going to happen.

'How did they even get this?' She groaned, her hand moving instinctively to cover the photograph, as if by doing so she could block it out. Except she knew that she couldn't, that hundreds, thousands of copies of this exact same photograph were appearing on the front page of this newspaper as it was distributed all over the country. The world, perhaps?

Her face paled even more as she realized the consequences of that happening. She really didn't want her father butting into her life right now!

She took her hand off the photograph, staring down at it intently now. She was just about to get into the cab, her face turned slightly away from the camera, but was it enough so that the casual observer wouldn't recognize it as being her? She was thinner than she had been six months ago, and her hair was shorter too, so maybe, just maybe—

'Actually, Tyler,' Bill cut in on her racing thoughts, his tone sarcastic, 'I'm more interested in why this paper have this photograph and we don't! Where the hell was your boyfriend Morgan when all this was happening?' He glared down at her.

'He *isn't* my boyfriend,' she responded automatically, still staring down at the photograph. 'You know, the downward angle of this photograph means the photographer must have been standing on the wall or something,' she said slowly.

'Who the hell cares where they were standing?' Bill exploded. 'He, or she, got the damned photograph and we didn't!'

That wasn't all he or she had got; the headline with the photograph screamed the caption, ZAK PRINCE TAKES HIS 'MYSTERY LADY' HOME TO MEET THE FAMILY! Zak was going to kill her. Slowly.

Except… This was all his fault. *He* had arranged that dinner last night with Stazy and Jordan. Maybe *she* would kill *him*. Slowly!

She grimaced. 'I doubt Stazy and Jordan Hunter will see it quite that way. Maybe they'll press charges for invasion of privacy,' she added with satisfaction.

'And a lot of good that will do them.' Bill snorted. 'Tyler, if you're having an affair with the man, then why—?'

'I am *not* having an affair with Zak Prince!' she cut in fiercely.

Bill raised his eyes heavenwards. 'Okay,' he sighed. 'If you're *involved* with Zak—'

'I'm not *involved* with him, either,' she insisted.

'Bill, you of all people know exactly why I'm spending time with Zak Prince.'

'And a lot of good it's doing me!' he snapped. 'From the looks of this photograph, you're too busy socializing with the man to have come up with anything on him of any interest!'

Anything sensational, Tyler knew he meant. Something, as she spent more time with Zak, she was becoming increasingly reluctant to do even if she did find out any deep, dark secrets about him!

A great reporter she was turning out to be! Maybe Rufus had been right after all—she really wasn't hard enough for the cut-throat career of journalism. Maybe she should just give up and— No, she mustn't even think that way. She *had* to succeed at this. She just *had* to. It was what she had said she would do when she had walked out on her life six months ago, and she had to do it!

'All I'm trying to say, Tyler…' Bill sighed his frustration with the situation '…is if you do get involved with the man then give us the heads up on it first, hmm? Remember where your loyalties lie, okay,' he added before going back to his office, the slamming of the door behind him enough to confirm his bad temper.

If Tyler had needed any confirmation. Which she didn't.

She looked down at the photograph again. Could anyone tell it was her? Really tell, unless—like Bill— they already knew she was spending time with Zak? Probably not, she decided critically. In fact, it could have been any one of hundreds, thousands, of tiny brunettes getting smilingly into the cab.

And yet, under any other circumstances, she would

have been proud to be photographed with Zak Prince, would have been ecstatic if she really were the 'mystery lady' in his life. If she were the woman in his life at all!

But this was different. This was deliberate stalking, and not just by one reporter or photographer, but a number of them. Which meant she had to take action immediately. If it was Jane Morrow behind this, then she had to somehow find her and stop this vendetta against the Prince family, as well as herself. Before someone really got hurt.

'Tyler!' A pleased voice broke into her reverie.

She looked up to see Perry entering the office, relieved to see the cheerful grin on his face. She had to admit to having avoided him since his declaration of love the other day, but there was nothing in his smiling face now to indicate the incident had ever happened. Which was fine with her. She liked Perry; in fact, he was the only real friend she had made in England, and she certainly didn't want to spend the rest of her time here avoiding him.

'Perry,' she returned warmly, at the same time turning the newspaper on her desk face downwards; she didn't want to start Perry off again on his dire warnings about Zak. She had already had enough of those this morning from Bill! 'I think Bill is looking for you,' she informed him.

Perry glanced across at their boss's office. 'Is that good or bad?' he asked as he sat on the side of her desk, as handsome as ever in casual tee shirt and denims.

Why couldn't she have fallen in love with nice, uncomplicated Perry? Why couldn't she have fallen in love with anyone except Zak Prince?

Because she hadn't, she accepted heavily. It was Zak that she loved, that she would probably always love.

She shrugged, standing up. 'I'm really not sure.' She avoided answering the question. 'And I'm afraid I have to get going now; I have an appointment this morning.'

'Zak Prince again?' Perry frowned.

'Just my luck, huh.' She deliberately made light of the subject.

'How about lunch later?' Perry stood up too, blue eyes intent.

She gave a regretful grimace. 'I'm really not sure, Perry. I'll call you, okay?' She smiled encouragingly. Although not too much so; she didn't want to give Perry the wrong impression. Again.

She was still a little stunned by Perry's proclaimed feelings for her. She didn't think she had given him any encouragement, but she couldn't be sure. Especially when Zak and Bill both seemed to assume that Perry was her boyfriend!

'Fine,' he said breezily, obviously determined to keep this conversation light and unpressured.

To her relief. They might never get back to that easygoing friendship they had once shared—at least, as far as she was concerned—but it would be nice if they could at least talk to each other without embarrassment.

'See you later, maybe,' she told him as she left.

The conversations with Bill and Perry had seriously cut in on her time, meaning she would have to go straight to Zak's hotel, rather than trying to find Jane Morrow first. But she would take the earliest opportunity to get to her—she had to stop this harassment before it got completely out of hand.

But she had other things on her mind now apart from Jane Morrow or Perry. Thanks to the photograph in that paper, she was absolutely dreading meeting up with Zak this morning. It would be just too much to hope that he hadn't seen that phograph. And even if he hadn't, she knew, in the circumstances, that she would have to tell him about it.

He had already seen it!

One look at his long-suffering expression as he opened the door to her knock, and Tyler knew there were no confessions or explanations necessary. Although she was a little taken aback by his first comment!

'I'm really sorry to be putting you through all this, Tyler.'

'I—you're sorry?' She blinked up at him; this was not the reaction she had been expecting from him.

'Yes,' Zak rasped. 'Someone, it appears, is playing games with us. And I don't like it.'

Tyler thought she knew exactly who that someone was, but she was still loath to bring Jane Morrow's name into the conversation. She had managed to make one brief call on her mobile on the journey over here, but Jane Morrow's last employer had refused to even talk about the woman. His secretary had been a little more forthcoming, commenting that she believed the other woman was now a literary agent.

Tyler hadn't yet had time to follow that lead up, but she would do so once she left Zak later today.

In the meantime, Zak's reaction to the photograph of the two of them was something of a surprise.

'Maybe someone just got lucky?' She shrugged as she walked into his suite.

'No, I don't think so,' Zak murmured as he closed the door behind her. 'It seems too—insistent, for that.'

'Insistent?' she repeated lightly—knowing exactly how insistent Jane Morrow could be! 'Because of the première on Saturday, maybe?' she suggested. 'After all, that's sure to increase the interest being shown in you by the press. And talking of Saturday,' she added determinedly, 'I hope you've found someone else to accompany you to the première?'

Zak shot her a mocking glance. 'Now why would I do a thing like that?'

Because there was this—thing, between them, that shouldn't be there. A sort of frisson that appeared whenever she was anywhere near him, which set all of her senses and nerve endings onto alert. It was there now, had sprung into action the moment she'd looked at him. No, even before she'd looked at him, the excitement singing in her veins having increased with every passing mile of the journey over here.

God, she loved this man. Loved everything about him. The way that his honey-blond hair fell endearingly over his brow, each of those handsomely chiselled features that so often contained such teasing mischief, the way he looked good wearing a faded tee shirt and scruffy denims that moulded to the hard contours of his waist and hips, even his bare feet sensual in their male perfection. And she wasn't even a person who particularly liked feet! But she loved Zak's feet, as she loved everything else about him…

She gave a wistful sigh before answering him. 'It really isn't my scene, Zak.'

Which was yet another lie on her part. Before

England, before she'd become simply Tyler Wood, she had attended numerous movie premières, as well as charity balls and fund-raising events for everything from underprivileged children to an endangered species of monkey in the African jungle.

In the States, she could have attended the première of *Gunslinger* with little reaction, except the usual prestigious mention of her having been there. As Tyler Harwood she would have been *expected* to be there!

What would Zak have made of her then? A vacuous social butterfly who picked and chose to put the weight of her name to whatever charitable fancy took her at the time.

Would he have even *liked* Tyler Harwood? Somehow she doubted that. Just as she knew he certainly wasn't going to like Tyler Wood once she had written her scandalous exposé on him!

What a depressing thought.

'Tyler?' Zak was looking at her searchingly now. 'Tyler, are you crying?'

She hadn't thought that she was. In fact, if anyone else had asked her that question she would have answered a scornful 'no'. But just Zak asking the question seemed to make it so, hot tears burning behind her lids before falling down her cheeks. Making it impossible for her to deny it!

'Damn it, you *are* crying!' Zak groaned even as he reached to take her into his arms, holding her closely against him, one hand cradling the back of her head, the other moving soothingly up and down her spine.

Oh, God…!

Those already alerted nerve endings and senses suddenly went berserk as the feel and smell of Zak bombarded them, her knees feeling weak and wobbly as she clung to the broad width of his shoulders.

'If you don't want to go to the première, then you don't have to!' Zak muttered, straightening slightly, both hands moving up to cradle either side of her tear-wet face as he kissed first one damp eye and then the other. 'I hate it when you cry,' he grated. 'Even if you do look more beautiful than ever,' he added huskily as he looked down at her.

Tyler gave a choked laugh. 'Then you're the first man I've ever known to find red eyes, soggy cheeks and a runny nose beautiful!'

'On you I do,' he assured her. 'Although I'm not sure I like the idea of other men having made you cry.' He frowned darkly.

'Just you, hmm?' she teased, very aware that at this moment the world had narrowed down to just the two of them, Tyler and Zak, Zak and Tyler, that anything else, her past, Zak's present, their lack of a future to-gether, had faded completely into the background.

Zak shook his head. 'I don't want to make you cry, Tyler. Making you cry doesn't come anywhere near the list of things I would like to do to you!'

Her heart actually seemed to stop beating com-pletely for a moment or two, her breathing catching in her throat as she stared up at him. The blue of his eyes was deeper than ever, her own image reflected back at her in the black depths of his dilated pupils.

She swallowed hard before drawing in a shaky breath. 'You have a list of things you'd like to do to me?'

'I have a list,' he confirmed softly. 'And last night's chaste kiss goodnight isn't anywhere on it!' he joked.

She had gone to bed dreaming about that kiss! Had

lain awake for hours, it seemed, hugging that kiss tightly to her.

Because she knew her time with Zak was limited? Because she knew that once she had found his Achilles heel, and written about it, that Zak would never want to see her again?

Yes, because of both of those things, she acknowledged heavily. Both of them, and at the same time neither of them. She could take, oh-so-briefly, the little Zak had intimated he was prepared to give, aware from what he had said just now that he was open to the suggestion of an affair between them. But when he learnt the truth about her, when *The Daily Informer* hit him right between the eyes with where that intimacy had taken him, he was only going to hate her all the more.

She didn't want that. Couldn't live with that.

'I have a list, too,' she told him brightly, stepping back from him to turn away from the sudden confusion she could read in his expression, to reach into the depths of one of the leg pockets of her combat trousers. 'Here it is.' She produced her notebook, turning it to the applicable page before handing it to him, at the same time hardening her heart to the disappointment she could now see clearly on his face.

She had made enough mistakes in her life already without adding a relationship with Zak to their number! It was far too late to stop herself from falling in love with him, but she couldn't further complicate that by entering into a full-scale relationship with him, a relationship he could later accuse her of using to her advantage.

Even if every instinct in her body cried out to be in his arms, in his bed, and damn the consequences!

Zak looked down at the notepad Tyler had handed him, taking longer than usual in his confusion to sort out the jumble of letters into some sort of readable order. But once he did, he realized this was the list of questions Tyler had intended asking him today in connection with the article she was writing.

How the hell had they moved from her being beautiful, and his having a list of things he wanted to do to her, to *this*!

'I know it probably looks a bit daunting,' Tyler continued in that bright, jaunty voice. 'But if we just go through them one at a time, I'm sure we can—'

'Tyler, don't talk to me as if I'm six years old!' he growled, closing the notepad with a firm snap before flinging it down onto the coffee-table. 'What the hell happened to the tears? A few minutes ago you were in my arms because you were upset, and now you're— well, now you're back to business!' And while she might be able to turn her emotions on and off at will, he certainly couldn't—his body was still hard from her close proximity. An arousal she must have been well aware of!

Was that the reason she had pulled back when she did? Was Tyler the one playing games now? Damn it, he was thirty-six years old—he didn't play that sort of game. With anyone.

She frowned. 'I think it's for the best, don't you?'

Whose best? His? He certainly didn't enjoy these hot and cold moods of Tyler's, having to draw back from the brink time and time again.

So it must be for Tyler herself. But why? She was attracted to him; he was experienced enough to be completely sure of that! So what was holding her back? Another man? She had told him she wasn't involved with Perry Morgan, that she lived alone, but that didn't mean there wasn't someone waiting for her back home in the States...

It was the only explanation that seemed to make any sense. And while he might applaud her will-power in resisting the attraction between the two of them, couldn't she see that the fact there was an attraction between them meant she couldn't be completely emotionally committed to this relationship back home?

'Tyler—'

'Zak, you may as well stop right there, because I am not going to have an affair with you!' she cut in forcefully as he would have made a step towards her, at the same time holding up one of her hands to ward him off.

He came to an abrupt halt, his eyes glowing with anger that she felt she had to hold him off at all. 'It's usually polite to wait until you're asked!' he snapped, not enjoying the way she flinched at his words, but at the same time needing to hurt her as she was hurting him.

Because he liked Tyler. Hell, he more than liked her! He had never felt this way before. Never wanted to kiss a woman, and yet at the same time protect her, in the way that he wanted to with Tyler.

He looked forward to seeing her every day, had woken up this morning with a smile on his lips because he had known that in a few hours he was going to see Tyler again.

He had spent most of yesterday trying to find out more about her—and not succeeding too well, he admitted—but now, today, he had realized that he didn't need to know any more about her than he already did, that it didn't matter any more, that just being near her was enough.

He was in love with Tyler!

And that emotion was completely alien to him. Totally. Oh, he'd had crushes on girls when he was in high school, had liked and enjoyed the company of several of the women he had been involved with over the years, but nothing he had felt for them was anything like what he now felt for Tyler. Just the anticipation of seeing her again was enough to make him feel good, being with her somehow making him complete.

That she didn't feel the same way about him was painfully obvious! Feeling as he did, he could never have pulled back from her in the way she had from him just now. Damn it, despite everything, he still wanted to take her in his arms and make love with her!

'I'm sorry.' Her gaze didn't quite meet his now. 'You're right, I shouldn't have just assumed—maybe I should just go now? I mean, I doubt you will want to continue with the interview today after—this,' she added awkwardly.

This? She called it 'this' in that way? He had just realized that he was in love for the first—and last?—time in his life, and she dismissed it as if what was happening between them was something rather unpleasant she would rather just forget!

Tyler didn't feel the same way that he did, he told himself again, feeling a sharp pain strike his heart. She couldn't, or they wouldn't even be having this soul-destroying conversation.

It was ironic really, if he thought about it. The Eternal Bachelor, Zak Prince. The Elusive Prince. The

Prince of Princes. All of the ridiculous names the media had labelled him with over the years! And when he did finally fall in love, when he no longer wanted to be elusive, or indeed a bachelor, the woman he was in love with didn't feel the same way about him!

It would even be funny—if it didn't hurt so much!

'You're right, I don't want to continue with the interview,' Zak bit out harshly, turning away; just looking at Tyler right now was too much.

Tyler looked uncomfortable now. 'Er—shall I come back tomorrow, then?'

Tomorrow? Would anything have changed by tomorrow? Would he no longer be in love with Tyler? Would she have suddenly discovered that she loved him, after all? None of those things was likely to happen, Zak chided himself bitterly—but especially the last one. Which was the only one that mattered.

'I'll call you,' he snapped. 'At the newspaper,' he added as he realized he didn't even have her mobile number. 'Later,' he rasped. Much, much later. Next century, maybe!

'Fine,' she accepted shakily. 'I—there's a few things I need to do today, anyway.'

What things? Zak wanted to know. And who, if anyone, was she doing them with?

This was unbearable!

Zak Prince, the man who never became seriously involved, was in love with a woman who refused to even tell him her private telephone number, let alone anything else about her life! She knew all there was to know about him, and he—

The phone rang. He had never thought he would be grateful for the interruption of the ringing of the telephone, and he scowled as he saw Tyler was just as relieved. 'Stay where you are,' he instructed grimly before picking up the receiver, his eyes widening as he easily recognized the voice on the other end of the line. 'Max, it's the middle of the night in LA!' he calculated after a brief glance at his wrist-watch.

'Still early,' his friend dismissed airily. 'Besides, you told me to call you if I came up with any answers for you on this Tyler Wood thing. Although I think I should warn you, old buddy, this isn't coming for free, I'm going to want some answers about her from you in return.'

'Fire away,' Zak invited, watching Tyler with narrowed eyes even as he listened to Max.

She had moved to look out of the window, giving every appearance of not listening to his end of the telephone conversation. Not that there was a lot to hear, Zak deliberately keeping his responses to Max to a simple yes or no.

Which wasn't to say he wasn't finding Max's conversation interesting. Because he was. *Very* interesting.

'I owe you one, Max,' he told the other man warmly when Max had finished talking. 'But later, okay?'

'The fair Tyler wouldn't happen to be there right now, would she?' Max guessed astutely.

'As a matter of fact, yes,' Zak confirmed. 'And it's brunette, not blonde.'

'Beautiful?'

'Oh, yes.'

'I'll leave you to it, then.' The other man chuckled before ringing off.

Zak put the receiver down slowly before looking across at Tyler as she turned to look at him, the silence stretching between them as his gaze narrowed.

'What?' she finally questioned, her chin raised defensively, her body tense.

'That was a friend of mine in LA,' Zak told her unnecessarily; she had to have been able to work that much out from his conversation. 'It appears that Tyler Wood never wrote an article on Gerald Knight in any publication in America.'

He watched with interest as she visibly paled.

'You've been lying to me, Tyler.'

CHAPTER TWELVE

TYLER stared at Zak, unable to speak, unable to think, it seemed. He— They— It—

'You've been checking up on me?' she finally managed to gasp.

She had suspected as much yesterday, but nothing had prepared her for this. So much for warning Gerald not to say anything!

With the release of her vocal cords, her thoughts began to race too. Zak had someone in America checking up on something she had told him. If he had gone to that extreme about a casual remark, what else had he done? That visit to Bill Graham yesterday—had that been checking up on her too, rather than discussing the première as Zak had claimed?

Dear God, what else had this Max in America managed to find out about her?

Zak's mouth twisted humourlessly. 'Don't go all pretend indignation on me, Tyler—'

'There's no pretence about it!' she said heatedly, an angry red haze blinding her to anything else but the fact that Zak had been making enquiries about a Tyler Wood back home.

How had Zak's friend got his information? Whom had he talked to in order to find out there was no article on Gerald Knight written by Tyler Wood? Because if he had talked to the wrong people—

She didn't even want to think about that! Besides, Rufus was in New York, not Los Angeles, and as such it was highly unlikely that he would get to hear about Max's enquiries. And even if he did, he might not connect her to the Tyler Wood they were talking about.

Keep telling yourself that, Tyler! Rufus, she knew from experience, had far-reaching tentacles in the media world, and it wasn't such a big step to take to get Tyler Wood from Tyler Harwood! She should have chosen a completely different pseudonym, but she'd stuck to something close to her real name because she'd known she'd forget to answer to it otherwise!

She glared at Zak. 'You had absolutely *no* right to pry into my personal life—'

'Your *professional* life, actually, Tyler,' he corrected her calmly. 'Something that, in the circumstances, I have a perfect right to ask about. And I'm still waiting for an answer,' he reminded her.

'And you'll continue to wait,' she spat. 'Because, after this, I have no intention of telling you anything. In fact, I think it might be better if we terminated this whole interview right now.'

She knew it would be suicide as far as her career at *The Daily Informer* was concerned; Bill Graham had left her in absolutely no doubts about that. But far better she get fired from the paper than Zak continued to probe into her background in this intrusive way. If she were no longer pursuing this exclusive with him, he would have no further reason to ask questions about her, here or in America.

The ironic thing was, if he just asked his sister Stazy the right questions, she could tell him everything about Tyler he might ever wish to know! Well, as much as Stazy was aware of, anyway.

'Running away, Tyler?' Zak jeered.

As far and as fast as her legs—and possibly a jet plane?—could carry her!

But where could she go? France? She only spoke a rudimentary French, certainly not enough to live and work in the country. Germany? Ditto. In fact, that applied to all the European countries. Canada, maybe? The same language, and yet still a separate country. Hmm, maybe that would be worth considering—

'Tyler?' Zak's voice brought her sharply out of her reverie, his narrowed gaze fixed shrewdly on her as if he had half guessed that running away might be closer to the truth—and a lot more permanent—than he had thought.

'You seem to have all the answers, Zak,' she hissed, eyes flashing. 'Work it out for yourself!' She was so angry with him that half of her just wanted to lash out at him. But the other half of her wanted to dissolve into tears again!

She had known Zak was trouble from the moment she had met him; what she hadn't realized was that he wouldn't be satisfied with just stealing her heart, he would completely knock her legs out from under her careerwise too. Bill Graham would have no other choice but to fire her for incompetence after she failed to get a story on Zak—and she wasn't sure she didn't deserve it!

She had come to England to prove herself, as a reporter and as a person, and so far she had completely blown the story of the decade by allowing Nik Prince to play on her emotions, and now she had compounded that mistake by falling in love with his brother. To add insult to injury, she also had another man, a man she thought of only as a friend, madly in love with her, which had made life decidedly complicated.

Maybe she really wasn't safe to be let out on her own!

Zak was shaking his head now. 'You have no reason to run away from me.'

'Oh, yes, I most certainly do. Why couldn't you just leave things alone, Zak?' Her voice, to her chagrin, broke emotionally this time, instantly betraying how distressed she was by his actions.

'What is it, Tyler?' He looked at her searchingly. 'Who are you running away from?'

She couldn't tell him—if there was still even the tiniest chance she could prove herself as a reporter, then she would. With or without Zak's input.

'Today? That would be you,' she snapped. 'But tomorrow it could be someone completely different.'

'I don't believe it—you aren't a woman who runs away. Towards something, maybe, but never away from it.'

It was what she had told herself when she had left New York six months ago, but maybe she had been wrong about that, too? Maybe she had been running away all this time?

The truth was, she could have found her own apartment in New York, could have found a job too— maybe not reporting, because Rufus really did have a finger in every media pie in New York. But she could have found a job of some sort, could still have proved her independence that way.

Couldn't she?

She just didn't know any more. Falling in love with Zak, having him talk to her in this way, having him believe she was fearless, had shaken her belief in what she was doing.

She swallowed hard. 'Zak, you don't know me. You

may think, with that call from your friend, that you know more about me now than you did last night. But you don't really know me,' she repeated flatly, not even sure she knew herself any more.

She needed to go somewhere, completely quiet and free from stress, and work out exactly what she was doing with her life.

'But, don't you see? I'm *trying* to know you!' Zak practically growled in frustration.

She gave a humourless smile. 'When you think that you do know me, give me a call, hmm? I'd like to know the answer to that one, too!'

'Tyler, is this reaction just because I had a call from a friend in LA?'

'Not really,' she sighed. 'But perhaps we should just forget doing the interview, and I'll do what I can to stop the invasion of your privacy that's been happening the last few days—'

'You *know* who it is?' He frowned as he glanced down at the photograph of the two of them in the newspaper.

'Yes, I think so. But don't worry, I'll deal with it.'

'You'll—!' Zak broke off exasperatedly. 'Tyler, just give me a name and I'll deal with it myself.'

She met his gaze unflinchingly. She still didn't want to bring Jane Morrow's name into any conversation with him. In typical protective Prince fashion, he was already up in arms about the mischief Jane Morrow had tried to cause between Nik and Jinx. If he thought Tyler was contacting her again, he'd probably assume Jinx's ex-editor was still intent on making mischief, and that Tyler was aiding and abetting her to get a good story!

'I don't think so.' She shook her head, turning away

so that he wouldn't see the tears gathering in her eyes—she had to get out of here before she shed any of those! 'If you'll excuse me, I think I should go now—'

'Just like that?' He grasped her arm and turned her back to face him. 'Tyler, what the hell is going on here? Three days ago you were desperate for this interview, and now you're just walking away? I don't get it.'

Desperate? Was that really how she had appeared to him on Monday morning? Yes, she probably had, she thought, feeling rather crushed.

Three days ago, before she'd come to know this man, she had been hungry for his story, determined to prove herself, no matter what the cost. Now she no longer knew what she wanted. Except she didn't want to do anything that would hurt Zak. And she didn't want anyone else to do anything to hurt him, either…

She gave a dismissive shrug. 'It isn't working out the way I expected.' And how! Despite her schoolgirl crush, falling in love with Zak had never been part of her plan.

'And just what did you expect?' Zak asked.

In all honesty? After the things she had read about him, the charmed life he led, the women he was involved with, she had thought Zak Prince would shatter all her girlhood illusions and turn out to be a pampered, arrogant man who revelled in being a movie star. What she had discovered was that she couldn't have been more wrong…

'Let me guess—more glitz and glamour!' Zak snorted in disgust as he read her thoughts. 'That isn't who I am, Tyler, it's what people like you make me out to be!'

People like her…

But she wasn't like those other reporters who would do anything for a story. That was the problem. If she had uncovered nothing else this week, she had at least realized that about herself. And if she were to leave here with any of her dignity intact, then she had to go now—before she made a complete idiot of herself and started blubbing all over the place again!

She smiled a little sadly. 'Unfortunately, glitz and glamour are what the readers of *The Daily Informer* like to read with their Sunday morning cereal and toast. You simply don't measure up to your pre-publicity, Zak.'

Ouch! That had hurt her to say, so heaven knew how Zak felt about it. If the tightening of his mouth, and the dangerous narrowing of his eyes were anything to go by, then not very good!

'I can honestly say that you don't measure up to yours, either,' he scorned. 'And I'm not referring to the fact that you weren't the man I was originally expecting!'

Ouch, again! On a more personal level this time. It was definitely time for her to go, before this conversation developed into a slanging match.

She feigned an unconcerned shrug. 'Then I guess we were both disappointed, weren't we?'

He nodded, a nerve pulsing in his rock-hard jaw. 'I guess we were.'

Tyler swallowed hard, knowing she had succeeded in what she had set out to do; if only alienating Zak like this didn't hurt so much! 'I'd better go, then,' she muttered.

'I think you better had,' Zak agreed icily before turning away from her.

Tyler gave one last, longing glance at the long length of that back turned so uncompromisingly towards her, knowing she hadn't just terminated her interview with Zak, that she had also effectively ended her career as a reporter. Before it had even begun, really.

She left the hotel suite, not knowing where she was going or what she was going to do now...

'Why are you looking so down in the mouth, Zak?' his brother Rik asked as he walked into Stazy's kitchen.

Zak glanced up from where he had been staring unseeingly into his empty coffee mug. 'When did you get back from France?'

'It's good to see you too!' Rik retorted sarcastically. 'And I got back a couple of hours ago, if you're really interested. Which, I suspect, you're really not,' he said astutely as he sat down opposite Zak at the kitchen table.

'Stazy didn't mention you were back,' Zak frowned. Although considering he'd been in this morose mood ever since he'd arrived half an hour ago, that wasn't really so surprising! 'And it is good to see you,' he added, trying to smile and at the same time doing his best to shake off his despondent mood.

His hotel suite had suddenly seemed small and oppressive after Tyler had left earlier, and so with nothing else to do, and nowhere else to go, Zak had come round to see Stazy. Their sister was upstairs at the moment bathing her baby son, Sam.

'How was Paris?' he asked Rik, more for something to say, really, than because he was actually interested.

Rik grinned. 'As beautiful and inspirational as ever.

I was on such a roll with this new screenplay I'm writing that I didn't really want to break off and leave,' he added wistfully.

Zak knew that, for some reason, Rik always worked well in Paris, that he loved everything about the place; which was why, when he was working on a new screenplay, he invariably chose to go there to do it.

'Then why did you?' he asked, making patterns in the sugar-bowl with his spoon now.

Where was Tyler now? Zak wondered. Had she so much as given him a second thought after leaving the hotel earlier? Or was she, having given up on this exclusive with him, already hot on the trail of some other so-called star? Someone a bit more cooperative than he had been, perhaps!

The latter probably, he decided with a heavy sigh. How could his life, the bachelor life he had always enjoyed to the full, suddenly seem so empty and pointless? Even the anticipation of the movie he was due to start work on next week didn't particularly interest him.

'What?' he questioned sharply, having glanced up to find Rik quietly watching him, dark brows raised.

'The première of *Gunslinger*,' Rik announced. 'Saturday. That's why I came back. I was the screenwriter, remember?'

'Oh. Yeah.' Zak gave an awkward grimace.

How could he have forgotten that Rik had written the screenplay to his last film? He was afraid he knew the answer to that only too well: because Tyler completely occupied all his thoughts—how she looked, how she talked, how much he loved her!

'What's wrong, Zak?' his brother probed gently.

He stiffened immediately. 'Why should you imagine there's anything wrong?'

'Oh, come on, Zak,' Rik reproved. 'I'm your brother, okay. I know when there's something wrong. You aren't your usual cheerful self, for one thing,' he continued as Zak would have protested again. 'In fact, I would go so far as to say—hey, this doesn't have anything to do with your "mystery lady", does it?' he pounced with a speculative raise of an eyebrow. 'It does have something to do with her!' He grinned as Zak scowled blackly. 'Who is she, Zak? Anyone that I know? Or that I'm going to know...?'

'Leave it alone, Rik,' Zak growled, blue eyes narrowed in warning.

'Leave what alone?' Stazy enquired as she returned from successfully bathing her young son and putting him in his cot for his afternoon nap.

'I was just asking Zak about the "mystery lady",' Rik answered.

'Tyler?' Stazy frowned as she turned from pouring herself a mug of coffee. 'What about her?'

Was it Zak's imagination or did Stazy suddenly look a little uncomfortable? No, he was sure he wasn't imagining it; there was a definite frown between Stazy's troubled grey eyes.

'I think Zak is actually in love,' Rik said as he stared at him in astonishment; all of Zak's family were aware of his reluctance to get seriously involved with anyone.

But it hadn't been reluctance exactly, Zak realized now. It had been more to do with the fact that he had never met the right woman before. Before Tyler...

'In love? With Tyler?' Stazy's voice rose in agitation as she looked at him with some concern now. 'I thought the two of you seemed—quite friendly, last night, but she assured me that— Zak, it isn't a good idea for you to get involved with Tyler. I—you—she isn't quite what she seems.'

Zak studied his sister through narrowed eyes. Stazy was obviously seriously anxious about something. And if it involved Tyler, then he wanted to know what it was. More than that, he *needed* to know what it was!

'Then what is she?' he asked, every inch of his body tense as he waited for Stazy's answer.

'I—she—' Stazy broke off awkwardly. 'I promised her I wouldn't talk about it—wouldn't tell you about it, unless I thought your not knowing was going to hurt you in some way.'

Zak stood up suddenly, staring at his sister incredulously. 'Stazy, you've known me for all of your twenty-two years. I'm your brother, for goodness' sake, and yet you're telling me that in spite of all that you've chosen to keep the confidence of a woman you *only met for the first time last night*?' His voice rose in volume the longer he talked without taking a break, so that his final few words actually came out as an accusing shout. And he never shouted. Had never found anything disturbing enough in his adult life to shout about.

A fact Stazy was well aware of, if her startled expression was anything to go by. 'It wasn't like that,' she defended herself heatedly. 'You told me—you both said— Zak, is Rik right? Are you in love with Tyler?'

His jaw clenched as he gritted his teeth. 'And if I am?' he finally grated through barely moving lips.

'Oh, Zak, no!' Stazy groaned. 'I realized who she

really was the moment I met her last night. And she didn't deny it when I challenged her upstairs.'

'Hey, don't cry, Stazy.' Rik stood up to go to their sister as she looked in danger of doing exactly that.

Great, just great! Zak thought; he had now succeeded in reducing both the women he loved to tears in one single day!

'You couldn't have known, Stazy,' he tried to soothe his sister, feeling like a complete heel now. 'I didn't discover myself how I really felt about her until this morning. But if I'm understanding you correctly, you're telling me that Tyler isn't really Tyler?'

That was something he didn't understand at all. How could Tyler not be Tyler? And if she wasn't Tyler, then who the hell was she?

CHAPTER THIRTEEN

'AND SO, you see, Tyler, the only reason I spoke to you the other evening was because I wanted to thank you,' Jane Morrow told her happily.

Tyler stared at the other woman in disbelief. True to her promise to Zak earlier, she had finally managed to track Jane Morrow down to the literary agency she now worked for, the two women going to a coffee bar nearby so that they could talk privately.

Only for the other woman to turn around and actually thank her for getting her sacked from her last job because she absolutely loved her new one!

Tyler frowned. 'You aren't angry? Resentful? Vengeful?' she probed.

'Heavens, no.' The other woman laughed. 'Of course I was all of those things at the time.' She grimaced ruefully. 'But I love what I'm doing now, and if I hadn't literally been given the push then I wouldn't be doing it.' She blushed slightly. 'There's also a man in the office who—well, my life has completely turned around, I can assure you. Which was why I tried to thank you when I saw you at O'Malley's on Tuesday.'

Unfortunately, this also meant that Jane Morrow wasn't the person responsible for the gossip, setting David Miller on them, or the photograph!

Then who was? Tyler was at a complete loss. The only consolation—if it could be called that!—was that now she had terminated her interview with Zak, perhaps those other things would stop too.

Zak…

God, how just thinking about him made her heart ache!

Enough for her to wish she hadn't turned down the chance of an affair with him?

Oh, yes! In fact, since she had left his hotel a couple of hours ago, she had twice turned around with the intention of going back, apologizing for the things she had said, and telling him she had made a mistake about having a relationship with him, however temporary.

It was always when she reached this part of her apology that she stopped herself from doing any such thing.

As Zak had pointed out so succinctly, he hadn't actually asked her to have an affair with him, so how could she go back and tell him she was more than willing, after all?

She couldn't. And after all those things she had said to him, those deliberately hurtful things, she couldn't ask him to resume the interview, either.

Besides, the interview wasn't something she wanted to do any more. She had realized, at some point during that hurtful conversation with Zak this morning, that she couldn't do this, that dredging up secrets and scandals in other people's lives, and then making them public, wasn't for her. That reporting wasn't for her…

A part of the reason for that decision, she knew, was because someone had been doing exactly that to Zak and herself the last few days, and she had found it despicable.

Oh, she had received her fair share of publicity as Tyler Harwood but, probably because of Rufus's influence, it had never been of a scandalous or hurtful nature; the hounding of the last few days had been both those things.

Quite what she was going to do next, stay in England or return to the States, she had no idea yet, but her time at *The Daily Informer* was definitely at an end.

Which was why, when Zak walked into the newsroom of the paper an hour later, she was in the middle of clearing all her personal belongings from her desk!

She could feel her face pale as she watched him stride across the room, tersely acknowledging a couple of reporters who said hello to him, while at the same time his razor-sharp gaze remained firmly fixed on Tyler.

What was he doing here? She had thought after this morning that she would never see him again, except on a movie screen, and yet three hours after they had parted so badly, here he was.

But perhaps he wasn't here to see her? He had come to see Bill Graham the last time, so perhaps—

'Tyler *Harwood*, isn't it?' he snarled as he came to a halt beside her desk.

Tyler instantly felt her legs go weak at the knees. He knew. How? His sister must have told him…

Zak looked at her coldly, his gaze raking over her with obvious contempt. 'I have absolutely no idea what game you've been playing with me, Miss Harwood—'

'Tyler,' she interjected, her lips feeling numb. If only her heart felt the same way! 'Didn't Stazy tell you? Explain why—'

'My sister,' he cut in icily, 'trusting soul that she is, is of the opinion that there are certain—aspects, of your pretence, that you should tell me yourself!' His acidic tone told Tyler exactly what he thought of that!

He was angry, and Tyler knew he had a perfect right to be with her. But not with his sister. Stazy wasn't the one who deserved Zak's justifiable fury.

'I was the one who asked her to help me, okay?' Tyler told him fiercely. 'And she assured me that she would only do so as long as it didn't hurt you.'

'Speculative gossip and damning photographs didn't qualify as that to you, hmm?' Zak growled.

He couldn't *still* think Tyler was in some way responsible for those things? But what could she tell him to convince him otherwise? Jane Morrow was so obviously out of the equation now, and Tyler had no one else to pin it on. And already lying to Zak about her identity wasn't exactly the best way to go about convincing him she hadn't lied to him about anything else either!

Zak looked disgusted. 'No wonder you were so upset this morning by my phone call with Max in Los Angeles; did you think he was going to expose you for who you really are?'

She flinched at his disparaging tone. 'Hardly,' she came back flatly. 'LA isn't somewhere I go too often!'

'Not glitzy and glamorous enough for the rich society darling of New York?' Zak returned pointedly.

Their obviously heated conversation was attracting quite a lot of attention, a hush having fallen over the newsroom ever since Zak had stalked in.

So much so that Bill Graham was curious enough to wander over to his open office door. 'Twice in one week, Zak?' he taunted the younger man. 'Careful, or I'll think you're playing favourites with my reporters.'

'I can't see a single reporter in this room I would

even give the time of day to!' Zak ground out, giving the other man a glacial glare, his hands clenched at his sides.

There was an audible gasp around the room, a certain hostility in the air now, too.

It was all her fault, Tyler realized dismally, knowing that it was her Zak was angry with, her he had directed that insulting remark to. But he had insulted every other reporter in the room to do it!

'Why don't you step into my office, Zak, and we can talk there?' Bill invited pleasantly, only those that knew him well able to recognize the steely edge to his tone. Tyler had come to know him quite well the last six months. Although not quite as well, she had discovered an hour or so ago, as she had thought she had...!

'Tyler can join us if she cares to,' Bill added persuasively as Zak made no move to join him.

She gave a fierce shake of her head. 'I won't if you don't mind, Bill, I still have some things to do here. But you two go right ahead,' she offered—and then she could make good her escape. Zak was pretty scary in this mood. Not that it wasn't wholly merited, but it was still scary!

His gaze speared her once more, before he turned back to the older man. 'Why not?' he bit out, not sparing Tyler so much as a second glance as he strode across to join Bill.

That was just fine with her! She wanted out of here, anyway. Even more so since Zak had just insulted half the people she had worked with for the last six months, all of them now looking at her with varying degrees of perplexity. And why not? They knew as well as she did that she was the reason Zak Prince had just been uncharacteristically rude to them.

The sooner she got out of here—and away from Zak—the better for everyone!

'Exactly what do you think you're doing, Zak?' Bill Graham queried as he closed the office door before moving to sit behind his desk.

Zak didn't answer, choosing instead to stride restlessly up and down the small confines of the room; his conversation with Tyler just now had left him feeling like a caged tiger who needed to bite someone!

To be truthful, he wasn't a hundred per cent certain what he was doing here himself. Except he had felt a need, after talking to Stazy, to at least let Tyler know the game was up.

Tyler Harwood. Pampered heiress. Society princess. The list of names the media had dubbed her was endless.

He should perhaps have guessed something didn't quite add up about Tyler Wood—her friendship with Gerald Knight, for one thing, the Vera Wang dress for another; they were hardly in keeping with the junior reporter she was supposed to be. Hell, he had guessed there was something different about her, just not the full extent of that difference!

And why was he so furious about it? Because she had lied to him? Hidden a huge part of herself from him? Did that make her other than the woman he had fallen in love with? He didn't know!

Bill tried again. 'Unless I'm mistaken, you were giving Tyler a hard time just now.'

Zak gave a derisive snort. 'I want to shake her until her teeth rattle!'

Bill pulled a face. 'Oh, I think you shook her up quite enough—without getting physical about it!'

Zak glowered down at the older man. 'She made a fool out of me! She made a fool out of you, too,' he pointed out. 'Do you have any idea who she really is?'

'I know exactly who she is, Zak,' Bill revealed softly. 'I've always known.'

Zak blinked, stopping the pacing to stare at the other man now. Bill Graham *knew*—

'Sit down, Zak.' Bill sighed wearily. 'Please,' he added as Zak didn't move.

He dropped down into the chair on the opposite side of the desk, still more livid than he'd ever been in his life.

'Better,' Bill approved. 'Now let's set the record straight. Of course I know who Tyler is; her only qualification as editor of her college newspaper certainly didn't merit me going to all the trouble of taking her on as a junior reporter! No, I did that as a favour to an old friend.' He shrugged. 'But, you know, Tyler surprised me,' he continued. 'She's good, Zak. Maybe not as a reporter on a tabloid newspaper,' he conceded ruefully. 'But her style of writing is excellent.'

'I wouldn't know,' Zak muttered.

The other man gave him a frown. 'Thirty years ago, when we actually reported the news and not this rubbish about who's sleeping with who this week, Tyler would have become a star reporter. Putting it bluntly, she's too good a writer to waste her talents on a newspaper like this one. Besides,' he added with a small smile, 'she has a conscience.'

Zak didn't want to hear that, or what a good writer she was; he was still too angry with her for that. 'You said you employed Tyler initially as a favour to an old friend...?' he prompted shrewdly.

'So I did.' Bill gave a laughing acknowledgement of that shrewdness. 'Tyler's father Rufus Harwood is a very old friend. I owe him more than one. He called me, explained about Tyler being in London looking for a job; I hired her.'

Rufus Harwood was someone Zak had heard of, a media mogul of mega proportions. He owned a television network in the USA, several radio stations, plus several newspapers.

Zak shook his head. 'But how could he possibly know, when Tyler walked out claiming she was going to make it as a reporter—' at least Stazy had confided some things in him! '—that she would come to this paper to get a job?'

'He couldn't,' Bill admitted. 'But Rufus was pretty sure she wouldn't get a job without proper experience on any other paper—and he was right! Even I wouldn't have given her a job without Rufus's request. As predicted, she was turned down by quite a few before she came here. And you know the rest!'

Rufus Harwood. Tyler's father. An extremely powerful man, not to be taken lightly, if the publicity about him was to be believed. And Zak had no reason to believe it wasn't. Why else would his only child decide to leave her home, her country, in order to become her own person and try to make it by herself?

Zak couldn't fault her for doing that. Only for using him, deceiving him, in order to do it.

'I was just lucky she came here,' Bill continued seriously. 'She's a lovely woman, Zak. Stubborn too, of course,' he added with more than a touch of admiration. 'She wasn't at all happy with the man Rufus picked out for her to marry.'

Marry? Tyler was *engaged*?

Zak must have looked as though he was about to do somebody some serious physical damage, because Bill said hurriedly, 'I said she wasn't happy, Zak. In fact she totally rejected any idea of marrying Richard Astor-Wilson.' He chuckled. 'That must have really upset Rufus!'

'Richard Astor-Wilson?' Zak choked.

That was yet another name he knew. Old family. Old money. One of the most powerful families in New York. And Tyler had refused to marry the only son and heir!

'Can you believe it?' Bill nodded as he saw Zak's expression. 'You have to like and admire Tyler just for doing that.' He sighed. 'It's a pity she's leaving. I'm going to miss—'

'She's leaving?' Zak echoed sharply.

'In fact, she was clearing her desk when you arrived—' He broke off as Zak stood up to walk over to the internal windows and look out into the main newsroom.

Tyler was nowhere to be seen. The desk where she had been sitting when he'd arrived was completely empty too.

'She messed up with that story on your brother Nik and his girlfriend—now his wife, of course.' Bill shrugged as Zak turned back to him accusingly. 'Plus she didn't deliver the story on you, either,' he added, eyeing Zak challengingly.

'So you just *fired* her?' Zak exploded.

Tyler had gone? To God knew where—because he certainly didn't!

'No, I did *not* fire her.' Bill bristled irritably. 'She may have thought I was going to, though. She was on a warning to dig up as much fodder for the gossip columns on you as she could, or she was out,' he explained. 'I was never going to do it, of course, but—'

'Because you *owed* Rufus Harwood!' Zak gibed.

'I just wanted to prove to her that she was in the wrong line of work.'

Tyler was gone! It was really all that Zak could think about at the moment. 'Did she know you only employed her initially because of who her father is?'

'She does now,' Bill replied.

Zak frowned. 'But not before?'

Bill quirked greying brows. 'What do you think?'

'I think—' Zak spoke between his teeth '—that if she had known, she would have told you to go to hell and your job along with you!'

'There you go.' The older man gave a satisfied smile. 'You know she's a good kid, too. So why are you giving her such a hard time?'

Zak opened his mouth to answer the other man, and then closed it again. Why *was* he giving her such a hard time?

Because she had lied to him about who she really was? Zak supposed she hadn't exactly lied—she had just been economical with the truth. Or was the real reason he was so angry because he had fallen in love with her, and she didn't return those feelings? Yes, that was probably closer to the truth!

'I didn't sack her, Zak,' Bill Graham repeated quietly. 'She resigned, effective immediately, because she couldn't bring herself to write that story on Nik and Jinx last month. Because, in spite of believing I was going to sack her if she didn't come up with some juicy gossip about you, she couldn't do that either. I told you, the girl has a conscience.'

Zak frowned. 'So there actually was no exclusive article for the Sunday magazine? No feature piece?'

'Nope,' the other man confirmed. 'I'm afraid that what *The Daily Informer* does best is scandal!'

Now Zak was totally confused. Tyler must have felt pretty strongly about making it on her own to have gone to the lengths she had, to have given up all the pampered luxury she was used to, the social recognition, to become a junior reporter on a less-than-reputable newspaper, using the tube for transport, living in a small apartment. And, at a guess, not always having the money to eat properly...

But given two assignments by her editor, first the story on Nik and Jinx, and now another one on him, Tyler had not written either and had simply packed up her things and left. Because her *emotions* were involved?

Zak fervently hoped that, where he was concerned, Tyler getting emotionally involved was a really good sign...

'I may not have sacked Tyler, Zak, but I did have reason to sack someone else this morning,' Bill Graham interrupted his thoughts.

Zak's interest sharpened, deepening further at the pointed way the other man returned his gaze. 'Morgan...?' he guessed.

Bill gave a humourless smile. 'Morgan.' He nodded, his mouth tightening. 'If anyone asks me I shall say he resigned for personal reasons, but within these four walls...? I don't take kindly to one of my staff giving stories and photographs to rival newspapers!'

'So Perry Morgan was responsible for the gossip about the "mystery lady" in my life? But why would he do something like that to Tyler? I thought the two of them were friends.' More than friends, he recalled jealously.

'It wasn't aimed at Tyler, Zak, it was aimed at you,' Bill said. 'He's in love with Tyler—I'm pretty sure she doesn't return the feeling,' Bill assured him. 'If she did, none of this would have happened.'

'I don't understand you.'

Bill sighed. 'He muttered something about a photograph he accidentally took of you and Tyler, that you were annoyed about it, and had told Tyler so in no uncertain terms. I think he reasoned—if it can be called that!—that if he could cause enough of a rift between you, if you thought it was Tyler responsible for those things, that he could stop any sort of—friendship, shall we say?—developing between the two of you. Did he succeed?' Bill asked with more than a touch of mockery.

'Only up to a point,' Zak admitted, remembering the accusations he had hurled at Tyler after each of those incidents. Totally undeserved accusations, it now seemed...

'I'm not even going to ask where you're going.' The seasoned editor laughed as Zak moved towards the door. 'Tell her she should write a book.'

'What?'

'Tell Tyler she should write a book. A biography, maybe. Her research is excellent, her style of writing even more so. Tell her to write Rufus's biography.' Bill grinned wickedly. 'Rufus would love that!'

Zak gave a rueful shake of his head, once again turning to leave, before stopping again, his expression rather pained as he turned back to the other man. 'I don't have Tyler's address,' he admitted irritably.

He wasn't sure that admission merited quite that amount of laughter from the other man!

CHAPTER FOURTEEN

TYLER stared apprehensively at her apartment door as the knock sounded for a second time.

Could it be Zak come to insult her some more? Well, she couldn't take any more today. She already felt so brittle she was in danger of snapping in two. One more insult from him and she was likely to do exactly that!

Today had already been so awful. So awful that, apart from a single telephone call when she'd got in, and a half-hearted attempt to pack a suitcase, she hadn't had the energy to accomplish anything else towards leaving.

'Tyler? Are you in there?' Perry's voice asked through the door. 'Open the door if you are; I really need to talk to you.'

It was Perry. Not Zak.

But of course it wasn't Zak, she derided herself even as she moved to answer the door; Zak had already said everything to her that he needed to say!

'Tyler!' Perry greeted her with obvious relief as she opened the door. 'What's going on?' he demanded as he followed her into the apartment. 'You didn't call me about lunch, and when I telephoned the paper Kelly told me that you'd been sacked.'

'Resigned,' Tyler corrected wearily. 'I resigned, I wasn't sacked,' she explained as he still looked puzzled.

'But—where are you going?' Perry frowned as he spotted the partly packed suitcase in her bedroom.

She moved to close the bedroom door. 'Home, I thought.' She attempted to smile.

'You were just going to pack up and go?' he said indignantly. 'Without telling me?'

'Of course not.' She sighed, not sure that was exactly the truth.

Perry had been the last thing on her mind today, hence her having completely forgotten to telephone him about having lunch together. Oh, she probably would have thought about calling him to say goodbye. Eventually.

'I'm not leaving right this minute,' she said flatly.

'I don't see why you have to go at all,' Perry objected. 'I—Tyler, I've resigned too—'

'Oh, Perry, no!' She groaned, knowing her own resignation had to be responsible for that. It was bad enough that her life had turned upside down; she didn't want to be responsible for messing up Perry's life too.

He shrugged. 'I don't want to continue working at the paper if you aren't there too.'

She already was responsible, she realized. This situation just seemed to be getting worse and worse.

'Look, I don't see why you have to go anywhere, Tyler,' Perry was saying eagerly. 'We can go freelance. In fact, this just might be the opportunity we've both been looking for— What do you mean, no?' he snapped as Tyler simply shook her head at his suggestion.

'Perry, I haven't been completely honest with you. I'm not who you think I am. My name isn't even

Wood. I—my father is Rufus Harwood,' she told him reluctantly.

'I already know that.' He waved a hand in dismissal of her revelation. 'You—'

'You do?' Tyler was stunned. Perry knew?

'Of course. I'm not completely stupid, you know. I recognized you within days of you coming to work at the paper,' he said. 'It doesn't have to change anything; I'll simply come back to America with you, if that's where you want to go. Once your father sees how much in love with you I am, then I'm sure he'll give his consent to—'

'Perry, stop!' Tyler cried; hadn't he heard anything she'd said to him the other day after he'd told her he was in love with her? Obviously not.

And it was more than a little disquieting to realize that Perry had known exactly who she was all along...

'You can't possibly be in love with me; you don't even know me,' she protested.

She couldn't believe the irony—such a short time ago she'd told Zak that he didn't know her either...not that he'd claimed he was in love with her!

Zak.

She had to stop thinking about him! Otherwise she was going to go quietly insane. But one thing was for certain: loving Zak as she did, she couldn't even give Perry the ghost of a hope that she would ever return his feelings.

'I'm sorry, Perry, I really am. But I—I'm going home alone.' It was going to be traumatic enough as it was, without dragging Perry into it.

He stared at her for several moments, and then he gave a thoughtful nod of his head. 'You're right, that's probably the best way to go about this. You can explain the situation to your family, and then I can join you in a couple of days—'

'Perry, you aren't listening to me!' she interrupted, upset that he was being so persistent. 'I—I'm not in love with you—'

'Of course you are,' he contradicted. 'You've just become a little confused the last few days. It's all Zak Prince's fault.' He scowled at the mention of the other man. 'The two of us were getting along really well until he came along. And we'll—'

'Perry, no!' The more he continued in this vein the more agitated she was becoming. 'I'm really not in love with you. I like you very much. You've been a good friend to me since I came here, but I—' Her words were cut off as Perry pulled her into his arms and tried to kiss her.

It was the end of the line for Tyler, and she finally started to get angry with him. She didn't want this. Didn't return his feelings. And she never would.

She wrenched her mouth away from his, pushing hard against his chest in an effort to release herself. 'I said *no*, Perry! And I meant it!' Her earlier unease, when he'd told her that he had known who she was all this time, returned as she saw the determination on his face as he glowered down at her.

'It's him, isn't it?' Perry accused, his good-looking face becoming positively menacing in his anger.

She swallowed hard. 'I don't know what you mean, but for the sake of our friendship—'

'It isn't friendship I want from you!' he snapped. 'You know what I want—' He broke off as a knock sounded on the apartment door, his expression becoming even uglier.

Tyler felt overwhelming relief at the interruption.

She didn't care who was on the other side of that door:
the landlord asking for his rent, someone conducting
a survey, or even someone trying to sell her something—she just wanted to kiss whoever it was. Perry
was frightening in this mood, and had become a man
she didn't even recognize. There was also the fact that
he had always known her real identity to contend
with…

'Is that him now?' Perry asked as she moved to
open the door. 'Zak Prince on his white charger come
to rescue the fair maiden?' he jeered unpleasantly.

She wished that it were Zak, even while she told
herself that it wasn't. But a door-to-door salesman
might not be enough for her to get Perry out of her
apartment.

'Zak!' Tyler stared incredulously up at the man as
he stood grim-faced on the other side of the door, that
grimness increasing as he looked past her into the
apartment and saw Perry there.

'Tyler.' He nodded tersely, the expression in his
eyes unreadable. 'I haven't caught you at an incon-
venient moment, have I?'

Despite the edge of sarcasm to his tone, Tyler could
still have laughed with the relief at his being here. 'Not
at all. Come inside.' She grasped his arm and practically pulled him into the apartment, only to find herself standing awkwardly between the two men as they
glared at each other.

She had no idea what Zak was doing here, and really didn't care if it was only to level fresh accusations
at her; he was here, and now she could perhaps get
Perry, who had turned into such a stranger, to leave.

'You aren't wanted here, Prince,' Perry announced
suddenly.

Tyler gasped at his insulting tone. Not only was it incredibly rude, it was also patently untrue; she so *did* want Zak here!

But Zak didn't look at all perturbed by the other man's aggressive tone, his expression slightly softened as he looked down at her. 'Is that true, Tyler?' he asked softly. 'Do you want me to go?'

'No!' she responded sharply, and then forced herself to take a deep breath and calm down. 'No, of course I don't,' she answered more calmly. 'Actually, Perry, I thought you were the one who was leaving?' She looked at him challengingly.

He raised dark brows. 'Hardly,' he drawled, reaching out to pull her against his side, his arm moving possessively about her waist. 'As it happens, Prince, you're here just in time to offer us your congratulations; Tyler has just agreed to marry me.'

Tyler stared up at him in consternation, more and more convinced that Perry had only become her friend because of who she really was.

Because he couldn't honestly think that she—

There was no way that she had ever agreed—

He just couldn't be serious!

But she could see, by the tight clenching of his jaw, the dangerous glitter in his eyes, that he was. Deadly serious.

Zak felt as if someone had just punched him in the stomach. Tyler couldn't be going to marry this man. If she was going to marry anyone, it was going to be *him*!

Now he really did feel as if someone had just knocked all the air from his lungs! He had never even contemplated marrying anyone before, and now, in the space of four days, he knew that his life would never be complete again if it didn't have Tyler in it, as his wife. That he would never be wholly alive again if she married another man!

And then he caught sight of the expression on Tyler's face: disbelief mixed with dismay. Hardly the look of a woman who had just agreed to marry the man she loved!

Zak straightened. 'Really? Then Tyler must have a very forgiving nature,' he said in a hard voice.

Perry's arm tightened about Tyler's waist; it was enough to make Zak feel like hitting him!

'What do you mean?' Tyler asked, a little confused.

Zak glared at the other man. 'Do you want to tell her or shall I?'

An angry flush darkened Perry's cheeks. 'I have no idea what you're talking about,' he protested.

'Neither do I, Zak.' Tyler still sounded confused.

If Perry Morgan didn't stop touching Tyler in that intimately possessive way soon, Zak knew he wasn't going to be responsible for his actions!

He thrust his hands into the pockets of his denims to keep them out of mischief. 'Only that your friend here is the one responsible for that article and photograph of us appearing in those newspapers. Or didn't he tell you that?' he added softly as he saw Tyler turn to stare incredulously at the other man.

Tyler finally moved out of the other man's grasp—instantly lessening the pain in Zak's chest. 'Is this true, Perry?'

'Of course it isn't true,' Perry scorned. 'He's just telling you that to try and drive a wedge between us. Prince probably organized it himself—people like him thrive on publicity so much that they have to create their own!'

So far Zak had held off hitting the other man because he wasn't sure how Tyler would react to him doing that, but at this precise moment he was in danger of forgetting all about that and hitting Perry Morgan, anyway!

'Strange,' he grated, his hands bunched into fists now. 'That isn't the way Bill Graham tells it.'

'Bill?' Tyler echoed, looking very pale now. 'But what—?'

'Just ignore him, Tyler,' Perry Morgan cut in angrily. 'Bill Graham wouldn't give him the time of day, let alone tell him anything of such a personal nature!'

But as Zak and Tyler both knew, Bill had talked to him, not once, but twice, and he could see the memory of this morning's meeting, of the two men being together in Bill's office when she'd left, in her wide brown eyes.

'What do you think, Tyler? Did Bill Graham tell me he'd fired this guy or didn't he?' Zak arched blond brows in query.

Tyler looked as if she couldn't take much more, and when Zak thought of all she had already gone through this morning—the photograph in the newspaper, the argument with him, leaving the paper—he really wasn't surprised she looked slightly punch-drunk. He wished he could make this easier for her, but, if nothing else, she needed to know the truth about Perry Morgan.

She swallowed hard. 'I believe you when you say he did,' she said, moving away from Perry as he momentarily relaxed his hold. She turned to glare at him. 'What I find hard to believe is that you did those things, Perry!' Her voice shook with anger and her eyes flashed. 'And you told me you'd resigned because you didn't want to continue working there without me! I think you'd better leave right now.'

Perry Morgan's face flushed angrily. 'But we're getting married—'

'We most certainly are *not*!' Tyler snapped. 'We never were. Even if you hadn't done those awful things, I still wouldn't marry you. I already told you, I don't love you.'

Zak felt such relief at hearing these words, and looked admiringly at Tyler. He knew it was something of a cliché, but she really did look magnificent when she was angry, all five feet two inches of her proudly tense, the colour in her cheeks adding depth and sparkle to those beautiful brown eyes. And for once it wasn't him she was angry with!

'I suppose you think Tyler *Harwood* is too high and mighty to marry a mere photographer!' Perry Morgan sneered nastily, obviously realizing he had completely lost any chance of a relationship with her.

Tyler gave him a scathing glance. 'Make that *ex*-photographer! If I know Bill you'll be lucky to get a job working for the *Hicksville Chronicle* photographing baby shows! As for me,' she went on to ram the point home, 'I never had any intention of marrying you, either as Tyler Wood or Tyler Harwood!' She frowned. 'Admit it, it's only because you knew who I was all the time that you became my friend in the first place!'

Zak felt for her as her voice shook emotionally, knew how much this must have hurt her.

Perry Morgan gave her a thoroughly unpleasant smile. 'Why else would I bother with a junior reporter—and not a very good one, at that?'

'It's time for you to go—past time!' Tyler looked

at the man with cold, compelling eyes as she walked over and held the door open for him. 'And don't bother to find your way back. Ever!' she bit out icily as Perry Morgan walked jauntily across the room.

'You know, you really are a—'

'Just go, Morgan!' Zak snarled as the other man seemed about to launch into some verbal abuse that Tyler could very well do without.

He watched tensely as Perry did exactly that, ready to leap to Tyler's defence if the other man should so much as try to talk to her again. In fact, Zak was inwardly somewhat disappointed that he didn't; hitting Perry Morgan would have been a pleasure!

Tyler closed the door firmly, taking several seconds to compose herself before turning back to face Zak. 'Thank you,' she murmured huskily. 'I still can't believe he—but I should have known.' She sighed. 'He was the one to introduce me to David Miller a few months back. I guess I just didn't want to think that Perry had sold me out.' She looked at him apologetically. 'I really believed, until a short time ago, that it was Jane Morrow who was responsible for setting the press on us. I didn't want to mention her name before because—well, I'm sure you understand why I didn't...'

Zak took a surprised breath. Jane Morrow! *That* was who that blonde who'd come up to them outside O'Malley's on Monday night was! It was no wonder he hadn't recognized her immediately—the only time he'd been introduced to her was when he'd bumped into Nik having dinner with her, some weeks before Nik had met his wife.

Tyler shook her head. 'What could Perry possibly have hoped to achieve by doing those things?'

Was this the time to put forward Bill Graham's theory: that Perry Morgan had sensed the deepening feeling between her and Zak, and was determined to put a stop to it? Would Tyler be ready to hear that just yet?

Zak shrugged. 'I guess he was jealous of the time you were spending with me.'

Her eyes widened. 'But that was work. Business.'

Work. Business. The two words hit Zak like a slap in the face. Was that all he was to Tyler—work and business?

'Perhaps he really was in love with you?' Zak grated.

Her eyes flashed chocolate-brown fire. 'My father's money and prestige is what he was in love with! If that's his idea of love, he can keep it!'

It wasn't how Zak loved her, no. He just wanted to be with her every minute of the day and night, to share everything with her, to know and cherish everything about her, to have her cherish and love him in the same way…

'So what will you do now?' he asked. 'Bill tells me you've resigned from the paper.'

'I've already called my father and made my peace with him. I'm going home.'

'Before or after our date on Saturday?'

Tyler's eyes widened. 'You still want me to go to the première with you?'

'Why not?' He forced his reply to sound casual. 'It's a bit short notice to ask anyone else at this late date,' he added so that she wouldn't think he was about to go all domineering on her as Perry Morgan had.

She gave a rueful smile. 'That's honest, at least.

And after Perry's deceit—' her mouth tightened at the mention of the other man '—I need that. So, yes, I would love to attend the première with you.' She gave him a shaky smile. 'As Tyler Harwood, if that's okay with you?'

She could go as Tyler Smith as long as she went with him! Zak inwardly acknowledged with a definite lift of spirits. 'Fine. Oh, before I go…I have some words of wisdom for you from Bill.'

She looked wary now. 'Yes?'

Zak smiled reassuringly. 'He said to tell you your writing is too good for the tabloid press, and that you should write a book. A biography. He suggested your father as the subject of that biography.'

He was completely captivated as Tyler burst out laughing. 'Oh, Rufus would love that! He would probably disinherit me just for suggesting it!' Her eyes glowed mischievously. 'He's always said that the only good biographies are the ones that aren't written. In fact, he…' She trailed off, her expression thoughtful now. 'You know, it's actually not such a bad idea,' she said slowly. 'Although getting my father to agree to it could be interesting!'

'Think about it,' Zak suggested softly, happier now that he knew he would at least see Tyler again on Saturday evening. 'You could always write one on me first just to show him how good you are.'

Where the hell had that idea come from? He was about as keen to have his biography written as he was to have a tooth extracted! Except that having Tyler write his biography would mean he could keep her in his life for several more weeks, months, years…

'You?' Tyler looked as stunned at the suggestion as he had felt making it.

'Why not?' Zak shrugged.

'You can still ask me that after the disaster of the last four days?'

He wanted to ask her a lot more than that! And with the time he might have bought himself with the idea of her writing his biography, perhaps he could do just that.

'None of that was your fault. And to give you something to think about,' he added, walking over to the door now, 'that night at O'Malley's, when I was—less than polite to the waiter?'

'Yes?' she responded warily.

'The reason I reacted so badly to the disappearance of the duck that I usually ordered from the menu was because I'm severely dyslexic. I could probably have figured out some of the other dishes on the menu given time—but it would have been too obvious to you and everyone else that I was having problems reading. So I stuck to the easy option and just ordered a steak instead.'

Zak didn't give her a chance to make a reply before letting himself out of the apartment and closing the door quietly behind him.

It was time for the trust between them to begin…

CHAPTER FIFTEEN

'WHY did you tell me that about yourself?'

'Tell you what?' Zak asked innocently.

Tyler sat beside him in the back of the white chauffeur-driven limousine he had arrived in to pick her up for the première, the glass partition between them and the driver firmly closed.

Zak looked absolutely wonderful in his tuxedo, completely relaxed as he lounged in the seat beside her.

Tyler had been wondering for the last two days why he had suddenly told her on Thursday about his dyslexia. She knew that it wasn't public knowledge, that it was exactly the kind of juicy gossip she had been searching for in order to keep her job at *The Daily Informer*. That would probably still assure her a job there—if she wanted it. Which she didn't.

But that still didn't explain why Zak had confided in her in that sudden, unexpected way...

'Your dyslexia,' she reminded him, looking at him searchingly in the early-evening sunlight.

He shrugged. 'Another of my secrets is that I actually hate film premières! Acting is one thing, being the focus of all eyes, as myself, is something else.'

Why was he telling her these things, intensely private things? Was it just because of the biography he was suggesting she write about him?

Or was it something else?

She frowned, deciding there was only one way to find out...

'I hate caviare,' she revealed. 'And I had a lisp until I was ten, when an orthodontist, a brace, and a speech therapist sorted it out.'

Zak nodded in acknowledgement. 'I can't stand dill pickles in burgers. And I didn't kiss a girl until I was in tenth grade.'

'The girls at school called me Metal-mouth for two years. And I hate oysters.'

'My first date was a disaster; I threw up all over the girl at the top of a Ferris wheel. I hate squid.'

Tyler still had no idea where this was going, but she carried on anyway. Hoping! 'My first date was a disaster too; my mother insisted on coming along! I hate syrup on my pancakes.'

'Oh, now that's just going too far, Tyler,' Zak protested laughingly. 'No red-blooded American could possibly hate syrup on their pancakes!'

'I do,' she insisted. 'But I love strawberries and cream.'

'I love cold pizza for breakfast.'

'I love chocolate for breakfast.'

'I love English roast beef with all the trimmings.'

'I love something they call toad-in-the-hole. I know it sounds disgusting.' She laughed at his expression. 'But it's actually just sausages cooked in batter.'

'I prefer cricket to American baseball.'

'I love tennis more than either of them.'

'I love you.'

'I love— Zak?' Tyler stared up at him, wondering if she could possibly have just heard him correctly. Had Zak really said that he loved her?

'I didn't mean for it to come out quite like that,'

Zak muttered, shaking his head in self-disgust as he turned towards her in his car seat. 'I know this isn't the right time or place,' he added as they rapidly approached the theatre where his film was showing. 'I was going to show you this evening that being seen with me isn't all bad. Persuade you into perhaps staying on in England with the idea of writing my biography. And then, after a couple of weeks, I was going to—damn.' He groaned, raking his hand through his hair. 'It's true, Tyler, I do love you. But I'm not expecting—'

'I love you too, Zak,' she cut in shakily, wondering if she could possibly be dreaming all of this. 'I love you, too!' she repeated, her eyes glowing.

Zak's hands moved to cradle either side of her face as he looked intensely down at her. 'You do? You really do?' he asked uncertainly.

Tyler gave a choked laugh, encouraged by this uncertainty from a man who was always so self-assured. 'I've had a crush on you since I was fifteen years old!'

He made a face. 'I had a crush on Elizabeth Taylor when I was fifteen, but I didn't fall in love with her when I finally met her ten years ago!'

'Whereas I fell in love with you the moment I met you,' Tyler assured him.

Zak raised a mischievous eyebrow. 'You couldn't have done; I was rude and arrogant.'

'I loved you anyway,' Tyler insisted. 'I do love you, Zak. Very much,' she reiterated.

'Enough to marry me?' he probed gruffly, his gaze searching.

Her heart leapt just at the thought of being Zak's wife. But... 'You don't have to marry me if you don't want to,' she offered.

Zak grinned. 'Anything but marriage and your father would probably have me put in chains somewhere and throw away the key! In fact, I very much doubt whether he's going to be thrilled at the idea of having me for a son-in-law.'

Tyler shook her head. 'What my father really wants is grandchildren; I don't think he particularly cares who I marry in order for him to have them!' That was perhaps a slight exaggeration, but, after the long telephone conversations she had had with her father and mother over the last couple of days, she really did believe that as long as she was happy then her father would be happy for her. 'Besides—' she reached up and touched the hardness of Zak's clenched jaw '—this really has nothing to do with my father, Zak. Only you and me. Zak and Tyler.' God, how wonderful that sounded!

'Then marriage it is,' Zak declared firmly. 'How about we forget Tyler Wood and Tyler Harwood, and go for Tyler Prince instead?'

It sounded like heaven. Like all of her wishes coming true, she decided as Zak took her in his arms and began to kiss her.

Two days ago she had felt as if the bottom had dropped out of her world, just the thought of never seeing Zak again after tonight making her feel totally miserable. In fact, her crumbled dream of becoming a reporter had completely paled into insignificance in comparison with never seeing Zak again.

And now this!

It was so much more than she had ever hoped for. Zak loved her. She loved him. It was all that mattered.

Zak drew back reluctantly as the limousine pulled up in front of the theatre, accompanied by the sound of dozens of women screaming as they realized Zak was in this car.

Tyler wanted to scream with them, but settled for smiling proudly at his side as those women cheered and clapped as they walked the short distance into the theatre, camera bulbs flashing.

Zak's arm tightened about her waist. 'Your photograph is going to be splashed all over the front pages of the newspapers tomorrow,' he warned her.

Tyler shrugged. 'Who cares?' And she didn't. She would be happy to be photographed at Zak's side for the rest of her life.

'Richard Astor-Wilson might,' he teased.

Her eyes widened. 'You know about Richard too?'

Zak grinned. 'Bill Graham did. He and your father go way back, you know.'

'I do now. So much for striking out on my own, hmm?'

'But that's exactly what you did, Tyler,' Zak insisted. 'I'm sure Bill is serious about you writing a book.'

Tyler smiled. 'I've already mentioned it to my father. He's thinking about it.' She chuckled. 'That usually means yes! As for Richard...' She sighed. 'I'm afraid I wasn't very nice to him before I left New York.'

'Good,' Zak said with satisfaction.

She laughed. 'That's quite a fan club you have out there,' she murmured as the women could still be heard screaming Zak's name.

Zak's eyes were a deep, deep blue as he smiled down at her. 'A fan club of one is all I want,' he assured her huskily. 'As long as that one is you.'

'For always, Zak,' she promised as she reached up and kissed him.

'Always,' he vowed in return.

'Does the fact that the two of you can't seem to take your eyes off each other mean that I'm shortly to have another sister-in-law?'

Tyler turned curiously to the tall, dark-haired man who had spoken to them, instantly recognizing him as the youngest Prince brother, Rik.

Zak's arm moved lightly about her waist as he grinned at the younger man. 'You take it correctly, Rik.'

'That's great!' Rik bent to kiss Tyler warmly on the cheek. 'He's been moping around like a bear with a sore head the last couple of days,' he confided to her with an affectionate glance at his brother. 'You're a lucky man, Zak,' he congratulated as the two men shook hands.

'Your turn next.' Zak waggled his eyebrows suggestively at Rik.

'I'm happy as I am,' Rik protested.

'Is he?' Tyler whispered to Zak as Rik moved away to talk to one of the other actors who'd starred in *Gunslinger*.

'I'll tell you about it later,' Zak promised.

And Tyler didn't doubt that from now on they would tell each other everything.

No more secrets. Ever.

Exactly as it should be!

PRINCE'S LOVE-CHILD

PROLOGUE

'RIK…! Rik Prince, can that really be you...?'

He froze at the first sound of that husky, sensual voice. No—it was worse than that, he actually felt paralysed, every muscle and sinew immobile with shock, his chest having stopped rising and falling, only his heart, with a will of its own, continuing to beat. But faster, so much faster than normal, as if trying to protect itself from the onslaught of remembered pain.

That voice!

So easily recognisable, so painfully remembered. It was the voice that had spoken to him in his dreams so often in the past. The voice that, for months, had motivated him to pick up the telephone a dozen times a day, hoping to hear its honeyed warmth on the other end of the line…

Calls he had never made. But, he realised now, he hadn't thought of her for months; his previous unhappiness was completely buried.

Or so he had thought…

'Rik…?' The precisely English-accented tones were closer now.

In fact, as her hand reached out to touch him gently on his T-shirted back, Rik knew she had to be standing directly behind him.

How the hell was he supposed to deal with seeing her again after all this time?

He wasn't dealing with it at all at this moment; just standing here in the middle of the street, paralysed with shock, couldn't be classed as dealing with anything!

Breathe, you idiot, he instructed himself firmly, relieved when his body obeyed the command and his chest began to rise and fall once again. Now turn around, he ordered determinedly. Just turn around and face her. It couldn't be any harder than walking away from her had been five years ago.

Could it...?

If anything she was more beautiful than ever; tall, golden and tanned, with the most incredible green eyes he had ever seen. Diamond McCall. And how she lived up to that name—her beauty was dazzling.

Even in a skimpy pink T-shirt and ragged denim cut-offs, there was no doubting that this woman was *someone*. In Dee's case, despite or because of her melodious English tones, she was the present highest-paid actress in Hollywood, her name at the top of the credits, and enough to guarantee any movie she was in would be a box-office hit.

She was also someone else's wife...!

'I thought it was you!' she exclaimed excitedly now, her face alight with pleasure as she smiled at him. 'But how marvellous!' she beamed, one long, slender hand reaching out to grasp the strength of his bare forearm. 'I had heard that if you sat outside Fouquet's on the Champs-Elysées for long enough you would eventually see everyone in Paris who was anyone walking by, but I never believed it until now!' She gave an amazed shake of her head, long, honey-coloured hair swaying against her tanned shoulders. 'What on earth are you doing in Paris?'

His mind had gone completely blank. Had been so since the moment he looked into those deep green eyes.

Why was he here? In fact, who the hell was he? Damned if he knew...!

'Rik...?' Dee gave him a quizzical look now. 'You aren't still angry with me, are you?' she cooed.

Angry with her? Had he ever been angry with her? Hadn't his anger all been reserved for her manipulative stepmother and stepsister, both so determined that Dee would marry the mega-rich and powerful Jerome Powers? As he looked at Dee now, so beautiful, so intensely alive, it was difficult to believe anyone could ever be cruel or angry with her.

She gave him a poutingly reproving smile. 'At least say something, darling!'

He wasn't sure that he could, his tongue seeming cleaved to the roof of his mouth, like some awkward schoolboy. Which for a man of thirty-five, with a succession of screenwriting awards to his credit, plus ownership of a movie company with his older brothers, Nik and Zak, was pretty pathetic.

It was because he had had no warning of this meeting, he consoled himself.

Today had begun like any other day of his two months' stay in Paris: he woke at eight o'clock, went for a brisk walk beside the Seine, returned to his hotel for a breakfast of coffee and croissants and lingering over the newspaper, before venturing out again later in search of somewhere to eat lunch.

Nowhere in any of that relaxed routine had he had the least premonition that he would also see Dee McCall again today!

But he had to say something, couldn't stand here like a speechless moron for ever.

'You're looking well, Dee,' he finally managed gruffly, his American accent totally at variance with her softer English tones.

'So are you, Rik,' she returned softly, her eyes flirting with him beneath lowered dark lashes. 'Are you—?'

'Is—?' He broke off as they both began talking at once. 'You first,' he invited wryly.

He might not have thought of this woman for months—years?—but when he had, he had never imagined the two of them meeting like this, awkwardly, stilted, like two strangers who had never been madly in love with each other. He hadn't imagined Cathy and Heathcliffe either, but this—this was just banal!

Dee gave him a mischievous smile. 'I was just going to ask if you're here with someone.'

He shook his head. 'And I was just going to ask if you were here with Jerome.' Her husband. The man she had married five years ago instead of him. Despite all his pleadings for her to do otherwise.

It wasn't a period of his life he was particularly proud of, but at the time he had been so much in love with Dee that nothing else seemed to matter.

At the time…?

Yes, at the time, he realised dazedly now as he looked at her, because he wasn't still in love with Dee; time, and absence, had made that impossible to sustain. It was the memory of what they once had together, those fierce, snatched times together, that had kept her memory so much alive.

She had been so young, only twenty, on the way up in the world of acting, pressurised by her step-mother and stepsister into becoming engaged to and marrying Jerome Powers, then a man of forty and even more powerful in the world of media and enter-tainment than the three Prince brothers.

Rik had argued, Dee had been stubbornly adamant, tearfully pleading with him to understand that she had to marry Jerome in order to get away from her grasp-ing stepmother and stepsister. His promises that he could—and would—protect her in the same way, had all been tearfully rebuffed.

No, he wasn't still in love with Dee, but the anger he felt towards her stepmother and stepsister was still there!

'Dee-Dee, you have to come and look at the most beautiful little purse and pocketbook we found for you!' a man's deep voice interrupted.

Rik didn't need to turn to know who that man was; only one person called Diamond McCall Dee-Dee in that possessive tone; Jerome Powers, Dee's husband of the last five years.

'Hello, who—Rik...? Rik Prince!' Jerome greeted warmly as Rik finally steeled himself to turn and look at him. 'What on earth are you doing in Paris?'

Jerome smiled at him warmly, at the same time dropping a lightly possessive arm about Dee's shoulders.

It was impossible not to like this man, with his genuine warmth and charm, his iron-grey hair and sophisticated good looks attracting women of all ages. Even Rik couldn't help liking Jerome, and it would have been so much easier to dislike the man who was married to Dee.

'I was working for a while,' Rik answered, 'but now I'm just taking a couple of days' holiday before returning to the States.'

Jerome nodded. 'How are Nik and Zak? I heard they both got married recently. Making you the last of the Eligible Princes, I guess.' He grinned good-humouredly.

A grin Rik found very hard to return; if things had worked out for him five years ago he would have been the first of the Prince brothers to marry. Except the woman he had loved had married this guy instead...

'They're both good,' Rik nodded. 'Very happy, in fact.' Yet another reason for him to spend this time in Paris. Not that he begrudged his older brothers their newfound happiness, because he didn't, knew both of them were married to lovely women. But the settled happiness of his siblings made his own bachelor state seem all the more lonely.

Meeting Dee again like this in the company of her husband wasn't helping that situation.

'Excellent.' Jerome nodded happily. 'Dee-Dee, would you like to come and look in the store? I just know you're going to love the purse and pocketbook, and—hell, where are my manners?' Jerome shook his head self-disgustedly. 'I totally forgot to introduce Sapphie.' He turned to smile apologetically at the woman standing slightly behind him.

Rik hadn't even noticed the petite, auburn-haired figure until then—what man would when in the company of a golden goddess?

But as she stepped forward at Jerome's encouragement, shoulder-length auburn hair gleaming brightly in the sunlight, amber-coloured eyes gleaming like a cat's as she looked up at Rik challengingly, he felt the last vestiges of colour fade from his already pale face.

Today was already turning out as something of a shock; first the unexpected meeting with Dee and her husband, then the realisation that his love for Dee had died long ago. But now, with this other lady's appearance, it had just taken on nightmarish proportions!

Because he knew her.

He hadn't seen her for five years either, and their acquaintance had been brief—very brief!—but nevertheless he knew her.

In *every* sense of the word!

CHAPTER ONE

RIK PRINCE *had* recognised her, Sapphie realised with inner dismay as he continued to stare at her in disbelief.

Not that any of her own emotions showed—she kept her own expression deliberately bland, and betrayed none of her shock, or the effects of the painful memories that were flooding back: the love that had shaken her world apart after she had spent a night with this man. Most definitely, she showed none of the horror she felt inwardly at finding herself face to face with a man she had thought she'd never see again!

But then, it might have been OK if he hadn't so obviously recognised her *and* remembered too…!

Her small, pointed chin rose defensively as she thrust her hand out in greeting. 'Sapphie Benedict, Mr Prince,' she introduced herself with a pointedness that only a complete idiot could miss. And, despite the fact she knew that Rik Prince loved Dee to distraction, she didn't believe he *was* a complete idiot..just a selectively blind one!

Rik continued to stare at her, making no effort to take her outstretched hand, giving every impression of a man who had just been poleaxed.

Sapphie's direct stare turned to a glare as she mentally willed him to pull himself together and say

12

something. Anything. Just staring at her in this way was sure to be noticed, and commented on, by the other couple who were with them, and—

'Miss Benedict,' Rik Prince finally bit out tautly after briefly touching her hand. 'Or is that Mrs…?'

'It's Miss,' she corrected abruptly, her hand dropping back to her side, unobtrusively massaging the slight tingling of her fingers where he had briefly touched her.

Incredible…! She couldn't believe, after all this time, that she could still be so totally aware of this man. It had been five years, for goodness' sake; she should have got over this long ago!

'Much too formal,' Jerome put in with cheerful reproach. 'Rik and Sapphie sounds much more friendly!'

Friendly was the last thing Sapphie wanted to be with Rik Prince! *Especially* with Rik Prince. Something she intended making clear to him at the earliest opportunity. In fact…

'Why don't you take Dee to see those accessories she was interested in, Jerome?' she encouraged lightly. 'Rik and I will order more coffee for us all, and by the time the two of you get back we may have managed to get on to a first-name basis!'

'You will join us for coffee, Rik…?' Dee prompted huskily.

Sapphie's brows rose as Rik dragged his gaze away from hers in order to answer Dee in the affirmative.

Really, did the man have no sense whatsoever? she wondered impatiently; Dee and Jerome's suspicions were sure to be aroused if he didn't stop behaving in this way.

Not that Jerome seemed to have noticed anything unusual as he turned, smiling, to his wife. 'Come on, honey, I want to buy you an anniversary present,' he encouraged Dee indulgently. Then the two of them departed to go shopping.

Leaving behind them the kind of silence that could be cut with a knife!

But what else could Sapphie have done but encourage Jerome to take Dee away from here—even though the last thing she wanted was to be left alone with Rik Prince? He certainly hadn't been playing his part in the drama of two strangers being introduced for the first time.

'I thought Dee and Jerome's wedding anniversary was in September.' Rik suddenly spoke as he turned back from watching the couple leave.

'It is,' Sapphie sighed, moving to sit down at the table where Dee's coffee was cooling. 'Please—join me,' she invited curtly as Rik Prince continued to stand in the middle of the pavement, as if unsure what to do next.

She had seen that dazed look before on dozens of men's faces after spending time looking at Dee—seen it and, in this case, lamented it.

She slipped her sunglasses up in her hair as she continued to look at Rik Prince. He was just as handsome as she remembered: perhaps slightly leaner, but his dark hair was still as vibrantly overlong, brushed carelessly back from his brow, and his eyes as deep blue, his good-looking face all strong angles, and his muscular frame visible beneath the faded denims and cream polo-shirt he wore.

Finally he moved, his movements fluid as he sat down in the chair facing hers, his expression under control now, his eyes guarded by lowered lids.

Sapphie gave a frustrated sigh at his continued silence. Jerome might have been unaware of the intimacy between Dee and this man a few minutes ago, but she certainly hadn't been. She also questioned whether the meeting had happened by chance; if anyone had known how devastated Rik Prince had been five years ago when Dee married Jerome, then it was her. He had been in love with Dee then, and Sapphie had every reason to believe he was still in love with her now.

'Today is the anniversary of the day Dee and Jerome first met,' Sapphie informed him softly.

'I see,' he bit out tautly, the expression in those deep blue eyes still unreadable.

Sapphie wasn't sure at that moment which of the sudden impulses she felt was the stronger—the need to shake or hit him!

It had been five years, for goodness' sake; surely he had got over his feelings for Dee by now?

It had to be obvious to anyone looking at Dee and Jerome that, for the most part, theirs was a happy marriage. It had its occasional hiccup—like any other marriage—but even in these days of quick divorces and remarriages, it had to be clear that Dee and Jerome were destined to last for some time yet.

'I never—'

'Before—'

They both began talking at once, only to come to an awkward stop, then stare enquiringly at the other.

'Please,' Sapphie invited before turning smilingly to the waiter to order more coffee, only to turn back and find Rik Prince looking at her in brooding silence. 'You were about to say something,' she reminded him, unnerved by his steadily intense stare.

He seemed to mentally shake himself, sitting up straighter in the cane chair. 'I was going to say that, after all this time, I never expected to see you again.'

Amusement curved her lips. 'You mean, you hoped never to see me again!'

He frowned. 'If I had meant to say that, then that's what I would have said.'

'Oh, please.' Sapphie brushed his protest away with a wave of her hand. 'The sentiment, I can assure you,' she told him with feeling, 'is mutual!' She had never wanted to see him again, never wanted to even hear of him again, just wanted to block his existence even from her memory.

And yet now that she had seen him and spoken to him, she could see just how dearly familiar were his dark good looks and piercing blue eyes. Too familiar…!

Rik gave a humourless smile. 'That's honest, at least,' he drawled drily.

'It's a trait too few people possess nowadays. And, continuing to be honest,' she added, 'what I was going to say just now was that I feel, before Dee and Jerome return, which won't be too long now, I should make it perfectly clear to you that under no circumstances—and I do mean that,' she emphasised firmly, 'do I wish for either of them to discover we ever knew each other before today.' She looked at him challengingly.

He frowned for several long seconds, and then his brow cleared as he looked at her with mocking blue eyes. 'By saying that the two of us knew each other, I take it you mean—'

'I mean,' she put in forcefully, 'that I would rather Dee and Jerome believed we met for the first time today,' she explained clearly and succinctly.

Rik Prince gave an acknowledging inclination of his head, whatever disadvantage he had felt earlier seeming to have evaporated as he relaxed back in his chair, his eyes clearly showing his amusement now.

Well, she was glad he could find something funny about this situation—because she certainly couldn't!

'How does that sit with the honesty you mentioned only seconds ago?' he ventured sardonically.

'Oh, don't be so obtuse!' Sapphie replied impatiently. 'There's a time for honesty, and—'

'A time for dishonesty?' Rik finished derisively.

'Please don't tell me you're any more anxious than I am to admit to Dee and Jerome that the two of us stupidly spent the night together after their wedding!' She was breathing deeply in her agitation as she glared at him.

But her impatient anger couldn't keep the memories at bay of that night, of no words having been spoken between them as they'd seemed drawn to each other like magnets, of the passion they'd shared—a fierce and wondrous passion, as they'd sought oblivion in each other's arms.

Even now Sapphie could remember each caress, each kiss, their need wild and uninhibited, both of them seeming to recognise and accept that, in the clear light of the following day, they would each go their separate ways, never to see one another again.

And that was how it should have remained. How, if she had had her way, it *would* have remained!

'That day, you had just seen the woman you love marry someone else!' she prompted angrily.

Colour darkened his cheeks, his eyes the blue-grey of a stormy sea now. 'And if I had?' he bit out icily. 'What was your excuse?'

She could be selective, make excuses, could even evade the issue. But the truth, she knew—or at least the part she was willing to admit to Rik!—was much more likely to put an end to this conversation. 'Me?' she echoed self-disgustedly. 'I had just watched the man I loved marry someone else!' She now met Rik's gaze unflinchingly.

Because it was only part of the truth of what had happened to her that day. Sapphie had gone to Dee and Jerome's wedding believing she was still in love with Jerome, and had felt nothing but misery as she'd watched him marrying Dee.

But then something—she wasn't sure what—had made her glance around the church, and her eyes had come to rest abruptly on Rik Prince as he'd stared broodingly down the aisle at the couple being married, obviously as unhappy about it as she was.

Until that moment, love at first sight had just been a phrase to Sapphie, not something that ever happened to real people like her. Well, except perhaps those people who realised the following morning, as they looked at the person beside them in bed, that it had probably been lust at first sight, rather than love!

She wasn't one of those people; she'd woken at dawn the morning after Dee and Jerome's wedding to gaze hungrily at the man sleeping beside her, knowing that not only did she love every hard plane and hollow that made up his physical being, but that she also loved his gentleness, his intelligence, and sense of honour too.

She had gone to the wedding the day before believing herself in love with one man, but after the celebration had realised that she was irrevocably in love with another.

A man who'd made no secret of the fact that he was in love with Dee...

Jerome?

Was Sapphie Benedict referring to Jerome Powers?

Sapphie, with her mesmerising, amber-coloured eyes, and her grim determination to discuss and dismiss their first and—until now—only other meeting, had been hurting as much as Rik had five years ago because she'd been in love with Jerome Powers? She'd spent the wedding reception with him, and the night with him, because she had just watched the man she loved marry someone else?

But hadn't he just admitted to having done the same thing? Wasn't that night—and Sapphie herself—something he had kept buried deep at the back of his consciousness, the door to it tightly locked and bolted?

Yes, of course it was. But that was because he had always felt guilty about that night, about the fact that he had used Sapphie as a way of blocking out his pain. Knowing she had used him in the same way added a dimension now that filled him with anger. His fury wasn't logical, and it certainly wasn't fair, but it was how he felt, none the less.

'Are you still in love with Powers?' Rik rasped contemptuously. 'Is that the reason you're still hanging around the two of them? Hoping to step into Dee's shoes if the marriage should falter?'

'How dare you?' Sapphie gasped incredulously, having paled dramatically, those amber eyes the only colour in her face now. 'For your information, Mr Prince, I'm not hanging around the two of them at all. I happen to have been in Paris for four days now, doing some research. Dee and Jerome decided to stop off here yesterday in order to see me on their way to Dee's film première in London next week.'

'How convenient for you,' Rik scorned.

He hadn't even attempted to see Dee since her wedding day five years ago, whereas this woman appeared to have remained friends with both Dee and Jerome. Masochistic or what?

'It isn't convenient at all,' Sapphie came back forcefully. 'And as for my wanting to step into Dee's shoes if the marriage should falter—if you listened to what I said just now, then you'll have realised I used the past tense concerning my feelings towards Jerome. I *was* in love with him then, but I'm not now.' She was breathing hard in her agitation, her eyes sparkling with anger.

Considering how defensive she was, Rik wasn't sure that he believed her.

But somehow, looking into those amber-coloured eyes and seeing the contempt gleaming there, he doubted Sapphie Benedict cared whether he believed her or not!

What was hard to believe, as he looked at her now, seeing how her eyes gleamed challengingly, twin spots of fiery colour burned her cheeks, and the fullness of her mouth had thinned to a taut line, was that he had ever explored every inch of that slenderly tiny body, that he had run his hands time and again through the auburn thickness of her shoulder-length hair, kissed every inch of her gamin-featured beauty and tasted the intimate delight of her luscious lips and mouth.

Sapphie, as if becoming aware of Rik's lingering gaze, of the thoughts running through his head, seemed to gather herself up to attack. 'Let me make one thing clear, Mr Prince—'

'I thought it was to be Rik and Sapphie,' he reminded her tauntingly, smiling his thanks at the waiter as he placed the pot of fresh coffee and cups down on the table.

'Mr Prince,' Sapphie enunciated carefully once they were alone again, 'I don't know you. I don't want to know you. Is that clear enough for you?'

She really was beautiful, Rik acknowledged slightly dazedly; not that he had thought—even five years ago when he needed to block out the pain—that he would have been attracted to someone who wasn't beautiful. It just came as a surprise to him now to realise quite *how* beautiful Sapphie Benedict was.

More beautiful than Dee? Well…no. But Dee's beauty was made up of golden hues, whereas this woman was all fire and light; her hair, for example, gleamed red as the sunlight caught it, and her eyes had taken on the colour of leaping flames.

There was also the fact that, notwithstanding how much in love he'd been with Dee five years ago, the two of them had never gone any further than a few clandestine kisses. Whereas he and Sapphie Benedict had shared the most complete intimacy there was between a man and a woman.

'Very clear, Sapphie,' he finally answered her slowly. 'But if that really was the case, how would I know about the birthmark you have on your—?'

'Will you stop that?' she snapped furiously, sitting forward. 'Dee and Jerome are on their way back now,' she hissed warningly after a brief glance over his shoulder. 'This conversation is over as far as I'm concerned!'

Rik turned to give a cursory glance in the direction of the married couple as they strolled along hand in hand, pausing to look in a store window now, his mouth twisting with distaste even as he acknowledged how right they looked together: Dee so tall and goldenly beautiful, Jerome with that natural confidence of a successful middle-aged man.

'I would keep that emotion under wraps too, if I were you,' Sapphie bit out impatiently. 'Jealousy can be so unattractive!'

Rik turned back to find her looking at him scathingly. Jealousy? Of Jerome's role as Dee's husband, was what Sapphie meant. Was he still jealous of Jerome? No, in all honesty, he couldn't say that he was, any more.

Did that mean that he really was over his love for Dee…?

He raised dark brows as he returned Sapphie Benedict's challenging look. 'You would know, I suppose,' he drawled mockingly, but took no pleasure in the way her face fell at his deliberate taunt.

How ironic, how absolutely incredible, that the two of them should both have been in love with other people five years ago. Although Sapphie denied that she still felt that way about Jerome. And he… He realised with another lightening of his heart that, without even knowing it, he'd got over Dee. She was still one of the most beautiful women he had ever seen, but he could now view that beauty dispassionately.

Sapphie eyed him dismissively now. 'I never took you for an idiot, Rik. Misguided in your love for Dee, perhaps, but never an idiot.'

He looked at her curiously. 'You don't like Dee very much, do you?' he realised wonderingly; he had never met anyone before, male or female, who didn't instantly fall under Dee's charming spell. Although being in love with the other woman's husband would probably do it, he allowed.

'Of course I like Dee,' Sapphie bristled resentfully. 'Knowing a person's weaknesses and faults doesn't preclude your liking them.'

Rik gave her a rueful grin. 'Knowing mine doesn't seem to have endeared me to you!'

She eyed him bleakly. 'There are always exceptions to every rule,' she retorted before turning to smile warmly at Dee and Jerome as they rejoined them, her expression affectionately indulgent as she took in the new handbag that Dee carried. 'I see you preferred the larger design,' Sapphie teased.

Dee grinned unabashedly, her pleasure in the gift obvious. 'If you're going to have a designer bag, then it may as well be a big one!' She dropped gracefully into the chair next to Sapphie before placing the new purchase on the table. 'Isn't it absolutely gorgeous?'

The white bag, printed with a pattern of the designer's motif in different colours, was certainly big, Rik acknowledged. However, it also wasn't the little purse initially suggested. But then, why shouldn't Dee choose a much more expensive number? Jerome was so rich he made the multimillionaire Prince brothers look like paupers!

'It's lovely,' Sapphie assured the other woman warmly.

Rik couldn't help but admire, on the other couple's return, the way in which Sapphie seemed to have shaken off her obvious animosity towards him. Anyone glancing in their direction now would be sure to think they were just four friends enjoying a cup of coffee together on this glorious Parisian day.

Rik wasn't actually quite sure whether he could really class the four of them as friends, given all the emotions teeming beneath their surface politeness!

Nevertheless, he was reluctant for their time together to end. It had taken five years for him to meet Sapphie Benedict again and—surprisingly!—he found he was so intrigued, that he didn't want there to be another five before it happened again!

'I was just suggesting to Sapphie,' he gave her a sideways glance, his mouth quirking humorously as he noticed the disapproving tightening of her full lips, 'that it would a good idea if the four of us were to have dinner together this evening.'

He had turned back to the married couple by the time he made this suggestion, so he didn't actually see Sapphie's reaction to his suggestion—but he certainly felt it!

Shock was quickly followed by waves of pure animosity in his direction which she made no effort to conceal!

CHAPTER TWO

'YOU'RE incredibly stupid or totally insane—and as I don't believe for a moment that it's the latter, I can only assume that it's the former!' Sapphie spoke vehemently even as she marched her way past Rik and into the sitting-room of his hotel suite, not sparing her obviously luxurious surroundings a second glance as she turned to glare at him.

'Come in, why don't you?' Rik drawled sardonically, taking his time about closing the door and joining her.

Giving Sapphie the opportunity to take in exactly how handsome he looked in the black evening suit and snowy white shirt and black bow-tie. Not that she hadn't ever noticed how devastatingly attractive he was, it was just that he just looked breathtakingly so in this formal attire, every inch the wealthy and powerful screenwriter that he was.

She had responded to the way he looked five years ago, but also to the way he'd made her feel; she'd been attracted to his inborn confidence and sophistication as much as to his handsome features. But this was something else entirely.

Now he wasn't just Rik Prince, the youngest, and reputedly the most sensitive, of the powerful Prince brothers; now he was also the link between herself and the past, between her and...

No, she mustn't even go there! She had spent a night of mindless passion with this man, and he had to believe that was all they had shared.

He arched dark brows now as he eyed her teasingly. 'Am I to take it from your previous remark that you aren't looking forward to the four of us having dinner together this evening?'

Looking forward to it—it had to be the worst torture she could ever imagine!

Spending hours in Rik's company. Aware all that time that he was probably still in love with Dee. In a constant state of agitation herself, in case either Dee or Jerome said anything that might arouse Rik's suspicions. No, she wasn't looking forward to it at all!

But when Rik had made his suggestion earlier about dinner at Fouquet's, and it was greeted with such enthusiasm by Dee and Jerome, Sapphie simply hadn't been able to think of a good reason for not joining them. Especially as it had already been agreed earlier in the morning that she would eat with Dee and Jerome tonight. Besides, she dared not dine with all of them, because she was still nervous that either Dee or Jerome might unwittingly say something about Matthew...

Even so, she was sure that Rik had known earlier exactly how she felt about having dinner with him, since she'd spent the rest of their meeting this morning in silence, nodding her agreement to the suggestion they all meet in the hotel foyer downstairs at eight o'clock.

'Idiot!' she snapped now, totally immune to his admiring glance as he took in the black sheath knee-length dress she was wearing, and the way her auburn hair fell loose on the bareness of her shoulders. She gave an impatient shake of her head. 'This is a dangerous game you're playing—'

'Dangerous?' Rik echoed, dark brows arched mockingly. 'You aren't suddenly going to launch yourself at me in a passionate frenzy, are you?'

'Oh, very funny,' Sapphie bit out disgustedly. 'You are such a funny man, Rik. In fact, with your wit, I'm surprised you've never turned your talent to writing comedies!'

He grinned unconcernedly, an endearing dimple appearing in one cheek, obviously feeling completely relaxed about the evening ahead. 'I've never really thought about it,' he shrugged, 'but now that you mention it…' He smiled in the face of her obvious frustration. 'It's a little early yet for us to go and meet Dee and Jerome; would you care for a drink before we leave?'

As it had turned out, Rik and Dee and Jerome were all staying at the George V, just off the Champs-Elysées, whereas Sapphie had decided to stay in a more obscure—and less expensive!—hotel in one of the avenues off the Arc de Triomphe, so it had been decided that the three of them would meet in the foyer of the George V before strolling along to the restaurant.

And yes, Sapphie was well aware of the fact that it was too early to meet the other couple. Deliberately so. As this man had to be well aware.

'A brandy would be nice,' she accepted abruptly, having already noticed the untouched bottles of whisky and brandy on one of the side-tables. 'Thank you,' she added awkwardly.

'So far this evening you've called me "incredibly stupid" and an "idiot"—don't you think it's a little late for politeness?' He eyed her laughingly.

Sapphie felt a leap of awareness in her chest at how very attractive he was in this teasingly friendly mood. It would be so easy to forget everything else, and just enjoy being in his company...

His company was something she dared not risk enjoying! In fact, she couldn't let her guard down for even a second, had been a mass of churning emotions since the moment they'd met again this morning, feeling as if she were remaining only two steps ahead of a tsunami—and while it was increasing in force she was tiring fast!

She had to find a way of stopping it—stopping Rik—in his tracks!

'Thank you,' she murmured again as she took the glass of brandy from his hand and took a sip of the fiery liquid, hoping it would give her the courage she so badly needed.

Courage...? She was going to need more than courage if she was going to completely alienate Rik Prince. And that was exactly what she had to do—if she could stop him finding her amusing long enough to do it, that was!

Under other circumstances, meeting Rik again could have been the highlight of her trip to Paris. But as it was...

'Mr Prince—'

'You know, you really can't carry on being so formal with a man you've shared a bed with,' he cut in smoothly.

And a sofa. And the floor. Even the shower—if her memory served her correctly. And she knew that it did.

All of which would be better forgotten, let alone talked about! 'Rik,' she corrected tautly, sitting down in one of the armchairs and instantly wishing she hadn't, as Rik's gaze was drawn to the amount of silk-covered thigh revealed by her dress riding up her legs. 'The danger I was referring to has nothing to do with me—'

'Pity,' he responded, relaxing back in an armchair himself now as he looked across at her with narrowed eyes.

'—and everything to do with Dee and Jerome,' Sapphie continued determinedly.

She had given this a lot of thought when she returned to her hotel earlier—in the circumstances, how could she possibly think of anything else?—and had decided she couldn't make this personal, otherwise Rik's suspicions would be aroused anyway. So she had decided to make Dee and Jerome the issue instead.

It seemed to be working as Rik's mouth tightened, his expression grim. 'What about them?' There was a definite edge to his voice now. 'As you've already been at great pains to point out to me, they are obviously a happily married couple.'

'Yes, they are.' Sapphie nodded. 'But beneath his genial façade, Jerome is a very jealous man.'

Rik gave a slight inclination of his head. 'Dee is a lot younger than him, and a very beautiful woman.'

'She can also be a very silly one,' Sapphie told Rik with feeling. 'Not that it's her fault,' she added, remembering all too well Rik's earlier accusation that she didn't like Dee. Of course she liked Dee, but if this was going to work, then she had to exaggerate some of Dee's less admirable traits. 'Dee was very overindulged as a child. Her father adored her, always referred to her as his perfect diamond.' Sapphie shook her head. 'Is it any wonder that she grew up expecting every other man to adore her, too?'

'I don't know,' Rik said slowly. 'Is it?'

'Of course it's not,' Sapphie shot back. She wasn't getting through to him at all! 'I mentioned earlier that Dee and Jerome have had their share of hiccups...? Well, those hiccups usually occur after one of Dee's—flirtations. Jerome, understandably, resents any man who gets too close to his wife.'

'Understandably,' Rik echoed tightly. 'Although I still don't see what this has got to do with me.'

Sapphie eyed him exasperatedly; this wasn't going at all as she had planned. She had intended giving Rik a little friendly advice—such as 'stay away from Dee because of Jerome's jealousy'!—and he obviously wasn't getting it at all. She felt like boxing his ears now!

'You're in love with Dee—'

'Am I?'

She frowned frustratedly. 'Of course you are!'

'If you say so.' He shrugged.

'Look, I'm trying to help you,' she pressed on impatiently.

'So it would appear.'

She sighed at his lack of cooperation. 'The last man to get too close to Dee ended up losing his job on the *New York Times* newspaper and going back writing about cattle shows in his home state of Texas!' A fate that was a vast improvement on the one that had befallen Dee's admirer before that, an actor who was sacked from his role in a major film and was now working behind the counter of a fast-food chain!

Rik looked amused. 'And you think that might happen to me?' he queried. 'It's very nice of you to be so concerned on my behalf, Sapphie, but it really isn't necessary.'

She really wasn't getting through to him, was she? So much for advising him to stay away from both Dee and Jerome—and, as a consequence, away from her too; he just seemed to find her advice amusing!

'I am not concerned about you,' she stood up, deciding to try a different tack; if he didn't care about himself, then perhaps he would care on Dee's behalf. 'It's Dee I'm worried about.' She glared down at him.

Rik returned her gaze with cool blue eyes, his thoughts now unreadable behind a cold mask.

'Are you telling me,' he finally spoke carefully, 'that Jerome is likely to become violent towards Dee if—?'

'No, of course I'm not,' Sapphie denied exasperatedly; she just seemed to be making this situation worse, not better. And she had thought it couldn't get any worse! 'For all that she's emotionally immature,

Dee really does love Jerome. Being older than her, he gives her the stability she felt she had lost when her father died—'

'You presume to know an awful lot about the emotions of the woman who married the man with whom you yourself were in love,' Rik rasped harshly.

Perhaps she was getting through to him after all..he certainly didn't seem amused any more!

'I don't presume to know anything—'

'I think that you do.' Rik stood up in one fluid movement. 'And in the circumstances, I find your so-called concern for Dee a little—suspect, shall we say?'

He was very overbearing, towering over her like this, but Sapphie refused to back down now, finally feeling as if she was getting through to him. If she succeeded in getting him to back out of Dee's life— and consequently her own!—then she didn't care how intimidating he appeared!

'No, we will not say,' she replied tartly. 'As Dee's sister, of course I—'

'As her what?'

Sapphie instinctively took a step backwards at the vehemence in his tone, her eyes widening now as she took in the look of complete shock that he was too disturbed to even attempt to hide.

He hadn't known, she realised belatedly.

Incredibly, somehow, with everything else that had happened between them that night five years ago, she must have forgotten to mention that Dee was her little sister!

* * *

Sapphie was Dee's sister? The same stepsister who, along with her mother, had pressured Dee five years ago into going through with her marriage to Jerome Powers?

But wasn't that what she was doing now, too? Warning him, and every other man by the sound of it, from going anywhere near Dee's marriage to Jerome.

'Your name is Benedict, not McCall,' he finally bit out forcefully. Stupidly. Dee was an actress; McCall probably wasn't even her real name. But it seemed so impossible that these two women, so totally physically different, could possibly be related in any way, let alone be sisters!

'We're half-sisters,' Sapphie told him dismissively. 'I was two years old when my mother married Fergus McCall. Dee was born a year later.'

Rik turned away to walk over to the window, staring sightlessly out into the Parisian night.

Damn it, he had been congratulating himself earlier on the fact that he was over whatever he had felt for Dee, that, without him even being aware of it, his emotions had moved on.

And now this!

He hadn't asked Sapphie five years ago what she was doing at Dee and Jerome's wedding, whether her connection was to either the bride or groom. In fact, they hadn't talked much at all, he realised now.

But, thinking back to that time, remembering the things Dee had told him about her stepmother and stepsister, of how they were pressurising her into marrying the rich and powerful Jerome Powers, he couldn't help but wonder if his meeting with Sapphie that night had been quite as by chance as it had appeared at the time...

'Let me guess.' Sapphie spoke behind him. 'If Dee spoke of her family at all, it was to regale you with the stepmother and stepsister story?' She grimaced as he turned sharply back to face her. 'My stepfather died when Dee was thirteen.' She gave a sad shake of her head. 'His death hit her very hard, and the only way she could deal with it at the time was to think of herself as the beautiful swan left in the nest of the ugly ducklings! It seemed harmless enough at the time, if a little hurtful to our mother.'

The picture she was painting of Dee wasn't a pretty one. Rik remembered Dee as a beautiful butterfly desperately trying to fly away from the two women who were trying to run her life for her.

This woman and her mother!

But her mother and half-sister, not stepmother and stepsister...

He gave a dismissive shake of his head; if he once started to doubt Dee's integrity five years ago, then he really was in trouble!

Sapphie gave a humourless smile. 'I can see that you don't believe me.'

It wasn't a question of believing or not believing her; he was newly coming to terms with the fact that he was no longer in love with Dee, and also with hearing Sapphie telling him that the woman he had thought himself in love with all those years ago had never really existed either—it was just too much to take in!

'Why the hell should I?' he came back harshly. 'You and your mother got your way five years ago, let's just leave it at that, shall we?'

Sapphie looked perplexed now. 'My mother? What does she have to do with any of this?'

'Oh, please!' he grated.

And to think he had actually been starting to like Sapphie, to admire the cool way she'd dealt with what had happened between them five years ago. Hell, he was no longer even sure that it had just happened between them all those years ago; in fact, the more he thought about the way they had met, their lack of conversation, that shared passion in his hotel suite, the more he began to wonder if it hadn't all been planned to keep him well and truly occupied while Dee married someone else.

Although this presupposed that Dee's mother and sister had been aware that there was someone else in Dee's life besides Jerome...

Damn it, he had to get out of here—before he let those thoughts take him where he didn't want to go and he actually resorted to strangling Sapphie Benedict for what he now suspected her motives might have been towards him all those years ago!

'It's time to go,' he instructed after a glance at his wrist-watch. 'Dee and Jerome will be wondering where we are.'

Sapphie looked up at him uncertainly. 'Rik, what—?'

'I said it's time to go!' he commanded, grasping hold of her arm and manoeuvring her towards the door, allowing no respite when she stumbled slightly trying to pick up her evening bag.

He was too angry at this moment, needed to be where there were other people. Because strangling was probably too good for this woman.

But kissing her, at the same time showing his contempt for her, certainly wasn't!

He came to an abrupt halt as he reached the door, turning Sapphie Benedict in his arms to lower his head and take possession of her lips with his.

It was a kiss that wasn't meant to be enjoyed, by either of them. And as Rik felt Sapphie tremble in his arms he knew that she certainly wasn't deriving any pleasure from it, that if anything she was wary of him, of where his anger might take them. Well, let her be wary. She deserved to be wary. He wanted her to be wary. He wanted to take her...

His deeper, inner, decent self took control at that moment, filling him with self-disgust for the way he was behaving. He had never treated a woman like this in his life before, but as he felt the shuddering sobs that shook Sapphie's slender body he knew that he was both hurting and humiliating her. Not that she didn't deserve that—and worse—for what she and her mother had done five years ago; he just didn't intend lowering himself to her level.

He wrenched his mouth away from hers, taking hold of her upper arms to push her away from him, emotion blazing in his eyes as he saw the wretchedness of her expression, her eyes glittering with unshed tears, her lips puffy and obviously kissed.

An act. It was all an act, he assured himself determinedly; this woman, as much as Jerome Powers, had robbed him of Dee, of the love they had once shared—and he would never forgive her for it.

He drew in a harsh breath. 'If you're expecting an apology—'

'I'm not!' She wrenched out of his grasp, stepping away from him, the colour returning to her cheeks. 'I don't expect anything from you. I never have,' she added bleakly.

Rik's eyes narrowed. 'And what the hell is that supposed to mean?'

She made a dismissive movement with her hand. 'Nothing. Absolutely nothing.'

It wasn't nothing. It had certainly been something, a slight undertone to that comment that he couldn't quite put a name to...

But he could put a name to how he was feeling—and it wasn't pretty. He had never had cause to feel ashamed of his actions before, but he certainly wasn't proud of the way he had treated Sapphie just now. Even if she did deserve his contempt. She and her mother both.

Except...

Again he thought of the fact that Sapphie's mother was also Dee's mother, and that neither were the stepsister and stepmother Dee had claimed them to be. Why had she lied to him about those relationships? He—

'Dee and Jerome will be waiting for us downstairs,' Sapphie reminded him softly.

Rik frowned darkly at the way Sapphie avoided actually meeting his gaze, effectively making him feel more of a heel than ever.

Though he didn't see why he should, he decided as his resolve returned. Not when this woman, along with her mother, were responsible for it not being 'Dee and Rik' who were waiting downstairs.

'Then we had better go and join them, hadn't we?' he returned, his mouth twisting grimly as Sapphie stepped back to avoid the hand he would have placed beneath her elbow.

Fine. He didn't want to touch her again, anyway. Still couldn't be responsible for his actions where Sapphie Benedict was concerned!

CHAPTER THREE

'YOU'RE very quiet this evening, Sapphie; is there anything wrong?'

Sapphie turned to look at her brother-in-law, forcing a smile to her lips as he looked at her concernedly.

Quiet? Jerome thought she was quiet? Well, maybe, but Dee and Rik had talked enough for all of them during the last couple of hours as they dined together, usually about people or things of which Sapphie had no knowledge. Rik was completely ignoring the advice she had tried to give him earlier.

Oh, well, it had only been a case of misdirection on her part, an effort to try and draw attention away from herself. And she had been insulted and treated with suspicion for her pains. Why, she still didn't understand...

'I have a slight headache,' she excused, giving Jerome a reassuring smile. 'In fact—'

'You have a headache?' Dee prompted as she took time out from her laughing conversation with Rik. 'I have some tablets in my bag you can take.' She began to root through it. The new designer handbag, of course.

'I don't think that would be a good idea when I've already had a couple of glasses of wine,' Sapphie refused politely. 'In fact, I was just about to make my excuses and leave. A good night's sleep is probably all I need.' And to get away from Rik Prince's oppressive company!

She doubted if Dee and Jerome had noticed, but Rik hadn't so much as spoken one word to her during the last couple of hours. Not that she had wanted him to, but she was finding his silence towards her more unnerving than anything he might have said to her. That, and the brooding way Jerome had been watching his wife and Rik as they'd talked so easily together.

Dee, Sapphie knew, was always in her element when flirting with a man.

Rik Prince had been so wrong earlier when he'd accused her of not liking Dee. She loved her younger sister very much; she was just very aware of the emotional games Dee liked to play. And of Jerome's reaction to them.

She might have been using Jerome's jealousy earlier when she spoke to Rik as a diversion tactic, but actually Jerome's possessiveness where his wife was concerned was all too real.

It was a trait that had never shown its ugly face when Sapphie had believed herself to be in love with Jerome; if it had, she would have fallen out of love with him all the sooner. Although disillusionment had come soon enough: it was difficult to remain in love with someone who obviously loved someone else to distraction.

Although Rik Prince didn't seem to be having any trouble doing exactly that where Dee was concerned…!

'I'm really sorry to break up the party,' Sapphie

announced lightly, placing her napkin on the table-top and picking up her evening bag, 'but I really think it would be better if I went back to my hotel now.'

'I'll walk with you.'

Sapphie was so stunned by the fact that Rik had finally spoken to her, let alone by his offer to walk her back to her hotel, that her hand moved suddenly and knocked one of the wine glasses on the table. It would have fallen over, spilling its contents, had Rik not reached out and caught it as it began to tip.

Sapphie looked across at him with startled eyes. 'I'll be perfectly OK walking back alone.' After all, she had walked over to the George V by herself earlier!

'Oh, but I insist.' He easily held her gaze as he stood up, his expression unreadable. 'It's far too late for a woman to be out walking on her own. Besides,' he continued as Sapphie would have argued, 'I'm sure that Dee and Jerome have had quite enough company for one evening; this is romantic Paris, after all!'

Exactly, so why on earth would Rik want to stroll up the Champs-Elysées with her, of all people? Dee wasn't too happy at the prospect of losing her admirer, either, if her pouting expression was anything to go by! And when Dee was upset about something, anyone standing in her way had better watch out!

Not that Sapphie was a willing participant in this current situation, but she knew from experience that wouldn't matter to Dee if she felt like hitting out...

'Don't be so silly, Rik,' Dee told him impatiently. 'Jerome and I have been to Paris dozens of times before!'

'And no doubt we'll come back dozens of times more, too,' Jerome put in emolliently. 'But Rik does have a point,' he smiled at his wife, 'a nice stroll beside the river, with the illuminated Eiffel Tower as a backdrop, would be very romantic.'

'Lucky you, Dee,' Sapphie told her quickly as she saw the rebellious sparkle in her sister's eyes; Dee clearly wasn't happy with the thought of Sapphie disappearing off into the night with her admirer. Well, Dee needn't worry; Sapphie intended dumping that admirer as soon as it was safe to do so.

Dee looked at her husband and his encouraging smile, then at Rik's bland expression, obviously trying to weigh up whether or not she wanted to create a scene by insisting that Rik stay. Sapphie held her breath as she waited for the result of that deliberation.

'That sounds wonderful, darling,' Dee finally breathed huskily, her fingers moving caressingly on her husband's arm now.

Causing Sapphie to breathe an inner sigh of relief. One thing maturity seemed to have done for Dee was to teach her when not to push her luck. Or perhaps not; Sapphie winced as Dee gave Rik a challenging smile—maybe her sister was just trying to make Rik jealous now?

One day, Sapphie was sure, this was all going to blow up in Dee's beautiful face. But not tonight, she noted with relief. Jerome seemed quite happy now that he was going to have his wife to himself for a while. Rik Prince's expression was much harder to read...

Well, if he was less than satisfied with his companion, that was his problem, not hers!

'You can leave now,' Sapphie told him tersely once they had walked a short distance down the wide avenue towards the Arc de Triomphe. 'Dee and Jerome have already disappeared in the opposite direction,' she added as Rik looked at her with raised brows.

There had been quite a lot of kissing, and 'we'll meet again tomorrow' as Dee and Jerome took their leave outside the restaurant. But Sapphie saw no reason to continue this charade now that the other couple were no longer around.

Besides, she really did have a headache, mainly due, she knew, to Rik Prince's tense silence as he walked beside her, hands thrust into his trouser pockets.

Probably a ploy to stop himself from reaching out and throttling her, Sapphie accepted ruefully; he had certainly looked as if that was what he would have liked to do to her in his hotel suite earlier this evening!

But instead of that, he had kissed her...

A kiss that was not meant to be enjoyed—by either of them.

And Sapphie really hadn't enjoyed it. But she had learnt something about herself that she would much rather not have known. Until tonight, until Rik kissed her again, she had believed that instant love she felt for him five years ago had withered and died through lack of nurturing. But tonight, held once more in Rik Prince's arms, she knew that wasn't the case at all.

She was as much in love with Rik now as she had been that night long ago!

Rik had absolutely no idea what he was doing walking along beside Sapphie!

It had been one of the strangest evenings he had ever known in his life.

On the one hand, there he'd been with Dee, the woman he'd believed himself in love with for the last five years—though now he knew that he no longer loved her at all.

Then there'd been Jerome, the man Dee had married instead of him: a man that Rik couldn't help but like.

And lastly there'd been Sapphie Benedict, a woman he had spent a burning night of passion with five years previously; Dee's half-sister. One of the women who had played a leading part in taking Dee from him all those years ago. He was still so angry about that, he hadn't even been able to bring himself to talk to her this evening!

Instead he had spoken to Dee, whom he could now view with dispassion—and with whom, he realised, he had absolutely nothing in common! Her conversation was of fashion and the artificial world of acting, from which he normally chose to distance himself.

Adding to his confusion was his disgust with himself for the way he had treated Sapphie earlier, which had been building up inside him all evening.

Yes, at the time he had been angry with Sapphie, suspicious of her motives for what had happened between them five years ago. And yes, the pain of that had erupted out of control. But the way he had behaved, the physical retribution he had exacted, seemed more in keeping with his eldest brother Nik's ruthless nature than his own. Rik was the serious, caring, sensitive one of the family, not some arrogant monster who heaped vengeance on anyone who got in the way of what he wanted.

At least, that was what he had believed of himself until earlier tonight…

He gritted his teeth and turned to Sapphie. 'I owe you an apology—'

'I believe we've already had this conversation, Rik,' Sapphie dismissed. 'I think we agreed that you don't owe me anything!' she added bleakly.

There it was again, he recognised frowningly, that something in her voice that he couldn't quite put a name to…

'I do owe you an apology,' he insisted firmly, his hands clenched into fists inside his trouser pockets. 'I don't— I have never in my life before behaved towards any woman in the way that I did to you earlier tonight.'

Sapphie shrugged her slender shoulders. 'I'm sure that at the time you believed you had due provocation.'

'Whether I did or not is totally…' Rik broke off frustratedly, breathing hard, realising that even his apology was coming out all wrong.

What was it about this woman that made him behave so uncharacteristically? He really had no idea—and he wasn't sure that he wanted to know, either!

He sighed his impatience. 'Sapphie, will you, for goodness' sake, just let me apologise?'

She gave him a cool glance. 'If it makes you feel better.'

'It isn't a question of making me feel better…!' But wasn't it? Wasn't he just trying to salvage his own conscience, rather than anything else? After all, his anger was no less now than it had been earlier; he had just been unnerved by his reaction. He hadn't even known he was capable of behaving in that coldly ruthless way. 'What sort of name is Sapphie, anyway?' he challenged in order to give himself time to think.

Amber eyes sparkled with amusement as she glanced up at him. 'Can't you guess?' she said drily.

'No, I— Sapphie…' he said slowly, wincing as the penny finally dropped. 'Short for Sapphire?'

'Short for Sapphire,' she acknowledged with a rueful smile.

'Diamond and Sapphire,' Rik murmured slightly incredulously; he had thought his own family names slightly bizarre, but naming your daughters after precious stones seemed even more so.

'It could have been worse,' she said. 'We could have been Ruby and Emerald!'

'Hm,' he grimaced. 'No doubt when you have children of your own you will name them Mary and John!'

'No doubt,' she replied stiffly, coming to an abrupt halt on the wide pavement to turn and look at him. 'There really is absolutely no need for you to walk me back to my hotel,' she told him determinedly.

'I've been on my own in Paris for four days without needing an escort!'

Her relaxed amusement, while they had been discussing her name, was gone now, her eyes as hard and glittering as the amber stone they resembled, her expression aloof.

Rik gave a slightly dazed shake of his head, having no idea what he had said or done this time to cause her withdrawal. But he had obviously done something; she had seemed almost friendly there for a few minutes.

Or maybe it was just remembered past intimacies that made any prolonged exchange between them difficult?

Despite his feelings for Dee, Rik hadn't led a celibate life the last five years. And each time he'd become involved with someone, he had hoped that she would be the one to overshadow the love he felt for Dee. It had never happened, of course—although meeting Dee again seemed to have done the trick; perhaps he should have arranged this meeting a long time ago! But he could never remember this present awkwardness happening with any of the other women he had been involved with, either at the end of their affair or afterwards. In fact, he had become quite good friends with some of them.

Somehow he couldn't ever see becoming friends as a possibility where Sapphie Benedict was concerned!

He straightened. 'Look, I'm sure that both you and your mother believed you were acting in Dee's best interests five years ago—'

'And I'm sure,' Sapphie cut in impatiently, 'that

despite the fact you've mentioned this several times today already, I have absolutely no idea what you're talking about!'

Rik scowled at her obstinacy. This really was asking too much. He was trying his best to salvage something out of this mess, to smooth things over between them, if only so that they could be polite to each other in front of other people. But Sapphie certainly wasn't doing anything to help the situation!

'You and your mother wanted Dee to marry Jerome—'

'I did?' Sapphie's eyes widened incredulously at this accusation. 'And why, when I was in love with him myself, would I have wanted her to do that?'

Rik frowned. It was a good point. In fact, it was a very good point. And, as he hadn't known of Sapphie's feelings towards Jerome until earlier today, it wasn't one he had thought about before, either.

But now he did and had, and the answers that came immediately to mind once again put a question mark over Dee's integrity five years ago. In the circumstances, that wasn't acceptable to him. It couldn't be. Because it made a lie of the love he had felt for her.

'I don't suppose it really mattered, as long as one daughter was married to him—and, of course, his vast wealth and media influence!'

'How dare you?' Sapphie gasped angrily, breathing hard, the curve of her breasts visible above the low neckline of her strapless dress.

A fact Rik was all too aware of as he looked down at her. She really was a firebrand, he acknowledged admiringly. In more ways than one, if his memory served him correctly. And he knew that it did.

Just as he was sure Sapphie remembered the night they had spent together. No matter how he wished it were otherwise, he knew there was no way they could ever meet as just casual acquaintances!

He gave a regretful sigh. 'Listen to me, Sapphie—'

'No, Rik, I want you to listen to me,' she cut in forcefully, every curvaceous inch of her rigid with anger. 'I have little idea what Dee told you about our family five years ago—although from the few things you've told me, I can certainly take a guess!' she said disgustedly.

'Believe it or not, at the time we had more important things to discuss than you and your mother!' he told her stiffly, already disturbed by the variations he had already discovered today in Dee's version of things.

'I'm sure,' she scorned. 'But now I'm telling you how it really was. At the time I lived and worked in America. I was Jerome's assistant. I was also his fi-ancée—'

'His fiancée?' Rik was too surprised to successfully cover his surprise.

She nodded. 'We flew back to England so that I could introduce him to my family. But once Jerome took one look at Dee, I knew that was the end of that.' She grimaced. 'Trying to stop the two of them falling in love would have been like standing in the way of an express train! Instead I decided to just bow out gracefully.' She looked up directly into Rik's eyes. 'You seem to have the idea it happened differently. It seems I can't do or say anything to change your opinion. What I can do, though,' she continued as he would have spoken, 'is assure you that my conscience—and, incidentally, that of my mother—is completely clear. Can you claim the same?'

Rik was still trying to take in all that she had just said. Sapphie had been engaged to marry Jerome and then had lost him to Dee? It was so different from Dee's version of events. But, at the same time, this made so much more sense than Dee's story about being forced into marriage with someone she didn't love—especially since Rik had been there for her, and professing his own love. Really, he couldn't help but doubt Dee's tale of what had happened.

Which brought into question the last five wasted years he had spent believing himself to be in love with Dee; had the woman he'd thought she was ever really existed?

The pugnaciousness of Sapphie's tone brought him back to reality. 'What do you mean?'

Her mouth quirked. 'Is this meeting-up in Paris with Dee quite the accident that it appears…?'

It didn't take too much effort to know what she was getting at. 'I do not have affairs with married women!'

'Not even if you're in love with them?' Sapphie taunted.

'Not even then!' But he wasn't still in love with Dee. He didn't know how he felt towards her any more. If what Sapphie said was true, then the love he'd thought he felt for Dee had been based on lies…Dee's lies…

'You don't believe me, do you?' Sapphie said.

'I didn't say that,' Rik grated.

He didn't want to believe it, that it was true, and yet…

Sapphie kept going. 'I wonder if Dee even knew how much you loved her…'

Or really cared!

The thought popped into his head completely unbidden, and now that it was there he couldn't seem to blank it out again. He had been in misery that day nearly five years ago when Dee had married Jerome. But, as far as he could see, Dee had been every inch the blushing bride, not so much as giving him a sideways glance. At the time he had thought it was because she didn't want to give the two of them away, but now he wondered if she had even been aware he was there, let alone the pain he was in.

All these years he had taken Dee's silence to mean that she was doing the best she could to get on with her life, just as she expected him to get on with his. But had that really been the case, or had Dee simply forgotten he existed?

What a fool he had been, if that was true!

His mouth tightened at what he saw as his own stupidity. 'I would rather leave my feelings for Dee out of this.' Especially as he no longer even knew what those feelings were!

'Can we do that? Could we ever do that?' Sapphie responded tightly. 'Besides, I don't even know what ''this'' is. Look, I realise it was a shock for you today to see me again after all this time, and to realise that I'm actually Dee's sister. But if you look at it logically, then you'll see that there's really no reason why the two of us should ever meet again. In fact,' she continued, 'it's amazing that it ever happened at all!' She didn't look any more pleased about it than he did.

Amazing wasn't quite the way Rik would have put it!

'Oh, do cheer up, Rik,' Sapphie admonished brightly, her eyes gleaming now. 'By this time tomorrow we can forget we ever did meet again. You see, there's a bright side to everything, if you only look hard enough!'

At this moment, his head full of conflicting impressions of Dee and this woman standing in front of him—a woman with whom he'd shared a night of passion—Rik couldn't for the life of him see the bright side!

CHAPTER FOUR

'WHAT on earth are you doing here?' Sapphie showed her displeasure at having been shown out to the terrace of the George V, where she was expecting to have breakfast with Dee and Jerome but instead had found Rik Prince sitting at the table set for four.

Alone.

Not the sort of shock she needed first thing in the morning!

Especially after the sleepless night she had just spent, going over and over in her mind her conversation with Rik the previous evening in an effort to see if she had said too much, or revealed more than she intended. That was what she had been afraid of all along, of course.

She had finally come to the conclusion that she hadn't said anything that would rouse his suspicions...

Rik put his coffee-cup down on the table, clearly no more pleased to see her than she was him. 'It may have escaped your notice, Sapphie,' he drawled hardly, 'but, unlike you, I happen to be a guest at this hotel!'

Sapphie had half expected—and prepared herself!—for seeing him again at some stage during her breakfast with Dee and Jerome. But she just hadn't been expecting him to be sitting here and expecting to eat with them. And all before she had even had her first cup of coffee of the day too!

'Jerome called me earlier this morning and suggested I have breakfast with him and Dee. At the time I couldn't think of any reason not to,' Rik confessed, confirming Sapphie's suspicions as she reluctantly sat down on the chair the waiter pulled back for her. 'I don't believe there was any mention of your being here too.' Otherwise he wouldn't be here either, his tone implied. A tone Sapphie chose to ignore as she turned smilingly to the waiter and ordered another pot of coffee; she had a feeling she was going to need it!

'Rather a sudden decision of theirs to go on to London later today, isn't it?' Rik opined, once the two of them were alone.

Sapphie had been a little surprised herself when Jerome had called her on her mobile and explained the reason for them breakfasting together, because the couple had originally planned to spend another couple of days in Paris.

Although perhaps, given Rik Prince's unexpected presence here, it wasn't so surprising, after all…

Jerome was, on the surface, the most genial of men, and his indulgence towards his wife seemed boundless. But Sapphie had been perfectly serious when she'd warned Rik that Jerome drew the line at pandering to Dee's flirtations.

Having witnessed her sister unashamedly leading Rik on the previous evening, Sapphie knew that Jerome would have had to have been blind not to see it too. Admittedly, despite talking to Dee exclusively,

Rik hadn't seemed to be giving her sister any encouragement.

Sapphie eyed Rik assessingly now. 'Isn't it?' she came back noncommittally, smiling her gratitude at the waiter as he poured her coffee before putting the pot down and departing.

Rik's gaze narrowed. 'And what's that supposed to mean?'

'Rik, I'm really not going to get into an argument with you before I've even had my coffee!'

He continued to look at her for several seconds, and then he gave a begrudging smile. 'It really isn't surprising that I never guessed you and Dee are related; besides the fact that you look absolutely nothing like each other, you really are nothing alike. I certainly can't imagine having a conversation like this with her!'

Sapphie sipped her coffee before answering, not sure whether or not to take his remark as a criticism. But considering that Rik seemed to think Dee was just about perfect—apart from the little fact that she already had a husband, of course—it probably was!

'Feeling better now?' he prompted mockingly as she rapidly finished one cup of coffee and poured herself another.

'Not particularly, no,' she answered flatly; where were Dee and Jerome?

Nine o'clock, Jerome had told her when he rang her earlier, and it was already ten minutes past now.

Rik grinned at her disgruntled attitude. 'Perhaps we should just go ahead and order breakfast? I noticed you hardly ate any dinner last night, so you're probably hungry.'

Sapphie gave him a sharp look, not having been aware that he had noticed anything the previous evening except Dee.

And that, she realised with an inner feeling of panic, felt distinctly like jealousy on her part!

No such thing, she instantly assured herself. What was the point of her feeling jealous about this man? Her feelings for him were going nowhere. Nowhere that she could allow them to go, anyway!

She put her coffee-cup down again. 'Shouldn't we wait for Dee and Jerome?'

'Mr Prince?' The waiter had once again appeared silently beside their table. 'Mr Powers has just telephoned down, sir,' he continued as Rik looked up at him enquiringly. 'He sends his apologies, but he and Mrs Powers aren't going to be able to join you, after all. He hopes that you and Miss Benedict will continue without them.'

An awkward silence followed the man's departure as Sapphie suddenly had an idea of what Jerome was trying to do, and Rik, she was sure, was desperately searching for a way to extricate himself from this situation!

'Hm,' he mused slowly. 'What's all that about, do you think? Why didn't Jerome call one of us directly on our mobiles?'

Sapphie had to admire Rik's shrewdness; most men wouldn't have realised that it was about anything!

But she didn't need to think about it herself; suddenly she knew exactly what Jerome was up to. It would have been laughable, if only Jerome hadn't chosen Rik Prince, of all people, to try and match make her with!

Ever since their broken engagement five years ago, Jerome had been suffering from a guilt complex where Sapphie was concerned, feeling as if he had let her down when he married Dee instead of her.

The result was that, whenever he could, Jerome sent an eligible bachelor in her direction, in the hope that she would fall in love. Rik Prince, it seemed, was his latest effort, and probably an attempt to kill two birds with one stone; if only he could encourage Rik to be attracted to Sapphie, Jerome would succeed at diverting the other man's attentions away from Dee!

However, Jerome couldn't possibly know that Rik Prince was the very last man Sapphie would ever allow into her life!

Into her own life. And into Matthew's…

Because she had no idea what Rik would say, what he would do, if he was to know that exactly nine months after they had spent the night together she had given birth to a healthy eight-pound baby boy.

Matthew.

Rik's son.

Sapphie had asked herself many times during her pregnancy whether or not she ought to contact Rik Prince about his impending fatherhood. A part of her said he had a right to know, but another part of her had argued strongly against it. Rik had made no effort to seek her out since their night together, had obviously never given a thought to the fact there might be any long-term consequences. If he had, perhaps her decision would have been a different one.

As it was, she had decided against telling him. It wasn't a night she was particularly proud of. She might have fallen in love with Rik on sight, but anyone with eyes in their head on Dee and Jerome's wedding day could have seen that Rik had had eyes for no one but the bride.

Sapphie had set out to deliberately bring herself to Rik's attention at the reception party, had noted his increasingly reckless mood as the evening wore on, even his invitation for her to join him in his hotel suite had been made in an offhand manner, as if he hadn't really cared whether she did or not.

The consequences of that night, she had argued to herself two months later when she'd learnt of her pregnancy, were hers alone. In fact, she had adamantly refused to tell anyone who the father of her baby was.

And when Matthew had been born, so beautiful, his hair dark and soft, with eyes the colour of the sky, she had been glad that she had decided not to tell Rik he was to be a father. This baby would be hers, and only hers.

It would have been too much to subject her beautiful child to a tug of war; even then she had known Rik well enough to know that was what it would have become, that he wasn't the sort of man to shirk his responsibilities. Matthew was too wonderful to ever be classed as someone's responsibility!

Which was the reason it had been such a shock to

see Rik again yesterday, why she had been desperately trying to alienate him ever since.

Unsuccessfully.

But one glance at him and she had seen how like his father Matthew already was; tall for his four years, his baby features already starting to show signs of the strength of his father's jaw, his mouth a perfect replica of Rik's, as was the deep blue of his eyes.

In fact, she had realised with a sickening lurch of her stomach, if anyone were to see Rik and Matthew together, their relationship would be unmistakable!

Not that she thought for a moment that Jerome had guessed the truth, and that was the reason for his trying to push Rik and her together; Dee and Jerome had last seen Matthew almost eighteen months ago, and he'd been very much a baby then. Also she was sure that the other couple really didn't have any idea that Sapphie and Rik had ever met before.

Something she had been at great pains to emphasise to Rik when she spoke to him yesterday. In fact, she felt as if she had been balancing on a tightrope since meeting Rik again.

But the worst part had definitely been the dread that either Dee or Jerome might mention her son, and that Rik would add two and two together and come up with the correct answer of four!

It hadn't happened, thank goodness, and luckily for her—and for obvious reasons of his own—Rik was no more anxious to reveal their past association than she was.

With any luck, with Dee and Jerome's departure

from Paris later today, Sapphie need never think of, or see, Rik Prince again!

And the sooner she got back to the house she and Matthew shared with her mother, to the peace and happiness that was their normal existence, the better she would like it!

'What do you think it's all about?' She answered Rik's question, deliberately turning the focus back to him and away from herself; he wouldn't be any more pleased by Jerome's matchmaking than she was.

Rik eyes narrowed, his mouth thinning. 'No matter what you may think to the contrary, Sapphie, I do not want to be, nor have I ever been, involved with a married woman!'

No, she could believe that, Sapphie accepted; he was too sincere for it not to be the truth. Which meant that he and Dee probably hadn't met again since Dee's marriage...

Not that it made a great deal of difference to her decision concerning Matthew. Guilt on Rik's part was not something either of them needed. Or pity, either.

Sapphie had had to rethink her life and career once she'd discovered she was pregnant and had decided to keep her baby, had known that her high-powered new job a personal assistant—Dee had insisted that Sapphie couldn't possibly continue to work for Jerome in the circumstances!—was not a suitable one for a single mother.

Even if she did say so herself, her career change, to a freelance society reporter, had worked out very well. She had made so many contacts and friends during her time as Jerome's assistant that finding people to interview hadn't been a problem, and neither had finding newspapers and magazines to publish her work. Jerome's publications had been amongst them, her brother-in-law assuring her that what Dee didn't know couldn't hurt her. And, as Sapphie had no personal contact with Jerome, she hadn't felt that she was betraying her sister's trust in any way either.

From writing those articles and meeting all those glamorous people—in some cases, unbelievably glamorous—had come the idea for writing a book. Ambitious, she knew, but it had been amazing how popular a novel with murder in Hollywood as its main theme had proved to be…

She gave Rik a scathing glance. 'I don't think I'm the one you have to convince of that,' she scorned. 'Do you?'

Rik was growing more than a little tired of bearing the brunt of Sapphie's derision. Especially as *he* was the one with a grievance, since he was still not completely convinced of her innocence when it came to what had happened five years ago.

He had thought over what she had said last night—in fact, he hadn't been able to sleep for thinking about it. But if he was to accept what Sapphie claimed had happened five years ago, if he was to believe her version of things, then that made him nothing but the idiot she had once claimed him to be, for believing in Dee so absolutely. And he wasn't ready to admit to that. Not yet.

But one thing he was willing to admit, to himself at least, was that he had never yet been bored in

Sapphie's company. As he had been by Dee's last night…?

Well…yes. But, he had also decided during his wakeful hours last night, maybe it was the five years' gulf between himself and Dee that had made it impossible for them to converse easily. That, and the presence of Dee's husband and sister!

'I think you're exaggerating Jerome's concern about Dee,' he rasped harshly, leaning back in his chair to look at Sapphie through narrowed eyes.

If she had suffered from any sleeplessness last night because of their previous heated exchanges, then it certainly didn't show, Sapphie looking refreshingly lovely this morning in a cream sundress that deepened her tan and brought out the red highlights in her hair, those amber eyes still clear and shining.

Damn it, her eyes were always challenging when she looked at him. Something else he was finding he disliked intensely.

Sapphie's feelings for Jerome Powers all those years ago could hardly have been mild, considering she had been engaged to him. In fact, she'd claimed they were the reason she had ended up in bed with Rik. Which, considering her continued scorn about his emotions towards Dee, he found highly hypocritical!

It was a no-win situation as far as he could see, no matter how they continued to argue about it.

'How about we order some breakfast?' he suggested. 'That should be a safe topic of conversation, at least!'

'I'm not hungry,' Sapphie refused.

Neither was he. 'Then how about you and I go for a walk? You might work up an appetite,' he persevered.

'How about you and I...?' Sapphie gave a frustrated shake of her head. 'Haven't I got it through to you yet that I don't want to spend any more time in your company than I have to?'

Rik held on to his temper with effort. 'I believe you may have mentioned it once or twice.'

Her eyes flashed like molten gold. 'Then you have your answer, don't you?'

Rik held up the palms of his hands. 'I was only suggesting a walk, Sapphie, not a morning in bed together!'

She gasped, colour darkening her cheeks as she hastily looked about them to see if anyone was listening to their conversation.

They weren't; Rik had already checked. His only fun in this situation might be in teasing Sapphie, but he had no intention of causing her a moment's embarrassment in front of others. There was a certain dignity about her, a self-possession, that stopped him from ever doing that.

'Come on.' He stood up, moving to pull back her chair so that she had no choice but to stand up. 'A walk in the sunshine will do us both good.' It might also help to clear the cobwebs in his brain after his sleepless night. 'My intentions are strictly honourable, Sapphie,' he declared as she looked slightly dazed at finding herself outside the hotel and walking towards the River Seine and the looming Eiffel Tower.

She shot him a quick, disapproving glance, keeping

her distance as they progressed along the avenue. 'I've only ever been that stupid once in my life!'

Stupid? Was that how she thought of their night together? He had considered her his salvation at the time and whenever he had allowed himself to think of her afterwards it had always been with a smile of remembered affection.

And no matter what Sapphie might have felt, he *had* thought of her during the intervening years, had often wondered where she was, what she was doing, if she ever thought of him with the same affection.

Obviously not, if her horror at seeing him again yesterday was anything to go by!

'I never thought of you as stupid, Sapphie,' he assured her huskily. 'Although, having talked to you, I do understand your reasons a little better now—'

'You think I was a diversion to stop you from interfering with Dee's wedding,' she reminded hardly.

He winced at the accusation, knowing it was deserved, and regretting that he had ever said anything so hurtful. But he had been hurting himself yesterday and had hit out at the only person that he could. No excuse, he knew, but it was what had happened.

One thing he did know; her description of her engagement to Jerome, her love for him, had definitely rung true...

Rik squirmed uncomfortably. 'I might have been a little hasty when I made that remark—'

'Might have been!' she echoed. 'I was twenty-three years old, Rik, and although I had been engaged to marry Jerome, the two of us had never been lovers.

You were my first. Or were you too preoccupied that night with your own emotions to realise that?'

No, of course he hadn't been; that was an aspect of their night of passion that had always puzzled him. But, until just now, time and distance had convinced him that he must have imagined that small initial barrier to their lovemaking—that, of course, Sapphie couldn't have been a virgin. Anyway, women simply didn't give their virginity away to a complete stranger, did they?

Though Sapphie had…

CHAPTER FIVE

Too much!

After all her care yesterday, all her thinking before speaking, she had now said far too much…!

Admittedly he had just made her angry all over again with his doubts concerning her motivation five years ago, but even so, as she saw the sharp intelligence of his gaze, the questions starting to form there, she knew it had been a mistake to have let that anger provoke her into saying as much as she had.

As a virgin, the possibility of her using contraception that night had to have been nil, and Rik knew that he certainly hadn't used any. Damn her reckless tongue!

'But I wouldn't give that too much thought if I were you, Rik,' Sapphie dismissed brittlely. 'I've had dozens of lovers since, and I'm sure they were all grateful for the fact that you had already taken away that particular barrier!'

She knew by the angry darkening of his eyes that by pretending she'd slept with other men, she had successfully diverted his attention from the original subject; her virginity. Although, as his gaze now turned to Arctic grey, she wasn't too sure she would be able to handle his change of mood. But for both their sakes, as well as Matthew's—he was already

fatherless, so it wouldn't do if his mother was throt-
tled in the street too—she knew she had better try!

'Perhaps I was right about this walk not being a
good idea,' she told him lightly as she came to a halt
on the pavement. 'We don't seem to be able to be in
each other's company for five minutes without one of
us insulting the other!'

A nerve pulsed in his tightly clenched jaw as he
obviously fought an inner battle to control his anger.
'Why is that, do you suppose?' he finally managed to
rasp between clenched teeth.

'We simply don't like each other?' she suggested
with a dismissive shrug.

Rik continued to glare at her for several long seconds, and then he seemed to force himself to relax,
his hands unclenching at his sides, his mouth twisting
into a humourless smile. 'But I do like you, Sapphie,'
he mused. 'I find your forthright manner, the way you
say exactly what you're thinking, very—refreshing.'

Sapphie's breath caught in her throat as her gaze
was met and held by his now warm blue eyes.

'Perhaps it isn't that we dislike each other at all,'
Rik continued gruffly, one hand reaching up to cup
the side of her face, his fingers seeming to burn where
they touched, holding her mesmerised. 'Perhaps it's
that we like each other too much?' he murmured before his head lowered and his lips claimed hers.

She had realised yesterday how she still felt about
this man, but it was an emotion she had denied by
being continually rude and antagonistic towards him.

But now, with his lips gently exploring hers, she
couldn't deny her feelings any longer. She loved this

man. Unbelievable as it might seem, after five years' absence, she was still in love with Rik Prince!

Perhaps it was because of her deep love for Matthew, and his undeniable likeness to his father. Or perhaps she loved Matthew as much as she did because of that likeness to his father; whatever the reason, she knew, as her body instinctively melted into Rik's, that she was still in love with him!

The summer sun beat down on them hotly, but Sapphie's heat was all coming from inside, making it impossible for her to think; she was only capable of feeling.

And what she felt was remembered desire; her hands clung to the broad width of Rik's shoulders, her body curved into his, making her completely aware of his own arousal.

'Well, well, well,' drawled a self-satisfied male voice. 'And you told me I was wasting my time, Dee, trying to get Sapphie and Rik together!'

Sapphie and Rik had sprung guiltily apart at the sound of Jerome's voice, Sapphie now shooting Dee a wary glance at Jerome's comment.

As Sapphie had suspected, Jerome was trying to throw her and Rik together, and from the furious expression on Dee's face—her eyes were sparkling a venomous emerald—her sister was far from pleased that he seemed to have succeeded.

Not that he had. Sapphie might still love Rik, respond to him as she had to no other man, but it would be an act of madness on her part to even contemplate becoming involved with him again. Dee's obvious displeasure, at the mere idea of Rik and Sapphie liking each other, had nothing to do with it!

As for Rik, Sapphie couldn't even look at him at the moment, didn't trust herself not to give away her feelings. Neither did she want to witness the apologetic expression that was sure to be on his face as he looked to Dee for forgiveness for what had, after all, only been an impulse on his part!

'Actually, Jerome,' Sapphie briskly took charge of the situation, 'Rik and I were just saying goodbye to each other; I've decided to return to England on the Eurostar train with the two of you this afternoon.' The idea had only just occurred to her, but the more she thought about it the more she liked the idea of going home. Safely away from the temptation of Rik Prince!

'That sounds like an excellent idea,' Dee grated, obviously only slightly mollified by this news. 'I'm sure that Matthew will be eagerly awaiting your return,' she added challengingly.

Sapphie felt her heart miss a beat, her face go pale, at Dee's deliberate mention of her young son. Had Dee somehow realised? Did she know why Sapphie had steadfastly refused to share with anyone all these years the identity of Matthew's father? It was what Sapphie had feared ever since meeting Rik again yesterday, the reason she had endured the dinner together last night; she simply couldn't let Dee or Jerome tell Rik that she had a young son.

No, Sapphie decided after a searching glance at her sister; Dee was angry at what she saw as this current defection of her ex-lover, rather than venting her fury at how quickly her ex-lover had turned to Sapphie for consolation five years ago and shared an unforgettable night of passion.

And it had been unforgettable. As far as Sapphie was concerned, at least.

She had always thought, following Matthew's birth, that it was her concentration on him that had robbed her of any desire to become involved with another man. Now she knew that wasn't the case at all...

Because, despite what she might have told Rik a short time ago in self-defence, she had only ever had one lover in her life—and that was Rik.

'Matthew?' Rik queried abruptly, a slight edge to his voice.

If Sapphie had needed any confirmation that Dee was still completely ignorant of the identity of Matthew's father, then she got it now. Her sister's expression was blazingly triumphant as she sensed Sapphie's discomfort with the subject. Besides, Sapphie acknowledged, if Dee had once realised that Rik was Matthew's father, then she certainly wouldn't want Rik to know about it now. Dee was out to make trouble, yes, but not the amount that would erupt if Rik were to discover he and Sapphie had a son! Rik's attention would be totally focused on Sapphie then!

Dee stepped forward, giving Rik a teasing smile as she linked her arm with his. 'Now, now, Rik, we women have to have our little secrets, you know,' she murmured suggestively.

Jerome frowned. 'I don't see what the big deal is. It's not as if Sapphie—'

'Darling, if Sapphie hasn't told Rik about Matthew,

then we really shouldn't do so, either.' Dee gave her husband a coquettish smile, still clinging to Rik's arm, glowingly lovely in a short cotton dress that exactly matched the colour of her eyes and showed off the long length of her tanned legs. 'Although I do think it's naughty of you not to have mentioned him, Sapphie,' she admonished.

Sapphie turned in Rik's direction, only to find him staring straight back at her with hooded blue eyes, that gave her absolutely no insight as to what he was thinking, either about the kiss the two of them had shared or the conversation since Dee and Jerome had joined them.

She quickly averted her gaze, her own emotions in turmoil; just looking at Dee's proprietorial claim on him upset her, not to mention how close Rik had come to learning that she had a young son.

He wasn't stupid—far from it, could count as well as she could, and Matthew's age of four years and two months, plus the nine months of her pregnancy, would take him exactly to the point the two of them had last met!

'As you say, Dee,' she muttered stiffly, 'we women must have our little secrets.'

Dee smiled, looking like a cat who had got the cream, obviously completely satisfied with the way this conversation was turning out. 'The waiter said the two of you had left without eating; shall we all go back to the hotel and have breakfast together?' she suggested brightly.

Sapphie couldn't think of food at this moment, knew that it would choke her. She couldn't even look at Rik right now, let alone sit and eat a meal with him as if nothing had happened.

But maybe it hadn't for him; after all, he wasn't still in love with her, neither did he have the secret of their son to guard with all the fierceness of a lioness protecting her cub!

'Actually, I think I'll just go back to my hotel and check the availability of seats on the Eurostar,' she answered evasively, having no intention of being left alone in Paris with Rik once the other couple had left, and feeling too disturbed at this moment to even try to monitor the conversation between Rik and the other two. 'I need to pack as well.'

'If none of you have any objections, I think I might travel to England with you, too,' Rik put in mildly.

Unbelievably.

Devastatingly!

Sapphie had thought she'd hit on the perfect way to avoid seeing Rik ever again, and instead it seemed she was to be stuck on a train back to London with him, and Dee and Jerome, for several hours.

It had to be her idea of purgatory!

It was impossible for him to mistake the look of absolute dismay on Sapphie's face at his suggestion!

Rik wasn't quite sure where the idea had come from. He'd intended returning to the States from here, rather than going to England. But, now he'd come up with the idea, it seemed the right thing to do.

Having believed himself in love with Dee for the last five years, and then discovering that wasn't the case at all, he now found himself drawn to Sapphie.

Whether it was because of their past association, or because she was the first woman he had been in close contact with since his startling realisation, he really wasn't sure yet. But he was very attracted to her and he wasn't comfortable letting her just disappear out of his life for a second time.

If the sense of jealousy that had shot through him at the mere mention of this guy Matthew's presence in her life was anything to go by, then he was right to pursue this attraction, and not just walk away. He had already done that once where Dee was concerned, and he knew he had been correct to do so. Sapphie wore no rings on her left hand, so this Matthew wasn't her husband or fiancé. In fact, if the man was anyone really important in her life, he would be with her in Paris right now, wouldn't he? What was that saying? *'All's fair in love and war'…?*

Well, he seemed to have been fighting a continuous battle with Sapphie ever since the two of them met again yesterday!

As for how he felt about her—he didn't quite know yet; he just had this feeling of unfinished business between them. And he wasn't going to spend another five years of his life wondering about what might have been!

He was totally aware of Sapphie, had in his possession an elusive memory of her lithe nakedness moving against his, of her legs wrapped about him, of her little cries of pleasure as he kissed and caressed her, of tiny teeth sinking into his shoulder as their pleasure reached its peak…

No, he wasn't yet willing to let Sapphie walk out of his life a second time.

'I think I'll give breakfast a miss too,' he told Dee and Jerome lightly. 'In fact—' he extricated himself from Dee's arm linked with his '—why don't Sapphie and I meet up with the two of you again later? Say, twelvish?'

Dee looked far from pleased at the way he had moved away from her and closer to Sapphie, her expression tight as she looked at both of them from beneath lowered lashes.

'Sounds good to me,' Jerome was the one to answer Rik smilingly. 'Come on, honey; I'm starving!' He smiled encouragingly at his wife.

'Well, I'm not,' Dee snapped uncooperatively.

To give Jerome his due, his smile didn't so much as waver for a second, whereas Rik knew that if his wife ever spoke to him in that petulant tone in front of other people he would be far from pleased.

His wife?

That was a joke; the only woman he had ever asked to be his wife was this other man's wife!

But even so, if Dee had ever spoken to him like that— What was he doing? Dee had always been perfect in his eyes, the woman he measured every other female against. And had always found them wanting.

But, he realised begrudgingly, the last twenty-four hours in Dee's company, the discrepancies he had found in what she'd told him and wondering what was actually fact and what was fiction, had made him question just how well he had actually known Dee all those years ago. They had really only been out on a few dates together before she'd told him of her impending marriage to Jerome, and the reasons for it. At which point Rik had decided he wanted to marry her himself, that he couldn't live without her.

And yet he had. Quite successfully, on a professional level. It might not have been quite so successful from a personal point of view, but even that side of his life had had its moments.

Of course, Sapphie had been one of its highlights…!

'You must be hungry, Dee,' Jerome told his wife firmly. 'I know you didn't feel too well this morning, but that's passed now. You're just feeling cranky because of your condition.'

Condition? What condition? Was Dee ill—?

No, Rik realised with a sudden intake of breath, Dee wasn't ill at all—she was pregnant!

Why was he so surprised? The other couple had been married five years now, a family was a natural progression, wasn't it?

And did he really care, or was it just force of habit that made him react…?

'Yes, do go and have some breakfast with Jerome, Dee,' Sapphie was the one to put in lightly, at the same time stepping forward to link her arm with Rik's.

He looked down at her frowningly, the force of the anger sparkling in her amber-coloured eyes was enough to make his own widen.

Idiot, her gaze scorned, why don't you just get a grip and stop making an idiot of yourself over Dee?

He straightened abruptly, not sure that was what he was doing. It was a bit of a shock to learn of the pregnancy, yes, but, there again, it wasn't really any of his business, was it?

'Yes, do go ahead, Dee,' he encouraged lightly. 'After all, you're eating for two now!' he offered, receiving a venomous look from her glittering green eyes for his trouble.

Really, these two sisters certainly knew how to let a man know exactly what they were thinking without saying a word! Sapphie was patently furious with him, and Dee was far from happy too—though, as far as he was aware, he was doing his best to keep things on a friendly basis with everyone.

Even if it was hard going!

It was his own fault, of course. He had put Dee on a pedestal, believing her to be perfect, that he could never love anyone else in the way that he loved her. How stupid was that, based on a few days of knowing each other? Especially as she had then told him she was about to marry another man!

Very, he acknowledged with a self-derisive wince. No wonder Sapphie made no effort to hide her scorn every time she looked at him!

Sapphie.

Surprisingly, he felt he knew her so much better than he had ever known Dee, personally as well as physically. The physical part was a fact, but the personal part was there every time she spoke to him in that bluntly truthful way of hers, every time she looked at him with those frankly assessing eyes.

And found him wanting…

Justifiably so, he acknowledged heavily. He had been an idiot to believe himself in love with a mirage for five years…!

'Don't be ridiculous, Rik,' Dee told him sharply. 'The baby is minute. No one looking at me would even know I'm pregnant!'

He certainly hadn't, Rik allowed. Dee had looked just the same to him when they met again yesterday, perhaps even more glowingly beautiful than he remembered. But then his sister, Stazy, had had an added glow about her when she was pregnant with Sam, so perhaps that was normal. His knowledge of pregnant women was limited. Obviously.

'You see? Cranky,' Jerome murmured indulgently as he put his arm about his wife's shoulders and turned her back in the direction of the hotel. 'We'll see you two later,' he added before leading away a disgruntled Dee.

Leaving an awkward silence in their wake as Rik, at this moment, couldn't think of a thing to say, and Sapphie—well, she was probably still disgusted with him!

'You didn't know, did you?'

He turned to look enquiringly at Sapphie as she spoke to him.

'You didn't know about the baby until just now, did you?' she persisted evenly.

He frowned. 'Why should I have known?'

'No reason. I just thought—'

'Don't bother to tell me what you thought,' Rik responded swiftly. Then his tone softened. 'I…It was kind of you to—help me out of what could have been an awkward situation.'

Her eyes flashed deeply gold. 'I didn't do it for you, I did it for Jerome. He's so excited about the baby.'

Rik nodded. 'And how does Dee feel about it?'

Sapphie gave him a cold look. 'You would have to ask her that, not me.'

'Look, Sapphie,' he rasped, beginning to feel angry all over again, 'no matter what you may think to the contrary, I really hadn't seen Dee since her wedding and we met again by chance yesterday outside Fouquet's. A fact I'm sure I've already told you more than once. And again, despite what you may think, I do not tell lies,' he added harshly.

'But how can you possibly have continued to be in love with someone you haven't even spoken to for five years…?' She broke off quickly, colour heightening her cheeks now. 'Forget I asked that,' she muttered dismissively. 'It's none of my business what you do.' She turned away. 'I really should get back to my hotel, check on the train and pack. If you'll excuse me?' She didn't wait for him to answer before hurrying off in the direction of her hotel.

Rik watched her go, the sunlight making her hair a deep red halo of colour, her body swaying tantalisingly as she walked.

Away from him.

Leaving him with the distinct feeling that Sapphie Benedict had no time for him, or what she considered his confused emotions.

Except they were no longer that confused to Rik. He had been in love with the mirage that was his vision of Dee.

Now he wasn't.

He wasn't sure what he felt for Sapphie yet.

But he did feel something!

CHAPTER SIX

WHAT on earth had possessed her to get into a conversation with Rik about his feelings for Dee?

If she had managed to be in love with Rik for the last five years without seeing or speaking to him, then why did she think it was ludicrous that he had felt the same about Dee?

Admittedly, she did have a day-to-day reminder of Rik in Matthew; tangible proof of that one night they had spent together. But even so, she should have got over her feelings for Rik long ago.

She certainly shouldn't have allowed him to kiss her—or have kissed him back—this morning.

Or have let Dee witness that kiss...

Because she was sure, as far as her possessive younger sister was concerned, she hadn't heard the last about that!

Sapphie was proved right, it turned out—she hadn't heard the last of it. Dee took the first available opportunity to talk to her about it, that very afternoon. Rik and Jerome had gone off in search of coffee for them all before they boarded the Eurostar train, leaving Sapphie and Dee seated together in a quiet corner of the departure lounge.

'Exactly what did you think you were doing, Sapphie?' Dee demanded, green eyes glittering angrily. 'Rik is mine, you know, and he always will be,' she proclaimed with confidence.

It really wasn't Dee's fault she was so utterly self-ish, Sapphie reminded herself patiently. Dee had been petted and spoilt by their family from the moment she was born; her father had adored her because, to him, Dee was perfection personified; her mother had in-dulged her because she was pleased to have a child with her second husband; Sapphie had been delighted to have a little sister to play with.

Which had all been fine when Dee was a little girl, but as she matured, and everything became 'mine', it had become less attractive. Dee continued to demand, and usually get, adoration from everyone she met. Even her career had fulfilled that demand, the public flocking to see every film she'd starred in—indeed, several people had already stopped her today to ask her for her autograph! Only her warmth and beauty were on show to her public, Jerome having so far managed to keep her temper tantrums, when she couldn't have her own way, from the Press.

But she was going too far when she put people under the heading of 'mine'—even if Rik Prince did give every impression of fitting that pigeon-hole!

'No one is disputing your prior claim to a friend-ship with Rik, Dee,' Sapphie answered soothingly, although she suspected that Jerome might have some-thing to say about that!

Dee raised blonde brows. 'It was much more than a friendship!'

Sapphie knew it was, didn't doubt for a moment

that Dee and Rik had once been lovers. She just didn't want to hear about it!

'Fine,' she replied uninterestedly.

'It is not "fine",' Dee snapped. 'The two of you were kissing earlier. And now he's decided to travel to England, instead of back to the States as he originally planned to do!'

'I really don't think the two incidents are related, Dee,' Sapphie responded wearily; she had no idea why Rik had changed his plans, but one thing she did know: it had absolutely nothing to do with her! 'I explained earlier about the kiss,' she continued evenly. 'And if Rik has changed his plans, then it probably has more to do with you than it does with me.'

'Do you think so?' Dee brightened.

Even at twenty-five, and expecting a child of her own, her little sister could still be so immature. 'I do. I also—thank you for not telling him about Matthew earlier,' Sapphie added quietly, still very aware of the narrow escape she'd had.

Dee gave her a feline glance. 'That doesn't mean I'm not going to,' she purred. 'It's just that Rik can be so—shall we say?—indulgent towards women, and I didn't want you coming on to him as some poor, pathetic, single-mother figure!'

Sapphie bit her bottom lip to stop herself from laughing; poor, pathetic, single-mother figure be damned! There was nothing poor or pathetic about her. She earned more than enough money to keep herself and Matthew very comfortably and, although she didn't go out that often, she still had plenty of friends she could see if she wanted to. But it would serve no positive purpose to point this out to Dee, who only ever saw what she wanted to see. At the moment she was making it very plain that she didn't want to see Sapphie anywhere near Rik!

Which was perfectly OK with Sapphie; once they reached London later today, she didn't want to be anywhere near Rik either!

Although it was a little difficult to avoid him once they were in the close confines of their train carriage!

Their first-class seats were the height of comfort, and the stewardess was very attentive. But the four of them were seated around a small table, two facing forwards and two backwards, and as Jerome wouldn't hear of anyone sitting next to Dee besides himself, that left Sapphie and Rik sitting next to each other, too.

Not that Dee had too much time to voice any objections to the arrangement. She fell asleep shortly after they left Paris, Jerome quickly joining her in slumber as he rested his dark head on her golden one.

The first few months of pregnancy could be extremely tiring, as Sapphie well knew, the body having to adjust to all sorts of changes. It had been a bout of morning sickness earlier today that had prevented Dee and Jerome joining them for breakfast, as planned.

'What were you researching in Paris?'

She turned back to look at Rik as his soft voice questioned her.

'Sorry?'

He turned to face her, his broad shoulders moving

beneath the black jacket he wore over a white T-shirt and faded denims. 'You mentioned yesterday that you were in Paris doing some research…?'

Yesterday? Was it really only twenty-four hours since her world had been turned upside down? Life was never going to be quite the same again after this chance meeting with Rik. Because it could happen again at any time, just as it had this time, when she least expected it!

'Once I moved back to England—'

'You left your job as Jerome's PA?'

She smiled. 'I was persuaded, shall we say, that it wasn't quite the thing to do. In the circumstances.'

'I see,' Rik murmured, glancing across at the sleeping Dee with narrowed eyes. 'So you not only lost your fiancé, but your job too?' There was a steely edge to his voice now.

'It was the best move I ever made,' Sapphie responded quickly; she was not about to give him a condensed version of all Dee's little faults and foibles. 'I became a freelance interviewer, doing profiles on the rich and famous, stuff like that. But truth really can be stranger than fiction, and some of the things I learnt…!' She laughed softly. 'I've just managed to have my first book published. And to answer your question, I was in Paris researching part of my second book.'

'You're a writer?' Rik looked impressed. 'What sort of—? Wait a minute!' He sat up straighter in his seat. 'You wouldn't happen to be the new thriller writer everyone is raving about—S.P. Benedict, the author of *Cold Night*—would you?'

Her mouth quirked. 'Sapphire Pearl Benedict,' she announced with feeling. 'A bit of a mouthful, don't you think? Although thank you for at least having heard of my book.'

'It's worse than that, I'm afraid, Sapphie—I've read it!' he told her teasingly. 'My brother, Nik, gave it to me. At one point he was thinking of trying to acquire the film rights, but I read it and...' He broke off. 'You know, Sapphie,' he continued, 'just for once, I would like the two of us to have a conversation without one of us insulting the other!'

Sapphie couldn't help her burst of laughter at the totally awkward expression on Rik's face, although she quietened it down to a soft chuckle as she saw they were disturbing the other couple. 'Perhaps it would be better if we didn't talk at all,' she suggested.

'Not an option,' Rik told her firmly. 'Why don't we just move over there?' He indicated the empty seats opposite them; the carriage was actually only half full. 'Then we won't be disturbing anyone.'

Oh, no? Sapphie was disturbed every moment she spent in this man's company!

Although she found it wasn't quite as bad sitting at the table opposite Rik, who was facing her now rather than sitting next to her, his denim-clad knee occasionally touching hers.

'So you're an author,' Rik said again admiringly. 'It seems we have more in common that I realised.'

'Not really,' Sapphie instantly denied, not wanting to get drawn into that trap. 'Although working with all those actors and actresses, you must be able to appreciate how easy it would be for one of them to murder the other!' she said lightly, hoping to lead the conversation off on another tack.

He pulled a face. 'As a lowly screenwriter, I'm more likely to be the victim than the murderer!'

There was nothing in the least lowly about Rik Prince's writing. He more often than not worked alongside his brothers, Nik Prince, the director, and Zak Prince, the actor. But he didn't collaborate with them exclusively, having worked with and for all the top Hollywood directors at one time or another.

She was hardly on his level, with only one book to her credit!

'Maybe I should make that the subject of my next book,' she said sharply. 'Screenwriter murdered with his own pen!'

'I use a laptop,' Rik drawled drily, at the same time indicating the slim leather case he had placed in the overhead rack opposite.

'Even better,' Sapphie retaliated. 'It would make a rather good blunt instrument, and I bet all the blood could easily be washed off afterwards too.'

Rik gave a rueful smile. 'Vicious little thing, aren't you?'

'I believe I could be,' she acknowledged. 'Given the right circumstances.' Such as someone trying to take her son away from her!

She was sure that most mothers must feel this way, that well of fierce protective maternal love driving them from the minute it swept over them when their newborn child was placed in their arms. Sapphie knew it drove her, and it was a feeling that hadn't diminished in the slightest the last four years. In fact, it had probably grown stronger!

Which was why one part of her—the part that still loved him—wanted to be closer to Rik, while the other part of her—the part that knew how dangerous he was to her son's future—wanted to keep him at arm's length. If not further. Much further!

'But let's not talk about me,' she dismissed briskly. 'You mentioned that you've been working while you were in Paris…?'

'Writing the adapted screenplay for *No Ordinary Boy*,' he explained. 'A labour of love rather than work. My brother, Nik, recently married Jinx Nixon; she's related to the author of the book.'

'I saw their photograph in the newspapers,' Sapphie recalled, also remembering that moment of panic she had felt at the time when she'd realised how much alike the eldest and youngest Prince brothers were, both of them dark and steely-eyed. 'They looked very happy together.'

'They are,' Rik agreed. 'I never thought I would see my big brother fall in love, but boy, when he did…!' He gave an affectionate shake of his head.

'I met him once,' Sapphie explained. 'It was when I was working for Jerome,' she elaborated at Rik's questioning glance. 'I remember Nik as being one of the most focused people I had ever met.'

'He still is,' Rik affirmed. 'But now he's focused on Jinx rather than anything else.'

'Lucky Jinx,' Sapphie murmured wistfully.

Rik looked at her searchingly. 'You aren't another

one of the legion of women who've fallen for my big brother's arrogant elusiveness, are you?'

'Certainly not,' she was stung into replying. 'I admired his attitude to his work.' Her cheeks became flushed. 'Anyway, I'm sure that's all changed now that he's married.'

'Jinx doesn't seem to have any complaints,' Rik agreed.

'Maybe she's already learnt not to,' Sapphie came back tartly. 'I certainly have no intention of ever becoming some man's possession.' She really had no idea whether or not Jinx and Nik's marriage was like that, her remark meant on a personal basis rather than as a criticism of their relationship.

She was her own person, and intended remaining that way. For Matthew's sake as well as her own.

'I don't think that's quite how it is with Nik and Jinx,' Rik rebuked her lightly. 'Jinx is far too strong a character to be dominated in that way. For instance, Nik is the one who has moved to England, shifting the base of Prince Movies to there. Jinx's work is in the UK, and so is her father. Who, incidentally, lives with them.' Having declared his love for Jinx, Nik's commitment had been total.

That sort of loving was obviously a family trait, Rik recognised—except that he had been in love with totally the wrong woman for the last five years!

No, perhaps that was being a little hard on himself. Until yesterday, the woman he'd loved had had Dee's face and body. But after another twenty-four hours spent in her company, he'd come to know that the woman he had loved wasn't real at all.

The woman he'd thought he loved had fire tempered with vulnerability, valued honesty above everything else. Dee wasn't that woman. She had lied to him about so much five years ago—about her family, as well as her reasons for marrying Jerome; so how could he now believe a single word she said?

It was going to take some adjusting to, but he knew with certainty that he really wasn't in love with Dee any more. If he ever really had been...

'You don't have to defend your brother to me, Rik,' Sapphie assured him. 'My opinion of him is totally irrelevant. I met Nik once; I'm unlikely to meet him again.'

Rik tensed. 'How can you be so sure about that?'

'Because people like the Prince brothers have no part in my day-to-day life.'

In other words, he wasn't going to have any part in her day-to-day life, then, either. Not that Sapphie had made any secret of the fact that she wasn't pleased to see him again after all this time. But still it hurt to be dismissed by her in this casual way.

'I'm a Prince brother, and I seem to be part of your life at this moment,' he pointed out mildly.

She gave a nervous smile. 'Once we reach London, and have gone our separate ways, I doubt there will be any reason for the two of us to ever meet again.'

Her tone implied that couldn't happen soon enough, as far as she was concerned. Which irritated Rik intensely!

'I was hoping that you might have dinner with me this evening?' he offered challengingly.

Sapphie gave him a startled look, too surprised to

even try to hide her reaction. 'Why on earth would you want me to do that?' she said incredulously. 'More to the point,' she went on, 'why on earth would you think I would want to have dinner with you, this evening or any other time?' She looked totally stunned by the suggestion.

Rik felt himself scowling darkly. 'Look, I know I behaved badly five years ago, Sapphie—'

'I would rather not talk about that, if you don't mind!' she hissed forcefully, before shooting a pointed look in the direction of the still dozing Dee and Jerome.

Rik sat forward to lean across the table towards her, keeping his voice to a whisper. 'I don't agree. I think we should discuss it,' his tone levelled reasonably, 'if only to set the record straight between us.'

'There's nothing to set straight between us!' Sapphie shot back at him fiercely. 'And I'm sure you don't usually return to discuss one-night stands after they've happened!'

He drew in an angry breath. 'I have never thought of that night in those terms—'

'Of course you have!' she ripped back. 'Stop trying to romanticise something that just wasn't that way at all!'

Perhaps he had been guilty of thinking of their night together in those terms, but he didn't think of it that way now any more—and he didn't care for the fact that she still did!

'That night was as much out of character for me as I'm sure it was for you,' he grated. 'Ask anyone who knows me: my brothers, my sister, and they will all tell you—'

'I have no intention of discussing that night with any third party, thank you very much!' she told him, drawing in controlling breaths. When she spoke again, her voice had softened and become reasoning. 'Why can't you just accept that I want to forget that night? That it would be better for everyone if you did, too?'

He sighed his frustration at her stubbornness. 'I want to get to know you better, Sapphie—'

'Well, I don't want to know another single thing about you,' she assured him. 'Now, would you just leave the subject alone?' she demanded with feeling as she observed Dee and Jerome beginning to wake up.

No, he was afraid he couldn't do that. Not now that he had met Sapphie again. Because she was much more real to him, their night together was so much more real to him, than the mirage of Dee he had carried around in his heart for five years.

But, in the circumstances, he knew that convincing Sapphie of that was going to be no easy task!

Still, a Prince had never been one to back away from a challenge...

Although none of his plans to see Sapphie again showed in his demeanour for the rest of the train journey as he conversed lightly with Dee and Jerome.

Only Sapphie remained distant and apart from the conversation. No doubt wishing the miles away so that she could get away from him all the sooner!

Was there something wrong with him, he wondered, some quirk in his nature that made him feel attracted to women who didn't want to know? Well…in Dee's case, that wasn't strictly true; she had given him the impression that she wanted him too, but couldn't have him. Sapphie just didn't want him!

Except that he was pretty sure he hadn't mistaken her response this morning when he'd kissed her…

He was also pretty sure that he wanted to kiss her again. And sooner, rather than later!

'I have a car waiting, if you would like to join us?' Jerome informed Sapphie and Rik, as they all made their way out of Waterloo Station. Other bystanders started recognizing Dee, and soon a crowd had started to gather around them.

'No, thanks, I think we'll just take a cab.' Rik was the one to answer for both himself and Sapphie, at the same time as he took a proprietorial hold of her arm.

'I'll see you later this evening, Sapphie, when I visit Mummy,' Dee had time to call out to her sister before she and Jerome were caught up in the crowd and their wave of adoration for the actress, Diamond McCall.

'Phew.' Rik breathed his relief as he and Sapphie escaped the throng.

Sapphie pulled out of his grasp before stepping away from him. 'I'm not getting in any taxi with you,' she told him stiffly, seeming even more distant now that they were back on her native soil.

He wasn't too surprised at having his plan to take Sapphie home thwarted, and at the same time find out her address; Sapphie was neither stupid, nor gullible.

Of course, there was always the possibility that she shared a home with the faceless Matthew...

Damn it, why hadn't he thought of that earlier?

'I wasn't seriously suggesting that you would,' he rasped harshly, more annoyed than he could ever have imagined he'd be at the idea of Sapphie living with another man. 'I just thought you would prefer not to be caught up in Dee's three-ring circus!'

Mobile phones and cameras were flashing further down the station now, as excited travellers took their chance to record the actress's arrival. There were even one or two paparazzi.

With a cynicism Rik hadn't known he possessed, he couldn't help wondering if Dee or Jerome hadn't tipped off the Press themselves. Dee certainly seemed to court adoration, and Jerome, as her agent, was too much of a businessman not to want to take advantage of that.

'Oh.' Sapphie looked slightly nonplussed at his explanation. 'I would.' She smiled awkwardly. 'Thank you.'

Rik felt his anger fading. 'Did it hurt you to say that?'

She gave a self-deriding grimace. 'Only a little,' she sighed before drawing herself up determinedly and thrusting out her hand. 'Well, Rik, this is goodbye. It's been—interesting, meeting you again.' She gave a humourless smile. 'Perhaps we can do it again in another five years or so!'

Rik reached out to lightly grasp the hand she held out to him, not to shake as she had intended, but to gently pull her towards him. 'This isn't goodbye,

Sapphie,' he warned, unable to fight the compulsion he felt to take her in his arms and kiss her.

And for a moment—too brief a moment as far as he was concerned!—he felt her response, her lips parting beneath his, the slenderness of her body pressed against his, her breasts warm and soft—

Sapphie pulled sharply away, her eyes blazing like molten gold as she glared up at him. 'I said goodbye, Rik, and that was what I meant!' She bent to pick up her bag before turning on her heel and walking away from him, quickly becoming lost in the crowd.

Rik stood where she left him, not even attempting to stop or follow her, knowing he had pushed his luck enough for one day where Sapphie was concerned.

He walked slowly out of the station, got into a cab and gave the driver his brother Nik's address, a slight smile starting to curve his lips as he settled back on the seat and began to formulate a plan for seeing Sapphie again.

Because no matter what Sapphie might think to the contrary—might hope to the contrary!—there was far too much left unsaid and done between them for him to allow this to be the last they saw of each other.

Far too much!

CHAPTER SEVEN

'HONESTLY, Mother, I have absolutely no idea what we're even doing here!' Sapphie grumbled as she looked around the star-filled reception room in one of London's top hotels.

'Don't be such a wet blanket, Sapphie,' Joan McCall chided her daughter affectionately. Joan was still a voluptuously attractive woman in her early fifties, the black sequinned dress she was wearing showing off her curvaceous figure to advantage, her shoulder-length auburn hair only needing a little professional help to maintain that vibrant colour. 'I, for one, am enjoying myself. This is the first time Dee has ever invited us to one of these parties.' Joan glowed happily.

Actually, technically, Dee hadn't done the inviting this time; Jerome had. And after a week of glancing nervously over her shoulder in case Rik should suddenly appear—there had been far too much of a determined glint in his eyes when they'd parted a week ago for her to be sure that he wouldn't!—Sapphie was treating the whole thing with suspicion. But so far—thank goodness!—there wasn't a Prince in sight!

And there was no doubting that her mother was enjoying this after-première party. They hadn't actually been invited to see the film itself—but Joan's face lit up excitedly as her hazel-coloured eyes spotted one star after another.

Sapphie, less trusting of the sudden invitation, had checked, and double-checked, to see if any of the Prince brothers—director, actor, or screenwriter—had had anything to do with the making of Dee's latest film. They hadn't. So, reluctantly, and under pressure from her mother, Sapphie had accepted for both of them.

She sipped her glass of champagne and looked around her—there had to be some consolation to feeling like a goldfish in the midst of a group of piranhas!—before answering her mother. 'Personally, I would much rather be at home with Matthew,' she muttered, not at all mollified by the fact that Matthew had told her she looked a lovely mummy when she went to tuck him in and kiss him goodnight.

To add insult to injury, she had even had to go out and buy a new dress for the evening! Occasionally Sapphie went to parties, or enjoyed just quiet evenings with friends. But there had certainly been nothing in her wardrobe to wear to a post-première party. Especially one that celebrated her sister as the star of the film!

Her mother had gone on the dress-shopping expedition with her, persuading Sapphie to spend some of her hard-earned royalties on a Chinese-style sheath of gold-coloured silk. With her hair lightly secured on top of her head, her legs tanned and silky and three-inch heels on her gold-coloured shoes, Dee certainly couldn't complain that she hadn't made an effort!

'Don't be silly, dear,' her mother dismissed distractedly now. 'It's eleven o'clock; Matthew has been asleep for hours.'

'Curled up in bed with a good book, then,' Sapphie persisted; who on earth went out to a party that only started at ten-thirty?

She would stay for an hour, an hour and a half at the outside, she had promised herself when she accepted the invitation. Just long enough to add weight to the happy-family image that Dee was promoting this week.

The news of Dee's pregnancy had appeared in the newspapers earlier in the week, photographs of an ecstatic Dee and Jerome printed along with them.

Although as she looked at Dee now, surrounded by friends and admirers, radiantly beautiful in a revealing green dress that exactly matched the colour of her eyes, her figure still slender and willowy, it was difficult to believe that in six months' time she would be a mother.

Sapphie shook her head as she turned back to her starry-eyed mother. 'I can't wait to leave!'

'I'm sorry to hear that, Miss Benedict,' a man drawled pleasantly behind her, his accent noticeably American—although thankfully it wasn't Rik Prince's! 'It is Miss Benedict, isn't it?' the man enquired lightly as Sapphie turned sharply. 'I believe we met in New York several years ago.'

The man was older than Rik, his eyes a cool grey, but nevertheless the likeness between the two men was obvious; the dark hair was the same, as was the powerfully lean body, and that sensually smiling mouth.

Nik Prince!

There was no mistaking those arrogantly sculptured features. And if Sapphie had any doubts—which she didn't!—the red-haired woman standing smilingly beside him gave his identity away; it was only weeks ago that a blaze of publicity had surrounded Juliet 'Jinx' Nixon, now Jinx Prince, and her photograph had been on the front page of every British newspaper.

Sapphie had met Nik Prince only briefly six years ago, and she very much doubted she was memorable enough for this man to greet her again like this. But the alternative of Rik having talked to his eldest brother about her didn't ring true either.

'Yes, we did,' Sapphie finally answered him politely.

'I thought I recognised you.'

Sapphie still wasn't convinced. 'This is my mother, Joan McCall.' She drew her mother forward into the circle. 'This is Nik and Juliet Prince, Mother,' she introduced guardedly, still wary at having Nik Prince's considerable charm turned on her.

A charm which he now turned on her mother. 'I can see why Sapphie and Dee are so beautiful; obviously they both take after their lovely mother!' he complimented Joan warmly as the two shook hands. 'You don't look old enough to be an almost-grandmother!'

Joan blushed with pleasure at this flattery from

such a gorgeously handsome man. 'How kind of you to say so, Mr Prince, but actually I'm al—'

'Mr Prince is a well-known film director, Mother,' Sapphie quickly cut in over what she was sure was going to be a mention of Joan's other grandchild, Matthew. Sapphie's son.

'Please call me Nik,' he invited. 'And most of my wife's intimate friends call her Jinx,' he went on warmly, the smile he bestowed on his wife one of intimacy.

Which was a good enough reason for Sapphie to stick to calling the other woman Juliet; she wasn't going to become intimate with any of the Prince family!

'I find these parties a little overwhelming too,' Juliet confided, clearly attuned to Sapphie's own discomfort. 'Perhaps when Rik arrives we can all go and have a quiet drink somewhere else in the hotel?'

Only one part of that suggestion registered with Sapphie—*when Rik arrives*!

She glanced quickly around the room, feeling like prey that was being hunted, but unsure exactly which direction the attack was going to come from!

Rik was coming to this party, too!

Now she was convinced that her invitation wasn't just the act of kindness on Jerome's part that it had appeared. But the question was, who had been instrumental in setting this meeting up: Jerome, as another act of misguided matchmaking, or Rik himself?

The fact that Nik Prince and his wife were here and

had made a point of coming over and speaking to her made her inclined to believe it was the latter...

But why? Hadn't she made it more than obvious—bluntly so!—that she didn't want to see Rik again?

And hadn't she also spent the last week just waiting for something like this to happen, convinced that Rik had meant it when he told her it wasn't goodbye?

She drew in a deeply controlling breath, her smile forced as she turned back to look at the Princes, her hand tightly clutching her evening bag. 'That won't be possible, I'm afraid,' she declined evenly, while inside her feelings were in turmoil; she had to get away from here before Rik arrived! 'I have to be home by twelve o'clock.' Thank goodness she had only booked the babysitter until then!

'Why is that?' drawled an all-too-familiar voice. 'Do you turn into a pumpkin at midnight?'

Sapphie froze, having been surreptitiously watching the main doors for Rik's entrance. However, it seemed he had chosen instead to enter by one of the fire exits at the back of the room. He couldn't have chosen a better way to disconcert her!

Well, if that had been his intention, he had definitely succeeded!

Actually, disconcerted didn't even begin to describe how she felt as she slowly turned to face him, her breath completely taken away by how gorgeous he looked in a black dinner suit, black bow-tie and snowy white shirt, his hair slightly damp, as if it was raining outside, or he had recently taken a shower.

His warm blue eyes echoed the companionship

he'd offered her on the train from Paris, his smile wide with pleasure as he took hold of her hand before bending to kiss her lightly on the cheeks. 'It's good to see you again,' he told her quietly, at the same time keeping a firm hold of her hand.

Everything else apart—her mother's presence, Rik's brother and sister-in-law, Matthew—she had to admit it was good to see him too. Her pulse fluttered erratically and her cheeks grew hot with the pleasure of being with him again.

But it wouldn't do—because there was no way Matthew could be kept apart in this situation. There never would be.

'It was the coach that turned back into a pumpkin at midnight, not Cinderella!' she teased.

He shrugged unconcernedly, still smiling warmly down at her. 'I never was very good where fairy stories were concerned!'

Sapphie was, had known them all when she was a child. But she wasn't a child any longer, and she knew there could be no fairy-tale ending to this particular story. All she could hope for was to limit the damage. And the only way to do that, she knew, was to get out of here, as far away from Rik as possible.

'No, as I recall, Rik always preferred adventure stories,' his brother put in mockingly. 'Swashbuckling pirates and the like!'

It wasn't too difficult for Sapphie to imagine Rik as a little boy—after all, she had one just like him at home!—with his head buried in a book, totally absorbed in the adventures written there.

But that image—Matthew!—reminded her all too forcefully of why she had to leave. Now!

'Thanks, Nik,' Rik drawled ruefully before turning to Sapphie's mother. 'I'm Rik Prince, Mrs McCall.'

'Oh, dear,' Joan fluttered flusteredly. 'If your brother Zak walks in too, I shall just faint away!'

'Don't worry, Joan,' Juliet Prince was the one to answer laughingly. 'Zak is still away on his extended honeymoon.'

'Yes,' her husband joked. 'We may never see him or Tyler again!'

Juliet gave him a playful punch in the arm. 'You're only jealous because you're an old married man of three months!'

Nik gave her a wolfish grin that totally belied the 'old' part of that statement. 'I'll ask you to say that to me again later tonight, Mrs Prince!'

This family banter was all well and good, Sapphie acknowledged impatiently, but it was holding her back from getting her out of here. Despite several discreet attempts to release herself, Rik still had a tight hold of her hand! 'I really do have to leave—'

'No, you don't, Sapphie,' her mother was the one to answer her firmly. 'I think it would be much more appropriate if I was to leave and you stayed on here with your friends. You get out so little as it is—'

'Mother, I went to Paris for four days only last week,' Sapphie protested sharply. For one thing, none of the Prince family were her friends. For another, she knew by the tingling in her hand and up her arm that she really did have to get away from here. From Rik.

Just being near him again like this was doing strange things to her. Her cheeks felt permanently hot, her stomach was churning nervously. And as his hand held hers—his thumb was lightly caressing her palm now—she trembled all over.

She had to get away from him—and it was no longer just for Matthew's sake!

Rik watched Sapphie from beneath lowered lids, able to feel the turmoil inside her through her hand as it trembled slightly in his. He could also see the flush in her cheeks, and the vulnerability of her neck and throat, which were exposed by the way her hair was swept up in softly loose tendrils that lightly caressed her nape and temples.

His lips longed to caress her too!

She looked absolutely beautiful this evening: her gold-coloured silk dress shimmered against her curves, the high-necked knee-length style somehow managing to look as sexy as hell.

Although he had to admit, she could probably have worn a sack and he would still have found her sexy!

This last week of waiting to see her again had seemed more like a month to him, his patience stretched to its limits as he chafed against the delay. Nik had been the one to arrange their presence at tonight's party. Rik hadn't dared risk even a breath of his own attendance reaching Sapphie's ear; he knew her well enough by now to know that she would simply not have come if she'd known he was going to be here as well.

It had done absolutely nothing for his ego to admit that, and Nik had laughed himself almost to tears once Rik had explained the situation to him. Especially as it turned out that Nik knew a lot more about Diamond McCall than Rik ever had; apparently, her flirtations with her leading men were legendary amongst the movie set, and she'd even tried it on with Zak on one memorable occasion, but had failed miserably because of Zak's aversion to being involved with married women.

Rik still inwardly winced at Nik's reaction when he'd told his brother he had thought himself in love with Dee for the last five years. 'With Diamond McCall?' Nik had exclaimed. 'The woman is a walking, talking Venus fly-trap!'

'That really isn't helping Rik right now, darling,' Jinx had reproved concernedly.

Thank goodness for Jinx! She had been the one to come up with this evening's party as a way for him to see Sapphie again, even offering her own and Nik's presence as moral support. Knowing how much she hated these things, Rik had deeply appreciated—and quickly accepted—the offer, on the basis that Sapphie was less likely to just tell him to go away in front of his family!

'That was work, Sapphie,' her mother gently refuted her protest. 'I can easily take the car home that Jerome has put at our disposal this evening,' she offered. 'And you can come along later,' she urged evenly, smiling approvingly at Sapphie's hand, which was still held fast by Rik's.

Joan McCall wasn't part of the conspiracy to get Rik and Sapphie together, but at that moment she might just as well have been, Rik acknowledged admiringly.

Although he wasn't quite so pleased a second later when Sapphie pointedly removed her hand from his, obviously having also seen her mother's smiling approval.

Sapphie shook her head. 'You know I have an early start in the morning—'

'It isn't going to matter if you sleep in a little this once, Sapphie,' her mother insisted firmly. 'I want you to stay and have fun this evening. In fact, I insist upon it,' Joan McCall told her eldest daughter determinedly. 'Matthew isn't going to mind a bit once I've explained it to him.' She smiled encouragingly.

Matthew…!

There was the mention of that man again!

But if he was in Sapphie's life, then why wasn't he here with her tonight?

Damn it, the one time Rik had casually mentioned this Matthew to Jerome, the other man had dismissed him as not being a problem.

But Matthew certainly seemed like one at the moment if it meant Sapphie had to leave early because of him!

Sapphie, surprisingly, had gone very quiet after her mother's last remark, a fact Joan took advantage of as she made her hurried goodbyes before crossing the room to say goodnight to her youngest daughter.

Dee, predictably, was at the centre of an adoring crowd, a brilliant green butterfly shimmering above lesser mortals.

The vision left Rik cold. In fact, the more he learnt about Dee, the less he liked her. Why, oh, why hadn't he tried to find out more about her long ago? He could have saved himself years of heartache if he had. Forget Dee, he told himself impatiently, it was Sapphie who was important.

Sapphie was still incredibly quiet, he realised suddenly, and she seemed to have gone slightly pale now, too. Because her mother had mentioned Matthew? What sort of hold must the man have over her if she reacted in this way just at the mention of his name?

'If Matthew means so much to you, then why the hell isn't he here tonight—?' Rik broke off abruptly as Nik began to cough as if he were choking. A frowning glance from Rik in Nik's direction was rewarded by an impatient glare from his brother. Cool it, Nik's angry grey eyes warned exasperatedly.

Rik gave an inward wince at that unspoken warning, glad of the diversion created by Jinx, who set about acquiring a glass of champagne—totally unnecessary, as it happened—to help ease her husband's coughing fit. It gave Rik a chance to regain his jealous temper.

Nik was right; what was he trying to do, alienate Sapphie before the evening was out? He had already known about Matthew; his mission tonight was to encourage Sapphie to get to know him, to like being with him—not to annoy her to the point where she decided to leave!

'He wasn't invited,' Sapphie answered him stiffly now. 'And I really don't think—'

'We were just about to retire to one of the hotel bars for a quiet drink,' Jinx put in, Nik's coughing fit over as he sipped his fresh champagne with obvious enjoyment. 'Come on, Nik,' she linked her arm with her husband's, 'let's go and see if we can find a nice, quiet corner somewhere for the four of us to sit.'

Briefly leaving Rik alone with Sapphie. A tongue-tied Rik, as it happened. He had been thinking of this moment all week, and now that it was here he just didn't know what to say. How did you go about explaining to a woman that the dream woman you had been in love with for the last five years was nothing but a figment of your own imagination? That in the short time he had spent with Sapphie she had become so much more real to him? That he liked listening to her talk? That he just liked being with her, full stop?

That he was falling in love with her!

If he wasn't already in love with her…

He had debated long and hard this last week how he felt about her. He knew that he longed to see her again. That he loved the way she spoke so honestly to him. That he found her company stimulating. That just looking at her excited him in a way he wouldn't have believed possible.

But he also knew from previous conversations with her that it was going to take a lot more than words to convince Sapphie he was no longer in love with Dee—although the simple truth of the matter was, he never had been!

'You look wonderful,' he volunteered.

Sapphie gave him a startled look from those incredible amber-coloured eyes of hers, obviously not expecting the compliment after his earlier sharpness—he really would have to try to control his jealousy. Thank goodness Nik had managed to stop him this time before he completely alienated Sapphie all over again!

'Incredibly beautiful, in fact,' Rik added softly, rewarded by the blush that heightened her cheeks.

But, despite the blush, she remarked, 'Dee has always been the beautiful one of the family!' He probably deserved that, Rik accepted. Until they'd met again last week, and he'd come to realise how feisty and beautiful Sapphie was; apart from the odd wistful thought of that passionate night five years ago—and the odd guilty one too!—he hadn't really given Sapphie's feelings too much consideration. Sapphie had gone from his hotel suite the next morning before he'd even awoken; nothing, not even a tissue or used glass, had betrayed her presence there.

Not that Rik had told Nik and Jinx everything about what had happened when he'd slept with Sapphie; that would remain their secret, was no one else's business but their own!

'Shall we go and join the others?' Sapphie suggested stiffly. 'As it would appear that I'm not going to be allowed to leave until I've had at least one drink with you all!' she added impatiently before turning and striding off after Nik and Jinx.

At least, she tried to stride, but her dress, its silk material fitting snugly to her breasts, waist and thighs to just above her knees, made it impossible for her to do more than take small, elegant steps.

Rik caught up with her easily, taking a light hold of her elbow, matching his steps to hers before grinning down at her. 'I'm beginning to like your dress more and more!'

Sapphie shot him an exasperated glare for his trouble.

But she didn't come back with one of her sharp put-downs. And she didn't try to pull away from him again, either.

It was a start...

CHAPTER EIGHT

SAPPHIE was enjoying herself!

A glance at her wrist-watch told her it had been over an hour since she and Rik had joined Jinx and Nik in a quiet alcove in one of the hotel's public bars. An hour during which Nik had ordered another bottle of champagne to be served to the four of them and then he and his wife had gone out of their way, Sapphie was sure, to put her at her ease, regaling her and Rik with stories of the funnier side of their brief courtship and their marriage.

Sapphie was sure the champagne was helping her to relax too, but all the same, this meeting with Rik hadn't been as difficult as she had imagined it would be. There was no Dee around to sour things, for a start!

Although Sapphie still suspected that this whole encounter had been arranged by Rik, somehow. She wasn't sure how he had done it—or even why he should have bothered!—but she nevertheless felt the chance meeting with Nik and Jinx, and then Rik's appearance, had all been choreographed.

But she was still enjoying herself!

In fact, apart from that brief moment of panic earlier when her mother had mentioned Matthew, the evening had turned out to be nowhere near as traumatic as she had might have feared.

Apart from that brief moment of panic earlier when her mother had mentioned Matthew...!

At the time Sapphie had thought she was about to have a heart attack!

So far, mainly due to Dee's coy behaviour on the only other occasion Matthew's name had been mentioned, Rik seemed to have the impression that Matthew was the current man in her life, and certainly had no idea he was only four years old.

But he had come pretty close this evening to discovering the truth...

She shouldn't be enjoying herself, shouldn't relax her guard for a moment when she was around Rik!

'More champagne?' he offered attentively, holding the bottle over her half-empty wine glass.

'I don't think so, thank you,' she refused. 'I really should be going soon.'

Very soon. Before she relaxed too much and became incautious about what she said.

'Why?' Rik topped her champagne glass up anyway. 'I would have thought you worked from home.'

She did. But just because she might have had only a couple of hours' sleep didn't mean that her son—their son—wouldn't come bouncing into her bedroom at his usual six-thirty in the morning, expecting her to be as bright and happy as he was!

Admittedly she shared a house with her mother, and had done so since Matthew was born. But that was really only as moral support, Sapphie preferring, whenever possible, to take care of Matthew herself.

She absolutely adored him...!

'Actually, I think we're the ones who should be

going,' Nik Prince put in lightly. 'My wife issued me with a challenge earlier this evening—I would like to go home and collect on my success!' He smiled suggestively at his wife as he stood up before pulling Jinx to her feet beside him. 'It's been really nice meeting you again, Sapphie,' he told her pleasantly, his arm about his wife's shoulders now.

'Very nice,' Jinx echoed warmly, obviously quite happy at the thought of going home. 'Perhaps the two of you would like to come to dinner, say—Saturday evening?' she prompted brightly.

Sapphie blinked, taken totally aback by the invitation, let alone the phrase 'the two of you'!

Surely Nik and Jinx didn't think that she and Rik were really a couple? Admittedly, Rik had kissed her when he arrived, and held her hand for longer than was really necessary, but even so...

No, she decided as she watched the two brothers exchange a knowing look. This was another ploy on Rik's part, she was sure; the invitation had nothing to do with what had happened this evening and everything to do with preplanning on the part of the Prince family.

Her mouth set mutinously, she shot Rik a resentful glare as she stood up. 'No, I don't think—'

'How about I call you tomorrow, Jinx, and let you know?' Rik cut in smoothly as he stood up too. 'Sapphie probably has to check her diary or something.' His arm moved lightly about Sapphie's waist.

Her diary, as Sapphie well knew, was completely empty of future engagements; she just didn't like being manoeuvred in this way!

'No—'

'Yes, please do call me, Rik.' Jinx moved forward
to kiss him warmly on the cheek before moving to
do the same to Sapphie. 'I really have enjoyed meeting you this evening, Sapphie, and we'd love for you
to come to dinner on Saturday.' Her clear eyes looked
steadily into Sapphie's.

There was no doubting the other woman's sincerity, just as there was no doubt in Sapphie's mind that
she had enjoyed meeting Jinx and her husband. Rik
was the problem here…just being anywhere near him.

Because she was so totally aware of him, found her
defences weakening the longer she was with him.
She'd already fallen into that trap once. Once was an
accident, twice was just pure stupidity!

'I'll try,' she murmured noncommittally, very
aware of the warmth of Rik's arm about her waist.

'Good.' Jinx squeezed her arm.

Sapphie managed to keep the smile on her lips for
as long as it took Jinx and Nik to leave. At which
time she turned furiously on Rik. 'You arranged all
this!' she accused, eyes blazing. 'Your brother and
his wife! The two of us meeting! The invitation to
dinner on Saturday evening!' She glared at Rik,
breathing hard in her agitation.

Rik continued to look at her for several seconds,
and then he nodded. 'Yes.'

Her eyes widened. 'What did you say?'

'I said yes,' he repeated patiently. 'It was all pre-
arranged. The meeting with Nik and Jinx to break the
ice. My own arrival a few minutes later. The dinner

invitation just now.' He sighed. 'Why don't we sit down and—?'

'I don't want to sit down,' she flung back, stung by his easy acquiescence to her accusations; she had at least expected him to attempt to deny them! But then, when did Rik ever do what she expected him to do…? 'I want to know the reason you did all that.'

'I wanted to see you again. You made it very clear, the last time we met, that you didn't want to see me—'

'For obvious reasons!' Sapphie reminded him. 'Just because Dee stole the man I loved does not mean I need you to fill the gap!'

Rik gave a smile. 'Dee doesn't love me. She never did.' Sapphie knew that, knew that Dee loved Jerome as much as she was capable of loving anyone other than herself. But that didn't necessarily change the way Rik had always felt about Dee…

'That may be so,' Sapphie retorted. 'But *you* still love *her*—and she knows it.'

He quirked dark brows quizzically. 'I'm not answerable for what Dee does or doesn't know—or thinks she knows,' he replied softly.

She looked at him searchingly. What did he mean? Was he saying that…?

She gave an impatient shake of her head. 'I don't have the time for this.' She bent to pick up her evening bag. 'It's been—different,' she said. 'But now I have to go.' Because she was past anger, and now felt as if she was about to cry…!

'I'll walk outside with you and make sure you—'

'Rik—don't!' she choked, her head down, her vision now blurred by unshed tears. 'I—I like my life exactly the way that it is. I was happy! I don't want—don't want—'

'Sapphie, are you crying?' Rik groaned, lightly grasping her arm to turn her to face him. 'You are! Damn it—I never meant to make you cry!'

'Then what did you mean to do?' she demanded emotionally. 'Why go to all this trouble—?'

'It was no trouble, Sapphie,' he assured her huskily. 'And I had asked to see you again,' he reminded her, 'but you said no.'

'For very good reason!' She nodded. 'I didn't want to see you again.' What she really wanted with this man, and what she could actually have, were two distinctly different things! 'No matter what impression you may have to the contrary, Rik, I do not indulge in affairs!' No matter what she might have told him—out of pure self-defence!—there had been no other lovers in her life but Rik. She hadn't wanted any...

But she did still want Rik; her traitorous body told her so every time she was near him. As she wanted him now...!

'I really do have to go, Rik.' Before she made a complete idiot of herself!

And they had already attracted enough attention for one evening, she realised as she saw the curious looks being sent their way by the other people in the bar.

Too much attention for Sapphie's comfort. She turned on her heel to walk quickly out of the room, across the reception area and outside into the refreshing night air, breathing it in deeply as she fought the compulsion to be sick.

'Sapphie…?'

She had no defences left, no strength to fight Rik, who had followed her outside. He took her into his arms, his brilliant blue gaze holding hers briefly before he lowered his head and his mouth claimed hers.

Oh…!

Her need for this man was just too much for her to resist, her lips parting beneath his even as her arms moved up over his shoulders and her fingers became entwined in the silky dark hair at his nape.

With a low groan in his throat Rik deepened the kiss, his arms tightening about her waist as he moulded her slender curves to the harder planes of his body.

Nothing had changed, Sapphie acknowledged achingly; she loved and wanted this man. Only this man. She realised now that she always would.

'Sapphie!' Rik husked now, his lips moving to the warm sensitivity of her throat. 'Sapphie!' he murmured achingly, his hands moving restlessly along the length of her spine, his tongue seeking the hollows at the base of her neck, his breath warm against her already overheated skin. 'I want you, Sapphie.' His voice was intent as he raised his head to look at her. 'Sapphie, please—'

'No!' she managed to gasp weakly, desperately seeking the strength to pull away from him. And failing.

'You want me too, Sapphie,' he insisted as her body continued to betray her. 'Stop fighting me, darling—'

'I am not your darling,' she burst out, at the same

time pushing ineffectually at his shoulders. 'Rik, let me go! You have to let me go!' she pleaded as he made no effort to do so. 'Don't you understand it yet that there's simply no room in my life for you?' This last was intended to hurt.

And she had succeeded if the darkening of his expression was anything to go by. His arms moved up to grasp her arms. 'I didn't imagine your response just now,' he grated harshly. 'Or in Paris. Or in London when we said goodbye—'

'Exactly—we said goodbye, Rik,' she reminded him. 'As for my responding to you...' She made her voice as hard as she could. 'So you're a more than competent lover—what does that prove?' She looked at him with challenge, while all the while her heart was breaking inside at the deliberate gulf she was putting between the two of them.

Rik frowned ominously even as he returned her stare. 'What does it prove?' he bit out. 'Well, for one thing, it proves you aren't in love with anyone called Matthew!'

Sapphie felt herself sway as her knees went weak, all of the colour draining from her face as she looked at him with wide, amber-bruised eyes.

Rik watched the change that came over her with ever-increasing dismay. And puzzlement. Why had the mere mention of the other man's name have such a physical as well as emotional effect on her? What hold did this man have on Sapphie to make her react in this way?

She drew in a deep breath, seeming to gather herself up, glaring at him with fiercely intense eyes now, the colour returned to her cheeks as her anger grew. 'You're wrong; I love Matthew with every fibre of my being!'

The words were like nails in Rik's flesh, his hands falling helplessly to his sides as he stared at her disbelievingly.

'He's the last thing I think of before I go to sleep at night,' Sapphie continued emotionally. 'The first person I think of when I wake in the morning. And if, for any reason, I should ever feel sad or dispirited,' her voice grew stronger, 'then I just have to think of Matthew's smile, a smile that's only for me, and then nothing seems quite as bad as I thought it was.' Amber eyes looked steadily into his now. 'Isn't that love?'

Rik blinked dazedly. It certainly sounded like it to him; was the way he had been thinking of Sapphie since they'd met up again in Paris.

Too late.

Damn it, he was always too late!

He didn't know what to say in answer to her challenge. Telling her how he felt now seemed a waste of time. His as well as hers.

He'd had his chance with this woman five years ago, and well and truly blown it; it was too much to hope, too much to ask, that a woman as beautiful as Sapphie would still be free after all this time. Sheer bloody arrogance on his part, in fact!

He gave a humourless smile. 'It certainly sounds a lot like it!' he allowed heavily.

'Good,' she dismissed briskly. 'At least we're

agreed on something! Now, if you don't mind, I'm going home.' She signalled the first cab waiting in the line outside the hotel. 'Why don't you go back inside and enjoy the party?' she suggested offhandedly as she got in the back of the cab and closed the door firmly behind her.

Rik stood on the pavement and watched the cab as it pulled away, continuing to watch it until it was swallowed up in the late-night traffic.

He couldn't move. Didn't want to move, felt as if once he went back into the hotel he would be shutting a door on Sapphie.

Instead he turned on his heel, hands in his pockets, and began to walk towards the River Thames.

He had always found something soothing about moving water; his mother had claimed it was because she swam in the ocean all the time when she was pregnant with him. Maybe she was right, because minutes later, staring down into the moon-reflected water, he felt a certain calm moving over and into him.

Sapphie said she loved this Matthew, and her sincerity had rung true. But at the same time Rik knew that she wouldn't—couldn't—have responded to him in that way if she really was *in love* with this other man.

But was that of any help to him in the face of Sapphie's obstinate claim that she loved Matthew?

He had absolutely no idea, he realised, of what he was going to do next.

Which was why he was in no mood, having walked back to the hotel—he had booked a suite there for the night—to get into conversation with Jerome Powers, of all people!

Sapphie had once loved this man, had been about to marry him, would have married him if Dee hadn't come along and taken him for herself. Ridiculously, Rik found himself jealous even of that past love.

'Hi, Rik,' the other man greeted him jovially, seemingly impervious to Rik's scowl. 'I just came out to check on where the four of you had got to.'

'The others have all gone home, and I'm just on my way upstairs to bed,' Rik answered Jerome flatly, just wanting to get away, to be on his own, to lick his wounds in private.

Jerome grinned unconcernedly. 'Feeling lucky, were you?' he said smugly. 'That sort of thing isn't going to work with Sapphie, I'm afraid. Once bitten, twice shy and all that.' Considering Jerome was the 'once bitten' part of that statement, Rik found his attitude less than charming.

He shook his head, his hands clenched at his sides as he resisted the impulse to actually hit the older man. 'I would really rather not talk about Sapphie, if you don't mind!' He had no objection to talking with Sapphie, but he certainly wasn't going to talk about her. Especially with Jerome Powers! 'And shouldn't you be getting back to your wife rather than out here looking for Sapphie?' he prompted pointedly.

Jerome's smile widened proudly. 'Doesn't Dee-Dee look absolutely stunning this evening?' now left him absolutely cold—it was auburn fire that he wanted.

'You're right, I should get back,' Jerome agreed.

'But I wouldn't give up on Sapphie if I were you; I can see that she likes you really.'

Liking him was one thing—and he wasn't convinced that she did like him!—but Rik wanted more than that. So much more! And he wasn't even sure when—or even if—he was ever going to see her again.

Simply going and knocking on her door hadn't seemed like an option after the way they had parted at the railway station last week, which was why he had organised such a convoluted meeting this evening. But, from Sapphie's reaction, he knew for sure that something like that wasn't going to work a second time.

After the things Sapphie had said to him tonight he wasn't certain there was any point, either.

Damn it, he had never bothered with a hotel-room bar before in his life, but right now it seemed very tempting! Drunk had to be better than this aching pain.

Somewhere after the fourth glass of whisky—or could it have been the third gin?—he must have drifted off to sleep, because when the loud ringing of the telephone woke him some time the next morning he found himself slumped in an armchair, still wearing his dinner suit.

He sat up quickly, only to collapse back down again as his head threatened to explode. And still the telephone continued to ring in that mind-shattering way.

He made a grab for the receiver, dropping it with a clatter the first time, then finally managing to bring the receiver up to his ear. 'Whoever you are, please go away,' he groaned, feeling as if he had scrambled eggs for brains and cotton wool in his mouth; this getting drunk was way overrated, he decided.

A hearty laugh sounding down the telephone line made him wince. 'You don't sound too good, little brother,' Nik drawled with obvious amusement.

'I'll let you know about that later—at the moment I'm just trying to keep my head on my shoulders!'

Nik gave another chuckle. 'I gather things didn't go well after we left last night?'

Rik shut his eyes at that understatement. 'You could say that.'

'I just did,' his eldest brother returned. 'But the reason I rang is that I've just had a very interesting business meeting with Jerome—did you know he and Dee are flying back to the States this afternoon?'

Didn't know. Didn't care. And he wasn't in any sort of mood to discuss business.

'What the hell is the time?' Rik opened his eyes and tried to focus on his wrist-watch, finally managing to make out that it was eleven-thirty; not surprising really when he must have gone to sleep—passed out?—at around four-thirty. At least he'd had the foresight to put the 'Do Not Disturb' notice on his door! 'Nik, I'm really not awake yet, so can I call you back after I've showered and dressed?'

'No problem,' Nik accepted. 'Although I really only called to tell you that, according to Jerome, the reason Sapphie is so wary of becoming involved with anyone is that she has a young child. The father left her literally holding the baby, apparently, and...'

Rik was no longer listening, felt completely numb. And this time it had nothing to do with the drink he had consumed into the wee small hours.

A child. Sapphie had a child. What the hell—?

'A little boy.' Nik's words penetrated again. 'By the name of Matthew.'

It wasn't another man at all that she talked of with such love, but her own child...

Rik knew what he had to do!

CHAPTER NINE

'Do you ever intend to tell him that he has a son?'

Sapphie's face paled as she looked across the kitchen table at her mother. The two of them were enjoying a late-morning cup of coffee together, while Matthew happily sat on the floor at their feet, totally engrossed in a box of special building bricks he'd been given on his fourth birthday a couple of months ago.

Sapphie hadn't slept well. In fact, when Matthew had come into her bedroom this morning at his usual time of six-thirty she wasn't sure she had been to sleep at all, images of the evening running again and again through her head.

'Sorry?' She looked dazedly at her mother, not quite sure she had heard her correctly.

'I thought, at first, when you introduced me to Nik Prince and his lovely young wife that he was Matthew's father, the likeness was so noticeable. Which, considering his recent marriage, would have been something of a disaster,' her mother opined. 'But once Rik Prince arrived, I realised how mistaken I had been. So, I repeat, Sapphie,' she pressed, her frown troubled now, 'are you going to tell him about Matthew?'

Sapphie swallowed hard, having had no idea until this moment that her mother had noticed Rik's resemblance to Matthew; Joan had already been in bed, fast asleep, when Sapphie got in last night. She'd checked on Matthew before she went to bed herself and had found that he was fast asleep too, his small, loose-limbed body sprawled sideways across the bed, dark curls framing his cherubic features.

His resemblance to Rik had made her heart ache.

But she was stunned now by her mother's quietly posed question; it simply hadn't occurred to her that once her mother had seen Rik she would realise he was Matthew's father!

She swallowed hard. 'I hadn't intended to, no,' she said gruffly, knowing there was absolutely no point in trying to deny something that was so glaringly obvious to someone who knew Matthew so well and had now met Rik.

Her mother sipped her own coffee before answering. 'Why not?'

'You can ask me that?' Sapphie gasped, shooting a concerned glance at Matthew as he looked up curiously, her reassuring smile enough for him to go back to his building bricks. 'Can you imagine what that would do to Matthew's life?' she asked her mother softly. 'An English mother and an American father; he would become a human ping-pong ball, bouncing across the Atlantic!' She looked worried at the thought.

'It may not come to that—'

'Of course it will come to that!' Sapphie insisted agitatedly.

'But Rik Prince so obviously likes you—'

'Well, of course he likes me—he wants to go to

bed with me!' Again, she could have added, but didn't.

Her mother looked troubled. 'I've never pressed you for the identity of Matthew's father; I've tried to respect the fact that you didn't want to talk about him and told myself that you knew best. But now that I've actually met him…!' Joan shook her head. 'It doesn't seem right somehow. He seems like a nice man, a responsible man—'

'He's both those things,' Sapphie allowed; after all, she was in love with him—she could hardly make him out to be some sort of monster!

'I thought so,' her mother rejoined. 'Couldn't the two of you try to make a go of it? Perhaps even get married—'

'And live happily ever after?' Sapphie cut in fiercely. 'This is the real world, Mother, not a fairy story!'

'I do know that, Sapphie,' Joan answered quietly. 'I'm fifty-two years old, and I've been widowed twice; of course I know that.'

Of course she did, Sapphie acknowledged guiltily; her mother never talked of loneliness, always seemed happy, kept herself occupied with her bridge and gardening clubs. But that didn't mean she hadn't sometimes been lonely and unhappy during the last twelve years.

Although Matthew, Sapphie knew, had helped to fill some of that gaping hole in her mother's life; Joan would be someone else who would be hugely affected if Rik was told of his son, though she doubted her mother had thought that far ahead…

'I know you do.' She reached over and squeezed her mother's hand understandingly. 'It's just—' She broke off as the ringing of the doorbell interrupted them.

'That will be the postman.' Her mother stood up. 'I'm expecting a parcel.'

Sapphie watched her mother leave before glancing down at Matthew, maternal pride swelling in her chest; he really was a beautiful boy, and so happily secure in the world they had made for him here. She would not allow him to become a tug-of-love child, or his security to be ripped asunder. No matter how much she might love his father...

'We've a visitor,' her mother said woodenly as she came back into the kitchen, her face slightly pale. 'You've got a visitor, Sapphie,' she added softly. 'I've put him in the sitting-room.'

Sapphie tensed. 'Him?' she repeated warily.

But she knew who her visitor was without her mother needing to answer; only one person could have had this effect upon her mother: Rik.

She put her cup down slowly and stood up. 'Will you keep Matthew in here with you?' Her eyes pleaded with her mother to co-operate, to continue to respect her decision where Matthew's father was concerned.

'I'll try.' Joan nodded ruefully. 'But you know what he's like about visitors.'

Yes, she did know. Her young son was gregarious, not at all shy about meeting new people; in fact, he loved them. 'Just try,' she encouraged huskily, her hands feeling icy cold, and yet at the same time her palms were damp.

What was Rik doing here?

More to the point, how could she get rid of him before he discovered the truth about Matthew?

She was sure that last night he had believed Matthew to be another man, that without actually resorting to lies she had compounded that impression by talking about how much she loved him.

And yet, less than twelve hours later, Rik was here, in her home. In Matthew's home...!

She ran her damp palms down her denim-clad thighs, then drew in a deep, controlling breath before entering the sitting-room.

If she looked bad after a relatively sleepless night, then Rik looked much worse, his face very pale, lines of strain beside his nose and mouth, though sunglasses prevented her from reading the expression in his eyes.

It was this that she grasped on to. 'I thought it was raining outside?' she said derisively.

'It is,' he agreed, reaching up to remove the sunglasses, revealing the dark circles beneath his eyes, the light actually making him wince. 'Never mix champagne, whisky and gin,' he drawled. 'It's a lethal combination!' He placed the sunglasses back on his nose.

At any other time Sapphie might have found his discomfort amusing. But not today. Not with Matthew only feet away.

She looked at him coldly. 'What are you doing here, Rik? What do you want?'

'A gallon of black coffee might help,' he suggested. 'Although I wouldn't put a bet on it!'

'Sounds like you had a good time after I left last night,' she said drily, not sitting down, and not asking him to either—even though he did look as if he might fall down at any moment. But she was too restless to sit down, and he wouldn't be staying long enough to make himself comfortable!

'A bad one,' he corrected her. 'And on that basis, I suppose things can only get better. In fact, as far as I'm concerned, they already have. Sapphie, why didn't you just tell me that Matthew is your son?'

Rik was wrong—this situation had just become a hundred times worse!

Rik watched as Sapphie moved to sit down abruptly in one of the armchairs, her face rigid with shock as she stared up at him with haunted amber-coloured eyes. 'Who told you?' she choked, her gaze sharpening suddenly. 'Was it Dee? Because if it was—'

'It wasn't Dee,' Rik assured her soothingly, noticing the look of relief that flooded her eyes. 'Look, Sapphie,' he moved to go down on his haunches beside her chair, taking one of her cold hands into the warmth of his, 'doesn't my being here tell you that it makes no difference to me? That you could have six children and I would still want you?' And he knew that it was true, that he wanted Sapphie, no matter what baggage she brought along with her.

As he'd stood beneath a stinging hot shower earlier for ten minutes, trying to see the situation from her point of view, he'd realised that it was love for her child that had made her behave so defensively, that had made her so determined to push other relationships from her life. To push him from her life. It was up to him to change all that.

Sapphie swallowed hard, eyeing him warily now. 'You would?'

'Yes—I would,' he came back firmly.

Nik had tried, in his usual big-brother fashion, to give him advice on the telephone earlier that morning, urging him to remember that a single mother came as part of a package, and that he would have to bond with the child as much as the mother, and to remember that all the time he was doing this bonding with the mother and the son the child's real father was out there somewhere doing his damnedest to ensure that he didn't succeed!

At which point Rik had come back with, 'And if it had been Jinx in the same circumstances?'

'I would still have fallen in love and married her,' Nik had answered without hesitation.

Exactly. That was exactly how Rik felt about Sapphie. OK, so she was a little prickly because of her circumstances; he would just have to overcome her distrust. And how hard could it be to bond with a small child who wasn't yet mature enough to have formed many likes and dislikes?

Although he wasn't quite so sure about that when, the very next moment, a small voice somewhere else in the house began to cry out, 'I want my mummy! I want my mummy!'

Sapphie tensed at the very first cry, snatching her hand out of his to stand up. 'You have to leave—'

The door was flung open suddenly, silencing her, a small tornado hurtling into the room and into her waiting arms. 'Mummy!' the little boy cried determinedly. 'I wanted to show you my tower, but Nana said you were busy.' He turned to give his grandmother an accusing look as she stood behind him in the open doorway.

Having expected a baby, or, at the most, a small toddler, Rik was rather surprised that Matthew was quite this big—and this vocal!

Sapphie bent down and swept the little boy up into her arms. Matthew's height and sturdiness showed him to be a little boy of about four—or five?—years old, with glossy dark curls framing his still-babyish features. As he turned, Rik found himself the curious focus of the child's deep blue eyes.

'It's a man,' he told his mother brightly.

No, not just a man, Rik realised as he continued to study the little boy. All of the colour drained from his face as he looked at a replica of himself at four years old: the same tall-for-his-age body, those dark, glossy curls, the same blue eyes. No, not just a man— Matthew's father!

This little boy—four years and two months old if Rik's memory was correct—was his son!

He couldn't breathe. Couldn't speak. Damn—he wasn't sure he was going to be able to stand on his own two feet for very much longer!

Sapphie's child was his child. His son. Matthew was his son!

'I'm so sorry.' Joan was the one to break the silence as she spoke pleadingly to her daughter. 'I tried to stop him, but…' She gave a helpless movement of her hands.

Joan McCall, a woman he had grown to like the previous evening, knew that Matthew was his son, too! Why else would she be quite this upset, so apologetic?

'It's OK,' Sapphie assured her mother huskily. 'Maybe—maybe it's for the best.' She turned to look enquiringly at Rik, her arms tightening about Matthew as she saw the completely stunned expression on Rik's face.

He still couldn't speak, could only continue to stare at Matthew. He was such a beautiful child, so much a little boy already, so—so his!

And he had already missed four years of his son's life…

Because of Sapphie. Because she had chosen five years ago not to tell him she was expecting his child.

Why had she done that? What right did she have to have made that decision alone, to have kept Matthew a secret from him for all these years?

Anger started to replace the numbness, blinding, white-hot anger. 'God damn you, Sapphie!' he rasped harshly.

'The man swore, Mummy,' Matthew gasped, blue eyes wide. 'He's a bad man.'

'No, not a bad man, darling,' Sapphie assured him huskily. 'Just a very angry one, I think.' She raised questioning brows in Rik's direction.

'Anger doesn't even begin to describe how I feel at this moment,' he ground out fiercely.

What he wanted, more than anything, was to reach

out and take his son in his arms, to crush him to him, to know the wonder of holding his own flesh and blood!

But he couldn't do that; he was nothing but a stranger to Matthew, a 'bad man' who swore at his mother…!

Sapphie drew in a sharp breath at the violence she must have seen in his expression. 'This isn't the time or the place for this, Rik,' she began to reason.

'You're right—it isn't,' he bit out forcefully, exerting every ounce of will-power he possessed to keep a lid on the anger that threatened to explode from him. For Matthew's sake. For his son's sake!

He still couldn't quite take all of this in, and yet he knew it was the truth, the evidence—Matthew's likeness to him so blazingly, obviously, right here before him. But if he needed any other confirmation then Sapphie's look of despair, and Joan's concern as she looked at both her daughter and her grandson were enough to convince him.

Over the last week he had grown to heartily dislike a man by the name of Matthew, to resent the part he played in Sapphie's life. But the overwhelming love he felt now as he looked at his son was almost enough to bring him to his knees!

He shook his head weakly. 'You're right, Sapphie; the time and place for this is a court of law!'

'No—' Joan cried.

'Rik, please!' Sapphie groaned emotionally.

'Please!' he repeated furiously. 'Please?' he said again less forcefully as Matthew scowled at him fiercely—for shouting at his beloved.

Sapphie was right, Rik acknowledged hardly, they couldn't talk about this in front of Matthew. That would only serve to alienate the little boy more. And that was the last thing he wanted.

What he wanted at this moment—Matthew!—he couldn't have. Which left him only one course of action.

'You can expect to hear from my lawyers,' he stated harshly.

'Rik, no!' Sapphie gasped again.

'Rik, yes!' he said coldly, taking one last knee-weakening look at Matthew before striding to the door, giving Joan McCall a look of reproach as he passed her in the doorway.

But he would be back.

And soon!

CHAPTER TEN

'WELL, that could have gone better, couldn't it?' Sapphie murmured weakly even as she sat down in one of the armchairs, Matthew on her knee. Her legs were shaking so badly that if she didn't sit down, she knew she would fall down.

Matthew climbed off her knee. 'He was a naughty man, Mummy. He swored.' But his last comment was only made distractedly as he spotted his box of toys behind the sofa and made a beeline for his favourite fire-engine.

'I think he had good reason to swear,' Sapphie's mother sighed, having stepped aside as Rik left or risked being trampled underfoot. 'Sapphie, can you imagine how that poor man feels—?'

'Yes! Yes, I can,' she acknowledged shakily.

And she could; she knew how she would feel if Matthew were suddenly produced as her child. Wondrous at the beautiful miracle of him, but angry too at the person who had deprived her of the first four years of his life. In this case, that was her…

'What do I do about this?' She looked at her mother desperately. 'You heard him—he's going to make it a legal battle!' Her voice rose in panic.

Because she knew it was a battle she was likely to lose. Rik hadn't abandoned his child, he simply hadn't known of his existence. Plus he was a rich and powerful man, and his reputation was unimpeachable.

'You can't let it get to that, Sapphie,' her mother echoed her own thoughts. 'Admittedly, a court usually comes down in favour of the mother, and I'm sure that they would this time too, but Rik is entitled to have access to his son. He's a wealthy man, and his lawyers are bound to be the best there are—'

'You aren't making me feel better, Mother!' Sapphie replied, her eyes welling with tears.

'I don't mean to upset you, Sapphie,' her mother sympathised, moving to squeeze her arm reassuringly. 'Really, I don't,' she urged. 'But I was watching his face the whole time, saw the way he looked at Matthew! Sapphie, it was that same look of pride and fierce protectiveness you see on every new parent's face!'

She knew that, had seen it too; Rik already loved Matthew with a fierce paternal love.

Taking that into account, and the way he felt about her at the moment—so angry he had looked capable of strangling her!—then she knew he wasn't likely to settle for anything less than complete access to Matthew. She doubted very much that Rik would succeed in taking Matthew away from her—her own reputation was as unimpeachable as his—but the ensuing battle would probably ensure that Sapphie and Rik ended up hating each other for the rest of their lives!

'I have to go and talk to him,' she decided determinedly as she stood up.

Her mother nodded. 'I think that's very wise—'

'But I can't!' Sapphie groaned frustratedly.

'You have to—'

'No, Mother, I meant that I can't go and talk to Rik because I have no idea where he's staying!' Sapphie explained desperately. 'It's just never come up in conversation,' she defended as her mother looked at her disbelievingly.

'But surely—someone must know where he can be reached,' her mother reasoned impatiently.

Dee, Sapphie thought instantly. Much as she hated to acknowledge it, Dee was sure to know where Rik was staying while he was in London.

But did she really want to go to Dee cap in hand and ask her about the whereabouts of her ex-lover?

Did she have any other choice?

'You're lucky to have caught us, Sapphie,' Jerome informed her lightly as he answered her call to his mobile.

Sapphie had totally forgotten that Dee and Jerome were leaving later today to go back to the States. Not surprising really, given the circumstances! She only hoped that luck would continue for the rest of what promised to be a traumatic day...

'Rik?' Jerome echoed after Sapphie had told him the reason she was calling—if not the reason she so desperately needed to find Rik! 'Well, he was staying here at this hotel last night—'

'That's all I needed to know!' Sapphie breathed with relief. 'And to wish the two of you a safe journey home, of course,' she added quickly as she realised how that must have sounded.

'Of course,' Jerome echoed drily. 'And you didn't let me finish just now; I said Rik was staying at the hotel last night, but it's my understanding that he booked out early this morning.'

Sapphie felt herself deflate again. Obviously Rik had come here after he'd signed out of the hotel, but where had he gone now? She had no idea. Had no idea of anything concerning Rik's private life! But his life had overspilled into her own now, and in the circumstances, she had to find him!

'You really do need to reach him, huh?' Jerome probed gently at her continued silence. 'Did the two of you have a fight or something last night? Only he seemed a little down, after you left.'

'A little down' didn't at all describe the way Rik was when he stormed out of her home a short time ago! Murderous was probably more apt!

'I just need to talk to him about something,' she answered evasively. 'But if you don't have any idea where he is, then—'

'I don't—but Nik Prince is sure to know. And I do have a number where he can be reached,' Jerome assured her with satisfaction.

Nik Prince? The man had been pleasant enough last night, but once Rik had told him of the way she had kept his son's existence a secret from him for the last five years, she very much doubted that would continue! Even on such a brief acquaintance, she knew that Nik Prince would be a formidable enemy.

More formidable than Rik was at this moment?

The answer to that was a definite no!

'OK,' she sighed. 'If you wouldn't mind giving me that number…?'

'Just a second,' Jerome dismissed. 'Dee, honey,

would you just come and talk to Sapphie while I get
my Filofax from my briefcase?'

'Hi, Sapph, what's going on?' her sister demanded
bluntly.

'I—er—I have one of the buttons from Rik's suit
in my bag,' she invented lamely! 'It dropped off last
night and I just wanted to return it to him.' Lame.
Very lame!

'Aren't you being a little obvious, Sapphie?' Dee
drawled, not fooled for a moment. 'Haven't you learnt
yet that if you have to run after a man, then he isn't
worth bothering with?'

Was that the reason that, even after five years of
marriage, Jerome was the one who still did all the
running? Probably, Sapphie acknowledged ruefully.
But if it worked for them…

But, unfortunately, their relationship bore absolutely no resemblance to her own present situation!

'I'll explain some other time, Dee,' she moved on
briskly, knowing that soon, if Rik was to continue
with his intention of involving lawyers, everyone was
going to know that Sapphie Benedict was the mother
of his son… 'Right now I just need to contact Rik.'

'Well, don't say I didn't try to warn you,' Dee replied before putting her husband back on the line,
with an audible caution to him not to be too long.

Sapphie forgot all about Dee's warning as soon as
the call was ended, staring for a good five minutes at
the piece of paper where she had written down Nik
Prince's telephone number.

What was she going to say to Rik's brother? Would

he, like Dee, think that the button was just a ruse, and that she was chasing his youngest brother?

What did it really matter what Nik Prince thought about her now when pretty soon he, and the rest of the Prince family were going to be told they had one more to add to their number!

For all she knew, Nik Prince might already have been told about his nephew!

'Will you just back up a few sentences?' Nik frowned darkly, standing across the room from where Rik paced up and down in front of the unlit fireplace.

Rik came to a halt. Sapphie hadn't told him he had a son. *A son.* Every time he thought of Matthew he felt as if he was going to fall down on his knees at the wonder of him.

He had arrived at Nik and Jinx's a short time ago and, so far, he knew, he hadn't made a great deal of sense. Because his brain wasn't functioning properly, and his heart felt as if it was about to burst!

'Does this have anything to do with what I told you earlier about Matthew?' Nik guessed shrewdly.

Did it have anything to do with Matthew…?

It had everything to do with Matthew. And he couldn't think about Matthew without thinking about Sapphie, too.

Sapphie…!

Every time he thought about her he felt driven to his knees, too. His emotions were so confused; on the one hand he was so angry with her for keeping her pregnancy, and consequently Matthew's birth, a secret, but on the other he was full of admiration for the way she had dealt so capably with both those things. She hadn't just dealt with them, with Matthew, she had excelled; Matthew was a beautiful and intelligent child.

He'd had Rik figured as a 'bad man' within minutes of meeting him!

And no wonder Sapphie had looked as if she hated the sight of him when they'd met again in Paris. It also explained her determination that Dee and Jerome shouldn't know they had ever met before. Met—they had created Matthew!

'Rik, what—' Nik broke off to glare impatiently at the telephone as it began to ring.

'I should answer that if I were you,' Rik advised drily, knowing that Jinx had gone out with her father this morning. 'I know I'm not making a lot of sense at the moment!'

Because this was just so big. So onerous. It was going to blow the family's minds once they knew about Matthew. Rik was the loner, the private, reserved one, the one who was always there to advise the rest of the family. But now he was the one who was falling apart!

He desperately wanted to see Matthew again. Just wanted to look at him, to breathe him in. All he had wanted to do earlier was pick him up and walk out of there with him. And what would that have achieved? A broken-hearted mother and son—and possibly a father in a police cell.

For once in his life he didn't know what to do next. In his anger this morning, he had threatened Sapphie with lawyers; he wasn't stupid enough—stunned enough!—to believe he would ever win a custody fight for a little boy who didn't even know him. But he would have a right to see him, despite the fact that his mother so obviously didn't want to share him.

He was back to Sapphie again…

He still didn't know how he felt about her now! Part of him could have strangled her for not coming to him five years ago, for not telling him about the baby she was expecting. His baby. But another part of him wanted to kiss her for giving him such a beautiful son. He wasn't—

His attention focused on Nik as he realised that, although his brother was talking into the receiver, he was actually looking at him while he did so.

'There's no need for that; he's right here.' Nik spoke tersely. 'No, I don't think he's going anywhere any time soon, so why don't you just come over here? No, it's no trouble,' he responded to the next question before reciting the address of the house he and Jinx shared with Jinx's father. 'See you soon, then, Sapphie,' he said politely before ending the call.

Sapphie. That had been Sapphie on the telephone? And she was coming here?

Why? To threaten him as he had threatened her? Or to cajole him into seeing that he had no part to play in Matthew's life? Neither of those options appealed to him!

Although he had to admire Sapphie for trying…

'Sapphie mentioned something about meeting on neutral ground,' Nik told him darkly. 'Exactly what have you been doing to that lovely lady, little

brother?' He glowered at Rik from beneath lowered
brows.

Rik hadn't actually done anything yet. Neither
would he, having already come to his senses enough
to know he was on a hiding to nothing if he took
Sapphie to court to gain custody. But Sapphie didn't
know that!

'I can't talk about it yet, Nik.' He shook his head.

'Fine,' his brother replied. 'I'll go make us both
some coffee.'

The coffee, and the waiting, didn't improve Rik's
mood; Nik was treating him as if he had been drinking this morning too. And maybe to his brother it did
seem that way; he certainly wasn't making a lot of
sense!

But when the doorbell finally rang to announce
Sapphie's arrival, he knew that he couldn't just leave
his brother in the dark like this, that he owed Nik an
explanation, at least.

He drew in a deep breath, standing up to pace the
room again. 'Nik, in a minute or two you're going to
hear something...' He stopped, not sure how to continue, but knowing time was running out, that the
housekeeper must have answered the door by now,
that Sapphie was on her way in here. 'Nik, Matthew
is my son, OK?' he burst out, having decided there
really was no easy way to say it.

The dark thundercloud that suddenly gathered in
Nik's face was probably very reminiscent of Rik's
own reaction earlier this morning!

'No!' Nik exclaimed. 'It is not OK.' He looked at
Rik as if seeing him for the first time.

No, Rik accepted leadenly, it really wasn't OK.

And from the bleak look on Sapphie's white face as she was shown into the sitting-room, it wasn't OK with her, either; the look she gave him from beneath her long, dark lashes was wary to say the least.

Rik's first instinct was to wrap her in his arms and keep her safe, to assure her that he would never let anyone hurt her. Except, to her, he was the one threatening her...!

Nik stood tall and powerful across the room, his sheer size forbidding. 'Do you want me to go or stay—'

'Stay!'

'Go!'

A humourless smile twisted Nik's mouth as they both answered at the same time. 'As the choice seems to be split down the middle, I think I'll go with the lady and stay. If only to see fair play,' he added with a warning look in Rik's direction.

Rik and Sapphie stared wordlessly at each other, the tension increasing as the seconds passed. She looked so fragile, Rik acknowledged, so vulnerable.

Finally, when Rik didn't think he could stand it a minute longer, Sapphie drew in a deep breath and began to talk. 'Rik, you had no right to come to my home this morning and—'

'I had every right!' he returned, all of his anger seeming to return in a split-second. 'You should have come to me five years ago!'

'And how was I supposed to do that, when it was Dee whom I would have to have asked where you were?' she reminded him. 'I had the same trouble this morning, as it happens,' she added. 'I had to call Jerome.'

'Proving that you could manage to track me down when the incentive was strong enough! You could have done the same thing five years ago if you had wanted to!'

'Asked Dee, you mean?' Sapphie came back.

'If necessary—yes!'

'Just have contacted the woman you were in love with and asked her where I could reach you?'

'Why not?' he returned. 'And I am not in love with Dee!' he added harshly.

'You thought you were five years ago!'

'I thought there was a Santa Claus until I was eight years old; that doesn't make him real!'

'Oh, very funny.' Sapphie glared at him, eyes sparkling deeply amber. 'And when I spoke to Dee, was I also supposed to tell her the reason I needed to reach you was because I was pregnant with your child?'

'Well, it would certainly have been a step in the right direction!' The last thing Rik wanted to do was argue with Sapphie, but at the moment he couldn't seem to help himself.

She drew in a sharp breath. 'You shouldn't have threatened me this morning—'

'What else was I supposed to do—pat you on the head and tell you what a clever girl you are?'

What little colour had stained her cheeks in her anger now quickly drained away, her hands clenching at her sides. 'I'll fight you, Rik. I won't let you take Matthew away from me,' she told him with quiet determination.

'Sapphie,' Rik lowered his voice reasoningly, knowing that shouting at each other wasn't going to help anything. Probably nothing was, but he had to try! 'I'm sure that we can sit down and come to some sort of reasonable compromise that doesn't involve a court battle..'

'That you threatened me with, you mean,' she reminded hardly, her eyes huge pools of accusing amber. 'I don't want Matthew to end up shuttled backwards and forwards across the Atlantic like some sort of human ping-pong ball—'

'You know, Sapphie,' Rik cut in, 'I think we reached the point some time ago in this conversation where what you want isn't of primary importance. Matthew deserves to have a father. Damn it, he has a father—'

'A father he doesn't even know!'

'And whose fault is that, do you think?'

'OK, OK, that's enough.' Nik moved to stand between them as they glared at each other across the width of the fireplace, jaws jutting out aggressively. 'Time out!' he added firmly as neither of them made a move to back down. 'Sapphie, would you please go and sit down in that chair over there?' he prompted gently, giving an approving nod as, after several lengthy seconds, she did so. 'You,' he turned impatiently to Rik, 'sit! And don't give me any arguments, Rik,' he added as Rik would have done just that. 'You're behaving like a child, so I'm treating you like one!'

As if to prove his brother's point, Rik found himself only just managing to clamp his lips shut. He gave a low groan of self-disgust before moving to sit down in the armchair opposite Sapphie's.

He was behaving like a child. In fact, they both were. When it was their son they should have been thinking about, discussing, like the two sensible adults they really were. Nik's was the only voice of reason...

Nik turned to Sapphie, his smile gentle. 'Do you have a photograph of Matthew with you, Sapphie? Of course you do,' he said as she took a small photograph wallet out of her shoulder-bag and shakily handed it to him.

Rik's fingers itched to snatch the wallet out of his brother's hand, to look at his son once again. But the warning look Nik shot him before he began looking at the photographs was enough to advise him against even trying!

Nik's expression was unreadable as he looked at the half-dozen snaps. 'Matthew's adorable, Sapphie,' he told her gruffly as he handed the wallet back before turning once again to Rik. 'He looks just like you did at four years old. It's a pity you had to grow up into an idiot!'

'Now, look—' Rik broke off his protest as Sapphie gave an involuntary laugh, instantly biting her lip as he looked across at her with annoyance.

'Better.' Nik nodded his satisfaction as Sapphie seemed more relaxed. 'Now, I didn't want to stay and listen to this conversation—I was asked to do so. And I'm glad I was. Left to your own devices, you two are just going to rip each other apart.'

He was right. Rik knew that he was. At the moment, he and Sapphie were just continuing to hurt each other.

'Now, I've listened to the two of you,' Nik continued softly. 'And I can see where all the anger and pain is coming from. But in reality there's a very simple answer to this whole problem.'

'Don't tell me.' Rik's mouth twisted derisively. 'We're back to the parable suggesting cutting the baby in two, and the one of us who loves Matthew the most will then back down—'

'Get real, will you, Rik?' his brother interrupted. 'There's absolutely no question about who loves Matthew the most—Sapphie does. She carried him inside her, gave birth to him, has loved and nurtured him for the last four years—Rik, you'll get your chance to talk in a minute, OK? At the moment it's still my turn!' Damn it, Nik always had a way of making him feel five years old!

'This is just a suggestion, you understand?' Nik continued gently.

Nik's suggestions had a way of being orders, but for the moment Rik was willing to give his brother the benefit of the doubt.

'The answer to the problem seems pretty clear to me,' Nik reasoned. 'The answer to all the problems; the lawyers, the tugging Matthew backwards and forwards across the Atlantic, the fact that you're both his parents—'

'Will you just get on with it, Nik?' Rik urged impatiently, having no idea where this conversation was going.

He received another narrow-eyed glare. 'Fine.' Nik nodded tersely. 'Then the obvious answer to all this confusion is for the two of you to marry one other!'

CHAPTER ELEVEN

'AND on that cheery little note,' Nik quipped, as both Sapphie and Rik stared at him in shocked disbelief, 'I will leave the two of you alone together to discuss the possibility!'

Sapphie was barely aware of him leaving the room and closing the door gently behind him.

Marry Rik?

For Matthew's sake, to give him stability rather than subject him to an emotional tug-of-war?

Wasn't it for the very reason that she hadn't wanted to be forced into marrying Rik—or for Rik to feel he had been forced into marrying her!—that she hadn't told him of her pregnancy five years ago?

And yet now, bleak and loveless as it was to her, she couldn't see any other way to resolve this argument...

Hadn't her own mother suggested it as a possibility only an hour or so ago?

And been ridiculed for her trouble, Sapphie acknowledged heavily.

With good reason!

Oh, Rik had made it pretty plain this morning that he wanted her, and she already knew that she loved him—had known that five years ago! But was Rik's desire, and her love, any basis on which to build a happy family life for Matthew? She didn't think so.

Her love for Rik wouldn't fade—it had already been tested to its limits and survived!—but desire certainly could, and probably would.

'It's a ridiculous idea,' she stated flatly; she didn't know what she had expected the outcome of this meeting to be, but it certainly wasn't this!

She didn't look at Rik as she stood up and walked over to the window. As far away from him as was possible in the confines of the Princes' sitting-room!

'Is it?'

Sapphie had been so immersed in her own churning emotions that she hadn't realised Rik had stood up too, that he was only inches behind her. But she could feel his presence now, his heat, the raw pull of his body on hers.

But it wasn't enough!

It would never be enough...

She gritted her teeth, clenching her hands at her sides in order to stop herself from turning and launching herself into his arms; that would solve absolutely nothing!

'Utterly ridiculous,' she confirmed determinedly. 'It would never work.'

Rik's hands came to rest lightly on her shoulders, tightening as Sapphie stiffened at the contact and the fresh assault upon her senses.

'It worked five years ago,' he reminded.

Oh, yes, it had, if Rik was referring—and she was sure that he was—to the explosive passion between them that had held them enthralled from midnight till dawn.

Sapphie had no idea how many times they had

made love, had lost track of time and space, aware only of Rik and the magic of his lips and hands.

Was it any wonder that they had created a child as beautiful as Matthew that night…?

If the two of them married, they could have more children, brothers and sisters for Matthew—

No, she mustn't even go there!

Her shoulders tensed beneath Rik's caressing hands as she dragged herself back from that daydream. 'You're talking about sex, Rik,' she dismissed. 'But even if we could recapture that, sexual attraction fades, and then what are you left with?'

'Liking and respect?' Rik put forward.

She shook her head, shrugging out from under his hands to turn and face him. A move she wasn't sure was a good one as she found herself mere inches away from Rik, his heat enveloping her, even his gaze burning hot as it fixated on her mouth.

Sapphie was almost able to feel, to taste, his lips on hers!

And then, his gaze holding hers now, she really could taste him, as his mouth softly possessed hers as he kissed her, the pent-up emotion inside him spilling out.

How she loved this man!

But how she feared him too, and what he could do to the security of her family!

A sob caught in her throat, caught and held, choking her, the sudden lack of oxygen to her brain making her feel dizzier than ever. This couldn't work, wouldn't work, no matter how many times Rik kissed her in an effort to prove otherwise.

She tried to pull away, but instead found herself held at arm's length as Rik looked at her searchingly. She waited for him to say something, but knew that there really wasn't anything he could say that would make this situation come out right. For any of them.

'OK, Sapphie,' Rik finally sighed. 'Maybe we should forget you and me for the moment and concentrate on Matthew instead.'

She could only stare at him wordlessly, had been expecting more threats, his calm logic taking her completely by surprise.

'Will you at least let me get to know him?' Rik continued softly. 'And allow him to get to know me?'

How could she even begin to stop that happening, if that was what Rik had decided he wanted to do?

She knew that she couldn't, he knew it too, but to give him his due, he was at least giving her the courtesy of asking rather than demanding.

'As what?' she said warily.

'His father, preferably.'

She shook her head. 'That's just going to confuse him.'

Rik's mouth hardened. 'Then, perhaps, get to know me well enough to realise that I'm not the bad man he thinks I am!'

That wasn't too much to ask. In fact, it was nothing really; Rik wasn't a bad man, and if Matthew spent any time in his company he would quickly know that.

'I think that could be arranged,' she accepted slowly.

It was so much more than she had hoped for—in fact, it seemed a little too good to be true!

Rik's hands dropped from her shoulders. 'Then that will have to do as a start. And maybe after we've convinced Matthew we can begin working on convincing you I'm not a bad man, too.'

She had never thought he was a bad man. Not five years ago. And certainly not now. She loved him too much to ever think that of him.

She had no idea whether or not this seemingly impossible situation could ever be resolved, but accepted that they did have to try.

One thing she was certain of; she could not marry Rik as a way of settling the situation. She simply couldn't. Not even for Matthew's sake.

What good would she be doing him when that loveless marriage would inevitably, ultimately, destroy her?

Rik watched Sapphie as the different emotions flickered across her intensely beautiful face, a fist turning in his stomach for what she was going through. She was so tiny and defenceless at this moment that he knew he couldn't take advantage of her fragility. Not when it was his own son that caused that vulnerability!

Sapphie could go, and already had gone, through several kinds of hell because of him, had faced her pregnancy on her own, not even confiding the identity of her baby's father to her family; no, she'd had only her mother's emotional support once Matthew was born, having no father or even stepfather of her own to help her.

She had even lost her job as Jerome's personal as-

sistant because of Dee, and had to find some other
way of supporting herself and her child!

He might have been angry with Sapphie earlier, but
she had every right to hate him, a man she had believed was in love with her own sister!

What he had once felt for Dee now seemed so shallow and unreal. This woman—Sapphie—was what
was real.

He went hollow inside just looking at her, and he
couldn't have spoken if his life had depended on it.
He admired Sapphie more than anyone else he had
ever known, he liked everything about her—and he
ached to make love to her again, to show her with his
lips and hands how much he…

He what?

Loved her, he knew with startling clarity. He loved
Sapphie. Absolutely. Completely.

And she could only look at him with apprehension.
Had done so since they met again in Paris.

She was looking at him that way now, too. And he
couldn't bear to see that, knew that he had to give
her back her sense of security where Matthew was
concerned.

'Please don't worry about it any more, Sapphie,'
he told her gruffly. 'We can just take each day at a
time, see where we go, hm?'

'If you say so,' she answered with that wariness
that tore at his insides.

'I do say so,' he assured her. 'Now, how about I
drive you home? I'm sure you must want to get back.
To Matthew.' He could see the little boy now in his
mind's eye, a beautiful child, whom Sapphie loved

with all her heart—no matter how she might feel towards his father!

Although Rik could guess at some of what she must feel towards him. Only days ago he had actually accused her of entrapment that night five years ago, of deliberately distracting him because she and her mother wanted Dee to marry Jerome.

What an idiot he'd been!

He still had no idea what had prompted Sapphie to spend that night with him, but he certainly knew it had nothing to do with entrapment. If that really had been the case she would have lost no time, once she discovered she was pregnant, in finding him again.

No, Nik was right, Sapphie really was a lovely lady—in every sense of the word.

Winning the love of a woman like Sapphie was not going to be easy but, loving her as deeply as he realised he did, he was certainly going to try!

'I would like to get back, yes,' Sapphie told him. 'But there's really no need for you to drive me. I came by taxi; I can easily go home the same way.'

'There's every need for me to drive you home,' Rik insisted firmly. 'I— Look, it's the least I can do, Sapphie. Besides,' he added ruefully, 'I don't feel like facing Nik again just yet! Would you?' He grimaced, Sapphie's tremulous smile reward enough for his deliberate self-deprecation.

'He is rather scary, isn't he?' she allowed, her smile less tremulous now.

'Nah,' Rik assured her with a grin. 'Underneath all that arrogance he's pure marshmallow!'

Sapphie looked less than convinced, and still very pale, her eyes huge and troubled.

Rik had taken a step towards her before he was even aware of what he was doing, but her sudden tension was enough to stop him from taking her into his arms again. Instead he lifted a hand and gently caressed one pale cheek. 'I shouldn't have been angry with you earlier,' he told her tenderly. 'I just— It was the shock. But still—' it still was a shock, but one that he was coming to terms with! '—I shouldn't have behaved in the way that I did.'

She looked up at him for several minutes, and then she gave a shake of her head. 'You really don't have to convince me that you aren't a bad man, Rik; I've never thought that you were.'

'Just a misguided one, hm?' he murmured, his gaze roving hungrily over her face; the skin of her cheek was soft and silky to the touch, her hair like living fire as he smoothed several tendrils back from the coolness of her temple.

'Just a misguided one,' she agreed heavily, her gaze no longer meeting his as she stepped away from him. 'Do we have to tell Nik we're leaving or can we just sneak away?' She attempted to be light-hearted.

An attempt that didn't quite come off as her voice shook slightly, but Rik admired her all the more for at least trying.

'Well, as I want to borrow his car to drive you home, I suppose I'll have to tell him.' He fell in with her mood. 'If you hear any shouting, followed by silence, then I'm probably a dead man!'

Sapphie obliged his own attempt at humour with a

smile. Not much of a smile, admittedly, but again, she did try.

It was enough for now, Rik decided.

Although as he walked through the hallway to Nik's study, he knew that he hadn't been completely joking about Nik's reaction; his brother had been a boxing champion in college!

As it was, Nik's ominous silence as he handed over the keys to his car was a lot more telling than anything he might have said; for all of his earlier calm in front of Sapphie, Nik took his role as patriarch of the Prince family very seriously. Matthew was a Prince!

'Not even a black eye!' Sapphie noted when Rik rejoined her in the sitting-room.

'Don't sound so disappointed!'

She eyed him teasingly. 'He's probably just waiting for the appropriate moment!'

'Probably,' Rik said with feeling. 'And it will be when I least expect it!'

Sapphie looked sad again. 'That's how I've felt for the last five years!'

He knew that, could only imagine the extra stress a possible meeting with him must have placed on her already stretched emotions.

'I'm surprised you didn't just hightail it out of Paris last week once you knew I was there.'

'I couldn't,' she replied. 'I didn't dare risk leaving and having either Dee or Jerome saying something to you about my four-year-old son.'

All he ever seemed to have given this woman— besides Matthew—was misery.

Was it any wonder she wanted to keep him at arm's length?

Whereas he just wanted to hold her, and love her, and take care of her. Something he knew she would never let him do!

It was his own fault she hadn't come to him five years ago; how could she have done, in the circumstances?

That knowledge was something he was just going to have to live with. Self-loathing was probably the least of what he deserved for being so utterly stupid.

'I really am sorry, Sapphie,' he said sincerely. 'For everything.'

'I think we both are,' she accepted. 'And there's no going back, so we can only go forward.'

It wasn't what he wanted, and perhaps it never would be, but they had reached some sort of truce. And he certainly wasn't going to give up, was in this for the duration!

Although the spitting virago who confronted him as he opened the car door for Sapphie to get out when they reached her home looked as if she might have other ideas about that!

CHAPTER TWELVE

'DEE...?' Sapphie said, surprised, as she stood by the car and next to Rik and watched as her sister strode forcefully down the pathway, blonde hair flying, her cheeks bright with anger, green eyes glowing like a cat's. 'But I thought you were flying back to the States this afternoon?'

'I was,' Dee confirmed, at the same time moving to stand in front of Sapphie, the full force of her anger directed at Rik as she faced him with all the ferocity of an Amazon warrior. 'Just who do you think you are?' she demanded. 'How dare you come here and threaten my sister in this way?'

Sapphie's initial surprise had turned to complete incredulity now; Dee was here to defend her? That had to be a first. And, given the circumstances, it was very surprising; she would have thought Dee would be angry with her, not Rik.

Dee turned to give her a reassuring smile. 'I was—concerned after your call earlier, so I telephoned the house and spoke to Mummy. She told me what happened this morning, the reason you absolutely had to find Rik.' Dee's mouth tightened as she turned back to face him. 'You may be one of the almighty Prince brothers, Rik, but—'

'Er—Dee—'

'No, Sapphie, I'm not going to shut up,' her sister

159

second-guessed her. 'You may think that you're all-powerful,' she continued to berate Rik, 'but you'll find I can be just as formidable an adversary if someone threatens my family. Or, at least, Jerome can.'

Sapphie's eyes widened in alarm. 'He isn't here too, is he?' This was already turning into something of a fiasco!

Dee shook her head. 'I persuaded him that it might be better if I came alone. But I'm sure he will be here like a shot if I ask him. You are not going to take Matthew away from Sapphie.' She poked Rik in the chest with one long painted fingernail. 'Not even if I have to give evidence against you myself,' she stated determinedly. 'I don't think a judge would look too favourably on a man who treated Sapphie in the way that you have. I realised long ago, because of the timing, that Matthew's father had to be someone Sapphie met at my wedding. But it never occurred to me that he might be you!' Angry colour had returned to her cheeks and her eyes were glittering with accusation as she stared at Rik.

'Dee, could we go inside and discuss this?' Sapphie suggested. Several of her neighbours were out washing their cars on this lovely summer's afternoon. She was still totally stunned by the fact that Dee was actually here to defend her, and that was without giving the neighbours a free show!

'Fine with me,' Dee acquiesced tightly. 'After you,' she invited Rik challengingly.

To give Rik his due, he looked as bemused by this changed Dee as Sapphie did. Admiringly so? Probably, Sapphie decided. Although, for once, she was sure her little sister wasn't out to impress anyone, that she really was *angry*. Rik was clearly impressed, anyway. She just couldn't win with this man, could she?

'Mummy has taken Matthew to the shops to buy some sweets.' Dee explained Joan and the little boy's absence once they had entered the unusually quiet house. 'I thought it best in the circumstances,' she added, giving Rik another venomous glare. 'You got my sister pregnant, and five years later you think you can just walk back into her life and claim your son? I don't think so!' she snorted.

If Dee had suffered any shock or hurt at this tangible proof of Rik's defection five years ago, then she wasn't showing it; her indignation was all on Sapphie's behalf.

Which Sapphie was still having trouble coming to terms with; what on earth could have happened to bring about this change in Dee? Not that Sapphie was complaining—far from it; it was nice to have her sister as an ally after all these years, rather than an adversary. It was just unexpected.

'There's a lot more to being a father than the act of procreation, you know,' Dee continued her assault.

And Rik continued to take it. Because he was as stunned as Sapphie? Or was it because of that increasing admiration for Dee that Sapphie could see in his eyes?

Sapphie turned away from him, shaking her head. 'Dee, I really don't think…' The pressure of Rik's fingers on her arm silenced her, her gaze questioning as she turned to look up at him once more.

'Let Dee finish what she has to say,' he said softly.

'Take your hands off her!' Dee slapped his hand away from Sapphie's arm. 'Being presented with a lovely four-year-old isn't fatherhood!'

'I do know that, Dee—'

'No, you don't,' she contradicted Rik forcefully. 'Being a father starts way before the babies are even born! It's getting up in the early hours of the morning when your wife is being violently ill with morning sickness. Bathing her face and hands before helping her back to bed. Putting up with her cranky moods. It's holding her hand during the scans, seeing your babies' heads and bodies clearly outlined. And then weeping together when the tests they've taken tell you that they're both healthy—'

'Dee…?' Sapphie looked at her sister wonderingly. 'Their heads and bodies? Both healthy?'

Dee's face softened, tears swimming in her deep green eyes. 'Twins,' she choked proudly. 'And I don't even know them yet.' Her voice strengthened as she turned once again to Rik. 'Haven't held them, kissed them, stroked their creamy cheeks—but I already know that if anyone attempted to take them away from me that I would fight them with every weapon available to me! As I will help Sapphie fight you where Matthew is concerned,' she stated fiercely. 'He's her baby, not yours. He doesn't even know you—'

'Sure he does,' Rik contradicted gruffly. 'I'm the bad man.'

Sapphie felt a knife pierce her own heart at how much that must hurt him. Matthew didn't mean it, of course, he just hadn't liked Rik being angry with his mummy. She would talk that through with Matthew, help him to understand that Mummy had been just as upset and cross.

'I'll talk to him, Rik,' she assured him quietly. 'Help him to understand—'

'How can he possibly understand something like this?' Rik said wearily. 'Dee, everything you've said about me is true,' he continued. 'Except for one thing.' He straightened. 'I will never take Matthew away from Sapphie—'

'Too damned right you won't!' Dee agreed.

'No, Dee—I meant that I won't even try to do that,' Rik explained evenly.

'Oh.' Dee looked taken aback now.

As was Sapphie. She knew that, for Matthew's sake, they had decided to drop hostilities, but she hadn't believed Rik would back down this far... Was it because he didn't want to hurt her and Matthew? Or because of the things Dee had said to him...?

Dee frowned. 'But my mother said—'

'Your mother thought that was my intention when I left here this morning,' Rik explained. 'The—situation has changed since then. I'll leave Sapphie to tell you.' He took his wallet out of his jacket pocket, writing something down on the back of a business card. 'Sapphie, you can call me on this number—any time, day or night—when you have decided I can see Matthew again.' He handed her the card. 'Call me. Soon,' he added, before turning on his heel and striding out of the room, the front door closing softly behind him seconds later.

'Well.' Dee stood like a deflated balloon in the middle of the sitting-room. 'Was it something I said, do you think?' She arched blonde brows.

No matter what he might have just said, Sapphie knew the situation with Rik was pretty bleak, and she still had no idea how it was going to be resolved.

But, at the same time, this change in Dee was so comical she couldn't help laughing. 'You were magnificent!' She hugged her sister before stepping back to look up at her admiringly. 'You had me pretty scared, anyway!'

Dee looked sheepish, then moved to sit down, more shaken by the encounter than she had been willing to show. 'I just hope he never realises that some of that dialogue was a direct steal from a film I made two years ago!' she laughed shakily.

Sapphie's eyes widened. 'Not the bit about the twins?'

'Oh, no, that bit's true,' Dee assured her happily. 'We cancelled our flight after the doctor called us earlier and told us the good news. We were going to come over this evening and tell you over a celebration dinner. Mummy is over the moon!'

'So am I,' Sapphie assured her warmly, relieved— and still slightly surprised!—at her changing relationship with Dee. This was the sort of closeness she had always wanted with her sister. She only hoped it lasted.

Dee looked at her sadly. 'I haven't been a particularly good sister to you so far, have I?' she admitted. 'And I doubt I'm going to change overnight, either. But I am going to try,' she promised. 'For instance,

I'm not even going to ask how you and Rik got together five years ago…!' She gave Sapphie a wry look.

'Best not to,' Sapphie agreed.

Dee smiled. 'It's strange, you know; the twins are here, inside me…' she covered her stomach protectively with her hands '…my bump is hardly showing. And yet I feel different.' Her eyes glowed with sudden laughter. 'I'm probably going to be an atrocious mother, but at this moment in time, now that the morning sickness has finally stopped, and I have my picture of the two of them, I feel as if I could right the world before breakfast and play tennis in the afternoon!'

Sapphie knew that feeling only too well, and, although it abated slightly, it never completely went away.

But, loving Rik as she did, and seeing the admiring way he had looked at Dee such a short time ago, she didn't think it was a feeling she was ever likely to know again…

'Have you been attempting to slit your throat—and failed!—or did you just cut yourself shaving?'

Rik continued to look in the mirror, glaring at his brother's reflection beside his own, his face pulled grotesquely out of shape as he attempted to stick a piece of tissue over the freely flowing cut on his neck.

'Not that I'm complaining either way, you understand,' Nik drawled as he leant against the doorframe to the bathroom. 'All this self-flagellation gets a little wearing after a while, anyway!'

Rik gave his brother a glare, before picking up a piece of fresh tissue and trying again to stop the blood flowing.

'Aren't you overdoing it a little?' Nik continued tauntingly. 'You're only going out for a pizza with Sapphie and Matthew, not off to meet royalty!'

Rik turned after finally succeeding in sticking the tissue to his cut, knowing that Nik was right; the evidence was in the adjoining bedroom—clothes he had tried on and discarded, before settling on faded denims and a white T-shirt. Only to cut himself shaving and bleed all over the T-shirt, meaning he had to start all over again.

Nik and Jinx had very kindly invited him to stay for as long as it took to sort out this situation with Sapphie and Matthew, but, considering this was the first time he had seen either of them since that meeting four days ago, Sapphie having telephoned him yesterday and made the invitation to go for pizza, he had a feeling Nik and Jinx were going to tire of his being here long before any progress was made. In fact, Nik's comment just now confirmed that his brother was already tired of him moping about the place.

Rik sighed. 'This is just so important—I don't know how to explain.'

'You don't need to explain anything to me,' Nik assured him. 'But have you considered that there may be a short cut to all this?'

Rik looked weary. 'I've already told you, Sapphie refuses to marry me!'

'I don't mean that,' his brother returned. 'In the circumstances, I can understand her saying no to that.'

Rik was puzzled; after all, it had been Nik's suggestion in the first place! 'You can?'

'Sure I can,' his brother rejoined. 'Rik, have you tried telling Sapphie that you love her, and then asking her to marry you?'

No, he hadn't told Sapphie he loved her—because he was too wary of what her answer might be!

He had messed this up from the beginning, hadn't appreciated what he had found in Sapphie five years ago; now he was determined to take things at the pace she set. And going out for a pizza with her and Matthew was as good a place as any to start.

The bistro where they were to meet was only a few minutes' walk from where Sapphie lived. However, Rik arrived ten minutes earlier than six-thirty, when Sapphie had suggested they meet, his anxiety to see them again was so acute.

He was sitting at the table drinking iced tea when Sapphie and Matthew walked in the door. His breath caught in his throat at how right they looked together, Matthew holding his mother's hand as the two of them talked and laughed.

Rik wanted to just gather the two of them up in his arms and carry them away to somewhere quiet where he could tell them how much he loved them.

Which would probably frighten the hell out of Matthew—and wouldn't exactly thrill Sapphie, either!

'Hi,' he greeted, standing up as they reached the table, not quite sure whether or not he should kiss

Sapphie and shake Matthew by the hand, or vice versa! Instead he did nothing except smile.

'Matthew,' Sapphie avoided meeting Rik's eyes as she bent down so that she was on a level with the little boy as he looked up curiously at Rik, 'you know we've talked about this, that this is your daddy?'

Rik's breath caught in his throat; whatever he had been expecting, it wasn't this!

If he had thought about it at all—and he had!—he had expected Sapphie to introduce him as 'Rik'; it had never occurred to him that she would have told Matthew—that his son would know—

'Hello, Daddy.' Matthew smiled up at him shyly, still holding tightly to Sapphie's hand.

He swallowed hard, emotion choking him. 'Hello, Matthew,' he finally managed.

Sapphie straightened, obviously not as composed as she appeared as her hands shook slightly, her gaze wary as she met Rik's searching one. 'I thought about what you said,' she said. 'We might as well start the way we mean to go on.'

That seemed practical. Logical, even; there would have been no point in Matthew calling him Rik if he was one day going to call him Daddy. Rik just hadn't expected—wasn't sure he deserved—such generosity on Sapphie's part.

'Thank you,' he accepted, pulling back the chairs for them. 'So, Matthew, what's your favourite pizza?' Not the most inspired of conversation openers, Rik accepted, but it was the best he could do right now, still stunned by the fact that Sapphie had told Matthew exactly who he was.

Actually, the only thing that Rik felt like eating was Sapphie, with his eyes, his mouth, his hands!

She looked wonderful, with her hair swept up in a pony-tail, her make-up minimalised to a light foundation and peach-coloured lip-gloss, her white T-shirt barely reaching the waist of her low-slung denims.

'What have you done to your neck?' Matthew asked a short time later as he wrestled with the trailing melted cheese on his pizza.

Damn, Rik had forgotten all about the tissue on his cut! Which meant he had been sitting here like a moron for the last twenty minutes—Sapphie was obviously too polite to have mentioned it.

In fact, Sapphie was being extremely polite, too polite, when he had hoped the two of them would get to know each other better too.

'An accident while I was shaving,' he explained as he removed the tissue and shoved it in his pocket; Nik could have mentioned it again before he left the house earlier!

'If you had a beard you wouldn't need to shave,' Matthew told him knowingly. 'Uncle Brian has a beard,' he offered, before turning his attention back to his enjoyable struggle with his pizza.

Rik frowned. Uncle Brian? Who the hell was Uncle Brian? As far as he was aware, the only uncle Matthew had was Jerome—he would find out about Nik and Zak later. Much later, as far as Rik was concerned; no doubt Nik had considered it a huge joke earlier to let him leave the house with the tissue still stuck on his neck!

'Brian Glover,' Sapphie offered. 'He's my agent.'

Her agent! Just her agent? Or was there something else between them? Matthew had obviously met the other man...

'Matthew comes with me to see him sometimes,' Sapphie explained at Rik's continued silence. 'When my mother is busy. He's a grandfather four times over, Rik,' she added drily as he just continued to look at her.

Ah. Probably not someone Sapphie would be involved with, then.

But she had already told him that, had said there was no one else in her life but Matthew. And Sapphie, unlike Dee, did not tell him lies. Even if some of her truths he would rather not hear!

Dee had really surprised him that day when he drove Sapphie home, and he had known from Sapphie's stunned expression that, as her younger sister defended her and Matthew with the ferocity of a tigress, she had been surprised too.

Probably it was the first time in her life that Dee had ever taken Sapphie's side in anything! He sincerely hoped it wouldn't be the last, that finally Dee was thinking of someone besides herself. Not that it particularly bothered him what Dee did; she was Jerome's problem—thank goodness!

'That's good,' Rik answered Sapphie's explanation about her agent, just enjoying looking at her.

He never wanted this evening to end, wanted to go right on sitting here, with Sapphie and Matthew, and never leave either of them again. Not that it was going to happen; they were deliberately eating at this early hour so that Sapphie could get Matthew home in time for bed. But it was what he wanted more than he had ever wanted anything before.

'How about dessert?' he suggested once they had finished their pizzas—though Sapphie had merely nibbled around the edges of one slice. 'What do you say, little buddy?' he encouraged Matthew. 'Would you like some ice cream or cake?'

'Chocolate cake, please,' Matthew told him without a moment's hesitation, at the same time giving him a beaming smile.

His son might look exactly like him, Rik acknowledged with a sharp intake of breath, but the rest of him was pure Sapphie. From that unpretentious smile, to his way of saying exactly what was on his mind.

'How about you, Sapphie?' He spoke gently, so full of emotion, of love, that he was surprised he could talk at all.

She smiled teasingly at Matthew. 'I usually have the remains of the chocolate cake that Matthew can't manage!'

Rik already knew from Sapphie that the two of them ate here every couple of weeks or so, and he felt privileged that this time they had invited him to join them; it really was progress, even if it was slower than he would have wished.

'Would you like to come back to the house for coffee?' Sapphie offered as she and Matthew stood waiting while Rik paid the bill—after a slight resistance he had at least won that argument!

Rik looked at her curiously, but her expression was unreadable. Deliberately so? Probably, he conceded;

he had no doubts that this evening was as much of a strain for her as it was for him.

But, Sapphie being Sapphie, he didn't doubt that she was willing to put herself through it for Matthew's sake.

But Rik wanted her to do it for *their* sake, because she wanted to see him again as much as he wanted to see her. It was a lot to hope for, but he could dream, couldn't he…?

'I would like that very much,' he accepted casually, taking one of the boiled sweets out of the basket next to the till and handing it to Matthew. 'There you go, little buddy,' he smiled at his son.

The little boy hesitated about taking it, glancing up uncertainly at his mother. 'Mummy?'

Rik felt something like a knife rip into his chest as he realized Sapphie had probably warned Matthew, as his own mother had him, about never accepting sweets from a stranger. Because, much as it pained him to admit it, that was what he actually was, a stranger to his own son.

Sapphie put a hand on Rik's arm. 'Matthew knows that I don't let him eat sweets in the evening,' she explained softly.

Not because he was a stranger at all! But simply because Matthew knew, and accepted, his mother's rule.

Sapphie smiled down at Matthew. 'But I'm willing to make an exception on this occasion!'

'Yippee!' the little boy cried excitedly before shyly taking the sweet. 'Thank you.' He gave another of those beguiling smiles that almost ripped Rik's heart from his chest.

Because he wanted to give this boy, this woman, the world, if only they would let him; it was a humbling experience to know that Matthew was more than pleased with just a sweet.

'Sorry about that,' Rik apologised once they were in Nik's car and on the short drive to Sapphie's house. 'I guess I'm going to need a bit of guidance on the rules.'

'It doesn't matter.' Sapphie shook her head, reaching up a hand to remove the band from her hair and shake it loose about her shoulders.

Completely taking Rik's breath away for what must be the dozenth time this evening. He wanted more than anything to kiss her, to hold her, to run his hands through that fiery hair. He had felt a need growing all evening, so that now, with her sitting so close to him, the smell of her perfume invading his senses, it was all he could think about, all he—

From the back of the car came the sound of Matthew choking!

CHAPTER THIRTEEN

'STOP the car!' Sapphie screamed as she turned and saw Matthew's face turning blue. 'Rik, stop the...' She didn't finish the second shrill instruction: Rik pulled the vehicle over to the side of the road and jumped out from behind the wheel to pull the back door open.

By the time he had Matthew's seat belt off and had taken him out of the car, Sapphie had joined them. If anything Matthew looked bluer than ever, his eyes wide and frightened as he looked up at her.

Rik didn't hesitate, turning Matthew away from him, putting his arms about the little boy's waist and pulling sharply inwards. A small orange object shot out of Matthew's mouth and he began to cry.

Sapphie gathered the child quickly up into her arms, tears streaming down her face too. 'Oh, God! Oh, God!' seemed to be all she could say, over and over again, as she held Matthew tightly to her, the little boy clinging to her.

'It was that damned candy,' Rik muttered angrily, kicking at the boiled sweet as it lay shattered on the ground. 'I guess Mummy knows best after all, huh, little buddy?' He ruffled Matthew's dark curls as he attempted a weak smile.

Sapphie could see that Rik was really as shaken as

she was by the incident, although she smiled too in an effort to disperse the fright Matthew obviously felt.

'It's OK now, baby,' she told her son huskily.

'I couldn't breathe,' the little boy cried, tears starting afresh.

'Nasty old sweet,' Sapphie declared, before looking up at Rik; his face was as pale as she felt hers must be! 'I'll sit in the back with him for the rest of the journey,' she said.

'Good idea,' Rik agreed, and saw that the two of them were settled in the back seat before getting back into the vehicle himself.

But he kept shooting the two of them anxious looks in the rear-view mirror on the remaining drive home. Sapphie smiled at him reassuringly as she felt the tension leave Matthew and he began to fall asleep.

She never ceased to be amazed at the way children bounced back from things; as a baby, Matthew could be burning up with fever one day and playing happily with his toys the next. Whereas she was usually an emotional wreck from the worry!

It was the same with the sweet, she realised as later they bathed Matthew before putting him to bed; she and Rik were obviously still feeling strained about the whole incident, but Matthew was splashing happily in his bath, completely reassured!

Although not quite...

'Will you be here in the morning when I wake up?' Matthew looked up at Rik with big blue eyes as he lay back in his bed, cosily ensconced under his Thomas the Tank Engine duvet. 'Susie, at kindergarten, she said her daddy is always there in the morning when she wakes up,' he added innocently.

Sapphie swallowed hard as she sat on the side of the bed. In the end she had decided to tell Matthew the truth about Rik because she felt it was best for both of them, even though she had known it was going to make things difficult for her. But she certainly had no idea Matthew had been talking to other children about his daddy at the pre-school he went to three mornings a week.

'Susie's daddy is a teacher, darling,' she explained.

'Oh.' Matthew nodded, obviously not understanding at all. 'What's my daddy?' He turned curiously to Rik.

'I write stories, like Mummy,' Rik answered him carefully, obviously totally besotted with Matthew already.

If he hadn't acted so quickly, hadn't known exactly what to do when Matthew started to choke...!

'Well, Mummy's always here in the morning,' Matthew said happily, as if Rik being here too would be the most natural thing in the world.

And maybe to a four-year-old it was, Sapphie acknowledged ruefully, as they took turns to kiss Matthew goodnight before going down to the kitchen.

To her surprise, Matthew had taken the news that Rik was his daddy with an acceptance that made her proud of him, his only comment being, 'Where did my daddy live before he came to us?' After days of working herself up to telling him, his calm reaction had been a welcome relief, the fact that he had once called Rik a bad man seeming to be forgotten in the excitement of having a father at last.

Sapphie moved about the room making coffee, Rik sitting at the table watching her. Her mother, with her usual tact and consideration, had decided to go to the cinema with a friend this evening. But with Matthew tucked safely in bed, probably already asleep if Sapphie knew him, she and Rik seemed very much alone...

'You're still looking a little pale.' Rik spoke concernedly as she brought the coffee to the table. 'He's OK, you know. And there shouldn't be any side-effects. Should there...?'

'No,' she reassured him, putting the cups down on the table as her hands started to shake as reaction began to set in, having kept herself under tight control in front of Matthew in an effort not to alarm him. 'If you hadn't been there—'

'If I hadn't been there he wouldn't have had the candy in the first place!' Rik put in, standing up to look down at her searchingly. 'But he seemed fine when he went to bed.'

'He is,' Sapphie agreed, tears welling up in her eyes and spilling hotly down her cheeks. 'It's only when something like this happens that you realise how vulnerable they are, how fragile life can be. If anything should ever happen to him—'

'It won't,' Rik told her firmly, clasping the tops of her arms.

Sapphie still shook. 'But if it did—'

'It won't, Sapphie,' he cut in firmly. 'I won't let it!'

She gave a humourless laugh. 'You won't be here to stop it—'

'I'll always be here, Sapphie,' Rik told her forcefully. 'You'll always have me.'

Sapphie became very still, staring up at him, totally bewildered by the intensity of his expression. What did he mean, she would always have him?

Rik gave a deep sigh at her bewilderment. 'Sapphie, I know you aren't ready to hear this, and I really don't want to completely blow any chance I might have of...' He broke off, breathing deeply. 'Sapphie, I love you. I love you!'

She couldn't move, could only continue to stare at him. He didn't really mean that he loved her, she finally decided; it was Matthew he loved, not her. If he was in love with anyone, then it wasn't her—

'You, Sapphie.' He spoke with intensity now, as if he could read her thoughts and was angry at them. 'Only you, Sapphie. It will only ever be you,' he insisted.

'But—but Dee?' she burst out. 'You love her, you've always loved her—'

'I was infatuated with Dee for a while; the fact that she was about to marry someone else intensified that feeling. But what I've remained in love with is another memory of warmth and giving, of fire and laughter.' He spoke as if he had just realised that himself. 'That was you, Sapphie, the night we met. I was all messed up about what I felt, and you and Dee became all mixed up inside my head, but the one I loved was the warm and giving one.'

Sapphie shook her head, afraid to believe him. 'But

I saw your face the day she was here, saw the way you looked at her as she defended my right to Matthew—'

'I do not love her. I have never loved her,' he added with finality. 'What you saw that day was the hope that there was some normal human decency in her, after all,' Rik explained. 'I hadn't seen any evidence of it until that moment! I love you, Sapphie. I always will.'

She looked up at him searchingly, wanting to believe him but was afraid to. She loved him so much that she simply couldn't settle for anything less from him. She wouldn't settle for anything less!

She had to believe him! Rik had never wanted anything in his life as much as he wanted her to believe it was her that he loved!

That he had always loved, he realised now.

That time with Sapphie, happening when he had believed himself in love with Dee, had stopped him from seeing, from acknowledging, that it was the woman he had held in his arms that night that he had continued to love. It had been her warmth and loving that he remembered, that he loved. Sapphie…

She shook her head now. 'You want Matthew—'

'I want you,' he corrected harshly. It was too soon, he knew that, but it was the way the evening had turned out, and he might never have another chance to tell Sapphie how he felt about her. 'I love Matthew, yes,' he acknowledged. 'And if I ever lost him it would half kill me! But if I lost you…! Sapphie, I wouldn't want to go on living without you.' And he knew it was the truth, that Sapphie meant everything to him.

He wanted to be there in the morning when Sapphie woke up, *every* morning for the rest of their lives. But still she said nothing, only continued to look at him warily.

'Sapphie, I want to marry *you*!' He released her, knowing that he couldn't be this close to her and not kiss her. Which wasn't going to help anything at this moment. 'I know, after all that's happened, how difficult it must be for you to believe me,' he groaned. 'I just—I don't know how to explain!' He drew in a shaky breath.

This was just so important, might be the only chance he would ever have to tell Sapphie how he felt. He had to do it right, or risk losing her for ever…!

'When I saw Dee again in Paris, when I first heard her voice, it all came rushing back, all the emotions I thought I had buried long ago. I couldn't breathe, couldn't talk—'

'You love her,' Sapphie stated flatly before turning away.

'I don't even like her!' Rik burst out frustratedly. 'It was you, Sapphie,' he spoke softly as she slowly turned back to face him. 'It was always you…! I just didn't realise it until I saw the two of you together in Paris. Dee is cold, selfish—and incredibly boring,' he admitted. 'You're warm, caring—and I have never known even a moment's boredom in your company.' He gave a rueful smile. 'In fact, the opposite! I can't even think straight when I'm with you.'

Sapphie continued to stare at him. 'That must be very—uncomfortable.'

Rik felt a glimmer of hope as he saw the flicker of amusement in those incredible amber-coloured eyes. Only a glimmer, but it was so much more than he had hoped for.

'No, not uncomfortable at all.' He gave a half-smile. 'Never that. Sapphie, you're the first thought in my mind when I wake up in the morning. All I can think of the entire day. My last thought before I fall asleep at night.' Although he hadn't been able to do much of that this last week! 'In fact,' he added self-derisively, 'Nik assures me that I'm the one who has become boring!'

Sapphie swallowed hard before moistening her lips with the tip of her tongue.

Rik's gaze hungrily followed the movement; he wanted her so much that he just wanted to forget all about caution, his promise to take things slowly, and make love to her here and now. Which would probably ruin everything!

'Nik doesn't know everything.' Sapphie spoke huskily. 'I can assure you, I'm not in the least bored in your company.'

'You aren't?' he breathed uncertainly.

'No.' She looked at him with clear eyes. 'Rik, I haven't been completely honest with you, either.' She swallowed again. 'I— Do you believe in love at first sight?' Her expression was anxious now. Rik frowned his confusion. He wasn't sure he could take listening to her explain her feelings for Jerome—

'You, Rik.' She spoke quietly. 'I'm talking about you,' she explained as he continued to look puzzled.

'Me?' he repeated sharply. 'But I've just tried to tell you that I don't love Dee, that I never loved Dee—'

'Forget Dee,' Sapphie interrupted.

'I would be happy to,' Rik assured her with feeling, wanting to forget that whole embarrassing incident in his life.

'Then it's done.' Sapphie smiled, taking a tentative step towards him. 'Rik, I told you that I was a virgin five years ago. I also told you that I'd had other lovers since. That last part isn't true.'

He could hardly breathe now, staring down at her, needing her so badly, wanting to touch her so badly that he trembled with the emotion.

Sapphie took another step towards him, so close now he could see the brown flecks in the amber of her eyes. 'Rik, I went to Dee and Jerome's wedding believing I was watching the man I loved marry my sister—'

'Don't, Sapphie,' he pleaded huskily. 'I think I can stand anything but hearing how much you love someone else—'

'I said I believed I loved him, Rik.' Sapphie was standing in front of him now, one of her hands reaching up to caress the hard line of his jaw. 'What actually happened that day, when I couldn't bear to even look at the two of them getting married, was that I turned and looked anywhere else instead. And I saw you.' She gave a shaky smile. 'That was when I knew what love was. It was— Rik, I fell in love with you the moment I looked at you. I love you, Rik,' she told him strongly. 'I've always loved you.'

Rik felt as if someone had just punched him, knocking all the air from his lungs. 'You—I—'

'Yes, Rik, you and I,' Sapphie echoed. 'And I don't know about you, but I really don't want to waste another five years of our lives together!' Her eyes glowed with love now.

For him. Only for him. What a fool he had been. What an idiot. He and Sapphie could have been together for the last five years if he hadn't been so blind.

He reached out and pulled her into his arms, crushing her to him. 'I love you, Sapphie! God, how I love you! I never, ever want to be apart from you again!' he promised before his mouth claimed hers in a kiss that left them both breathless and shaking as Rik finally lifted his head to gaze down at her wonderingly. 'Marry me, Sapphie. I think I'll go quietly insane if you don't agree to be my wife!'

She gave a husky laugh. 'I'll marry you, Rik,' she assured him emotionally. 'I'll marry you!' She beamed up at him, her face flushed, her eyes full of love.

It was the way Rik always wanted her to look at him. In fact, he intended doing everything in his power to ensure that she did!

EPILOGUE

'MATTHEW is really into this Santa Claus thing, isn't he?' Rik grinned as he joined Sapphie in the kitchen after going up to say goodnight to their son. 'Not that I'm complaining,' he continued as his arms slid about her waist from behind and he began to nuzzle her neck with warm lips. 'It makes it so much fun for us, too,' he murmured distractedly.

Sapphie turned, almost four months of marriage only having deepened the pleasure she always felt in his arms. 'Makes what so much more fun?' she encouraged laughingly.

'Er—Christmas. I think.' Rik looked down at her with adoring eyes. 'I find it hard to think straight when we're together like this,' he admitted.

The last four months had been the happiest Sapphie had ever known, too, being Rik's wife, being with him all the time, more wonderful than she could ever have imagined. And she knew he felt the same way about her.

Being part of the Prince family really was like being wrapped in warm, protective arms, the four sisters-in-law, Stazy, Jinx, Tyler and Sapphie, having become firm friends. And Matthew absolutely loved his brand-new family, was greatly looking forward to them all spending Christmas together in the Canadian ski resort of Whistler—once they had reassured him that they would leave a note for Santa Claus to tell him where they all were!

Sapphie reached up to kiss Rik lingeringly on the mouth, then she moved away to pick up the two glasses she had filled while he was upstairs, champagne for him and orange juice for her.

'Champagne for me?' Rik murmured appreciatively. 'What are we celebrating?'

'Three things,' she told him glowingly. 'Jerome called while you were upstairs—'

'The twins?' Rik prompted excitedly.

The twins. Not Dee. It had never been Dee, Sapphie knew now with certainty; she and Rik loved each other so completely. And she knew they always would.

'Fergus and Fiona,' she nodded. 'Both six pounds and one ounce,' she announced with a wide, beaming smile. 'Dee is fine. And Jerome sounds over the moon.'

It had continued to be a good pregnancy, Dee's only complaint that she could no longer see her feet by the seventh month!

Her sister hadn't exactly changed overnight, and Sapphie very much doubted that she ever would, but they were closer now than they had ever been as children, and that was more than Sapphie had ever hoped for.

'That's great.' Rik gently chinked his glass against Sapphie's before they both took a sip of their drinks.

'Mm,' Sapphie murmured appreciatively. 'The second thing is that my mother has decided to sell the house.'

'She's decided to move in with us, after all,' Rik said with satisfaction.

Joan had flatly refused to share the new house that Rik and Sapphie bought after their marriage, preferring to stay in the house she and Sapphie had shared after Matthew's birth, claiming the newly-weds needed time together with Matthew as a family, and none of their arguments to the contrary had managed to convince her otherwise.

'Actually…no,' Sapphie grinned, hardly able to contain her excitement. 'She's moving in with Jackson!'

Rik blinked. 'Jinx's father? That Jackson?'

Sapphie couldn't blame him for looking so surprised; she had been a little stunned herself when her mother told her the good news earlier today. Pleased, but definitely stunned.

'Yes, *that* Jackson,' she confirmed happily. 'Apparently the two of them got on so well at our wedding that they've been seeing each other ever since. They didn't tell any of the family, in case things didn't work out. But last night Jackson proposed—and Mummy said yes!'

'Well, I'll be damned…!' Rik exclaimed.

Jinx's father had been widowed a couple of years ago, and Joan had obviously been on her own for many years; Sapphie couldn't have wished for, or imagined, anything more wonderful than her mother falling in love again.

'You said three things…?' Rik reminded softly once they had drunk a toast to Joan and Jackson.

'Oh. Yes.' Colour blazed in Sapphie's cheeks. 'I

know that *No Ordinary Boy* is going into production in the New Year, but could you try and keep the end of July and the beginning of August free?' she prompted shyly.

Rik waggled his eyebrows at her. 'Why, what did you have in mind?'

Sapphie's eyes glowed with love as she looked up at him. 'A quick visit to the hospital before we bring home a brother or a sister for Matthew…!'

Rik went completely still, his face paling, all the teasing leaving his expression as he stared down at her as if he couldn't believe his ears. 'You mean—we're—you're—'

'I'm pregnant, Rik!' she announced excitedly. 'I went to see the doctor this morning when you thought I was out shopping, and—we're going to have a baby,' she breathed huskily, the words catching in her throat.

He swallowed hard, seeming unable to talk, deep blue eyes awash with emotion.

'Isn't it wonderful?' Sapphie smiled, radiant.

'Wonderful! God, I love you, Sapphie,' he groaned as he was finally able to move, gathering her up into his arms and holding her against him with tender possessiveness.

'I love you, too, Rik,' she declared. 'So very much. I always will.'

Always.

It had to be the most wonderful word in the entire English language—

No—that was love.

Something Sapphie had no doubts she and Rik would share for a lifetime…

millsandboon.co.uk Community

Join Us!

The Community is the perfect place to meet and chat to kindred spirits who love books and reading as much as you do, but it's also the place to:

- Get the inside scoop from authors about their latest books
- Learn how to write a romance book with advice from our editors
- Help us to continue publishing the best in women's fiction
- Share your thoughts on the books we publish
- Befriend other users

Forums: Interact with each other as well as authors, editors and a whole host of other users worldwide.

Blogs: Every registered community member has their own blog to tell the world what they're up to and what's on their mind.

Book Challenge: We're aiming to read 5,000 books and have joined forces with The Reading Agency in our inaugural Book Challenge.

Profile Page: Showcase yourself and keep a record of your recent community activity.

Social Networking: We've added buttons at the end of every post to share via digg, Facebook, Google, Yahoo, technorati and de.licio.us.

www.millsandboon.co.uk